D0503488

GLASS PREDATOR

ALSO BY CRAIG SCHAEFER

GLASS PREDATOR
CRAIG SCHAEFER

47N◉RTH

Published by 47North, Seattle

www.apub.com

Amazon, the Amazon logo, and 47North are trademarks of Amazon.com, Inc., or its affiliates.

ISBN-13: 9781477822982
ISBN-10: 1477822984

Cover design by David Drummond

Printed in the United States of America

Dedicated to the tireless staff of the McKittrick Hotel in New York City, who provided a wayward scribe with hospitality and inspiration on a particularly dark and stormy night.

PROLOGUE

At the end of the hall, the elevator chimed. It wasn't supposed to.

The sound jarred al-Farsi from his thoughts. A first edition of *Wuthering Heights* lay open before him. A warm fire was crackling in his office hearth, and his chubby white-and-beige cat was perched on the edge of his desk, happily purring. A perfect evening, until the rattling of the elevator heralded the arrival of an uninvited guest. She threw open his office doors and strode in like she owned the room. Her scarlet lips curled into a malicious smile, every strand of her blonde bob perfectly in place.

Al-Farsi sucked air between his teeth. *"Najidanere,"* he said. "I don't believe you have an appointment."

"I don't believe I need one," the woman replied. "And, please, no need for formalities, dear. You can call me Nadine. So this is where it all happens, hmm? The nerve center of your little . . . freelance intelligence operation."

She looked around, taking in the shelves upon shelves of identical notebooks, thousands of them. All the way to the vaulted ceiling, where shadows squirmed and twisted in patterns that didn't match the firelight.

"This is my home," he told her.

"For the moment. You've been a naughty boy, al-Farsi. Running your business in the heart of my prince's territory? You know who I am, and, yet, have you ever reached out to me? Have you ever offered me access to your records? Offered even a token gesture of respect? No. I'm very disappointed."

She approached the desk, taking slow, sauntering steps. He lifted his chin and adjusted his silk cravat, squaring his shoulders against the high-backed leather chair.

"I have an understanding with the hound," he said.

"You have an understanding with the *current* hound," Nadine said. "He's on his way down. I'm on my way up. If you want this adorable nightclub of yours to stay in business, you'd better get right with me. Otherwise, we're going to have a problem."

"Are we?" he asked, glancing upward. She followed his gaze.

Above their heads, a tarantula the size of a car clung to the ceiling. It stared down at her with beady, gossamer-purple eyes, its shadowy husk lined with rippling hairs of darkness. More shadows swarmed around Nadine's feet, bristling black centipedes that rose up from the carpet and skittered on thousands of twitching legs. Nadine looked back to al-Farsi and slowly arched one perfectly groomed eyebrow.

"That's adorable. Maybe you didn't get the memo: I am the grand matriarch of the House of Dead Roses. I have seven assassins downstairs, seeded among your unsuspecting clientele and ready to start a bloodbath. Another thirteen outside, with enough military-grade firepower to level the building on my command. Now be a good boy and put your pets away, or I'll make you *eat* them."

Al-Farsi's lips twitched. He broke eye contact, glancing down, as the shadows receded into the walls. "This is harassment," he said. "I'm reporting this to the hound."

"Good. Then you can tell him all about—what was it called? Oh, right. Operation Cold Spectrum."

He froze. He slowly lifted his gaze, meeting Nadine's smirk. She strolled around the desk and reached out to stroke the purring cat with her fingertips.

"That's right," she said. "I know. More important, I know that *you* know. You've had information on Cold Spectrum all this time, and you never volunteered it to my people. Never warned us. How much would your 'understanding' be worth if that got out, hmm? My prince would order this place burned to the ground and your soul offered up on a roasting spit."

She shoved his chair back with a sudden burst of strength. Then, slowly, she swung one leg over and straddled his lap, facing him, fingertips of one hand brushing his cheek while the other toyed with the neatly groomed strands of his beard.

"It's all right," she said. "I can keep a secret. As long as you make it worth my while. You should be thankful, you know. I'm aware you had another couple of visitors recently. Harmony Black and Jessie Temple."

"I don't—" He paused, swallowing hard. "I don't speak about my clients."

Her fingertip ran along his bottom lip. "Even if I ask nicely?"

"I am . . . quite immune to your tricks. Your magic won't work on me."

"Do I even need to use it? I have something even better: leverage. And you'll do as you're told. Do you know what they did to my little girl, back in Talbot Cove? They ruined her hunt. Humiliated her. Handed her rightful victory to a sniveling worm of a rival. Do you have any children, al-Farsi? It's a sacred thing, the bond between a mother and her daughter. I'd do anything to protect her. And yet, even though you extended the hand of friendship to my enemies and snubbed me, I'm not angry. I'm even going to give you a choice."

He stared at her, uncertain. "A choice?"

Her hand slipped down from his beard and closed around his throat. Her fingers curled, squeezing. Not hard enough to cut off his breath. Just enough to get his attention.

"A choice," she said. "You can be a willing slave, or an unwilling one. One option is far less painful than the other, but I'm content to leave the decision up to you. We have a saying in the House of Dead Roses: *In the end . . . all serve.*"

Still as a statue, he held her gaze. Her fingers squeezed tighter.

"What do you want from me?" he whispered.

Nadine raised one hand and snapped her fingers, sharp as a drumbeat. She nodded to the desk. Now, in a spot that had been empty a moment ago, a plain brown folder awaited. To al-Farsi it felt like a bomb, primed and ready to explode.

"Sometime in the next couple of days," Nadine said, "you're going to get a call from Bobby Diehl. You know, Diehl Innovations? They make the smart refrigerators and the overpriced phones?"

"I know him," al-Farsi replied.

"Then you probably know what he's going to call about. He's got his own score to settle with Temple and Black. He's going to offer you an exorbitant amount of money for everything you have on them."

"I never sell information about my clients. Under any circumstances."

Nadine giggled. "And that's what you'll tell him. But you *can* give him the contents of that folder without breaking your rule. And you will."

She shifted her weight on his lap, giving him room to reach toward the desk. His outstretched hand, faintly trembling, opened the folder. He read the paper inside in silence.

"I understand," he said. "And then?"

"And then you're going to call her." Nadine leaned in close, the air awash in her honeysuckle perfume, her hot breath gusting across his ear as she whispered. "Call Harmony Black, and warn her. I'll tell you exactly what to say."

"Why? What are you trying to accomplish?"

"You could call this a 'target-rich environment.' I'm going to destroy my enemies, win a boon for my court, and pave the way to the seat at my prince's right hand, all without lifting a finger. And you're going to help."

She pulled away from his ear. Sitting on his lap, almost nose to nose, smiling. But now her eyes were orbs of molten copper, burning bright, and her teeth were curved and pointed like a great white shark's.

"You're going to help," she repeated, "because if you don't, I'll expose you and that nasty little secret you've been sitting on all these years. And then I'll drag you straight to hell."

ONE

A life in the clandestine services means a new challenge every day. Sometimes it's an endless stakeout, waiting hours for a suspect to make a move. Sometimes it's combing through reams of accounting ledgers, looking for a single out-of-place digit that points toward the truth. And sometimes you find yourself in a burning building, ducking behind an overturned hospital gurney while the Phantom of the Opera throws bolts of fire at you.

The air boiled. Sweat beaded on my forehead, and my blouse clung to my clammy skin. My reflection in the stainless-steel gurney was a distorted fun-house ghoul, with flames roaring at my back and licking along the operating room's wall. Just to my left, the gurney's previous occupant sprawled out on the lime-green tile floor like a fallen puppet. He was naked, dead, with his scalp peeled back like a bad toupee, and his face cut away with surgical precision. He stared at me with lidless eyes, set into a perfect oval of wet, red muscle.

The woman in the doorway shrieked louder than the fire. Half of her face was concealed behind a white porcelain mask, twisted burn tissue peeking out along the edges, and her surgical scrubs were stained with enough blood to fill a slaughterhouse. Serpents of fire wreathed her hands, rippling in the air, curling figure eights around her clenched fists like a Möbius strip of raw magic. I smelled gasoline and tasted black smoke, the air wavering like a desert mirage.

"Just returning the favor, Agent Black!" She thrust out her fists and screamed.

One of the fire snakes lanced toward me like a burning arrow. It sizzled just over my head, hitting the back wall with a splash of Halloween orange and feeding the blaze.

"Just returning the favor!"

We'd first encountered Victoria Carnes—or Hostile Entity 138, according to her new target file—back in Detroit, where she and her partner were running a chop shop for human beings. She got away, but I'd left her with scars to remember me by. And apparently drove her from nutty to batshit psychotic in the process, too. When plastic-surgery patients started popping up in Nashville with their organs scooped out and their faces carved off, I had a pretty solid hunch that Dr. Carnes had gotten back into her old line of work.

Sometimes I hate being right.

A voice crackled over my earpiece. Calm, collected, tinged with a faint Irish brogue. "Harmony? Do you have eyes on the target?"

"Yeah," I gasped, hunkering down behind my makeshift cover. "You could say that."

"Is Jessie with you?"

I glanced to my right. My partner found her own cover, crouched low behind a flame-seared cabinet, but she was miles away inside her own head. Her turquoise eyes, inhumanly bright, reflected the growing blaze as she clutched her knees and rocked back and forth. A faint, keening whine escaped her throat.

"Something's wrong with her." I waved my hand, snapping my fingers at her. "Hey, Jessie. *Jessie*. Damn it. Could really use some covering fire here!"

A torrent of flame washed over the gurney's edge, pressing me flat to the floor while Victoria cackled at the top of her lungs. I made a mental note to choose my words more carefully.

A ceiling tile broke away and fell, hitting the floor at my back with a shower of sparks. On one side, a growing blaze inched closer by the second. On the other, a fire-tossing lunatic blocked the only way out. No time to wait for Jessie to snap out of it, no time for backup to get here. I took a deep breath—then coughed myself hoarse, sputtering and spitting smoke. Another, slower breath and I reached into my inner core, unfurling the heart of my power like the petals of a steel flower.

Earth, air, water, fire, sang the ritual trigger, whispering in my inner ear. *Garb me in your raiment. Arm me with your weapons.*

I called to my element, to the water, to the *idea* of water. I crooned a song of swift, icy rivers and bottomless ocean, of purity and flow, of the quiet, relentless strength that could carve through mountains. Tendrils of aquamarine shimmered around my right hand, driving back the smoke and the heat.

My left hand flipped back my jacket and pulled the Glock from my shoulder holster. I counted to three, braced myself, and made my move.

I leaped up from behind the gurney just as Victoria unleashed another burning serpent. I lashed out with my right hand and painted the air with water, a glistening diamond shield. The serpent hit the shield and burst in a screech of sparks and blue-hot light. I was already on the move, bringing up my gun and snapping off shots as fast as I could squeeze the trigger. One went wide, pounding into the wall and shattering tile. The second hit her in the shoulder. Victoria yelped, staggering back, clutching her wound. She turned and ran. I leaped over the gurney, dead set on bringing her down, but I froze in the doorway where she'd been standing a heartbeat ago.

The fire was still spreading, but Jessie didn't move a muscle—hadn't moved? She stared at the encroaching flames, unblinking, paralyzed. I cursed under my breath and holstered my gun. She snapped at me and growled as I put my arm around her shoulder, struggling to pull her to her feet.

"It's *me*," I said. "Come on, don't fight me."

Step by plodding step, I hauled her out of the operating room. "April," I said, "Carnes is gone. We need extraction, right now."

"On our way," she replied. On the other end of the earpiece, an engine revved to life.

I pulled Jessie through the abandoned clinic, past surgical suites filled with the mad doctor's recent handiwork—ragged red corpses and stacks of organ coolers under gore-spattered plastic—and through the dusty, empty waiting room. She started to come around once we made it out from the smoky haze and into the warm Nashville sun, and pulled away from me as she squinted and wobbled on unsteady legs.

"What happened back there?" she asked me.

I stared at her. It took a second to find my voice.

"You tell me."

The clinic burned at our backs, black smoke rising in thin, rippling plumes to touch a cloudless blue sky. A van roared up to the curb. The livery shouted out an advertisement for a local plumbing company, but the side door rattled open to reveal banks of flickering screens and control panels. April Cassidy sat at the heart of the surveillance suite, leaning back in her wheelchair. The woman—in her sixties, with steel-wool hair and eyes like frozen sapphires—beckoned us on board with a nod. Behind the wheel of the van, Kevin leaned to one side and glanced over his shoulder at us. He pointed to the wide-band radio on the cluttered dashboard.

"Police and fire incoming, ETA two minutes," the lanky teenager said. "We gotta *go*."

I slammed the door behind us. "Hit it."

April turned to the bank of screens. Whatever she was thinking, I couldn't guess. Her cool, expressionless face was a poker player's dream.

"Linder is waiting for a status report," she said.

The van screeched away from the curb, making a beeline for the highway. I held on to a monitor to steady myself and thought about what to tell our boss. Between some ruined real estate and a scrubbed operation, I didn't have any good news to share.

"Tell him we have positive confirmation that the Face Collector is Victoria Carnes, H. E. 138. She ambushed us and managed to escape. Tell him . . ." I shook my head. "Tell him the mission was a failure."

# # #

An hour later I stood in a motel parking lot, watching the sun go down and the Nashville lights rise up, cherry neon shimmering against a dusty violet sky. I didn't have anywhere particular to be.

Normally after a mission, the team would get together for a group meal. It didn't have to be anything fancy; with our per diems, we spent a lot of time in greasy spoons and chain restaurants. Fancy wasn't important. We just needed that time together to catch our breaths, to get our footing back, to quietly celebrate a job well done. Another target crossed off the Hostile Entities ledger, neutralized before any more civilians could get hurt.

Tonight, we didn't have anything to celebrate.

April had gone to bed early, claiming she felt a migraine coming on. Kevin hid in the glow of his computer screen, huddling behind the laptop lid like it was a bunker. And I paced the parking lot, trying to figure out how everything had gone sideways.

"You hungry?"

I turned. Jessie stood behind me, holding out the keys to our temporary ride—a Bureau-issued Crown Vic with rust spots and a patina of dead bugs—like a peace offering.

I opened my hand and caught the keys.

We ended up at Hattie B's, a chicken joint with a line wrapped around the building and a jumping patio out front. Country-western music washed out over the street, jangling guitars competing with the rumble of the traffic. Weaving around packs of drunken college kids, we eventually made it to the front of the line and placed our order at the counter.

"Chicken and waffles," Jessie said. "We gotta do that."

"I'm not even sure how to eat chicken and waffles."

"Two," Jessie said to the girl behind the counter. "Mild for her, and . . . what's the hottest temperature you've got?"

"We call it Shut the Cluck Up hot."

"I like this place already."

The restaurant was crowded, bordering on claustrophobic, but we found a spot to squeeze in. Our meals came in baskets with dill-pickle spears and sides of pimento-spiced mac and cheese. The chicken melted right off the bone, tender as butter under a crispy fried skin.

"Hot sauce on the chicken, maple syrup on the waffles," Jessie told me. "The trick is to get a little of both in a single bite. You wouldn't think the flavors would work together, but trust me, it's magic. The perfect team-up."

"Jessie, we have to talk about what happened out there."

She didn't meet my eyes, shifting her glance sideways while she talked around a mouthful of chicken. "It's a little fuzzy."

"You froze up. I've *never* seen you freeze up in a crisis. Not even once. What happened to you?"

She shrugged. "The fire, I think. Got overwhelmed. I'm sorry, okay? I let you down. Won't happen again."

I reached across the table. My fingers brushed against hers.

"I'm not asking for an apology," I said. "I'm trying to figure out what went wrong and . . . well, *help*, if I can. Fire's never bothered you before. Back in Oregon, Mikki burned that lodge down around our ears, and you were cool and collected the whole time. Cooler than I was, that's for sure."

"I was me, then." Her gaze dropped down to her lap as her bottom lip curled in a guilty twist. "The beast doesn't like fire. Just about the only thing in the world it's afraid of."

The beast was Jessie's constant companion, the curse pulsing through her bloodstream. Her father had inflicted it on her. He'd wanted her to follow in his footsteps: a butcher, a serial killer, a bloody-handed servant of a creature known only as the King of Wolves. Jessie chose a different path. A better one.

But the beast wasn't going anywhere.

"We had Carnes handled," I gently told her. "I mean, it's one thing to let it out when we *need* that extra burst of power to pull through a fight, but she's just a human psycho with some magic tricks. Bullets would have done the job. And you knew Carnes might use fire against us, so why would you risk . . ."

My voice trailed off. She finally looked at me, her turquoise eyes narrowed under the hot restaurant lights. She didn't have to say a word. Her face told me the whole story.

"You didn't let it out," I said. "Did you? The beast came out on its own this time."

TWO

Jessie finished her last piece of fried chicken, wiping down her greasy fingertips with a paper napkin.

"Let's go," she said. "Gotta walk off some of this food."

We headed out into the night, side by side down a long stretch of sidewalk, the street ahead blazing with signs for dive bars and honky-tonks.

"Last week, in New Jersey," Jessie said.

"That sloth-demon cult? What about it? We got the job done."

"I killed their high priest."

I nodded. "He was on the list. The man had seven victims in his basement, buried up to their waists in concrete. It was a righteous kill, Jessie."

"I was *trying* to capture him." She took a deep breath and glanced sidelong at me. "I didn't say anything before now because I thought it was a fluke. I had him in my hands, and the beast just . . . came out. I didn't call it. I didn't want it. Next thing I know, the guy's lying on the floor in three pieces, and I can't remember how he got that way. Today? Same thing, but worse. The second my heart rate went up, once Carnes showed her face, that was it: boom. Gone. Aunt April and I have worked for years to lock this thing down tight inside me. I know every trick in the book to keep control, to keep the beast chained up in the back of my brain, and they all *work*."

"Until now," I said.

"Until now. I'm pissed off about what happened out there today, and I'm embarrassed, which just pisses me off more. But mostly . . ." She stopped walking. "Harmony, I'm . . . I'm starting to get a little scared."

I took her hand.

"So we'll figure it out. Together, okay?"

She squeezed my fingers and nodded, then let go.

"Yeah. Okay."

My phone chimed. April, on the other end, didn't give me time to say hello.

"We need you back here, immediately. Linder wants a word."

I sighed. Getting called on the carpet was the last thing Jessie needed right now. She was already using herself as a punching bag, no outside help required. I wasn't looking forward to it, either, considering I was going to have to make up a story to explain our failure in the field, anything to keep Linder and his bean counters from finding out Jessie had lost control over her powers. They would have sanctioned her as a Hostile Entity years ago if April hadn't stepped in.

"Can't he debrief us tomorrow? We're all exhausted, and there's nothing time-critical—"

"It's a briefing, not a debriefing. We have a new mission. There's been an incident in New York; he wants us on the hunt while the trail is still hot."

"We'll be back in fifteen minutes." I hung up and looked Jessie's way. "Duty calls."

"No rest for the wicked. Fine. Good. I wanna get back out there. Don't know about you, but I feel like chalking up a win right now."

Kevin met us at the door to his motel room. Behind drawn curtains, the lights turned down, pinpoint text in neon green scrolled along his laptop screen. He'd patched the computer to some kind of phone-size dongle on a chunky USB cable, a second screen spitting out rapid-fire calculations.

"Ever since our run-in with Roman Steranko, I've been working on our network security," he explained. "Came up with a few new innovations to keep our data bulletproof. I passed it all along to the home office, too, so they could beef up Vigilant's network code. We won't get blindsided like that again."

We sat on the edge of a lumpy mattress. Beside us, April leaned back in her wheelchair and gazed silently at the laptop, eyes inscrutable behind her steel-gray bifocals. Kevin hunched over the keyboard and rattled off a burst of code. The text vanished, replaced by a glowing symbol that swallowed the screen: a violet padlock emblazoned with spiky, hard-angled wings.

"Vigilant Lock communication protocol two-point-oh is live," Kevin said, proudly folding his arms as he pulled over a chair. "As far as any peeping eyes are concerned, we're ghosts in the machine."

A webcam window popped up on the screen. The man on the other end could have been a ghost himself, with a forgettable face and a forgettable suit—a carefully cultivated blandness that defied memory. Linder had spent a lifetime lurking inside the gears of Washington, DC, and in the underbellies of the alphabet agencies, places where being forgettable was a survival skill.

"Agents," he said, "I'm sure you're eager to press your pursuit of H. E. 138, but something more critical has come up."

Bird's-eye footage of a bustling street corner filled the screen. Film from a news chopper, as police cordoned off the sidewalk and away from a curb lined with ambulances and squad cars. Two black SWAT vans camped out in the intersection, blocking off the road.

"At 4:15 p.m., eastern time, an armed robbery took place at the National Equity Bank in midtown Manhattan. Multiple civilian casualties. Bank robbery is a federal offense, so we have the green light to insert you as assets under FBI cover. I pulled strings to have the case passed over to the Bureau's Critical Incident Response Group. From there, it was passed to Special Agent in Charge Walburgh in the Crisis Management Unit."

"The completely nonexistent SAC Walburgh," Kevin muttered.

"And as of 7:12 p.m., Agents Temple and Black have officially been assigned to the investigation. You'll be rendezvousing with local police, then proceeding with the case on your own once you've interviewed them."

"Sir?" I said. "A bank robbery? I'm not clear on how this falls under Vigilant Lock's remit."

"This footage," Linder said as the screen shifted to a grainy picture from a cell phone, "was taken by a customer inside the bank. Watch carefully."

The unsteady hand with the camera was down at floor level. So were a dozen trembling, pale faces, customers pressed flat to the polished white marble with their fingers laced behind their heads. The shaky footage panned across the bank lobby, catching the ruffle of a black trench coat as a man in a balaclava and tinted goggles stalked past. He hoisted a duffel bag over one shoulder and a matte black carbine on the other, dangling from a strap.

"Do we have anything from the security-camera feeds?" Kevin asked. "It'd be easier to see what's going on."

"The footage was destroyed—" Linder started to say. The crack of a gunshot cut him off. The camera swung left, and a bank teller hit the floor. Wide-eyed and dead, a chunk of her skull decorating the alabaster wall.

"She was going for the silent alarm," said a man's voice. Another gunman, his face concealed behind a mask and goggles, stood over the teller's corpse and put two more bullets in her back. A couple of the hostages screamed, more of them whispering, frantic. Then another voice, a woman's, snapped out over the commotion with the force of a bullwhip.

"Shut. The *fuck. Up.*"

The camera's eye snapped around. The woman stood on the front counter, her rifle propped up against one shoulder. The neckline of her rumpled trench coat tugged back on one side, exposing the heavy Kevlar vest underneath. Even under her black balaclava, her voice was unmuffled, strident.

"Some of you aren't paying attention," she said, "so I will repeat myself. You stay down, you stay silent, and you get to live. You get in our way, you interfere with us in *any* fashion, you die. We do not care about you. This means we have no reason to hurt you. This also means we have no reason *not* to hurt you. So make this easy on all of us."

While the woman talked, I had my eye on the left side of the screen. Another robber—if I was counting right, this made four in all—stood sentry by the door. He didn't see the elderly security guard inching to his feet behind him. *Oh, no,* I thought. The old man had gotten the notion to play hero. This wasn't going to end well.

Creeping up behind him, the guard crouched, took a deep breath, then threw himself onto the gunman's back. One hand went for the rifle, the other clawing at the robber's face. The goggles ripped away as the gunman spun around and clamped his hand around the old man's throat. Then I learned why Linder wanted us on this case.

The gunman threw him like he was weightless. The guard went flying, ten feet across the lobby floor, and I heard his neck snap like a piece of peanut brittle as he hit the wall face-first. He crashed to the ground in a broken heap, his head bent back at an impossible angle.

"Wait," Jessie said. "Rewind that."

The screen froze on the dead guard's face.

"I thought you'd notice that, Agent Temple," Linder said. The footage inched backward, a frame at a time. I watched the feat of superhuman strength in reverse, the old man flying through the air, his throat landing in the hand of his killer. For just a second, with his goggles pulled off, the gunman's masked face had turned toward the camera.

His eyes were an unnatural, bright turquoise, inhumanly blue. Just like Jessie's.

"It would appear," Linder said, "that your father wasn't the only devotee of the King of Wolves. Given that they all took pains to conceal their eyes, it's a safe assumption that all four of the perpetrators have been . . . infected, much like yourself. They remained inside the bank for forty-seven minutes; a customer on the outside, finding the bank doors locked, called the police. When a squad car arrived to investigate, the thieves killed both officers and made their escape. Their coats and masks were found in a dumpster two blocks from the scene of the crime."

"Why did they stay in there for so long?" I asked. "Were they going for the vault?"

"No. They cleaned out the cashiers' tills and drilled into a few random safe-deposit boxes. The bank estimates their final take was roughly four thousand dollars."

Jessie shook her head. "That doesn't make sense. Huge risk, multiple casualties . . . who the hell goes to that much trouble for that little reward?"

"What was that you were saying earlier, about the security-camera footage?" Kevin asked.

"The footage isn't stored on-site," Linder said. "It's automatically transmitted to a server at Greenway Security, in upstate New York, and archived there. Twenty minutes before the robbery, Greenway's systems were compromised by a sophisticated Trojan-horse program. Everything *appeared* to be functioning normally, but the authorities later found that all incoming footage from this specific location was automatically deleted instead of being saved."

Kevin whistled. "Sophisticated."

April glanced his way. "Could you do that?"

"If I had a lot of time," he said, shrugging. "It's not just the doing—the logistics in setting up a hack like that are huge. You'd have to find out how the bank's security operates, who they contract out to, where the server farm with the data you want destroyed is located . . . none of that is public info."

I sat back and stared at the screen. The gunman with the turquoise eyes stood in freeze-frame, looking back at me.

"So they had inside information," I mused, "access to a skilled hacker, access to weapons and equipment. The heist was planned, executed, they made a clean getaway . . . but the actual robbery was amateur night, and they barely made any money. And they would have *known* that going in. It doesn't make sense."

The footage vanished. Linder's image hovered on the screen, his hands clasped before him. "Making sense out of chaos is your job, Agent Black. Needless to say, after the situation with the Red Knight satellite and the King of Silence, gathering intelligence on these so-called Kings is a top priority. We need to know exactly what they are, what they're capable of, and how to eliminate them."

"And if these four have the same juice my dad did," Jessie said, "they can tell us exactly how they got it."

"Indeed. The National Equity Bank thieves have been designated Hostile Entities 144 through 147. Locate them, interrogate them, and save at least one for offshore delivery so our specialists can perform a comprehensive physical examination. Terminate the rest. I'm transmitting your flight data now; you have tickets on an American Airlines flight leaving from Nashville International in two hours. Oh, and Agent Temple?"

Jessie lifted her chin, her eyes narrowed. "Yeah?"

"Under the circumstances, my superiors will be paying exceptional scrutiny to your field reports. Bear it in mind. Linder out."

The screen went black.

THREE

"Exceptional scrutiny?" Kevin asked, looking between Jessie and the dead screen. "What'd he mean by that?"

Jessie stood up. She shook her head, her nose wrinkling.

"Meaning years of faithful service ain't enough to buy me a pass. They wanna make sure I don't go native."

"To be fair," April said, "the King of Wolves was a long-dormant threat. Then we learned about the King of Silence, and Huburtus Becke intimated there were more than just the two."

I remembered Becke's words, echoing in the vast hangar beneath the wing of the space shuttle *Endeavour*. "Our research plumbed beyond the boundaries of this dimension," he'd told us, "but we were not alone, nor were we the first. There are Kings in the outer dark, young lady. The King of Wolves, the King of Worms, the Kings of Lament and Rust. And others."

A madman had conjured the King of Silence, pulling it from a nether realm that some had dubbed "the Shadow In Between." Becke and his allies couldn't send the thing back where it came from, so they shot it into outer space. We'd staved off an apocalypse out in California when Bobby Diehl—billionaire tech magnate and closet sorcerer—tried to put the thing on a leash. It had been a close call, too close, and the idea that more of these creatures were lurking out there made for a lot of sleepless nights.

"I'll be in the next room," Jessie grumbled. "Gotta pack my shit. Everybody be ready to roll in ten."

I followed her over. She slung her suitcase onto an unmade bed, grabbing clothes from the dresser and tossing them in by the fistful. I unzipped my own case. Packing for me is easy: two black suit coats, neatly folded. Two pairs of black slacks, pressed. Two ivory blouses. Underwear, toiletries in a clear plastic zip-top bag, and a row of neatly rolled neckties, each in a different color. Years of traveling, usually with less than an hour's notice, made the process of packing and folding mindless, mechanical. I glanced over at Jessie, silently stewing as she took out her aggression on her clothes.

"They're just scared," I told her.

"They're just *stupid*. What, they think if I cross paths with some-body who's got the same condition I do, I'm gonna get all buddy-buddy? Give 'em a big hug and switch sides so we can hang out together and do evil-monster shit?"

"They don't know what to think. These creatures . . . it's a new kind of threat, Jessie. Demons and rogue mages, we know how to handle. We're flying blind here, and you're the only living lead we have. Until now, anyway. You gonna be okay?"

Jessie sighed. She tugged a rumpled, balled-up top from her suitcase and made a halfhearted attempt at folding it before putting it back.

"It's just insulting. We're out here on the front lines, sweating and bleeding and getting the job done, while Linder and his buddies sit on their asses in some smoky boardroom in DC. The hell do they get off, questioning me?" Her shoulders sagged. She fell silent for a moment. When she spoke again, the fire in her voice was gone. "Besides, under the circumstances, what we talked about at dinner . . . the timing on this mission kinda sucks."

"Hey, this could be just what we need. They've been touched by the King of Wolves, and they've got the power that goes with it, same as you. Maybe they know how to keep it under control."

"I guess. Maybe. Just gotta track 'em down without me flipping out and killing anybody in the meantime." She looked my way. "You sure you're okay with this, working with me right now?"

"You're my partner."

"That's not an answer."

I nodded. "To me, it is. What'd I tell you, back in Talbot Cove? I don't have time to be afraid of the Bogeyman *and* the Big Bad Wolf."

She flashed a tiny smile. "Yeah."

# # #

We flew from Nashville International into LaGuardia, with a long stop-over on the way. Five and a half hours squeezed into coach, my shoulder slumped against hard plastic and moonlit clouds streaming outside the porthole as I tried to get some sleep. I faded in and out, lulled by the vibrations of the engine. I woke as the sun rose over a gray and stony October morning, casting spears of hazy light down into the canyons of New York City. It started to rain as we touched down on the runway. The landing gear jolted, squealing, and the jet's brakes roared while droplets of drizzle flecked the windows, offering us a cold welcome to the crossroads of the world.

The city had seemed endless from the sky, sprawling as wide as it was tall. It had filled every last foot of earth, nowhere left to go but up. We rode a black rental SUV across the Queensboro Bridge and headed for Manhattan. Seagulls wheeled in the sky above the East River, and along the water's edge, mighty cranes swung girders and slowly added height to four newborn skyscrapers.

April and Kevin set up our center of operations in a junior suite at the Grand Hyatt while I called ahead, touching base with a lieutenant at the Midtown South Precinct. He'd already been briefed, pulled into the loop by the nonexistent SAC Walburgh; he didn't bother pretending to be happy to hear from us, but he gave us the bank's address and said he was sending a couple of his people to play tour guide.

"You ready for this?" I asked Jessie as we got back in the SUV.

"Let's see," she said. "We've gone up against a sorcerer with his own pocket universe and a monster from outer space. Yeah, I think tracking down a few bank robbers—juiced up or not—should be a pretty light day for us."

Famous last words.

# # #

Behind a web of yellow tape, I stood in the foyer of the National Equity Bank and listened to ghosts. The bodies were all gone, carted off to the morgue, but they'd left signs of their passing: faded rusty smears on the marble and crumpled holes in the sleek white walls, the spent rounds already dug out and measured and photographed.

This was how I saw the world: a long string of crime scenes. The aftermath of violence, of chaos, of fear, arriving too late to help anyone or change anything. That was the nature of the war; the bad guys always got to throw the first punch. All I could do was walk the empty, silent span, listening to my flats click on the cold marble floor, count the clues, and offer my silent promise to the victims: *I couldn't save you, but I'll make sure this doesn't happen to anyone else.*

I couldn't save you, but for whatever it's worth, I'll make sure somebody pays for it.

The locals were on the scene to let us in and pass the torch. A pair of NYPD detectives, looking like mismatched bookends. One was a tall, dark peacock, draped in a tailored suit a few dollar signs above his pay grade. By comparison, I could only assume his partner had dressed in the closet with the light turned off. A mop of ragged and windblown blonde hair complemented her mismatched wardrobe. Still, her pale hand gripped mine like a steel vise, and her all-business attitude had me liking her from square one.

"Detective Marie Reinhart," she said. "This is my partner, Tony Fisher. We caught the case yesterday. I assume you're taking point?"

I nodded. "Special Agents Harmony Black and Jessie Temple. What are we looking at?"

"Hell of a lot of nothing." Marie pointed to the dried blood spatter on the floor. "Vics here, here, and two of our brothers in blue took it on the sidewalk outside. You saw the cell-phone footage?"

"We did."

Marie rounded on me, one hand on her hip. "Well, we *didn't*. Our witness's phone got confiscated twenty minutes after we brought him in, by some desk jockey with a cheap suit and Homeland Security credentials. You want to tell me what that was all about?"

I shared a glance with Jessie.

"Just what it says on the tin," Jessie told her. "The boys in ICE flagged one of the bank patrons as an immigration risk and kicked it up the chain. They wanted the footage so they could do further photo verification. Sorry, not our call. And nothing to do with this case."

"Really," Tony said, his voice cool and smooth. "So multiple eyewitness accounts of a security guard getting thrown fifteen feet across the lobby, like something out of a superhero movie, had nothing to do with it."

I shook my head. "Like I said, we watched the footage. Your witnesses were jacked up on adrenaline and seeing things. One of the thieves flipped a guard, sure, some kind of judo move. It was more like five feet, tops."

"His neck was broken in three places," Marie said.

"He was eighty-something and had severe osteoporosis. It didn't take a lot to kill him."

Marie's eyes locked with mine. I was used to the local authorities knuckling under as soon as we flashed our badges. They'd grumble sometimes—nobody likes being upstaged by the feds—but most of them were just grateful to shuffle a problem case onto somebody else's work pile. Not her. There was something fierce behind her eyes, bordering on feral.

Tony caught the look, too. He gestured to Jessie, nodding to one side.

"Hey, sister. Can I talk at you for a sec?"

They gave us a little space. Marie took it away. She closed the gap between us, her voice low and hard.

"I get it," she said. "You're a globe-trotter. Town to town, case to case, you fly in and you pull the reins and win the glory. Can't trust the local yokels, because if we knew what we were doing, we'd be in the FBI like you."

"That's not—"

"This is *my city*, Agent Black. I have two dead civilians, two dead cops, and the shooters are in the wind. I think your partner's story about immigration is a crock. I think you're holding back evidence. And you should consider yourself lucky I'm not inviting you to talk it over in the alley around back."

I held my ground and my gaze steady.

"Are you threatening a federal agent, Detective Reinhart?"

"When I'm threatening you," she said, "trust me, there won't be any room for misinterpretation. I swore an oath to protect this city. If you want to yank this case away from us, I can't stop you. But don't you dare try to keep me from doing my job."

"I wouldn't dream of it. You've got me all wrong, Detective. I'm here for one reason and one reason only: to help. You're right. We've got four shooters on the loose, and time isn't on our side. So can we extend a little trust and work together, or do you really want to step outside?"

She stared me down. One eyelid twitched, just a little, as she squinted at me. There was something . . . off, behind her eyes. Bad wiring. I recognized something in that. Something like me.

I waved my hand, taking in the lobby, the aftermath, the silence. "You feel this, don't you? You're not going to sleep until these people have been caught."

"Until they've been punished," Marie said.

"Neither will I," I told her.

She nodded slowly. I think she saw something familiar behind my eyes, too.

"All right," she said. "Sorry. I . . . take this job a little personally sometimes."

"You and me both."

The faintest hint of a smile. "If you've seen the footage, not sure what else I can tell you. We know there were four perps, possibly with off-site support: depends on whether one of them hacked the security feeds or if they had outside help. They ditched their gear two blocks from here, then vanished. Given the drop site, I think they escaped on the subway; there's an entrance less than a hundred feet away. Of course, without knowing what they look like, security footage from the underground won't tell us a thing."

"I understand they got away with less than five thousand dollars?"

Marie spread her hands. "Which they would have known in advance. There's a reason bank robberies like this just don't happen anymore. Sure, you get some lone nut with a gun—or a note claiming he has a gun—making a go at it, but if you've got the resources to put together a heavy crew, there are about a thousand places in this city you could rob and come away with more cash than that. Hell, rob any place *but* a bank: you could probably make more money strong-arming a McDonald's. Safer, easier, and the crime doesn't carry federal weight."

"And they didn't demand access to the vault? They didn't even try?"

Marie cast a glance across the empty teller lanes, past the collapsed ropes of blue velvet. "No, didn't even ask for a manager. They came in, cleaned out the tills, drilled a few safe-deposit boxes, and left."

"Any idea what their take was from the boxes?"

Marie shook her head. "The bank's cooperating. They're reaching out to all the box owners, asking them to volunteer a list of what was taken. Likely wasn't much, though: FDIC insurance doesn't cover safe-deposit boxes. People put passports in 'em, birth certificates, documents that might be *personally* valuable but worthless to your average thief unless they're working some kind of identity-theft scam."

Smart criminals, stupid crime. Back in my old life as a field agent—before I was drafted into Vigilant Lock, recruited to fight a shadow war against things that shouldn't exist—I usually saw it the other way around. I'd lost count of how many idiots I'd put in cuffs, convinced they were the next best thing to Professor Moriarty when they were really just thugs with delusions of grandeur. Not these four, though. They'd prepared themselves and put it all on the line . . . for next to nothing. It didn't make sense, which meant I was missing a piece of the puzzle.

"Show me the safe-deposit boxes," I told Marie. "I want to see what they *didn't* take."

FOUR

The safe-deposit vault was a little bigger than a walk-in closet, walls of tiny doors with double-key locks surrounding a narrow white laminate counter. A clutter of steel boxes littered the counter, sitting in a mess of loose paper. Just like Marie had said, nothing an average thief would want—birth certificates, marriage licenses, a couple of car titles, all crumpled in a rough hand and tossed aside.

My gaze slid along the walls. Here and there, a scattering of doors hung open, their locks punched out with brutal efficiency. A few had been drilled too fast, too sloppily, mangling the inner door and leaving the prizes inside untouched.

"Careless," I murmured, my fingertips brushing a patch of warped, twisted steel. "Why get careless now? Why do it at all?"

Marie stood in the doorway, a hand on her hip. "You figure it out, let me know. I'll be over at the tills. I want to take another look at yesterday's receipts."

I nodded, and she left me in the silence, under the hot white glare of overhead lights. There was something here, something I wasn't seeing yet. I reached into my breast pocket and took out a pair of glasses. Thick, black Buddy Holly frames, and the lenses were nothing but simple, untinted glass. The glasses were a gift from the enemy, a mole who'd used a hidden bug to follow our every move. The bug was gone, the mole was dead, and now they served a new purpose. One click of a button paired the concealed electronics to my earpiece and my phone.

"April," I said, "I could use some of your insight here."

"I'm receiving," she said. The pinhole camera in the glasses streamed a live video feed back to a laptop. She could see and hear everything from the safety of a hotel room, five blocks away.

"Why drill the boxes? They wasted time, they probably didn't find anything worth stealing, and they would have known that going in. Every minute they spent in the bank brought them closer to getting busted or dead."

"They had a reason," April said. "So look for the incongruity. What's out of place?"

The glasses recorded a slow sweep across the room. The pile of ransacked boxes, the scattered papers . . . and then a lone box, lying discarded in the corner of the room. I crouched down and picked it up gently. The black metal lid swung back, nothing inside but dust.

"Empty," I said, trying to put myself in the thieves' shoes. "Did you find something worth stealing in this one?"

My fingertips brushed the marble floor. Tracing a chip in the stone that matched a dent in the corner of the box. I stood up slowly and pantomimed hurling the box to the ground.

"No," I said softly, "you didn't. And you were angry. Frustrated. But you wouldn't be . . ."

"Unless they expected to find something in that particular box," April said.

I looked to the doors. Drilled locks here and there, some neat, most fast, sloppy. Like they'd gone faster and faster, driven by fury and the ticking clock.

"Interesting fact," April said in my ear. "It is exceedingly difficult for humans to create truly random patterns. We're driven by the need for symmetry and order."

Three pristine doors, then a pair of drilled locks. Two columns over. Five pristine doors, then a pair of drilled locks. Two columns over. Seven pristine doors—

"It's not random," I said. "It's just supposed to *look* random."

"Find the door that doesn't fit the pattern."

Now that I saw it, I couldn't unsee it. The perfectly symmetrical layout of ravaged doors, wrapping around the room, except for one. The one with the slowly, carefully drilled locks, removed with surgical precision.

I swept out into the lobby. Jessie and Tony, talking in low voices by a rack of brochures, looked over with a question in their eyes. Marie, behind the tills and buried in thick ledgers, barely glanced my way.

"This wasn't a bank robbery," I said.

Now I had her attention. "Beg your pardon?"

"It's a smoke screen. The heist, the random boxes—all of it was just a ruse to throw us off the scent. To hide the real crime."

I held up the empty safe-deposit box, the one with the dented corner.

"They didn't rob a bank," I said. "They robbed one customer. Box 1017. This is what they killed four people to get."

Jessie walked over, eyeing the empty box. "Any idea what was inside?"

"If I'm reading the scene right? Nothing. Whatever they *thought* they were going to find, it wasn't here."

Marie held up a finger. "Hold on. Like I said, the bank's cooperating. The honchos at National Equity handed over their low-level passwords so we could pull customer info. Give me a minute and I'll find out exactly who rents that box."

She hunched over a terminal, typing furiously, and Jessie pulled me aside.

"Nice sleuthing," she said, her voice low. "I've been making friends with the locals. Which is easy, considering Tony's been hitting on me since the second we walked in."

"Did you tell him you're not into guys?"

Jessie shrugged. "Nah. Anyway, he warned me his partner has something of an anger-management problem."

"I noticed."

"Apparently she's an obsessive workaholic who treats her job like a holy crusade against the forces of evil. I said I couldn't possibly imagine working with somebody like that."

"Cute," I said. "Get anything useful out of him?"

She shook her head. "Just damage control. I confirmed that nobody got a copy of that cell-phone video before Linder's guy scooped it up."

Marie looked up from behind the terminal. "Got it. And as if things weren't weird enough already, the customer isn't a local. He's got a Michigan mailing address."

That perked up my ears. I had history in Michigan. Bad history.

"What's his name?" I asked her.

"Douglas Bredford."

# # #

We knew Douglas Bredford.

Jessie and I had crossed his path on our first case together. He'd been drinking himself to death in a backwoods bar, burned out and broken. A life in the occult underground had left Bredford with a head full of horrors. We thought that was his whole story, until he dropped a name, one he obviously wanted us to follow up on. Cold Spectrum. We woke a sleeping beast. One of Kevin's hacker buddies had to flee across three states to get out from under the avalanche as encoded traffic from the DoD to the NSA to some backwater IRS office flew fast and furious, all asking the same question: *Who wants to know about Cold Spectrum?* Even our boss got in on the act, Linder subtly prodding us to find out if we'd been in contact with Bredford.

"There's only one thing that involves this much back-channel cooperation in DC," Kevin's contact had told us. "Heavy, heavy black-ops shit. Leave it alone, man. Just leave it alone."

Then Douglas Bredford's trailer exploded. Just before he died, he paid a neighbor to watch for us at the crime scene and pass on an envelope full of photographs. A scattering of candid shots, morgue photos, and news clippings—nothing that made sense, nothing we could use. And a photo of Linder, walking down the steps of the Capitol Building with a pack of suited men, a bloodred bull's-eye drawn around his face.

Whatever Cold Spectrum was, Bredford had been hip-deep in it. And he'd chosen his way out, his way of silencing the nightmares: tipping us off had started the chain reaction that ended his life. Now we were the heirs to a mystery and the custodians of a fistful of clues that didn't point anywhere.

"They knew who they were targeting," I said, working it through. "They knew what they *thought* they'd find in Bredford's safe-deposit box. But it wasn't there. Somebody else emptied it out first. They keep logs of everyone who accesses the boxes, right?"

Marie held up a spiral binder stuffed with tattered pages. "You have to sign in. You show your ID, sign the log, then a bank employee escorts you in. You've got one key, they've got the other, and both have to fit to open the box."

"Can we find out when Bredford was here last? He must have cleaned his box out."

"There's eight of these behind the counter," Marie said, thumping the binder down on the edge of the teller's booth. "Everybody grab one, let's get to work."

I started from the back, and even then I suspected we'd have to dig into the bank's archives. When we were in Talbot Cove, Bredford was in no shape to travel; I didn't know how he managed to drive to the bar and back without getting into a wreck. Whoever these thieves were, whatever they were after, they were going on outdated information.

Or I was. Barely five minutes after we started the hunt, Tony thumped his finger down on a scrawled signature.

"Bingo," Tony said. "And damn, looks they just missed him."

I frowned. "What do you mean?"

He spun the binder around to give me a look.

"Douglas Bredford was here yesterday," he said. "Accessed his box a little after one in the afternoon, just a few hours before the heist."

FIVE

Jessie and I shared a look. The authorities wrote off the blast at Bredford's trailer as a meth-lab explosion; there wasn't much evidence left behind, and what was left of Bredford's body could be picked up with tweezers.

Jessie leaned close and whispered what I was already thinking. "Mikki died in an explosion, too, before she turned up alive and well in Oregon. Easy way to fake a death—just get a fresh corpse with your height and build and make sure there aren't enough pieces left for a positive ID. You think Bredford hoodwinked us?"

"Only one way to find out." I looked to Marie. "The security-footage hack, erasing all the feeds from the bank cameras . . . did it cover the entire day's recordings?"

She shook her head. "Just the time of the robbery, plus maybe forty minutes on either end."

"Any chance they could give us a look at the feed from when Bredford signed in?"

Something in my voice tipped Marie off. She had good instincts. That, and a stare like she was trying to crack open my head and look inside.

"You know something about this Bredford guy, Agent?"

"No. But if we get a visual, I can run his image through the Bureau's facial-recognition software. It might help track him down faster. If these thieves were after his belongings, and he got here first, it stands to reason they'll be hunting for him."

She gave me a grudging nod, accepting the lie.

"Let me make a few phone calls," she said and pushed herself away from the counter.

"That envelope full of pictures," Jessie told me. "That hasn't sat right with me since day one. Bredford knew he was gonna die—or maybe knew he was gonna fake it. If he wanted to put us on Cold Spectrum's trail, what's with the cryptic hints? He could have just written a letter and laid it all out for us instead of sending us stumbling around in the dark."

"Unless that was the idea all along. It's just like Fontaine did, back in Talbot Cove: he gave us a few clues and sent us stumbling into his enemy's path to draw fire while he tried to get ahead of the competition. I'm starting to think we've been played, big-time."

Marie strode back over to us, checking her phone.

"All right, they're e-mailing a clip over. The log gave us the exact time he signed in, so isolating the footage was easy." She pointed at the nozzle of a thin gray camera, angled down at us from the back wall of the lobby. "Should give us a nice, clear shot of his face."

It was a clear shot, all right. From the brim of his fedora to his gleaming teeth to the creases on his secondhand suit.

"Son of a *bitch*," Jessie breathed.

Marie's eyes narrowed. "What?"

"That isn't Douglas Bredford." I tapped the screen, freezing the image on his obsequious smile. "That's Tucker Pearlman. He's a tabloid reporter."

Tucker ambushed us with a video camera in Talbot Cove, camping on the sidewalk outside a victim's house. The way he saw it, my hunt for the Bogeyman—the criminal who murdered my father when I was six years old—was a cage match for the ages. In the end, we'd traded a false lead for a real one and scored a clue that broke the case wide-open. I thought—hoped—that we'd never hear from him again.

And here he was, sticking himself right into the middle of our case. And probably getting himself killed, if we didn't find him before the thieves did.

"If he's not our man, he had the key to his box," Tony said. "And a driver's license with Bredford's name on it. Wouldn't have gotten past the teller without both."

"You know where to find this guy?" Marie asked me.

"I've got a pretty good idea. And if he cleaned out Bredford's box yesterday, I can all but guarantee he's crossed state lines by now, heading home to Michigan."

"All the same," Marie said, "we'll shoot an APB to LaGuardia, JFK, and Newark International. Bus and train terminals, too. If he's still in the city, good chance we'll nab him on his way out."

I gave her my card. Not my official FBI one, with a bogus address and a voice-mail box that routed to an empty office somewhere in Virginia. The one I gave to informants, cream embossed with a cell number in crisp black type. That's all. No name, no identifying marks, just a number. Marie raised an eyebrow.

"If you run him down before we do," I said, "call me."

"Agent? A word?"

The two of us stepped off to the side. She twirled my card in her fingertips.

"First, Homeland Security yanks the only footage of the robbery we've got. Then I name the box owner, and I clocked you *and* your partner recognizing it. Read it all over your face, so don't waste my time pretending otherwise. I've got a pal in the Bureau. I've seen his business card. This doesn't look anything like it, which tells me this isn't a government number, which in turn tells me you're running a back-channel operation. You want to tell me what the hell is going on here?"

I met her gaze. "I bet you're really good at poker."

"I'm not much for games in general."

"Douglas Bredford," I said, tiptoeing around the chasm of her suspicion, "is a person of interest in another case. An unrelated one, or at least that's what I thought. To be honest, the name caught me by surprise."

"That, I believe. And the cloak-and-dagger business?"

Detective Reinhart was a bloodhound; her partner characterized her as a crusader, someone who lived and breathed the job, and I could see it in her every move. How do you throw somebody like that off the scent? If I was standing in her shoes, what would work on *me*?

She needed validation, to feel like she was on the right track. So I gave it to her. Sometimes you can cover one lie with an even bolder one.

"You're right. The story about ICE is a cover. This has nothing to do with immigration or the other bank customers."

Marie unfolded her arms, opening up her body language. "What are we dealing with here, Agent?"

"That other investigation, where Bredford was a POI . . . it involves a domestic terror cell with ties to al-Qaeda."

Her jaw clenched. "These thieves—they're terrorists?"

"We don't know that for certain. We don't know anything just yet, but this other case involves several years of surveillance and deep-cover infiltration. We're on the cusp of taking this entire cell down before they can hurt anybody, but *only* if nothing blows our operation. We can't take any chances; I'm endangering my career, just telling you this much."

"I was in Manhattan," Marie said, "the day the towers came down. Just tell me what you need. I've got your back."

I caught the flash of pain in her eyes and managed to only hate myself a little. I knew exactly what I was doing: playing the odds, getting into her head, betting that a subtle invocation of 9/11 might be the perfect spur to get her on my side. Manipulating people is part of my job. Doesn't mean I have to like it. What I needed was a vow of silence, and assurance that if Tucker Pearlman showed his face, they'd shove him into a solitary cell and keep him quiet until we showed up to collect him.

# # #

I still figured Tucker was long gone, but I got Marie's card and we agreed to keep in touch; I had a feeling I'd be seeing her again. Jessie and I headed back to the hotel, where Kevin had the front page of the *New Perspective*, Tucker's rag of a digital newspaper, up on his screen. I watched him click past articles on UFO sightings and secret celebrity scandals, hunting for bylines.

"I'm already inside their server," he told us. "Hold your applause. It only took about five minutes on the telephone with tech support, pretending to be Tucker's boss. They asked for personal information that I scooped off the guy's public Facebook profile, then they handed me full access to his account. Pro tip: if your official password reminder is your dog's name, maybe don't post about your dog every five minutes."

I stood behind his shoulder, leaning in. "Okay, so how does this help us?"

"Tucker's about as off the grid as you can get without going full-on survivalist. The guy chases conspiracies for a living; no surprise he thinks everybody's out to get him. His job's the only exception. For that, he *has* to leave a footprint. This site's running a basic template, and all of the *Perspective*'s so-called reporters—there are only three of them, including Tucker—have full access privileges. They upload articles straight to the site, then the editor gives 'em a once-over and approves them to go live. The site logs the IP addresses that everyone connects from."

He clicked a button, and a subwindow popped up on the screen, a scrolling table of numbers and decimal points connected to page addresses.

"This article, about some guy at an auction spending a million bucks on a hat? Tucker posted this yesterday morning. The IP tracks to a Starbucks on Broadway."

"Okay," I said. "So he was here. We already know that."

Kevin held up a finger, then pointed to a line at the bottom of the list. "But this morning, about four hours ago, he uploaded this little gem of journalistic excellence."

He clicked through to the article. GRAFFITI GONE VIRAL, the headline screamed.

> A marketing ploy, or proof of Illuminati mind control? Over the past week, the images have spread from Miami to Houston to LA, painted by ordinary citizens who claim to have no memory of the deed. Plagued by nightmares, these afflicted souls are . . .

My eyes glazed, sliding over the lurid copy down to the photograph in the corner of the screen. Scarlet paint splashed a dirty brick wall. It took the shape of a great horned owl, mad eyed and razor clawed. And scrawled on the bricks beside it, a message: THE OWL LIVES.

"Five bucks says it's viral marketing for a horror flick," Kevin said. "Anyway, the IP points to Three Oaks, Michigan. A breakfast-and-lunch diner called the Cozy Corner Café. Now, look farther up the list. Tucker's last three articles, before his jaunt to New York, got posted from the exact same place. We might not have his home address, but we know he likes to write in public, and it looks like Three Oaks is where he hangs his fedora."

"He likes his routines," I said. "His familiar, comfortable hangouts. That's where we'll find him."

SIX

Three Oaks was a kissing cousin to Talbot Cove, three and a half hours west of Detroit and separated by ten miles of forested backroads. A mint-green sign at the edge of town, shaded by a tiny shingled roof, read WELCOME TO THREE OAKS. HOME OF *PRANCER* THE MOVIE.

Jessie let out a long, low whistle as our SUV cruised on by. "We are no longer in Manhattan. Does it feel like home, Mayberry?"

"You know damn well I left Michigan when I was six," I told her, "and don't call me Mayberry."

"I'm just surprised you haven't asked about tonight."

"Asked what?"

She stared at me. "Seriously?"

I drummed my fingers on the steering wheel, not sure what to say.

"Sun's gonna be down in fifteen minutes. The Cozy Corner Café is already closed, and it doesn't open until six in the morning. We've got all night and nothing to do with it."

"Speak for yourself," Kevin said from the backseat. "I've got a laptop and a World of Warcraft subscription. I *always* have something to do."

"And you state this fact as if you're strangely proud of it, instead of feeling a proper level of nerd shame," Jessie told him. She looked my way. "Talbot Cove is like, five minutes away from here. Why don't you swing over and drop in on your boyfriend?"

"What? I don't have a—oh."

"Yeah," Jessie said. "Deputy Cody? Cowboy hat, washboard abs, tight jeans? Hell, if I was into guys, you *might* have competition."

I shrugged. "I hadn't really thought about it."

"I say again: seriously?"

"We're on a mission, Jessie. Personal time is for when the mission's done. I like to keep things . . . compartmentalized. Life is cleaner that way. More orderly."

"Have you ever been tested?" she asked me.

"Tested for what?"

"Anything."

April coughed delicately into her hand.

"As it happens," she said, "I do have a bit of research I could use a hand with this evening. I've acquired some scanned documents from the turn of the century, dealing with obscure historical fables about wolves. Thought we might poke through them and see if anything relates to our current quarry."

I met her gaze in the rearview mirror, a silent look of gratitude. She nodded in response, a faint smile on her lips.

Jessie turned around, staring at April over the seat back. "You do understand that I'm trying to get Harmony laid, right?"

"I am aware, yes."

"As your fearless leader," Jessie said, "the mental and physical well-being of my team is extremely important to me."

"Duly noted," April replied.

"Given that you are a psychologist of considerable renown, you'll surely agree with my diagnosis: that given her emotional state and generally high-strung personality, if Harmony doesn't get some high-quality boning as soon as possible, she may literally explode. Literally."

I gripped the wheel and sighed. "I'm sitting *right here*."

"Don't look at me," Kevin said, head buried in his laptop. "I checked out of this conversation thirty seconds ago."

We rented a couple of rooms at the Comfort Inn, then called around until we found a pizza place that delivered. I spent most of the night sitting beside April at the tiny table by the window, poring over blurry scans of old storybooks while Kevin battled orcs on his laptop, and Jessie alternated between doing calisthenics, looking for something to watch on the room's grainy TV, and complaining about the sad state of modern television programming. For all that we found in the texts—eyestrain and a fat load of nothing—I think Jessie and Kevin might have gotten more accomplished than we did. Still, I was glad for the work. It kept my brain busy until I was tired enough to sleep.

By the time I found a genuinely engrossing passage, recounting fables of the often-benevolent *vilkolakis* werewolves of Lithuania, fatigue was tugging my eyelids shut. I pushed my chair back, said good night, and stumbled to the room next door. Jessie wasn't far behind me, brushing her teeth and throwing herself onto the queen bed beside mine while I shifted under the thin, starchy sheets.

"Mayberry," she whispered. "You awake?"

"Mmm-hmm."

"You know I only tease 'cause I love, right?"

"Sure," I said.

"But I don't get you. You *like* Cody, don't you?"

"That's . . . a fair way to put it."

"So why the hell didn't you go see him tonight? I mean, even if just to say hi?"

I wanted to say, *because there was work that needed doing.* My knee-jerk response, caught before the words could leave my mouth. A lie so easy I almost believed it myself, but we both knew the truth: April had tossed me a bone, a piece of busywork she could have handled on her own.

"I don't know," I told her. That was the truth.

"Do you think we would have thought less of you? Because we wouldn't have. You don't have to eat, sleep, and breathe this job, Harmony. You can't. You gotta take time for yourself, find some balance, or you're gonna burn out. Or worse."

"I've done okay this long. I just . . . we're on a mission. I can't get distracted." I rolled onto my side. Jessie's eyes glinted like faint, glowing sapphires in the shadows, studying my face. "I don't always . . . process things, in my head, the way other people do. I've always known that. It's not better, or worse, just different. I'm good at puzzles. I'm bad at people. That's just how I am."

"You're a lot better at people than you give yourself credit for."

"*You're* good at people."

"I'm good at *hitting* people," she said. "Just watch. Tomorrow morning I'll prove it."

"You might not have to hit Tucker."

"I don't believe the words *have to* were anywhere in this discussion. And for the record, I still think you need to get laid."

"Good night, Jessie."

Her response, less than a minute later, was a slow and steady snore.

# # #

The Cozy Corner Café filled up at first light. A stream of retirees, vacationers, and locals packed into the tiny restaurant's beige vinyl booths, trading the October chill for the steamy aroma of strong black coffee and eggs over easy. Jessie and I stood in the foyer, shuffling to one side as a waitress in a striped pink apron darted past, holding a tray laden with fluffy pancakes high above her head.

I squinted at the crowd, searching faces. "See him anywhere?"

"Neither hide nor fedora," Jessie said.

A harried-looking young woman scurried up to us with a pair of laminated menus. "Good morning, and welcome to Cozy Corner. Party of two?"

"Looking for one of your regulars," I told her. "Tucker Pearlman. Do you know him?"

Her face scrunched up like she'd just bitten down on a lemon wedge.

"I know him," she said, looking us up and down. "Haven't seen you two around town before. Are you friends of his?"

"Not even close," Jessie said. "We need to talk to him about some outstanding business matters."

The woman tilted her head, her voice dropping just below the din of the crowded restaurant. "Like . . . bill collectors?"

I saw where Jessie was going, and nodded. "We're not legally allowed to tell you that we work for a collection agency. Just like we're not legally allowed to say Mr. Pearlman is several months behind on his car payments."

She beamed. "You're gonna *repo* the creep? Oh, wow. Couldn't happen to a nicer guy. Maybe for once I'll actually get through an entire shift without him trying to grab my ass."

"Legally," Jessie told her, "we can't say if we are or not. But if we hypothetically were, and if he hypothetically used a false address on his loan paperwork in order to hide from us, do you know where we might find him?"

"Wait right here."

You've got to love a small town. In five minutes the waitress had talked to Tucker's cousin's roommate, who pointed her to Tucker's aunt on the other side of the room, and came back with an address scribbled on her order pad.

# # #

Tabloid work didn't pay much. Tucker lived on the edge of town, his cramped little house plopped down on a weed-choked lot. He'd only patched a few of the holes in his frayed screen windows, and old mud caked the dirty white siding. His car, a rust-eaten Ford, sat out on the dirt driveway. A warped board creaked under our shoes as we walked up his low porch. Jessie hammered on the door.

"Tucker Pearlman," she called out. "Open up, FBI."

Nothing. I leaned closer to the door, ears perked. A faint, frantic rustling from inside. Jessie pounded the door again, then looked my way with a question in her eyes.

I nodded and got out of her way. She took a step back and then thundered in, her foot lashing out against the brittle wood. Flecks of white paint and splinters flew as the door blasted open, slamming on its hinges. I was first through the door, Glock drawn and sweeping across the filthy living room, and Jessie smoothly filled in right behind me.

Empty pizza boxes, empty cans of beer littering a crusty carpet. Gnats buzzed in the stifling air, drawn to the glow of a computer screen set up on a folding card table in one corner. A password prompt flashed on the screen. From the number of failed attempts scrolled up behind it, Tucker had been playing guessing games.

There wasn't much more to the house beyond a closet-size bath, a bedroom where eight days of clothes lay rumpled on the floor, and a kitchenette. Jessie took the kitchen while I broke left, squinting in the shadows as I checked under Tucker's bed.

"Got him," Jessie snarled, running past the bedroom door. I poked my head out and looked in the direction she'd come from. A crawl-space hatch lay open, a patch of yellowed linoleum flooring pried up and tossed aside.

When Tucker trench-crawled out from under the front porch, covered in dirt and a twist of spiderweb in his tangled hair, we were patiently waiting for him.

CRAIG SCHAEFER

"I'm sorry," Jessie told him. "When we said, 'Open up, FBI,' were you under the impression that doing so was *optional*?"

His gaze swung between us, his defeated face lighting with sudden recognition.

"It's you. You two. Again."

"Uh-huh," I said. "Now get up, let's go back inside—through the front door this time—and we can have a nice long chat about how much trouble you're in."

Back in his living room, Tucker sat in his folding chair with his cupped hands in his lap while I went through his wallet. He had a driver's license in Douglas Bredford's name, a perfect twin of his own real one. And stuffed in between a couple of tattered singles, a key: a safe-deposit key, bound with twine to a tiny tag bearing the address of the National Equity Bank in Manhattan.

"Misrepresenting your identity to access another person's bank holdings. What's he looking at, Jessie?" I asked.

"Oh, ten, fifteen years easy," she said. "Unless he cooperates, in which case I could be convinced to look the other way on a charge or two."

"I was following a story," he told the floor, head bowed.

"This is going to come as a shock," I said, "but the First Amendment doesn't extend to identity theft."

He looked up at me. "Who's it going to hurt? The guy's dead. And this is a big story, a *real* one. The kind of story that's going to put me on the map."

"What'd you find?" I asked.

"If I tell you everything, will you let me walk?"

Jessie loomed over him.

"Let's hear the story," she told him. "*Then* I'll decide."

SEVEN

"When I heard about the explosion at Bredford's trailer on my police scanner, I hustled over as fast as I could," Tucker told us.

"Did you know him?" I asked.

He shook his head. "Never heard his name before. Didn't matter. I just knew it was a meth-lab explosion in a trailer park, and that sounded like a great lead. I could write it up as a 'corruption and depravity in small-town America' kind of thing, you know? If it bleeds, it leads."

"And what did you find?"

"At first, nothing. Something just felt wrong about the whole scene, though." He tapped the side of his nose. "I sniffed out a story. So I greased a few palms and got a look at the crime scene after all the techs had cleared out. First problem: the explosion was all wrong."

Jessie stood over him, one hand on her hip. "Wrong how?"

"Meth labs have a very distinctive smell, and you can't hide it. It's kinda like . . . well, cat piss. Sniff it once, you'll always recognize it. That's why most meth labs are either mobile or way out in the boonies. None of Bredford's neighbors ever caught an odor coming off his trailer until *after* the explosion. Like someone coated the wreckage with chemicals to simulate the smell. Second, cooking meth involves putting some seriously nasty chemicals under extreme pressure. I'm talking red phosphorus, lithium metal—when that brew goes up, you've got an *incredibly* hot, fast fire on your hands. The best you can do is let it burn itself out. Once the fire department hit the scene, they had that blaze out in less than five minutes. They shouldn't have been able to do that. Then . . . there's this."

He reached under his card table and lugged out a charred black box, about a foot wide and half as deep. The table rattled under its weight.

"Found this, secured *under* his trailer. Or what was left of it."

"You took evidence from a crime scene," Jessie said.

Tucker gave her an indignant look. "It was a lead. This is a SentrySafe 1200 model. Designed specifically to protect against fire damage. Got a buddy of mine to pick the lock."

"And what was inside?" I asked.

"The key to his safe-deposit box. And the tag attached, telling me exactly where to find it. I started digging into Bredford's life, and none of it made sense. Ages ago he was a cop, out in Jersey, and then he just . . . dropped off the face of the earth. I mean, the man vanished. Then about a decade ago he suddenly reappeared in a trailer park outside Talbot Cove, living like a hermit and drinking himself to death."

That part, we knew. Douglas Bredford had sidestepped into the shadows, just like Jessie and me, swallowed up by a world few people knew existed. The things he'd seen drove him to the bottle. What he'd been *doing* all those years—that was the part we couldn't figure out.

"I might have gotten access to his bank account," Tucker said, dipping his head.

"I like how you keep confessing to new crimes," Jessie told him. "It makes our jobs so much easier."

"He rented his box by automatic transfer, a hundred bucks a year. Now here's the kicker: all he ever *had* in that account was a hundred bucks. He'd put the money in about a month before the due date, like clockwork."

"Meaning," I said, putting it together, "that if he ever skipped a payment, the bank would reclaim the box. And open it."

Tucker's head bobbed. He poked a finger at me, his eyes bright.

"See? You get it. The fireproof box, with a key and a tag telling me where to look. Nobody would put a tag on their *own* key—I mean, you *know* where your bank is. It wasn't meant for him. It was meant for whoever cleaned up after he croaked."

"He wanted it to be found," Jessie said. "And the way he rented it, that was an insurance policy in case nobody did. One way or another, if Douglas Bredford died or disappeared, that box *would* get opened."

Tucker spread his hands. "You see? I had to know. I had to be the one to open it. If you ask me, Douglas Bredford was no meth cook. He was murdered. And he knew it was coming."

"So you got a fake ID and flew to New York," I said. "Pretending to be a dead man."

"Damn right I did. I'm a *journalist*."

"That's a very charitable interpretation," Jessie told him. "So what was in the box?"

Tucker jerked his thumb toward the computer screen and the blinking password prompt. "That's where I'm stuck. It was a USB stick. That's all. And it's protected. I don't get it. He *wanted* this to be found, so why put a password on it?"

"Out of the chair," I told him, and got Kevin on the phone while I slid in behind the keyboard.

I thought back to our meeting with Bredford. Then to the envelope of photographs he'd left behind, maddeningly cryptic. He'd wanted the USB stick to be found, all right, but I had a feeling he wanted it to be found by *us*.

"Mirror the screen to my computer," Kevin told me. "It's easy, I'll walk you through it."

While we connected, I tried a few obvious passwords. *Cold Spectrum*, as two words or one, kicked me back to the prompt. No dice.

"Decent encryption," Kevin said. "I can get through it, but it'll take me a while. I'm downloading a copy of the entire stick to my laptop now."

"Might not have to," I said. "Do you have that envelope with the pictures?"

"You think I let it out of my sight? Ever?"

I remembered the first picture in the stack. Douglas Bredford, in younger, happier, and more sober days, standing arm in arm with a pretty brunette in a sun hat. Then the second picture—the same woman, lying dead on a mortuary slab with a bullet between her eyes.

"That first photo in the stack," I said. "It had a phrase written on the back, but I can't remember the words. What was it?"

I heard him rummaging, the sound of ruffling paper. While he looked, Jessie came over and lightly touched my shoulder.

"We gotta get him out of here," she murmured. "If we followed the bread crumbs here, the competition can, too."

"What's that?" Tucker asked, blinking.

"Maybe you heard about the bank heist yesterday? The one where four people got shot? The robbers were after the box, just like you. And there's a good chance they're looking for you."

"Oh," Tucker said. "Oh. Shit."

"Yeah," Jessie sighed. "Nice going, ace reporter."

Kevin came back to the phone. "Got it. It says 'Paris in New York.'"

"I think that was her name," I said. "And she was important to him. Try it. Try 'Paris.'"

The fast rattle of keys. "Got it. We are *in*. Damn, this archive is big. Lots of pictures, looks like some scanned spreadsheets, accounting stuff . . ."

"You've got it all saved on your end?" I asked. "Good. We're on the way back to the motel, just have to get our witness someplace safe first."

"You said they killed *four* people?" Tucker asked, thumping his shoulders against the wall.

"That we know of," Jessie said. "Good news is, you're getting a pass on the identity theft. Frankly, we don't have time to deal with you right now. Bad news is you need to disappear until we catch these guys. You got anywhere you can hole up for a while?"

I was about to hang up when Kevin said, "Whoa. Uh, Harmony? You definitely need to get back here and see this."

"Why? What's up?"

He mirrored his screen back to Tucker's and flashed a grainy photograph on the monitor. A candid shot from across a ballroom. I wasn't sure what year it was taken at first: the flat-screen televisions on the walls clashed with the sea of vintage brown uniforms and red-and-black armbands. And then there was the man behind the podium, dressed in death's-head silver and black, flashing a too-familiar smirk beneath the tight brim of his SS officer's cap.

"Bredford was running deep surveillance on Bobby Diehl," Kevin said. "And pictures of him playing Nazi dress-up is only the tip of the iceberg. This isn't just random data. It's a blackmail file."

Tires rumbled up outside. I pulled my gun and pointed at Tucker.

"You, stay put. I'll check it out."

I emerged into cold autumn sunlight, wary, gun drawn, and my brain had just enough time to register two things. The black Land Rover pulled up lengthwise on the weed-infested front lawn, a piece of mobile cover, and the man in the black balaclava and shades lugging a matte-black rifle from the backseat. A belt of ammunition clattered to the ground at his boots as he swung the barrel around and pulled the trigger.

I threw myself to the grass and rolled as the rifle unleashed hell, chewing a long, ragged streak across the grimy siding and blasting out a window. I recognized the weapon: M249 SAW, man portable but intended to be shot prone, from a tripod mount. Instead, the masked man held it like a pistol in a single hand, firing from the hip. He wasn't alone: the rest of his crew, three more masked killers, boiled from the Land Rover and scattered for cover.

Bullets cracked from the doorway. Jessie, crouched sidelong just inside the door to maximize her cover, emptied her clip. One of the Rover's doors buckled, a side mirror blowing out, and the rifleman stopped shooting long enough to dive for cover. Long enough for me to scramble to my feet and run back inside, firing wildly and keeping his buddies pinned down for a few precious seconds.

While Jessie popped her magazine and reloaded, I looked Tucker's way. "You got a back door?"

He flailed his hands. "The—the kitchen, but it's been stuck forever. That's why I tried going out through the crawl space."

Jessie grabbed his shoulder, and we all hit the carpet as another blast from the SAW perforated the wall, letting in bullet-size streaks of daylight.

"I will *get* the fucker open," she growled, her eyes blazing bright. "Let's go."

We ran to the back of the house, keeping low. Jessie never had the chance to try the door: one of the masked men kicked it open from the outside and hit the kitchen like a blur, halfway across the room and knocking the gun from her hand before I could take a breath. I caught the glint of steel, a fighting knife with a serrated edge in his gloved hand. It flashed out, swinging for her neck. Jessie caught his wrist in an iron grip, twisted, and spun him around. He slammed his elbow into her gut, throwing her back against the kitchen table.

Tucker dived for cover, squirming into the crawl-space hole and throwing his hands over his head. Up the hallway, two more invaders broke in through the shattered front door. While one went for the computer, the rifleman turned my way and raised his weapon. The hall was about to become a shooting gallery, long and deadly straight, and I was the lone target in his sights.

EIGHT

I flung out my open hand as I called to my magic, feeling it flood through my body and down my spine. A rope of raw energy that grasped for the air all around me, corralling the foul-smelling miasma in the stifling house, and pulled it close. My ears popped and my skin prickled as the air congealed before me, streamers of amber mist projecting from my outstretched fingertips and forming a misty shield.

When the rifleman pulled the trigger, the world lurched into slow motion. I heard the hammer of the gun as if I were underwater—a faint and booming echo—and saw the bullets flying my way. The lethal steel wasps slowed as they hit my shield, then froze, hanging suspended in the air.

To my left, Jessie grunted as she hit the refrigerator door. She swung a hammering fist and I heard a jawbone crack. The masked man kept fighting, trading blow for blow, the two of them locked in a lethal dance of clinches and reversals. Moving faster than any normal human, throwing punches that could dent concrete.

Then she got hold of his knife hand, twisted it, and swept his leg out from under him. They hit the filthy floor, hard, and her weight punched the dagger straight through his breastbone.

Blood roared in my ears as the rifleman kept firing, more bullets hitting my shield, inching through it, straining to reach me. I was straining, too, the constant flow of power tearing through my body as I fought the kinetic energy. My arms trembled and my legs nearly buckled, like I was lifting a hundred-ton weight, and an electric pain seared down my spine. The other invader yanked the USB stick from Tucker's computer. It was the woman, the one who seemed to be in charge in the footage from the bank heist.

"Come on," she barked. "I've got the package. Fall back!"

The rifle's muzzle snapped upward, his finger sliding off the trigger. I crashed to my knees on the kitchen floor. My hand swooped down, the last of my energy spent, and the shield came down with it. Shells clattered to the hallway carpet in a rain of jacketed steel.

I had one shot. One chance. As the woman turned, following the rifleman out the front door, I raised my Glock in a weak and shaking hand and aimed for her back.

Jessie hit me from the side. She knocked me flat, pinning my gun hand under her knee, and straddled my chest. My head snapped to one side as she lashed out with a vicious backhanded slap. I tasted blood on my tongue, my vision blurring, and her fingers clenched around my throat.

"Jessie," I croaked. "Jessie, stop. It's me, Harmony. *Stop.*"

She froze.

She stared down at me, blinking, her hands still wrapped around my neck. She pulled them away, slowly, as her mouth opened in horror.

"Oh God," she breathed. "Oh God. Harmony. I'm . . . oh God."

She clambered off me, standing, then stepped backward. Getting away from me, as far as she could, until her shoulders thumped against the broken door.

Tucker peeked his head up from the crawl-space hole. He slowly looked from her, to me, to the dead man on his kitchen floor. "Is . . . is it over?"

I pushed off the floor, sitting up, rubbing my sore throat, and gave him a weak nod. "Yeah. For you, it is. Get out of here, Tucker. They got the USB. Probably won't come after you again, but just to be safe, get out of town for a few days."

"*Probably* won't come after me again?"

"We'll take care of it. Go. Now."

I didn't have to tell him three times. He raced through the house, throwing rumpled clothes and his toothbrush into a duffel bag, while I watched the yard from the window and kept my ears perked. Once a few more minutes had passed, long enough to make sure the gunmen were long gone, I gave Tucker the nod. He booked it. I heard the rattling wheeze of his battered Ford's engine as he peeled out of the driveway, bound for anywhere but here.

All the while, Jessie stayed frozen where she was, her back to the door and her eyes on my reddened cheek.

"I hurt you," she whispered.

"I'm fine."

That wasn't entirely true. My stomach tied itself in a knot, the bill from my magic come due, and it felt like I was being gut-punched with every move I made. The more power I called upon, using my body for a conduit, the steeper the price in the end. The room swam around me. I felt like I was going to throw up. Or that I wanted to throw up, but I couldn't. I focused on my breathing, nice and slow, closing my blurry eyes.

"I could have killed you," she told me.

"I'm fine." I stretched out my hand. "Help me up?"

I could have managed it on my own, but I wanted her help anyway, her hand trembling but strong around mine as she pulled me to my feet. I think, seeing the look in her eyes, lost and afraid, I just wanted her to know it was okay to touch me.

I looked for something to focus on, something other than the fact that I'd just been attacked and nearly strangled by my own partner. So did she. The dead man would do. I pointed to his goggles and mask.

"Want to do the honors?"

The balaclava peeled away. Early thirties, white, with stubble on his face and long, stringy blond hair that gave him a surfer look. Jessie pulled back one of his eyelids with her fingertip. Turquoise eyes. Same as hers.

He'd been wearing a black jumpsuit, like a janitor's coverall, buttoned up the front. Jessie pulled back the snaps and tugged it down off his arms, shifting his deadweight around and tearing the thin fabric around the jagged blade of the dagger where it impaled his chest. Underneath, he wore a Kevlar vest over a thin olive tank top. His arms were decorated in tattoos. Not full sleeves, but bits of ink picked up here and there over a lifetime, some pieces vibrantly colored and others dull and faded. Military, some of it: his left shoulder bore the biggest single piece, crossed rifles behind a beret-wearing skull and the motto AIRBORNE.

"I knew they moved like ex-military," I murmured, studying the art. "The way they covered one another, their tactics. Thought they might be . . ."

I turned his other arm, and froze. Jessie squinted at me. "What?"

I showed her a fresh-looking tattoo, inked in slate black just above his elbow. A sharp-edged triangle behind the Greek letter *chi*, shaped like a wavy-armed *X*. The logo of Xerxes Security Solutions.

"Mercenaries," I said.

I'd first run up against Xerxes on a solo operation in Las Vegas, where the private military corporation had been operating illegally on American soil, lending their firepower to a real estate mogul as part of a ritual-sacrifice scheme. I never did work out the whole story there, but the aftermath saw Xerxes stripped of its corporate charter, most of its recruits arrested, and the remainder—including Angus Caine, their CEO—fleeing with arrest warrants on their backs.

Then we crossed paths in Oregon and almost didn't make it out alive. A new backer—one with deep pockets and long arms, one of their soldiers hinted—hired what was left of Xerxes to retrieve the Red Knight satellite. Caine escaped, but not without leaving even more of his soldiers dead on a shopping-mall floor.

"Looks like somebody's been recruiting new troops," Jessie said. "They didn't have anybody like me back in Oregon."

I photographed the dead man and patted him down. Jessie called in the locals. The house filled up with part-time cops while Jessie swapped credentials with a sheriff's deputy and laid out the sanitized chain of events: we'd gone to interview Tucker Pearlman about a possible threat to his life, based on an article he'd written about meth cartels operating in the Michigan backwoods. Hitters showed up, we drove them off, end of story. Except in her version, the black Range Rover became a powder-blue Voyager. The mercenaries had already proven they'd start shooting at the drop of a hat, and no normal human had a chance at going hand to hand with them; the last thing we wanted was some local cop pulling them over and getting a closed-casket funeral. We'd have to track them down ourselves.

As for the dead mercenary, we weren't thrilled about giving some local coroner a look at a Wolf King–infected corpse, but we couldn't exactly take it with us. We'd report in as soon as it was prudent. Vigilant Lock's cleaners would move in, probably posing as ops from the Centers for Disease Control, and remove the body quietly and cleanly. Standard operating procedure.

First, though, it was time to stop back at the motel and get a look at our copy of Douglas Bredford's files. Whatever was on that stick drew a connection between Bredford's secret life, Cold Spectrum, and Bobby Diehl. And it was something worth killing for.

# # #

Jessie didn't talk. I wanted to, sitting helpless behind the wheel, but I wasn't sure what to say. I didn't want to make things worse. I tried, anyway. Silence wasn't doing either of us any favors.

"I really am okay."

My face and throat had faded to a faint pink, like the last remnants of a sunburn. I still tasted blood, my tongue playing over the hairline split inside my cheek, feeling a sting.

Jessie didn't answer. Her brow furrowed, eyes glancing to the left and down, as if searching her memories. Trying to put it all together.

"They had a scent," she finally said.

"A scent?"

Jessie nodded. "I caught it when I was tussling with the one at the back door. Like a . . . a musk, sort of? I felt it as much as I smelled it. It got into my head. Whispered in my ear. Telling me not to fight. That I *shouldn't* fight them."

"Didn't seem to work the other way. He was doing his best to kill you."

"That's the thing, though. He wasn't. I could see him tense up. Pulling his punches. He was trying to kill me, sure, but his body was fighting him every inch of the way."

Jessie slumped against the passenger-side door, her hand in her chin.

"Got worse when *she* came in."

"The woman?" I asked. "It looked like she was calling the shots at the bank."

"If I got a little hint of that musky scent from the guy I was grappling with, she was . . . like a fire hose on full blast. From the other side of the house. And I don't think she was doing it on purpose, like you and your magic. The scent was just *her*."

I stopped at a four-way intersection, a lonely rural road littered with October leaves.

"That's why you attacked me."

I didn't want to finish that thought. Didn't want to say the words. But I had to.

"I raised my gun to shoot, and that's when you jumped me." I glanced over at Jessie. "You were protecting her."

She took a deep breath, puffing it out through pursed lips. Sinking deeper into the seat, deflated.

"You gotta go on without me, Harmony. I can't go out into the field again, not until we fix whatever the hell is wrong with me. I could have killed you out there. I can't control myself. I'm not mission functional anymore. Jesus. If any of this gets back to Linder, he'll put out a kill order on me in a heartbeat. Vigilant's got a zero-tolerance policy for rogue agents, especially under the circumstances."

"I won't follow that order."

She snorted. "We're not their only team. He'll call in Panic Cell, have them do it. Or Redbird Cell, if he managed to recruit some rookies to replace the ones who got wasted in Miami. And they'll kill you for harboring me. Maybe they'd be right to take me out. Hell, you saw what happened. I couldn't stop myself. Maybe I'm just as bad as they are, I'm just better at faking it."

"You got sucker punched by a power we haven't figured out yet. That's not the same thing as being bad. You *choose* to be good or bad."

We drove in silence for a little while.

"Did some interesting reading last night," I told her, "looking up old werewolf legends with April. I mean, I know you don't *literally* turn into a wolf, but all legends come from somewhere, and we don't know how long the King of Wolves has been around. I thought maybe I'd stumble across a seed of truth, something we could follow back to the source."

"Let me guess," Jessie said. "You found a whole bunch of stories about psycho killers who howl at the moon. Like my dad."

"Mostly. But not everywhere. Did you know, in Lithuania, there's folklore about good-hearted werewolves? They watch over villages. Protect people."

"Do I look Lithuanian to you?"

We pulled into the motel parking lot, wheels rumbling over loose gravel. I stopped just outside our door.

"I'm only saying, it's not about the power, it's about the person who wields it. The King of Wolves didn't create the woman you are today, and neither did your father. You did. And I believe in you. Now how about we go inside and find out what kind of dirty little secrets Douglas Bredford was hiding all these years?"

NINE

Kevin was right: pictures of Bobby Diehl dressed like a Nazi were just the tip of the iceberg. Especially when the next string of snapshots, captured at the same event, showed a bound and naked potbellied man being led into the banquet hall by a noose around his throat.

We clustered around Kevin's laptop, wide-eyed.

"When were these taken?" Jessie asked.

"Can't tell by the file date," he said. "Looks like they were taken by a digital camera, but those went mainstream in the mid-'90s, and intelligence agencies had their own versions even earlier than that." He paused on a close-up of Diehl's beaming face.

April pointed a crooked finger toward the screen.

"He's younger, though," she mused. "Considerably younger. I'd say this was ten years ago, perhaps? Fifteen?"

The concealed camera had documented the event, watching as the man was bound to a table a masked woman approaching Diehl with a sacrificial dagger on a red velvet pillow. As Diehl raised the blade in one hand and took hold of the man's genitals with the other—

"Okay," Kevin said, fluttering his hand at the screen. He cupped his palm over his mouth, going pale. "I'm out. Somebody else take the wheel here."

April shooed him aside, rolling her wheelchair around to take his spot.

"Seriously?" he said, moving to stand behind the screen. "You're not even a tiny bit queasy right now? You're making me look bad, Doc."

"I spent over a decade in the Behavioral Analysis Unit before I ended up in this chair, young man." April slipped her steel-gray bifocals on and leaned closer to the screen. "This isn't *remotely* the worst thing I've seen."

We paged our way through the ritual slaughter. It wasn't just a murder. It was sheer, gleeful overkill, to the point my own stomach started to churn. Finally, mercifully, it was over, the string of photographs replaced by a scan from an accounting ledger.

"So," Jessie said, "we've got photographs tying Bobby Diehl to a neo-Nazi murder cult. I'm not even a little bit surprised by this. What we *don't* know is why Douglas Bredford, alcoholic man of mystery, had them first."

"Let's keep looking." April glanced over at Kevin. "You can come back now. The scary pictures are all gone."

The next set of photographs was innocuous enough. Security-camera footage from an underground parking garage, following a well-dressed man with a thin leather valise. From the other direction, a woman in black, holding a valise of her own. Bredford had included images from a second camera, making sure he'd saved crisp, well-framed shots of both of their faces.

The stream of pictures showed them meeting, crossing inches apart, then going their separate ways.

"I don't get it," Kevin said. "After Bobby Diehl's murder party, that was a whole lot of nothing."

I shook my head. "No. Back it up, three pictures ago."

Blowing up the photo only made it blurrier, but the details were still there. The bend of a wrist, the lift of a finger.

"They switched cases," Jessie said.

"It's a covert handoff." I pointed to the two valises. From this angle, it was clear they weren't identical. Close, but one was a light tan, and the other was longer, heavier looking, a deeper shade of brown. "And if we can find out who those two people are, I guarantee whatever is in those bags is something they're *not* supposed to be trading. Kevin, I think you were right. Bredford was blackmailing these people."

Next, a parade of numbers streamed across the screen. Ledger pages, bank drafts, dollar signs.

"Forensic accounting is my thing," I said to April. "May I?"

She slid the laptop my way.

"Okay," Jessie said, "while Harmony crunches the numbers, let's get cracking on IDs. We've got pictures of the two people in the parking garage, and the dead man at Tucker's house. Kevin, run all three through the Interstate Photo Service."

He nodded. "On it. I'll pass 'em through a few third-party analysis apps, too, in case any of them have their photos on the Internet somewhere. Long shot, but it's worth trying."

"Good," Jessie said. "April, can you contact your buddy at the Department of State? I'd like to run these through their visa database, too. It looks like the hitter we took out was working for Xerxes—if not now, at some point in his career—and they used to recruit globally, so he might be a foreign national."

We all got down to business. The ledgers painted a picture, drawing each brushstroke line by line and payoff by payoff, slowly coming together until I captured what Bredford wanted me to see.

"We got a hit." Kevin's voice jolted me from my thoughts. "Nothing on our dead wolf guy, but we've identified both of the people in the garage. Harmony's right, though I don't know if you're gonna feel like celebrating. The guy is Gerard Nowak, formerly a high-level mover and shaker at the Department of Defense, currently retired."

"And the woman," April said, "is on record as one Jianhong Min, a low-level administrative assistant at the Chinese embassy in Washington, DC."

Jessie's lips curled in a humorless smile. "Low-level administrative assistant. Right. Moving clandestine operatives onto foreign turf using embassy jobs for cover is an old CIA trick. I bet the Chinese do the same thing."

"Nowak was selling secrets," April said. "And Jianhong was buying, meaning either or both of them could have been under Bredford's thumb. Though as far as I can tell, Jianhong was recalled to China three years ago, so she'll be a bit hard to find."

"It gets worse," I said, turning the laptop screen around.

They gathered in close as I walked them through it, laying out what I'd found.

"Meet Burton Webb. Founder and president of RedEye Infometrics, an advertising and trend-tracking company he founded twelve years ago . . . with Bobby Diehl. Webb was a VP at Diehl Innovations until he spun off to do his own thing, with Diehl's blessing and seed money. Which is good, because according to these ledgers, RedEye only has a single client."

I tapped the screen, tracing a line from one column to another, drawing a map. "These transfers all pass through a shell corporation, which is owned by another shell. And I've seen it before. It's an NSA front. RedEye isn't a civilian company at all. It's a government op with backdoor funding."

"NSA being part of the Department of Defense," Jessie said, pacing the carpet. "And Gerard Nowak was a DoD employee. Add Bobby Diehl into the mix . . . all of these men could be connected."

"There's one more name in Bredford's files." I turned back to the screen. "This is Senator Alton Roth. I never met him directly, but I know him. He's a Vigilant Lock asset."

April lowered her head, peering at me through the top half of her bifocals. "What does he know, and what has he done?"

"Can't say what he knows, but according to this, he's done some very naughty things. Back when I was working that Nevada operation, before I joined the team, Linder called on him to deliver a back-channel favor. I needed Roth to pull some strings and sponsor a multijurisdictional task force in Vegas. Basically, a cover, and a justification for whatever needed doing. Turns out, according to this, he was working both sides the entire time. Remember those Xerxes troops? Senator Roth *hired* them."

Jessie stood behind my chair. Her hand closed over my shoulder as she leaned in, checking out a scan from a corporate bankbook. "The hell? Are you sure? *Why?*"

"Don't know, but he's all kinds of dirty. This is the Nevada Heritage Coalition, a PAC that pretty much exists to get Roth reelected. We've got money going out to Xerxes here. Over here we've got money coming from all *over* the place. Half these corporate donors are in receivership, bankrupt, or just don't exist. It's a big pile of weird. More importantly, it's a pile of evidence tying Roth to everything that went down in Vegas. He might be able to wriggle out of criminal charges by passing the blame, but this would wreck his political career if it ever got out."

April held a notepad on her lap, and a list of names in neat, tight script. She tucked her pencil behind her ear. "So. Four men: Bobby Diehl, Gerard Nowak, Burton Webb, and Alton Roth. Bredford had evidence that could damn all four of them, and may have been blackmailing them in exchange for favors unknown. We also have reason to believe that our wolf-infected thieves are hired guns. Hypothesis?"

"If this was blackmail," I said, "they all knew he had dirt on them. And the second his death hit the news, they would know it was only a matter of time before that dirt got a public airing. One of these four is the man behind the curtain: he hired the team to go and get the evidence back. Find the moneyman, we find the Wolves."

"Let's hope it's not Diehl," Jessie said, "considering we've still got a hands-off order on his evil ass."

Bobby Diehl was a big fish. He was also bait for an even bigger one. Word was, Diehl was worming his way into the Network, a criminal organization with worldwide reach and occult technology. According to Linder, he was our way in: a golden one-shot opportunity to take the Network down from the inside. Until he made the call, nobody was supposed to harm a single hair on Diehl's murderous, sadistic head.

Kevin rubbed his jaw and sat on the edge of the motel bed. "I don't think it's him. When have we seen Diehl do anything . . . normal? Or sane? The guy attacked you with *cyberzombies*. And, you know, the whole trying-to-unleash-an-alien-god thing. That, too."

"More to the point, he also has access to his own gunmen," April mused. "No need to outsource. Senator Roth, on the other hand, has worked with Xerxes before. He's the most obvious candidate. It's your call, Jessie: Who do we pursue first?"

Jessie's brow furrowed, her turquoise eyes glinting. She wagged a finger at the laptop screen. "I keep looking at the intersection. Diehl and Webb are tight, and maybe Nowak, too; it all comes back to RedEye. Y'know, maybe it's just me, but I'd really like to know what those folks are doing with my tax money. Harmony and I are going to check it out. While we do, Kevin, I want you to dig into Senator Roth. Get me *everything*. Every dollar coming in and out of his personal accounts and his campaign coffers. Who he pays, who pays him. April, I need you running interference."

April lifted her chin. "How so?"

"Everything circles around to Douglas Bredford and Cold Spectrum. Including our boss. Linder is involved in this mess, and until we figure out exactly how, I need you to come up with a grade-A cover story to conceal what we're really doing out here. Let's face it, this entire operation went rogue the second Bredford's name came into the picture."

Jessie shut the laptop lid and handed me the car keys.

"And until we get some answers, we're *staying* rogue. Let's roll."

TEN

To reach RedEye Infometrics, we would have to go back the way we came. Retracing our trail in the sky, all the way back to New York City.

"Same hotel?" Kevin asked as we were leaving.

"Yeah," Jessie said, "this one. You and April are staying put. You can coordinate logistics from here, and considering Harmony and I are about to walk into the middle of what looks like a covert NSA op, I'd feel better if you were a few states away. Besides, I don't want Linder tracing our movements, so I'm paying for the plane tickets out of my own pocket. Two is cheaper than four."

"I'll keep our tracks nicely covered," April told her. "Do let me know when you land."

Jessie and I stepped out the door together, into the motel parking lot. A cold breeze in the air smelled like old, dry wood. An early winter, coming in fast.

"So that was half-true," I said.

Jessie shrugged. "Until we figure out what's wrong with my head, I don't want them anywhere near me. Hell, I don't want *you* near me, but I know that's not gonna happen."

"Nope. You're stuck with me."

A yellow taxi with City of Detroit livery squealed into the parking lot, thumping over a curb and spinning hard, kicking up rocks. My hand shot under my jacket, going for my gun, but I didn't draw. The man behind the wheel had jaundiced skin and stringy hair plastered to his scalp with sweat. The cab jolted to a stop right in front of us, and he leaned toward the open window.

"Get in. Now," he said.

"I beg your pardon?" Jessie said.

He let out a heavy sigh. His voice was a slow, syrupy drawl.

"Darlin's, much as I'd like to turn this into a proper reunion with hugs and butterflies and glasses of Sazerac all around, time is something we're blessedly short on."

I blinked. "Wait . . . *Fontaine?*"

He pulled back the collar of his plaid flannel shirt, baring the trail of a Y-shaped autopsy stitch.

"In the borrowed flesh. And—" He paused as my phone began to ring. "I believe, my dear, that someone is looking to whisper dulcet tones of treason into your pretty ear. Go ahead. Get that. I'll wait."

I put the phone to my ear. "Black."

"Agent." Al-Farsi's voice gusted over the line, fast and flustered. "I'm so glad I found you. I must offer my humblest apologies, I—I appear to have made a terrible mistake."

Al-Farsi was an information broker, the man behind the curtain at a nightclub catering to Chicago's occult underground. He had a reputation for knowing everything about everybody, including us. Not the kind of person you ever wanted to hear say the words *terrible mistake.*

"Slow down. What's going on?"

"I was contacted by Bobby Diehl. He offered me a rather exorbitant sum of money for identifying three people in a photograph. I'm sending it to you now."

I lowered my phone and turned it sideways. Jessie leaned in against my shoulder, watching as the picture came through. I knew it instantly: a security-camera shot of Jessie, Cody, and me, standing in the heart of Diehl's Santa Monica R&D lab.

"Of course, you know my ethical code. I would never disclose information about a client, under any circumstances."

Leaning halfway out the car window, ears perked, Fontaine rolled his eyes. He curled his fingers and made a tugging motion in the air.

"I appreciate that," I said.

"Not . . . knowingly," al-Farsi said. "You see, I have quite the extensive file on your organization. It's safe to say I know considerably more about Vigilant Lock than you do, Agent."

"And you said you'd keep it all to yourself. You gave me your word of honor. So what's the problem?"

"The young man, Mr. Cody Winters . . . he isn't *part* of Vigilant Lock. I didn't even know he was a traveling companion of yours, and Mr. Diehl refused to give me the context of the photograph."

A burst of cold wind washed over the parking lot.

"Tell me," I said, feeling my throat go tight. "What did you do?"

"I gave him what he wanted. Nothing on you or Ms. Temple, but . . . everything on Mr. Winters. His name, his place of business, his home address. I assure you, if I had known—"

I hung up on him.

"The man lies like a cheap rug," Fontaine said. "He rooked you on a technicality, as he is prone to do. Now, then: unless you're feeling inclined to arrest me for stealing this car and/or this body, how about you hop in and we go save your boyfriend?"

"He's not my—" I shook my head. Too much to deal with, too many problems at once. "Jessie, go ahead without me. Get to New York and recon the RedEye facility. *Just* recon. I'll be right behind you."

"Are you sure?" Her gaze flicked between us, eyes narrow. She leaned in close and lowered her voice. "Maybe hitching a ride with a *demonic bounty hunter* is not your most rational decision?"

"He played straight with us in Talbot Cove," I whispered. "Well, not at first, but he did when it counted."

"He also has excellent hearing," Fontaine drawled, playing with the fare meter.

"We can't let the trail go cold," I said, "especially now that the Wolves have that USB stick. Right now, they're probably delivering it to whoever paid them off. I want them, and I want their boss. Just let me stash Cody someplace safe, then I'll be on the next flight out."

"Bring him back here," Jessie said. "April and Kevin can get him off the grid. Looks like he's joining the team whether he wants to or not."

She squeezed my arm, tight. I got in the cab.

"You'll have to forgive my driving," Fontaine said. We lurched out of the parking lot, tires squealing as we swung onto a hilly road. "My last car was a Studebaker. Mmm, they don't make 'em like that anymore."

"What's your angle, Fontaine?"

He gave me a sidelong glance and a slow, easy smile. "Why so suspicious, darlin'? Can't I extend a little professional courtesy to a fellow hunter? You said it yourself when we first met: we're all just officers of the peace here. I heard your beau was in trouble, and I came just as fast as I could."

"And I'm thankful for the backup. But you still have an angle."

He drummed his fingers on the wheel and let out a theatrical sigh.

"Fine, fine, if you must know, I'm on a job. The particulars of which led me to the realization that our mutual rival is making some curious moves. I had hoped, when we sent Nyx packing, that'd be the end of that business in Talbot Cove."

I still saw Nyx in my nightmares. Fontaine's competition faced us in the shape of a skeletal horror, flaming and chitinous, fueled by pure rage.

"She's coming after us?" I asked.

"Not her. Worse. Her *momma*. She goes by Nadine, and she's the head honcho of the House of Dead Roses. Spies. Assassins. Dirty deeds at a premium price."

The name jogged my memory. I thought back to the Red Knight case, to a chance meeting at a wine-tasting party . . .

"Nadine," I echoed. "About five eight in heels, blonde bob of hair, looks a lot like—"

"That's her. She introduced herself, didn't she? That was just her playing games while she got a close gander at you. She wants you and your lovely lady friend dead in all the worst ways, and if she can get her claws into your immortal soul, that's just the start of the fun and games. You thought Nyx was a sore loser? That's who she gets it from. She can't just take you head-on, though."

I tilted my head at him, shifting in my seat as he wove hard around a delivery truck then swung back into the right lane.

"Why not?"

Fontaine chuckled. "When you've got all eternity ahead of you— and half of it behind you—nothing matters more than face. She could send her boys after you, or just kill you with her own hands, but a noblewoman with Nadine's standing is expected to have . . . style. A certain panache. No, she's gotta redeem her family honor; that takes a *statement*. Also, scuttlebutt around the watercooler says she's angling for a hound position. That's the right hand of a demon prince, about as high as you can climb on the infernal ladder without committing regicide. I don't know what her long-term game is—believe me, we've *all* got one—but I think she's angling to play you against her enemies. If you die, she wins. If you live, she still wins. And tries, tries again."

"So she got at al-Farsi. Made him give up Cody's name, hoping I'd square off with Bobby Diehl." I worked it through, frowning. "What does she have against Diehl?"

"I was hoping you could tell me, seeing as a little birdie told me you just had a run-in with the man. Whatever happened, he seems to have it in for you and yours. And, more curiously, he's still breathing. Why is that?" Fontaine asked.

As he leaned into the accelerator, skeletal trees and dead leaves whipping past the cab's grimy windows in a blur and the chassis rattling, I weighed my options. Fontaine had helped us out in Talbot Cove, but he'd helped himself first; he was a smooth operator, an opportunist I could trust so long as we both wanted the same thing.

He was also a demon.

"Word from the top," I said. "There's a no-kill order on Diehl. Can't tell you why."

"He's not the only one."

I glanced his way. "What do you mean by that?"

"Oh, just the little incident that tipped Nadine's rage over the edge. The *other* reason she's not coming after you with her claws out. I could tell you about it . . . if you tell me about Diehl. Fair trade."

We rode in silence for a moment.

"There's a criminal organization," I told him. "Worldwide. Occult connected. Impossible to infiltrate. It's called the Network."

Fontaine's eyes narrowed. "I'm familiar with it."

"Diehl's trying to join. He's our way in."

When Fontaine spoke again, he spoke slowly. Carefully choosing every word.

"As one hunter to another, Agent Black . . . stay away from the Network. Far, far away."

"What are they? Are they connected to the courts of hell?"

He shook his head.

"They're something . . . different. Very different indeed. And there are other hells than mine." His shoulders clenched, a nervous shiver, then relaxed. "Well, this casts a new wrinkle on things. And I believe I owe you a story. A meeting was held in Las Vegas, between the hounds

CRAIG SCHAEFER

of Prince Sitri and Prince Malphas. Reportedly, Nadine invited herself to the party, and she didn't like what they decided."

"What was the meeting about?"

"You," Fontaine said. "You and your partner. Normally when humans get too close to the truths of our dour universe—especially if they have a reputation for, say, plaguing our kind?—a swift and violent retaliation is in order. Can't have the evolved apes figuring out who really runs this show. Instead, they've made it clear that for the moment, no subject of their princes—unless acting in self-defense—is to harm a hair on your heads."

"But . . . why? We're the enemy. Vigilant Lock was created to stave off supernatural threats to the United States. The courts of hell are pretty much the definition of a threat."

"It's a question I'd love an answer to myself. Don't get too relaxed, by the way. That's only two courts out of seven—in the United States alone—and your amnesty will only last so long as you're useful. As soon as that's over and done, they'll probably send assassins after you." He drummed his fingers on the steering wheel. "You're useful. Just don't know what you're useful *for*. Caitlin and Royce are formidable on their own; on the rare occasion when they team up, well . . . something big is in the wings. They need something done, and they're under the impression that you and the ferocious Ms. Temple are in the perfect position to accomplish it for them. Assuming Nadine doesn't get you both killed first. Then again, it's also possible they actually *wanted* Nadine at that meeting, expecting she was going to do exactly what she just did, because that's also part of the master plan."

Royce. I'd heard that name back in Chicago when we visited an informant at the Field Museum. Either it was a coincidence, or Dr. Khoury had some explaining to do. It'd wait, for now. In the back of my mind, a distant suspicion reared its sleepy head.

"So basically everyone is manipulating everyone else, and Jessie and I just got sucked into the game. Whether we want to play or not," I said.

74

"It is, sad to say, our nature."

"Fontaine . . . who did you say hired you? And what exactly is this job that brought you here?"

He smiled and gave me a wink. "I didn't. I didn't say either of those things. And I believe this is our stop."

We barreled past the forest-green sign at the village limits, fast enough to rattle its aluminum posts. **WELCOME TO TALBOT COVE: THE TOWN THAT WORKS! POPULATION 2,032**.

Coming in hot, and racing for a world of bad memories and pain.

ELEVEN

I never intended to come back to Talbot Cove.

Maybe that's what kept me away, more than my obsessive need to put things in tidy boxes, to keep mission time and Cody time separated by a clean stretch of wall. Every time I came to this town, people died. Like I was a curse, bringing the troubles of the outside world with me, splashing blood over the Cove's Norman Rockwell–perfect facade.

Not today, I resolved. *Nobody dies today.*

Cody wasn't answering his phone. Straight to voice mail, three times in a row. I told Fontaine where to turn, guiding him around the edge of town and taking a shortcut to the police station. The broken stacks of the old paper plant rose up over the trees in the distance, crumbling brick and steel curved like clutching fingers.

As we swung into the lot, the taxi's rear end fishtailing hard, Barry was rushing out the front door. The burly town sheriff charged for his squad car, red faced and sweating, stopping dead in his tracks when I jumped out of the cab.

"*Harmony?* Hey, I didn't know you were comin' to town! Can you come around later? Love to catch up, but we got a little situation."

"Yeah. We do. Where's Cody?"

Barry jerked a thumb toward his car. "Main Street. I'm headed there right now to help him out. Some damn fool out-of-towner crashed a truck straight through the front window of Hank's Hardware. Nobody got hurt, thank God, but it was a close call. Cleanup's gonna take all day."

I glanced back and met Fontaine's eyes. No need for words—he was thinking the same thing I was. Good way to draw a small-town cop into the line of fire? Cause an accident and wait for him to show up.

Thirty seconds later we were in Barry's car, rocketing toward the middle of town. He cast a dubious eye at Fontaine in the rearview. "Happy to see you and your, uh, friend, but I don't think a car crash really needs the attention of the FBI."

"Cody may be in danger. There's a credible threat. I can't go into details, just trust me on this," I told him.

He nodded, slow, his eyes narrowing. "A threat like . . . last time you were in town?"

"Very possibly."

Barry sighed. "Well, shit. Faced down a demon once and lived to talk about it. Or *not* talk about it. Guess I can do it again. Got a shotgun in the trunk."

Festive banners in orange and gold dangled over Main Street, stretched between lampposts to celebrate autumn and the town's upcoming Halloween festival. And farther down the boulevard, wispy black smoke congealed in the air over thrift shops, diners, and bakeries. A small crowd gathered on the street, a dozen people or so all murmuring and pointing. The rear end of a delivery truck jutted from the ruined facade of the hardware store, bleeding oil onto a river of glistening, broken glass.

And there was Cody, his own squad car pulled off to the curb, walking toward the gathered onlookers with a weary smile and his open hands raised.

"C'mon, folks," he called out. "I know it's an exciting day, but you need to back it up to the sidewalk at least. This wreck's leaking, could be dangerous. Why don't y'all go and have a cup of coffee at Norma's? You can stare all you want from the windows."

Barry slammed on the brakes, screeching to a halt next to Cody's car. I jumped out and the world went into hyperfocus. Threat-recognition mode. No driver in the truck, the door open, cab empty, no signs of a body. Nothing from the windows lining the street, no one on the rooftops, no glint of gunmetal or the gleam of a sniper's scope. Perfect place for an ambush, though: Main Street was a box canyon of old brick, running north and south with no alleys or side exits. Blocking the street on either end would turn it into a shooting gallery.

My gaze shot to the crowd. Clustered locals, mostly elderly, curious and excited faces. Except for one. A man in a black raincoat, tall, only the hint of a pale and stubble-lined jaw under his hood as he shouldered his way to the middle of the crowd.

A hooded raincoat, under a clear blue sky.

I ran for Cody, shouting his name. The stranger reached under his coat, moving in slow motion. One hand came out with a tiny metal remote, antenna up. The other held a plastic jug. He triggered the remote as he tossed the jug to the pavement, then raised one foot, stomping down hard.

I hit Cody from behind and tackled him to the street as the back doors of the truck exploded. A crump of sound and a flash of white light as the doors rocketed open, then came the fog. A bilious-green mist that gusted from the belly of the truck and from the ruptured jug at the stranger's feet, washing over the crowd, stinking of sulfur sprinkled with the faint hint of sweet cinnamon.

Cody fought me, struggling as I pulled him back. "Damn it, let me go, I have to *help* them—"

"It's too late," I snarled, putting my arm around his neck and forcing him away one flailing inch at a time. "Get away from the fog, don't let it touch you!"

Then came the screams. People buckled to the pavement, coughing, choking, clawing at their eyes as the fog swallowed them whole. And in the heart of the chaos, the stranger ripped off his raincoat and tossed it to the wind, emerging from the green mist as he strode toward us. His naked skin bristled with wires and plastic tubes, pumping luminous slime in and out of his bulging muscles. His eyes were baleful, scarlet LEDs, segmented like a fly's, locking in on us with laser precision.

We had just enough time to jump behind Barry's car before the creature raised a pistol in each hand and opened fire, raking the air with bullets.

Barry hunkered down beside me, his hand shaking as he tugged the service revolver from his holster. "What the hell *is* that thing?"

"It's called a Quiet One," I said. "Long story, no time. Stay down. Your gun won't work on it."

Cody had to prove me right. He sprang up from cover, snapping off two quick shots. The cyberzombie staggered back a step as bullets slammed into its cheek and chest. The pale flesh tore away, baring glistening titanium plate beneath. The creature sidestepped, fast, darting behind the ruined body of the truck.

"It's taking cover," Cody said as he dropped down on my other side. "What the hell? These things weren't *smart* last time."

Barry gaped at him. "What last time? Never mind that, how do we *stop* it?"

"I think they've gotten upgrades," I said. My mind raced, putting together a plan. Jessie could have taken the thing down with brute force; back in Santa Monica, her fists had been the only thing that *did* slow down Diehl's monsters, short of blowing up the entire room. I could only work with what I had, and what I had was . . . I turned to Fontaine.

"Look, that thing is basically a corpse hooked up to a computer. Do you think you can do your body jump on it? Possess it long enough for us to put it out of commission?"

Fontaine peered over the hood, giving the creature a dubious squint. He ducked fast as it stepped from cover and opened fire, bullets tearing into the squad car's hood. "I'll give it the old college try, but I've gotta get up close and personal. Think you can distract it for me, darlin'?"

I drew my Glock, holding it close to my chest.

Earth, air, water, fire, I thought. *Garb me in your raiment. Arm me with your weapons.*

"Let's find out," I said, and broke from behind the car. Bullets followed me, slamming into the cruiser's windows, shattering glass. I flung out my open hand and wove the air around me as I charged across the open street, returning fire with pinpoint shots. I knew I couldn't bring the creature down with my gun, but every hit, every patch of torn dead flesh and dented titanium, made it that much angrier.

The fog began to clear, leaving the air hazy and tinged vomit-yellow in its wake. I could taste it in the back of my throat, a foulness that made my skin itch. My eyes watered like I'd been chopping onions, burning and stinging, and my focus nearly slipped as the Quiet One turned its full attention toward me. Bullets froze in the sky between us, spiraling and crawling in the magically hardened air. Another few seconds and I wouldn't have the strength to hold my shield up any longer. I'd stranded myself out in the wide open with no cover, nowhere to run, and the creature's faceted eyes flashed crimson as it drew a perfect bead on me.

Then Fontaine slipped around behind it, running low along the ruined truck, and clasped his hands on both sides of its skull.

Fontaine dropped to the street. The Quiet One lowered its pistols, arms going slack, head slumped, like its plug had been pulled. The scarlet lights behind its eyes flickered as its head shot back up again. It jerked from foot to foot, limbs spasming, the creature—or the malevolent electronics driving it—fighting its demonic intruder.

I checked my gun. One bullet left. I was figuring out where to put it, how to do the most damage, when Fontaine settled the issue for me.

The creature's hands shot up, fingers curling over its bulging mechanical eyes. And slowly, inch by wet, squelching inch, tore them out. Cables glistening with shreds of meat and splintered bone ripped free as emerald ichor spurted from the dead man's eye sockets. It stood there for just a moment, bleeding green and clutching its eyes in its hands, before crashing to the pavement.

Fontaine's borrowed body shuddered, and he grimaced as he pushed himself up. I ran over, taking his hand, helping him to his feet. He leaned against me.

"That," he said in a shaky voice, "was the most unpleasant thing I've experienced in my entire life. And I'm 574 years old. I don't mean the assisted suicide, either, though that was no picnic. They're not dead, Harmony. At least they're not dead when he makes 'em what they are. There was a mind in there, trapped, trying to scream, locked in their memories of the operating table . . ."

His voice trailed off. I squeezed his arm. "Thank you," I said.

The last of the fog lifted, and as Barry and Cody came out from behind the bullet-riddled squad car, we got our first clear look at the gifts Bobby Diehl had brought to this little town. A glimpse of the sheer depth of his madness.

TWELVE

I'd assumed the fog was a poison gas, a chemical weapon designed to kill Cody if the Quiet One couldn't get the job done. I was half-right.

It was a mutagen. And as my skin itched and my eyes burned in the aftermath, I tasted the tang of twisted magic in the air, occult contamination mingling with Diehl's toxic creation. Bodies littered the street, nine or ten of them—anyone who'd been standing at ground zero when the jug burst. Bodies with twisted limbs, their bones turned to rubber and their skulls like slack, deflated basketballs. Flesh turned to dead-white snakeskin, or bristling with fine black fur like a tarantula's legs.

"Lord have mercy," Barry whispered, his forehead beaded with sweat. "Who would do something like this? *Why?*"

I knew the answer. Because he wanted Cody to suffer. And if he had the opportunity to field-test one of his sick technosorcerous creations at the same time, all the better. The collateral damage, the innocent lives lost, wouldn't mean a thing to him beyond raw data.

"Deputy," croaked a raw and faint voice, "help me."

A woman crawled from the pile of bodies. Her fingers had become spears of bone, tearing through her own skin, and her back bristled with ivory spurs. She lifted her head. More bone spurs jutted out from her cheeks; her chin oozed trails of black blood down her ravaged face.

"Norma," Cody said. He rushed over to her. "It's okay, we're gonna get you some help. You just hang on. Barry, call the ambulance!"

I held up a hand. "Cody, don't touch her. She might not be safe."

He shot me a murderous glare, dropping to one knee and pulling Norma into his arms. "She needs *help*, Harmony. Either lend a hand or get the hell out of the way."

"So hungry," Norma rasped. Then her gaze dropped to Cody's throat. *"Meat."*

She opened a mouth lined with barracuda teeth and lunged for him.

I used my last bullet to put her down. Norma's blood spattered across Cody's face and stained his uniform shirt. He dropped her corpse and stood, slowly, his eyes lost in a thousand-yard stare.

"Lord have mercy," Barry said again. He didn't move an inch.

Somebody had to. I holstered my gun and took the reins. "Fontaine, run into the hardware store and look for tarp, sheets, anything we can use to cover these bodies. Barry, you need to rope off this scene right now. Spread the word that there's been a chemical attack, possibly sarin gas, and you can't guarantee anyone's safety if they're out on the street until the CDC gets here."

"That," he said, staring at Norma's corpse, "wasn't sarin gas."

I stood between him and the body, locking eyes with him.

"Yes," I told him, "it was. I'm going to make a phone call now, and in a couple of hours, you'll be visited by some very polite men with CDC credentials, as well as a Homeland Security officer. They will tell you exactly what you saw here today, which is *nothing*. A colorless, odorless gas was emitted from the back of that truck, which instantly killed the people who breathed it. You will repeat this story until you believe it, and this is what you'll tell the media."

He kept looking past me, at the bodies. I snapped my fingers in his face until I got his attention.

"Barry? You will do this, or those polite men will visit you again. And they will hurt you."

Barry finally met my gaze. His eyes glistened with tears.

"I thought . . . ," he started to say, then fell silent.

"What?"

He shook his head. "I thought you were the good guys."

I took another deep breath. Then I got out my phone and called April.

"We are," I told Barry as the phone rang, "on a good day. This isn't a good day. Please cordon the area. We'll talk later."

I cradled the phone against my chin as I helped Fontaine with the tarps, covering the fallen zombie and his mutated victims with sheets of heavy, green oilcloth. April knew the routine; we needed a fast cleanup job, with help from Linder and the home office.

"And what story shall I give to explain your presence in Talbot Cove?" April asked.

"Following up a loose end from the Bogeyman investigation," I told her. "Diehl's agents tracked my movements, and the attack was meant for me. He'll buy that."

Cody stood motionless on the open street, staring shell-shocked at the shrouded dead. Once I got off the phone with April, cleaners on the way, I turned my attention on him.

"I know you didn't want to join up," I told him, "but consider yourself drafted. Now that Bobby Diehl knows who you are, he won't stop coming after you. Safest place for you is with me and Jessie. We'll keep you safe until we get a green light on—"

"No," he said.

I blinked. "What? Cody, you can't stay here."

"I know." He looked my way. "Doesn't mean I have to go anywhere with you."

"But . . . why?"

He balled his hands into fists, clenching and unclenching them. "Can you just . . . give me a minute? Can you maybe take into account the fact that I just watched nine people, people I've known my entire life, die right in front of me?"

"I feel their loss, Cody, but time isn't on our side here."

"Do you? Really?"

"Do I what?" I asked him.

"Do you feel a goddamn thing?" He put his hands on his hips. "You say the words, Harmony, you say all the right words, but it's like this doesn't touch you. Like you're some kind of fucking robot."

I sucked in my lips and bit down, hard. Counting to four before I answered him.

"Emotions are for after the mission. Right now, we're in a crisis situation, and we have to get moving. I understand you're upset—"

"Upset?" He pointed to the tarp at his feet, the lump that vaguely resembled a human being. "Norma babysat for me, Harmony. Probably did for you, too, if you can even remember. And I just watched you put a fucking bullet through her brain."

"I just saved your *life*."

"Normal people don't do this. Normal people don't murder somebody and just get back to business like it was nothing bigger than swatting a damn fly."

My self-control fractured at the edges. Chunks of ice falling from the shifting glacier, plunging into the ice waters of my heart.

"You know what, Cody? *Fuck* you. When we were hunting down the Red Knight, you had a gun in your hand half the time, just like me. And you pulled the trigger, just like me."

"In self-defense!" he shouted. "In self-defense. And then I came home and drank myself to sleep. That's how I've been getting to sleep every night since I came home from your little spy adventure. That's how normal people react when they've been fucking traumatized. And now you think I'm gonna leave my life behind and do it again? No. You go your way, I'll go mine. And maybe I'll do what you apparently can't—hunt Bobby Diehl down, and *finish* the evil son of a bitch."

I swallowed the lump in my throat. It came right back again.

"I can't let you do that, Cody." I took a breath through my clenched teeth. "Look, we're both under a great deal of stress right now. You're grieving, you're distraught, and you have every right to be. Come with me. Let me take you someplace safe. I won't even be there, if you don't want me to be. We can talk again when you're feeling . . . more yourself."

"I'm going after Diehl. He's gotta pay for this, Harmony. He's gotta pay."

"And he will. Just not yet."

Cody looked at me, lost. His mouth opened, then closed again. He shook his head.

"And how many more innocent people are gonna die before he does? I'll see you around, Harmony. I got stuff to do."

He started to turn. We drew almost at the same time. Both of us standing there, separated by eight feet of pavement and a dead body under a shroud, as we pointed our guns in each other's faces.

"Really?" he said. "You're going to shoot *me* now?"

"Bobby Diehl is going to kill you. Or worse. And I can't protect you if you leave. You have to come with me. I'm not giving you a choice."

We stood there, eyes locked, our gun hands high.

Then he lowered his revolver and slid it back into the holster.

"Sure you are," he said. "Because if it's a choice between shooting me or letting me go . . . you're going to let me go. And we both know it."

"Damn it, Cody—"

"I'm sorry, Harmony. I really am. I'm sorry for a whole lot of things. Maybe I'll see you around sometime. Maybe next time . . ."

He shrugged. Then he turned his back on me.

"I know you've got a good heart, Harmony. I just wish you could dig it up from wherever you buried it."

He started walking, heading south on Main Street.

"By the way, I was counting your shots. Your pistol's empty."

I watched him go. My arm fell limp, useless gun dangling from useless fingers. I put it back in the holster. A gentle hand rested on my shoulder, Fontaine standing behind me.

"Under the circumstances," he said, "I'm not sure if I should offer condolences or congratulations."

"Ha," I said, my voice flat. "Funny."

"I wouldn't worry too much, *ma chère*. Soon as he gets his head right, he'll come calling."

"I just hope he does before he pulls something stupid. Diehl isn't going to stop, and next time I won't be there to save him."

"He won't stop pursuing you, either." Fontaine nodded to the covered body of the Quiet One. "And unless you reckon that poor creature was smart enough to set all this up on its lonesome, that tells me good old Bobby has operatives in the vicinity. Probably a fine time to make your exit."

"I'm not leaving Cody behind."

"And doesn't this . . . little monster-hunting club of yours have resources you can call on, somebody to keep an eye on the boy while you tend to your business elsewhere?"

"He's not a registered informant, for his own safety," I told him. "And I've piled up so many lies at this point, trying to keep our boss in the dark, I can't dig my way out from under them. I'm out of options."

Fontaine gave me an appraising eye. "Not entirely."

"Meaning?" I gave him a sidelong glance.

"I've been saddled of late with an apprentice, and I'm supposed to be teaching her the tricks of the trade. Surveillance being one of those aforementioned tricks. You let me worry about Cody; we'll keep an eye on him while you do what needs doing."

I frowned, looking for some hint of a catch in his easy smile, his syrupy drawl.

"And the price would be?"

"A favor for a rainy day. Something I can keep in my hip pocket, in case I ever need it. Nothing onerous, nothing that'd shock your vaunted sense of honor, chivalrous creature that you are. Just an even trade."

I doubted that. I also didn't see any other options. I could either abandon Cody to the winds, leaving him with a target on his back and no way to protect him, or make a deal with a literal devil. I knew it was wrong. I knew it went against everything I stood for.

Just like I knew I was going to say yes. And so did Fontaine. I held out my hand and we shook on it.

"Besides," he told me with a wink, "maybe I just like having an excuse to call you. Now do me a favor and get packin'. I think you're headed for a world of trouble, and I'd like a few thousand miles between us when the shooting starts, just for safety's sake."

THIRTEEN

"Cody wasn't entirely wrong," Jessie told me. "Sounds like he was a dick about it, and I probably would have shot him in the leg and trussed him up like a prize hog, but he wasn't entirely wrong."

We were in a shabby hotel room in New York City, on the Lower East Side, sitting next to each other in a couple of rickety chairs pulled up to the window. A fourth-floor view looking down on a line of buildings on the far side of a busy street. Gentrification had hit the neighborhood like a whirlwind. My binoculars swept the street, where an old bodega struggled to stand shoulder to shoulder with a Whole Foods and a cell-phone store. Then a temp agency with a line falling out the front door, and at the end of the block, two stories of anonymous beige brick and glazed windows—the headquarters of RedEye Infometrics.

"Wasn't entirely wrong about which part?" I asked, my attention focused on the sidewalk. Looking for anything out of place, like the pair of pedestrians in heavier coats than the weather warranted, who'd been pretending to wait for a bus for more than two hours now. And the way they gave a sketchy eye to anyone venturing too close to RedEye's front door.

"Sanctioning Bobby Diehl," Jessie said.

"You still don't believe the Network is real," I said.

"Show me some proof and I'll start believing. Right now we only have Linder's word and Agent Cooper's story to go on. And even *Cooper* told you not to trust Linder."

"Fontaine said it's real."

"The demonic bounty hunter says it's real? The creature from hell who's pretty blatantly trying to manipulate us? Well, shit, Harmony, that's all I needed to hear. Why didn't you say so earlier?"

I passed her the binoculars. I hadn't mentioned my deal with Fontaine. I wasn't planning on it, unless I had to.

"Point taken."

"Look, I get it," she said. "*If* the Network is real, and *if* we could use Diehl as a wedge to get in and take it down, that'd be huge. But the Network didn't just pull off a terrorist attack in your goddamn hometown. That's on Diehl, and the longer we let him keep breathing, the more people he's gonna hurt."

"What do you suggest? Think we should go behind Linder's back and take him out?"

"It's a thought." Jessie handed me the binoculars. "Okay, mailman's coming. Check the window."

The lobby window gave me a glimpse into RedEye's world. Not much to see, just a span of checkered linoleum, a row of powder-blue chairs by the glass, and a small reception desk. As the mail carrier stepped in, brushing his shoes on a dusty mat just inside the door, the receptionist rose and gave him a smile. Something was off about her posture, though, and the way she reached for his bundle of letters.

"Her right hand never comes out from behind the desk," I murmured. "She's got a weapon back there."

"She probably sees that guy every single day, and she's *still* primed to blow him away if he pulls anything. There's some professional-grade paranoia for you."

I tracked the postman as he left, and so did the two watchers on the street, a quick hand signal passing between them. Giving the all clear.

"They're definitely cooking up something shady in there," I told her. "That said, I don't think Burton Webb is our guy."

"Why not?"

"We've got four names in Bredford's file," I told her. "Bobby Diehl, Gerard Nowak, Senator Roth, and Burton Webb. We've got good reason to believe one of them hired the Wolves to steal Bredford's blackmail goodies. Bredford was sitting on evidence of Diehl committing a murder. Nowak trading secrets with the Chinese. Roth hiring mercenaries and God knows what else."

Jessie nodded, following my train of thought. "But with Burton, the incriminating material was about his company being an NSA front. Nothing about him personally, like the other three men."

"And unlike the other three, he could survive his secret getting out. You know who went down when Snowden blew the whistle on NSA surveillance? Nobody but Snowden. Worst-case scenario, RedEye goes out of business, and Burton has to find himself another cushy corporate gig. That's not a guy who's looking to hire a team of killers."

"But we know he's tight with Bobby," Jessie said. "More important, we know Bredford had his eye on this place. He had to have a reason. I say we cross Burton off the suspect list and, while we're at it, find out what's really going on in there."

"How do you want to play it? I'm not comfortable with going into an office building guns blazing. Even if these people are spies, they're presumably *our* spies. And considering we're going behind Linder's back, what happens if they tell him we came around, asking questions?" I asked.

"Linder might have worked with the NSA back in the day, but these days, all his assets seem to be Bureau and Secret Service. Man's a chameleon, always shifting his colors, and there's no reason to assume his old buddies even have his phone number. This is one time when DC's right hand never knowing what the left hand's doing might just work in our favor."

Jessie glanced at her phone, scrolling past list after list of file names. Kevin had sent her the entire mother lode from the stolen USB, a ticking bomb under her short-cropped fingernail.

"Now, we don't know if Bredford was in direct contact with all four of these men, but it's a strong possibility. Meaning Burton Webb might be buttoned up in his office right this minute, knowing the blackmail data is out in the wild, just waiting for the other shoe to drop." She glanced up at me, a mischievous glint in her eyes. "Let's be the other shoe."

# # #

We flashed our badges at the front desk.

"I'm sorry," the receptionist told us in a tone that sounded anything but. "Mr. Webb is unavailable. He's in meetings all afternoon. Can I take a message for him?"

"No," Jessie said. "You can send him out here, or we can go in and get him."

The woman behind the desk slid her gaze toward the sealed, windowless door at her back. Her right hand stayed out of sight. I wondered what she had back there. A pistol? Sawed-off shotgun? I wondered if it was pointed at me.

"This is private property, Special Agent . . . Temple, was it?" She stared at Jessie's badge like she was memorizing the details. "I believe you need a warrant for that."

Jessie slipped her badge into her jacket. Then she pressed her palms against the edge of the desk, leaning in.

"Well, that's up to him. See, we need to talk to him about a sensitive matter. Just talk. But if he doesn't want to talk, well . . . we'll just take that sensitive matter to a judge, and we'll be back here in ten minutes with a warrant for his arrest. Call your boss. Let him know I said that. Use my exact words."

She picked up the phone. Talking in a low whisper, eyes locked with Jessie the entire time.

"He'll be right down," she told us.

We waited long enough that I started to wonder if he'd given us the slip. Then the door behind the desk wobbled open, and Burton Webb came out to face the music. I wasn't sure what I'd been expecting, but given he was a friend of Bobby Diehl's, it probably wasn't a doe-eyed man with a tight-cut Afro, wearing a plaid sweater-vest and a bow tie.

"Um, hi," he said, almost stumbling over his own feet as he crossed the lobby to meet us. "I'm Burton."

He held out his hand to Jessie. She stared at it, her lips pursed in a tight, bloodless line, until he put it down again. He tried me. I didn't shake it, either.

"Your office," I said, "would be a more appropriate place for this discussion."

"Right." He tucked his chin down. "Let's, uh, do that. Right."

Claustrophobia closed in on me as we stepped beyond the windowless door. RedEye was a warren of tight halls and locked doors, every bend under the watchful eye of a whirring security camera. The walls were aggressively beige.

We took a ride in a closet-size elevator with dull steel walls. Burton's office was on the second floor. It was the office of a low-level flunky, not a successful CEO. No outside light, a chunky desk with '70s-era woodgrain laminate—his only concession to vanity was a plush, high-backed leather chair. He sat down. We didn't.

I followed Jessie's lead and did what she did. Absolutely nothing.

Burton looked at her, then at me. He ran a finger along the inside of his collar, loosening his bow tie. He forced a smile. "Can I, um, get you anything? Coffee? Soda? I have diet."

We kept staring at him.

"Anything?" he asked. "Anything at all?"

I silently counted. Once I hit thirty, Jessie finally spoke. "We. Know. Everything."

Burton clasped his hands together, tight, as his jaw dropped. He sank into his chair.

"Oh God," he whimpered. "I'll pay the money back, okay? I swear, I didn't even take that much. You have to believe me."

Not the reaction I'd expected. I decided to give him a nudge.

"Not that much?" I said. "Are you sure about that?"

"I mean, people embezzle money all the time. And this was a government gig. You hear all the time about contractors ripping off the government for tens, hundreds of millions; I only skimmed a little off the top. And I stopped. I stopped years ago. I've been honest ever since, you can check my books. *Oh, please, God, don't kill me—*"

His head hit the desk, shoulders shaking as he struggled to keep from bursting into tears. Jessie looked my way, arching an eyebrow. I shrugged.

"You stopped when Douglas Bredford confronted you," I said, taking a stab in the dark.

His head, flat to the desk, nodded weakly.

"I knew this was coming," he whimpered. "The second I heard Bredford's luck finally ran out, I knew somebody would follow the trail back to me."

Jessie held up a finger. "One second. Need a word with my partner."

We stepped out into the hallway. Jessie held the office door open just a crack, keeping an eye on Burton while we talked in low voices.

"We apparently didn't get his *only* blackmail file," Jessie said. "There was nothing about any embezzlement on that USB stick."

"That, or Douglas didn't want this guy burned. He wanted to point us at him, point us at this *place*, without risking getting Burton hurt.

He deliberately held back anything that could land him behind bars. Or worse."

"Let's find out why," Jessie said, and led the way back inside.

Burton mopped his face with a damp tissue, trying to get himself under control. One look at us and he almost lost it again. Jessie put her hands on her hips, looming over his desk.

"Good news is, you're not going to prison," she told him.

"And we're not here to kill you," I added.

He sank deeper into his chair. "Y-you're not?"

"Well, probably not," Jessie said. "That's gonna depend on you."

He swallowed, hard.

"Let me guess," I told him. "You thought we were really NSA operatives, here to check on our investment."

His head bobbed. "You . . . aren't?"

"We're from a friendly but parallel agency. And we're only interested in one thing: Douglas Bredford. He came to you years ago, didn't he? Showed you evidence that you were stealing from RedEye. And he wanted something in return for his silence. What was it?"

Burton looked from Jessie, to me, and back again, his bottom lip trapped between his teeth, and his cheeks bulging like a frightened chipmunk. "Which agency did you say you were with, again?"

"The kind that doesn't exist," Jessie told him. "The kind you should cooperate with if you don't want this entire building to turn into a smoking crater. Fewer questions, more answers: What did you give Bredford?"

"I can't," he said. "I can't. Stealing a little cash is peanuts compared to what I had to do to get out from under Bredford's thumb. It was . . . it was treason, okay? And considering this place shouldn't exist in the first place, not the kind of treason you get a trial for."

"Burton," I said, "listen to me. We just want information. Tell us everything, and I mean *everything*, and we walk out that door and you never have to see us again."

Jessie leaned into his desk. "And whatever you think the NSA can do to you, trust me: we can do a whole lot worse, right here, right now."

Burton sagged into his chair, resigned.

"He knew I had a back door into the RedEye system. He wanted me to write a patch, a secret alteration of the operating code."

"Start from the beginning," I said. "What *is* RedEye?"

He glanced to the door and took a deep breath.

"I think I'd better show you."

FOURTEEN

We stood in a cavernous chamber beneath the building, in a sub-sub-basement past three card-locked doors, bathed in cool blue light. Rows upon rows of server racks stretched out before us, brushed steel and amber lights glowing in the shadows, separated by aisles paved with black rubber mats. Antiseptic blanketed the air, pungent and strong, the stink of chemicals and plastic pine trees sinking into my clothes.

"My pride and joy," Burton said. "The RedEye system. I wrote the algorithm it runs on when I was at Diehl Innovations. Bobby's a visionary, though, always was—he knew we couldn't put it to use, get the most out of it, without splitting off from the main company. So we started a subsidiary with his seed money, he put me in charge, and I took a trip to Washington to make my sales pitch."

"Are you . . . close to Bobby Diehl?" I asked him.

Burton shrugged. "I don't get invited to his house parties, if that's what you're asking. He was a decent boss. Still is, technically, though I've barely spoken to him in years. He just takes his cut from the NSA funding."

"So what does this thing do?" Jessie asked.

For the first time, Burton looked animated. He ran a hand along the server racks, like a father ruffling his child's hair.

"My field is encryption. At Diehl Innovations, I worked on security for our last three generations of smartphones; the work my team did was ahead of its time. Of course, encryption is only one side of the coin. *Breaking* codes, that's what I do for fun. Bobby came to me, early on, with a proposal. A way of winnowing down our competition. If we could crack the encryption on some of the leading cell-phone brands, then quietly farm out the information—blame it on Anonymous or some other hacker group—we could tank our rivals and make Diehl phones the only secure option."

"The Apple hack, a couple of years ago—" Jessie started to say.

Burton held up a hand, grinning like a kid with a slingshot. "Guilty. You cannot *imagine* what that felt like. Sixty-four-bit encryption was supposed to take about a billion years to manually crack. Literally. The first generation of RedEye did it in eight."

He spread a hand, taking in the room.

"This is generation three."

"So you built a computer that can break into cell phones," I said, "and sold it to the government. Now the NSA keeps you funded while you run the facility."

"Oh, more than that. Much more. Once we had the capability to crack pretty much anyone's cell, I took it to the next level. I assume you're familiar with the Echelon program?"

Jessie nodded. "Sure. Signals intelligence, sniffing satellite traffic for keywords. Say a magic word into a telephone—like *terrorist* or *bomb*—and Echelon probably picks it up."

Burton continued. "Probably. Or probably not. Echelon can only process data from communication satellites, can only decrypt half of it, and misses half of *that*. Not my baby, though. RedEye offers constant, sweeping surveillance of every major cell-phone carrier in the United States. And unlike Echelon, the NSA doesn't have to share the data with the CIA or any of our friends overseas. You know how the alphabet agencies are about sharing. Keywords—be it voice or text—are trapped, logged, and relayed to human analysts in real time."

"But not Diehl's phones," I said.

Burton chuckled. "Oh, especially those. Every Diehl-brand phone has a back door I designed. We don't have to crack the encryption—it cracks itself."

"So this is moderately horrifying and a gross violation of civil liberties," Jessie muttered. "What did Bredford want in exchange for keeping quiet after he caught your hand in the cookie jar?"

Burton's smile vanished.

"Shortly after RedEye went online," he said, "I was approached by some government men. Not the ones I usually worked with. They wanted me to upgrade the system, to make it better at tracking individual suspects. They gave me a name, Affan Sarraf, and said he was a member of al-Qaeda. An American citizen, in the process of formulating a terror attack, and they needed to find him. So I found him. With RedEye's help, it was easy."

"Then what happened?" I asked.

"Then I read the newspaper the next day." Burton glanced away. "Affan Sarraf committed suicide, shooting himself in the motel room I tracked him to."

He turned his back on us, taking a step down the black rubber mat between the canyons of his creation.

"Turns out it was a test. An unwitting demo for what I later learned was a black-bag project. See, you can't kill American citizens without a trial, not even ones with terrorist connections. Hell, not even overseas: remember the shit storm when al-Awlaki got smeared by a drone? And that happened in *Yemen*. But obeying the law leaves us with a bunch of bad actors running loose. People the government want gone, without all that messy due process."

"An assassination program," Jessie said. "That's what they wanted your invention for."

Burton nodded. He turned back toward us.

"They called it Glass Predator. We live in a post-9/11 world, is what they told me. An attack could happen anywhere, at any time. Can't take chances. Have to be ready, have to be strong." He chewed his bottom lip. "This was beyond off the grid. The program was created by a sealed presidential order. Only the president, and the three men who came to talk to me about it, knew it existed. And me, of course. And the hit team. I never met those people. Didn't want to. Apparently they used some kind of Delta unit for the job. Tier-one operators, the kind of guys who can parachute behind enemy lines with nothing but a knife between their teeth and come out alive."

"Did Bobby Diehl know about this?" Jessie asked.

"Him, too. He thought it was a great idea. See, that was a value-added service. Our funding, and his cut of the profit, doubled overnight."

I took out my phone, pulling up my copy of the blackmail files, an idea tugging at the back of my mind.

"The men who visited you," I said. "Was he one of them?"

I showed him the parking-garage photo of Gerard Nowak. Burton squinted at his face.

"It's a little grainy, and this was a long time ago, but . . . yeah. I think so."

Next, I pulled up Alton Roth's Senate profile page.

"How about him?" I asked.

"*Definitely* him. I remember, because he looked as nervous and sick as I felt. The third guy took him aside at one point and said, 'Don't worry, none of this can come back on you.' That's when I realized he wasn't queasy because he knew we were doing something wrong. He was queasy because he was afraid of getting caught."

The third man. I didn't go to Bredford's blackmail files for that one. I pulled up the scanned copies of the pictures he'd left behind in the wake of his death. I held the picture up so Burton could take a good, close look.

He pointed at Linder's face in the crowd of men on the Capitol Building steps, circled with a red-marker bull's-eye.

"That's him. That's the third man. He didn't talk much, but his body language said it all. He was running the show."

Now we knew what Linder had been doing for the government before Vigilant Lock.

It all fell together. When Agent Cooper warned me not to trust Linder, it was because her team had found something disturbing in Bobby Diehl's files. They must have seen a link, the connection that drew both men—and Gerard Nowak and Senator Roth—together. United here, in the belly of a mechanical beast designed to hunt and kill.

Jessie tugged my sleeve. We stepped back. She leaned in, her breath hot on my neck as she whispered, "Explains why Linder went out of his way to quiz us after the trailer bombing and find out if we ever spoke to Bredford. Harmony . . . you realize there's a very good chance that *our boss* is the one who had him killed, right?"

"He's out of the loop, then. Linder never would have sent us to investigate the bank heist if he knew Bredford's box was the target, or if he had anything to do with the Wolves. Sounds like he's not on speaking terms with his former partners in crime."

"Let's do everything we can to keep it that way." Jessie looked over at Burton. "So back to Douglas Bredford. What was this patch he wanted you to write?"

He clasped his hands together. "You have to understand, Glass Predator wasn't killing people around the clock. It was a side project, adjunct to the main RedEye program. I had a dedicated, encrypted line from the men in charge. Once a year, maybe once every fourteen months, they'd send me a name. Then, one morning . . . they sent eight at once."

"And Bredford was one of them," I said.

Burton nodded. "I thought it must have been a mistake. I actually reached out, on what was supposed to be a one-way channel, to ask for confirmation. They said the names were sleeper agents, members of a Taliban cell operating in the United States. Well, that night, Douglas Bredford was waiting in my kitchen when I came home. Five minutes into the conversation, I knew he wasn't a terrorist."

"What was he?" Jessie asked.

"In over his head. He had a team, some kind of black-ops thing, operating without any official sanction—I didn't know what they did, and I didn't ask. I only knew their code name."

"Let me guess," I said. "Cold Spectrum."

Burton sighed. "He wanted me to turn them invisible. To write a patch that would make it *look* like RedEye was hunting them, but quietly delete any positive hits. They could stay off the grid and have a shot at survival so long as they kept their heads down. I told him I couldn't do it. RedEye had a one hundred percent success rate. There's no chance eight people could escape scrutiny forever, not without my handlers coming in and demanding an audit of the system. In the end, we compromised: I gave him three."

"Three people who your system wouldn't be able to track?"

"Him and two names of his choosing," Burton said. "The other five would have to fend for themselves. And no target, once RedEye traced them, had ever survived more than a week. Bredford had to look at his team and decide: who would live, who would die."

"Jesus," Jessie breathed. "No wonder he ended up a drunk."

"Did he give you any indication of why they'd been marked for death?" I asked.

"We cracked open a bottle while he made his choice. Twenty-one-year Glenlivet. I still remember the taste. We drank to his team, to his friends. I kept apologizing. The drunker I got, the more I apologized. I told him I thought . . . you know, up until that night, I thought we'd been fighting the good fight here. Killing terrorists, protecting innocent people. We were breaking the law, but it was still the right thing to do, wasn't it? I thought we were the good guys. And he just gave me this *look*."

Burton held up his hand, cradling an invisible glass. His gaze went distant, lost in memory.

"He said, 'Let me tell you about the good fight, Burton. Let me tell you who I am. I'm the soldier who fired the last shot, at the last battle, for the future of humanity. The war is over. Humanity lost.'"

He looked away from us. Staring at the server racks, the cold and glimmering green lights. The machines hummed in the shadows.

"Bredford left, and I wrote the patch, and that was the end," Burton told us. "The end of the Glass Predator program, too. The encrypted line went silent. No names, no kill orders, not until two days ago."

"That's a long wait," Jessie said.

"Believe me, I was hoping I'd never see that line light up again. I thought the program had gotten mothballed. Hoped it had. Weird thing is? Not an American this time. They wanted help tracking a guy named Yousef Masalha. Alleged bomb maker with ties to Hamas, in the States on an expired visa."

"Did RedEye find him?" I asked.

"In about fifteen minutes flat. Masalha's a gabby guy, and he uses a Diehl smartphone. System hit a voice-print match."

"What about the two people you helped Bredford to hide? Do you know if they're still alive?"

Burton waved a helpless hand at the server racks.

"It's been years. I honestly don't remember their names. I could undo the patch and use RedEye to find them for you, but the feed to the NSA is still active. If we can find them, *they* can find them. You'd be putting these people at risk. I mean, I'll do it if you ask me to, but I can't stuff that genie back in the bottle. Think it over."

I pulled Jessie aside and said, "I know you want answers as badly as I do, but we don't have time. The Wolves are still out there, and so is the person paying them. Finding whatever's left of Bredford's team has to come second."

"Agreed." She turned to Burton. "Congratulations. You get to live."

He bit his lip again. "Thank you. I . . . I really mean that."

"That money you embezzled? You should think really hard about paying it back."

"I will." He clasped his hands together. "I'll think about it. And then do it. I mean, I'll do it. Every cent."

"I'm curious," Jessie said. "Given all that you've seen, everything you know . . . why are you still breathing? You could drop a dime on a lot of important people if you felt like turning whistle-blower."

He gave her a sly, almost prideful smile.

"You're standing in the reason why. I'm no dummy, okay? System access is calibrated to my biometrics, and I've infested it with logic snares. I'm literally the only person alive who can operate RedEye, and the day I disappear, my baby does, too. So, until the government finds somebody who can do what I do, and duplicate my work, they kinda need me around. And it's not like I don't get paid. I make enough money to keep my lips nice and zipped. It's a mutually beneficial arrangement."

Burton Webb wasn't our guy. That left three names on the list of suspects. Bobby Diehl we could find with ease: the only thing keeping the madman alive was Linder's no-kill order, and that smelled fishier by the minute. Senator Roth was a public figure; we could get a meeting with him as easily as picking up the phone. That left a single mystery man, our secret seller from the Department of Defense.

"There is one thing you can do for us," I told Burton.

Finding Gerard Nowak wasn't hard. He'd gotten sloppy in retirement, handling his business over an unsecured line. Not that he was doing much business; once RedEye sniffed him out, a quick call to Kevin filled in the rest of the picture. He was an occasional lecturer at the CUNY School of Law and spent most of his idle hours playing chess in Central Park.

"Nice, peaceful life for a guy who ran an assassination program," Jessie said.

"Or *is* running," I said, "and his retirement's a cover. Somebody's still feeding names to RedEye. One name, anyway. The timing can't be a coincidence."

Jessie said, "Considering Nowak might have a hit squad on speed dial, we need to show a little uncharacteristic caution here." She tapped her chin with her fingertip. "Encourage him to play ball and talk to us instead of calling in the big guns."

"I think I've got that covered. May I?"

We had Nowak's phone number, so I used it. I sent him a picture. The photo from Bredford's files, showing the handoff in the parking garage. I kept the accompanying text message simple and to the point: We need to talk, or this goes public.

Thirty seconds later, my phone rang. The voice on the other end was terse as a bullet.

"Chelsea Piers. The Maritime Center. One hour."

He hung up.

"Looks like we have a meeting."

"Good. Let's roll." Jessie turned to Burton. "You need to get lost for a little while. Leave town for a couple of weeks."

His brow furrowed. "What? Why?"

"Somebody hired a team of mercenaries to rob a bank, then invade a reporter's home, and they murdered four people to get their hands on a file stuffed with blackmail material. Material on the men behind Glass Predator. It's a fair bet that one of them is responsible.

No telling if that's the end of it or if they're going to wipe the *entire* chain clean. You're a link on that chain, and they don't care about RedEye or keeping the NSA happy, so that won't save you if they decide to put you on the hit list. You're probably in the clear, but for safety's sake, this would be a great opportunity to cash in some vacation time."

"I've been meaning to go on a cruise," he told us. "Now sounds good."

FIFTEEN

We got out of a cab at the edge of Chelsea. I tasted salt on the air, blown in on a cold breeze that rippled the green waters of the Hudson while gulls wheeled and squawked in a slate-gray sky. The winds of October couldn't keep the city indoors: joggers in sweats puffed their way along the river walk, alone or in packs, darting around retirees out for an afternoon stroll and the occasional pair of hand-holding lovers.

The Chelsea Piers Maritime Center was as massive as the ships docked alongside it, eighty-foot charter yachts with sleek lines and tinted windows. A pair of race-worthy schooners bobbed along a shorter pier, their sails stripped, crews in white dress uniforms scrubbing the boats down and locking them up ahead of the winter snows. Smaller sailboats coasted along the river, reaping the wind.

Gerard Nowak stood at the water's edge, his hands on a faded wooden railing as he gazed out across the Hudson. A gray trench coat and a cashmere cap staved off the cold. His eyes were gray, too, the color of faded newsprint, set into a long and tired face. He didn't look back as we approached him.

"That was quite the memory," he said. "Haven't thought of Min in . . . well, it was a long time ago. I assume there are other photographs as well?"

"Enough to make your life difficult," I told him.

"A lovely euphemism. I retired from a life filled with lovely euphemisms. Let's get down to business, then. The price of your silence?"

"What was Douglas Bredford's price?" I asked.

"Bredford." He reached into his coat. I did, too, my hand closing over the grip of my pistol. Instead of a gun, he took out a silver lighter and a slim cigarette. "Haven't heard that name in a very long time. Is that where you got the photographs?"

I nodded. Nowak dangled the cigarette from the corner of his mouth, cupping his hand over his lighter to protect it from the wind. A tiny flame danced as he clicked the igniter. He took two quick puffs, kindling the cigarette, and tucked the lighter away.

"So he had leverage on me all these years, and chose not to use it. Interesting. I presume he wanted to burn me from beyond the grave. That or ensure my cooperation with anyone who came to avenge him. Well, you have it, for whatever the aid of a washed-up bureaucrat is worth. Now what will you do with it?"

"Tell us about Glass Predator," Jessie said. "Why did you target Bredford and his team?"

"The answer to that question is above my pay grade. I was just the liaison between RedEye and the Department of Defense. I did what I was told: passed on the names of the condemned and supervised our field analysts. Glass Predator was . . . a mistake. A well-intentioned error, but far too much risk for too little reward. In the end, we quietly sacked the entire program. Cut ties, buried loose ends, and silenced the operatives."

"Silenced?" I squinted at him.

"We had a fire team of highly trained Delta operatives—beyond lethal and, frankly, psychopathic—who had committed over a dozen illegal executions of American citizens. When a predator in the wild develops a taste for human blood, you don't try to rehabilitate it. You put it down. Or in this case, you put a bomb in their Blackhawk and send them on a nice long flight over the Atlantic."

"So who's running it now?" Jessie asked. "The program is still active. RedEye just got a new target a couple of days ago."

Nowak turned away from the rail. His weary apathy vanished, his gray eyes turning razor sharp.

"Impossible. The encrypted line we used for sending targets to RedEye had one operator: me. And I haven't used it in a decade."

"Then somebody's doing a good job of impersonating you," I said. "The new name's a Hamas bomb maker named Yousef Masalha. Mean anything to you?"

Nowak took a drag from his cigarette. He looked back to the water, exhaling a long, slow plume of smoke.

"No. But there's no team of analysts to receive the data on the other end, and no assassins to send after him. No idea why someone would go to the trouble. What's your interest in this matter?"

"You weren't the only one Bredford was collecting data on," Jessie said. "Somebody hired a team of mercs to go after his intel and kill anybody in their way. We've got a short list of suspects, and it's getting shorter all the time."

Nowak's eyebrows knitted. He took his time, and another slow pull on his cigarette, then spoke his answer to the river.

"I hear Alton Roth is gearing up for a shot at the White House."

"A man in that position," I said, "couldn't afford a scandal. Not a hint of it. Doesn't take much to trip up a presidential bid."

"Certainly couldn't." Nowak ashed his cigarette on the rail, then flicked it out, into the water. "Certainly couldn't. He'd want to eliminate anything from his past that might be . . . untidy."

"Like Bredford's data. And any connection to Glass Predator," I said.

"You'll notice I haven't asked what agency you claim to represent, or whose authority you're acting under. I don't care. My career in the DoD taught me which questions matter and which questions don't. You're going after Roth, aren't you?"

"If he's our man," I said.

"Roth is a hard target. He's protected through channels I don't fully understand. He has the patronage of a political fixer who works on the outer fringes of the DC scene, a man who calls himself Calypso. Wide resources. Deep pockets. And if they've decided to scrub Roth's past squeaky-clean, I wouldn't be surprised if I'm on his hit list."

"Sounds like you're going somewhere with this," Jessie said.

He turned to face us, putting his back to the rail.

"I have a copy of the complete Glass Predator dossier. My name's been redacted, of course. Roth's hasn't. I'm too old and too disconnected to fight in the shadows these days; nobody in Washington will pick up the phone for me, and my allies are scattered and gone. I can't stand up to Alton Roth, and frankly, what little I've heard about his patron . . . frightens me. You, though—you might have a shot."

"You're offering it to us?" I asked.

"A trade. You delete all evidence of my youthful indiscretion with my lovely Chinese lady friend, and I give you the dossier. How you use it—if you dare to use it at all—is up to you."

"Can't keep that promise," I said. "The thieves already have a copy of Bredford's files, including those photographs. We can't erase what we don't have."

"A risk I'll have to take. If you succeed, I suspect the man who now holds that copy—be it Roth or another conspirator—won't be in a position to threaten me with it."

Nowak shook another cigarette from a cellophane pack. He didn't reach for his lighter. He contemplated the unlit cigarette, slowly turning it in his fingertips.

"I don't have to tell you ladies that you're swimming in dark waters now. There are sharks down here. Vast. Hungry. And very, very powerful. Assassination programs are just the beginning of what these people are capable of. When you find the man you're looking for, you'll get one shot at him. Just one. So think it through, plan your attack with absolute precision, then burn him down."

He put the unlit cigarette back in his coat pocket and met my gaze. "Burn him *all* the way down."

SIXTEEN

Nowak couldn't get the dossier, not right away. It was, as he put it, "hermetically sealed" in a hidden cache. Out of state, and buried deep, a safeguard he'd stashed away for a day like this one. He wouldn't give us the details; I got the impression it wasn't the only souvenir he'd saved from his old career. Just like Bredford, Nowak was prepared for his own death, ready to throw punches from the grave.

Jessie and I walked along the pier, looking out at the foggy shadows of the New Jersey skyline in the distance. Late afternoon and the wind was colder, ruffling my hair with icy fingers.

"It's Roth or it's Diehl," Jessie said. "One we're not allowed to touch. The other was involved in an illegal assassination program with our boss. Oh, and in any event, it all ties back to Douglas Bredford. And people who knew Bredford—like us—have a habit of getting killed. And it might be our aforementioned boss giving the kill order to keep the truth about Glass Predator buried. No matter what we do, we're putting our necks on a chopping block."

I tried to shrug, but the weight on my shoulders was too heavy. I felt the world pressing in on me, looming like the shadow of a mouse-trap's steel jaw. "It's a mess. Safest thing we can do is wash our hands of it. Go back, tell Linder the trail's gone cold, and call it a day. Move on to the next mission."

"That'd protect us, protect April and Kevin. Bad guy wins, but that happens sometimes." Jessie glanced at me, sidelong. "Is that what you want to do?"

"No."

"No," she echoed. "But it's my call. My team. Harmony, I really need you to do something for me right now."

"What's that?"

She stopped walking and turned to face me.

"Help me out here. Be my compass. Tell me what the right thing to do is, because I'm feeling lost."

"We're overthinking it," I told her. "Confusion, conspiracies, but at the end of the day—for me, anyway—only four things matter."

"What's that?"

I ticked them off on my fingers. "One bank teller. One elderly security guard. Two beat cops who died on the sidewalk of the National Equity Bank. Forget everything else. All that matters is that four people were murdered, and it's our job to catch the criminals responsible. If we don't, nobody else will."

"So we stay in the game," Jessie said.

"So we stay in the game. But Nowak is right. Whether it's Diehl or Roth at the end of the line, we've never had a fight this big ahead of us. We've got to think it through and get every scrap of information we can before we make our move."

"We've got a day or two before Nowak comes back with the dossier," she said. "What have you got in mind?"

"A change of angle. We've been coming at this from the top, spending all our time trying to figure out who hired the Wolves. Why don't we attack the problem from the other end?"

"Xerxes," Jessie said.

I nodded. "The one you killed in Three Oaks had a company tattoo, and they didn't have anybody with your powers when we fought Xerxes over the Red Knight. Either the Wolves were on a side mission at the time, or they're recent recruits."

"We find out where they're doing their recruiting—more specifically, we track down Angus Caine—and we find the Wolves."

"And once we do that, we'll know exactly who hired them," I said. "Because they'll tell us. Whether they want to or not."

Jessie gave me a slow, eager smile.

"Mayberry, have I mentioned how nice it is to have a partner with an actual brain?"

"Have I mentioned you should stop calling me Mayberry?"

"Nope. Hmm. So, how to track down an allegedly disbanded, decidedly disgraced pack of mercenaries who keep coming back like a bad rash?" She snapped her fingers. "Seeing as we're in the Big Apple, I think it's time you met our team's best asset in person. Let's go pay a visit to Vlad."

# # #

Rasputin was alive and well in Queens, New York. His thick, bushy beard shook as he leaped from behind the counter. He was draped in quilted Mongolian brocade and strings of golden coins that jingled like bells. He flailed a hand dripping with gaudy, oversize rings at Jessie.

"No. No, no, no," he said in a thick Russian accent. "You cannot be in here. That was our deal! You do not come to my shop, vhe are never seen together—"

"Harmony, lock the front door and flip that CLOSED sign around. Vlad, this is Harmony. I mentioned her on the phone, I think? She's Mikki's replacement. I traded up."

Vlad's shop, the Crystal Crow, was a shoe box cluttered with occult bric-a-brac. Paperback manuals for aspiring witches shared shelf space with "crystal" balls of tinted glass, pewter pentacles, and packets of dried herbs. A stuffed dragon dangled from an oversize iron chandelier, its tail thumping me in the face.

"*Vhat?*" he said, wide-eyed. "Vhat happened to Mikki?"

Jessie pulled him into a bear hug that quickly became a headlock.

"Long story. Faked her death, came back, tried to kill me, now she's in *special* jail. Drop the accent or you're getting a noogie."

"Vhat do you mean? I do not understand, how you say—" He yelped as Jessie's knuckles ground into his bushy hair, and his accent vanished. "Ow. Ow! Jeez, enough already!"

I glanced over from the door, flicking the lock shut. "You just went from Moscow to Brooklyn."

Jessie let him go.

He stood up, wincing, and smoothed his rumpled outfit.

"Yonkers, actually. Born and raised." He shrugged. "Hey, gotta keep the rubes happy. I give 'em the old 'wise Russian mystic' patter, and they pony up a few bucks to get their tarot cards read."

"Do you actually know how to read the tarot?" I asked.

"Nope. But neither do they."

"Vlad's real business operates out of the back room, peddling antiquities of dubious provenance," Jessie told me. "*Somebody* was doing business with grave robbers and got caught. Now he gets to stay out of prison and even earn a few shady bucks on the side, in exchange for certain considerations and favors. Like vouching for us in occult-underground circles when we're pulling a sting."

"Which is gonna get my ass killed sooner or later," Vlad moped. "So, ya know, thanks."

Jessie said, "You're welcome. Aw, cheer up, Vlad. I like you. And I'll like you even more if you can tell us something good. I hear Xerxes is hiring."

He spread his hands wide. "Like I hang out with hired guns? I don't like guns, Jessie. They make loud noises and put holes in you. I try to keep my blood inside my body, where it belongs."

"Their new recruits are magically amped up." Jessie pulled her sunglasses down on her nose. "They've got eyes like mine."

"I woulda heard about that. I definitely woulda heard about that. Sorry, sweet cakes, I got nothin'." He held up a finger. "I might have something else, though. You know that terrorist attack in Michigan, been all over the news all day? Word from a guy who knows a guy is, that wasn't sarin gas. Whole thing's some kinda cover-up. Possibly, just maybe, *aliens*. Might be worth checking out."

"We'll do that," Jessie sighed. "Thanks, Vlad."

Out on the curb outside his store, Jessie looked my way. "Well, we tried."

I nodded, distracted. Counting our options and not finding much to choose from.

Jessie said, "We know the name of one Xerxes member who's still alive. We could go back to RedEye, see if Burton can plug him into the system."

"Angus Caine's a survivor," I said. "He's careful. Besides, we sent Burton on a cruise, remember? Even if we could call him back to town, it'd be too dangerous for him. That said, we do have one other place to turn for information."

"Al-Farsi," Jessie said, reading my mind. "Who just gave Cody up to Bobby Diehl and got a whole bunch of people murdered in the process."

"Safe to say he owes us one, don't you think?"

"He owes us an even dozen, at least, but according to Fontaine, this Nadine asshole has him wrapped around her little finger. Anything he tells us, he'll probably turn around and tell her, too, and pass it along to Bobby for good measure. We don't need *another* ambush waiting for us."

"Do we have any alternative, beyond sitting around and waiting for Nowak to cough up the goods?"

116

Jessie frowned. Then she shook her head.

"No. Make the call."

At first I didn't think al-Farsi was going to pick up. Then again, after the stunt he'd just pulled, I wouldn't have, either. Finally the line clicked, and I heard his voice. Timid, strangely soft.

"Agent."

"Don't know if you've been watching the news," I told him, "but nearly a dozen people are dead in Talbot Cove, Michigan. That's my hometown."

"Yes, I . . . I saw. I can't tell you how sorry I am."

"I'm not the one you should be apologizing to."

I paused. If everything I said really was getting relayed to Nadine—and Bobby Diehl, by proxy—this was my chance to throw down a smoke screen. I couldn't stop Cody from going off on his own, but at least I could muddy his tracks a little.

"I'd tell you to apologize to Cody Winters," I added. "But that's going to be hard now. Maybe you can do it at his funeral."

Jessie gave me a thumbs-up.

"He . . . didn't make it?" he asked.

"He died right in front of me. Actions have consequences, al-Farsi. This isn't the first time you've played games with your little information business and gotten innocent people killed."

"Again, I'm terribly sorry—"

"Save it. You *owe* us, and it's time to pay up. Angus Caine is recruiting new soldiers for his Xerxes outfit. I want to know where he is."

He didn't answer right away. A strange, muffled silence, like he was cupping his hand over the phone and talking to someone in his office.

"I might be able to find that information for you," he said, "but not over the phone. Can you come to the Bast Club?"

"You want us to fly all the way to Chicago to get an address? Why can't you just text it to me?"

Another long pause. Jessie caught the look in my eye, my furrowed brow, and leaned closer to the phone so she could listen in.

"It's . . . a security issue," al-Farsi said. "I don't do business over the phone. Just come to the club, and directly to my office. I'll have a waitress invite you up, like I did last time."

That was wrong. The first and only time we'd met al-Farsi in person, we'd hijacked a ride on his private elevator after following one of his flunkies. There hadn't been an invitation—at least, not an overt one.

"Keep your voice even," I said, "and be casual. Can you speak freely?"

"No," he said, injecting a forced, soft chuckle into his voice. "I'm afraid not."

"Are you being held against your will?"

"That's correct, Agent Black. I'm glad we're in agreement, and I look forward to seeing you again. I'm afraid I really must be going now."

He hung up. Jessie scrunched up one corner of her mouth, thinking.

"So. Hostage situation."

"Looks like," I said.

"Could be Nadine in there. Or Nyx."

"Feel like going a second round with her?" I asked.

"We've been needing a solid win. And if saving al-Farsi's ass gets us the intel we need, even better." Jessie put a hand on her hip. "You think you can punch in Nadine's weight class? We *saw* what her kid is capable of."

I gestured toward the facade of the Crystal Crow, its dusty window display stuffed with pseudo-occult trinkets and Halloween decorations.

"You said he deals the real stuff out of his back room?"

"Yeah, it's like the warehouse from *Raiders of the Lost Ark* in there. In the mood to go shopping?"

"If we're going to take down an incarnate demon, we need to gear up—and I don't mean guns. Not *just* guns, anyway. And to answer your question, I don't know if I can beat her. But I know I'm damn well ready to try."

SEVENTEEN

In a back room packed with dusty crates, their wooden slats bearing stamps and customs seals from a dozen far-flung nations, we got down to business. I haggled with Vlad while Jessie paced the concrete floor, talking to April on her phone.

"Let's start with herbs," I told him. "I need powdered wormwood, acacia, chicory, garlic, and an intact mandrake root—"

"Hey, half of that I got. Garlic? It's New York, hit up the pizza place down the block."

"I want you and Kevin on the next flight to Chicago," Jessie was saying. "Once you land, get to the FBI field office on West Roosevelt. Use my credentials and tell 'em CIRG is going to be conducting a high-speed warrant service on their turf. I want the streets around the Bast Club *clear*: no feds, no cops, no law enforcement, period. Nobody so much as glances in that building's direction until we move in. We'll still have to deal with the civilian traffic, but we'll figure that out when we get there."

"I also need a soul bottle," I said.

Vlad took a crowbar to a long, narrow crate. The lid ratcheted up, inch by inch, old and corroded nails pulling free. Inside, a row of bottles—some covered in glittering sequins, some of them old sea glass with cork stoppers—nestled in a bed of shredded newspaper.

"Take your pick," he told me.

Jessie paced by, phone to her ear. "No, shotguns barely slowed Nyx down, but they might not be alone in there. Requisition a couple of SMGs in case we have to go room to room. Vests? Yeah, but go light, I want maximum maneuverability—"

I lifted a bottle from the crate. The faded green glass caught the overhead light, shining like an emerald as I turned it in my hand. The bottom of the bottle bore a carefully etched inscription, a pentacle ringed in Hebrew letters.

"This'll do," I said. "Now, then . . . marrowgoode?"

Vlad's eyebrows went up. "The question ain't 'Do I got it?' The question is, 'Can you afford it?' That shit's more rare than a four-dollar bill."

Jessie paused in midstride, glancing over. "What's marrowgoode?"

Vlad and I answered at the same time: "Powdered bones of a saint."

"Give her whatever she needs," Jessie told Vlad, then went back to her conversation.

After a few minutes of rummaging and griping under his breath, Vlad handed me a gray velvet pouch, fat and heavy with what felt like ashes.

"The right foot of Saint Padre Pio," he said. "Certified chain of custody through four buyers, all the way back to the guy who dug him up. That gonna be cash or credit?"

"That's funny," Jessie said, glancing over from her phone call. "It sounds like he thinks we're paying him."

Vlad tugged at his bushy beard. "You're killing me here, you know that?"

"Look on the bright side," I told him. "If we screw this up, you'll never see us again."

# # #

April and Jessie met us at O'Hare International Airport, twenty miles outside downtown Chicago. They'd picked up a surveillance package from the local Bureau office, disguised as a pizza van and loaded with electronic goodies.

"Linder's been haranguing me for a mission update," April told us. "On the bright side, he accepted the story about Diehl's men tracking Harmony to Talbot Cove."

Jessie nodded. "And the containment?"

"Under way. The corpses of the gas-attack victims were removed from the local morgue under the pretense of being a public-health risk, and witnesses were spoken to. The sheriff has been very cooperative."

Good. Barry would be safe, at least. For the time being.

"Any chance this means the hands-off order on Diehl's been lifted?" I asked.

April shook her head. "Quite the opposite. I was asked to remind you both that you are under no circumstances to approach him."

"A rule I look forward to breaking," Jessie said. "Let's do some recon. I want to see what we're walking into."

What we saw, taking a slow cruise down the back streets that led to the Bast Club, was nothing at all. No cars, no people, not a crow in the overcast sky. It'd be fully dark soon, normally time for the nightclub to start jumping, but the lot was nearly empty. Just a couple of windowless panel vans, like ours, and a neon-pink Maserati Quattroporte parked near the sheet-metal door.

"I don't like it," Jessie said. "There could be anything from a machine-gun welcoming party to a fire-breathing dragon in there. I'm not taking us in blind. Gotta be a way to get eyes inside."

"Drone with a camera?" Kevin offered, glancing back from the driver's seat. "No windows, but if we could get it inside the front door somehow . . ."

April held up a finger. "We do know an inside man. Anton Scudder, the creature who delivered notebooks from al-Farsi's listening post. He could be . . . convinced to aid us."

"I'm told I can be highly persuasive," Jessie said.

Scudder worked out of an appliance-repair shop, a little rathole crammed with dead toasters and gutted washing machines. Last time we came to town, we'd only watched him from a distance. This time we'd introduce ourselves. Jessie and I walked in the front door as copper bells let out a discordant jangle. Scudder glanced up from the pile of scrap on his desk, his bitter, pinched face magnified behind an oversize jeweler's glass.

"I'm backlogged," he snapped. "Drop off if you feel like it, but I can't get to any new work till next Tuesday."

My skin crawled. Scudder was a demon, a hijacker like Fontaine—but unlike Fontaine, Scudder's long-term victim was very much alive, trapped inside the prison of his own mind while Scudder wore his flesh like a suit.

"I can imagine," Jessie said. "Between your repair shop and running errands for al-Farsi, you must be pretty busy."

He scowled at her. "Don't know who that is. And I'm closed now. Get out."

"I'm going to be frank," I told him. "The only reason I'm not casting you out of that man's body, stuffing your spirit into a bottle, then burying that bottle in a very deep pit, is because we need you. What's going on with al-Farsi? Why is the club empty?"

Scudder shrank in his chair. "Private party."

"A private party named Nadine?" Jessie asked.

"What are you hassling me for? Sounds like you've got all the answers already."

"Do you *want* your boss dead?" I asked him. "Because if you don't start cooperating, that's probably what you're going to get. We're trying to help."

"You really think you can stand up to her? I'd pay to see that. Yeah, Nadine's there. And some of her thralls. Assassins from the House of Dead Roses. Al-Farsi slipped me a message. He said to stay clear of the club until they got what they came for."

"Which is?" I asked.

He shrugged. "I ain't in a position to ask, and I don't wanna know. The Roses scare the shit out of me. Nadine's got people chained up in her tower back home, who she's been torturing for so long she can't remember why she was mad at 'em in the first place. A couple, she can't remember who they *are*. You might think that'd be time to bury the hatchet. Her? No. She just invents new ways to hurt them. It's how she gets off."

"Sucks to be you," Jessie said, "because you're going in there, under the pretense of delivering a package to al-Farsi. When you do, I want you to note how many people Nadine has with her, what they're armed with, and where they've been stationed."

Scudder flicked his fingers under his chin. "Go pound sand. I don't know who you people are, but I don't take orders from you."

I set the soul bottle on his desk.

He stared at it, recognizing the glint of magic, and swallowed hard. I shoved a handful of junk aside, metal parts rattling to the floor, and leaned in close.

"You ever heard of the Bogeyman, Scudder?"

He twitched, looking between me and the bottle. "Y-yeah. What about it?"

"I'm her big sister," I told him. "And if you think Nadine can hurt you, well . . . you haven't met *me* yet."

He started to see things our way. Jessie babysat Scudder, making sure he didn't run for the hills, while I sourced the rest of the gear I needed. A mortar and pestle, sea salt, water from a pure spring. I took the herbs from Vlad's shop and made camp in the dusty, cluttered back room of Scudder's, sinking into isolation and silence as I reached for my magic. Grinding the mandrake root, measuring grains of wormwood, water turning mingled herbs into a cold and congealing broth. In my mind I was a child again, standing on a step stool at my mother's side in the kitchen while she taught me her secrets. Rhymes echoed through my thoughts, old witches' mnemonics, tricks to hold my focus in place. Funneling my intent into the work.

I emerged, holding out my open palm. "We're ready," I said.

Jessie tilted her head at me. "There's nothing in your hand."

"Look closer. Let your eyes go out of focus a little bit."

She squinted. "Still nothing."

"Don't look at my hand. Don't look at anything at all. Just kind of . . . feel with your eyes."

"Feel with my eyes." She stared at me. "Really?"

"Try it."

Jessie looked back to my hand, then nearly choked, her jaw dropping.

"Is that an *eyeball*?"

The gelatinous orb nestled in my hand, bloodshot and rooted in a mire of red-veined mucus. Its iris dilated, swiveling to look back at Jessie.

"Witch's Eye," I said. "If I trance out, I can see everything it sees. You did say we needed to get eyes inside the club."

"Thanks, Miss Literal. Good thing I didn't ask you to give me a hand."

I took Scudder by the arm. With a soft, slurping sound, the eyeball grafted itself to the back of his wrist. He shuddered, grimacing.

"You ever use one of these?" I asked him.

"No, why the hell would I?"

"Interesting fact," I said. "When I break the link with the Eye—which I can do from miles away—one of two things will happen. One outcome, it dissolves into a harmless puddle of goop. Wash your wrist off, you'll be good as new."

"Or?"

I smiled sweetly. "Or it detonates. So don't even think of running away. Go inside, deliver the package, and walk out. That's all you have to do. After that, you go free. I promise."

Kevin had been hard at work on the package in question: a stack of notebooks like the ones Scudder usually ferried from al-Farsi's listening posts. He'd superglued the covers and the pages together, turning them into a solid block. A solid block with a hollowed-out core inside, just big enough to send the hostage a little secret surprise.

"When you give it to him, make sure to say it has the new surveillance data on Huburtus Becke," I said. "Can you remember that?"

Scudder stared at his wrist, his face pale. "Yeah, sure, let's just get this over with."

When we were tracking down the Red Knight satellite, Huburtus Becke was the name al-Farsi gave us. If everything went right, he'd understand the message: that we were close, and we were coming for him.

EIGHTEEN

I cleared a space on the repair-shop floor, sitting cross-legged on the grungy tile. We'd sent Scudder off with his stack of notebooks and his mission; this was our best and only chance to find out what kind of nightmare we'd be walking into.

"Let's hope he doesn't say something stupid and give the game away," I told Jessie. "At least he won't run, as long as he believes he's got a bomb on his wrist."

"Doesn't he?"

I shrugged. "Nope. They're totally harmless. It'll melt into goop in about an hour, no matter what. Okay, I'm going to need some quiet time. Watch my back?"

"I'll be right here," Jessie said, standing over me.

I closed my eyes, sliding, sinking down into my own slow and steady breath. Warm waters closed over me, a bath of white light that glimmered on the other side of my eyelids like sunlight on a swift-flowing stream. Time melted away, and the world melted with it.

Then I was moving, swinging, riding on Anton Scudder's wrist. Lurching up as he hammered his fist on the metal door of the Bast Club.

It wasn't the usual doorman. The man on the other side wore a three-piece suit, but he had a boxer's nose and a long scar along one cheek. He flashed missing teeth as he snarled at Scudder.

"What?"

Scudder held up the stack of notebooks. "Delivery for the boss."

The man waved him in. "He isn't the boss anymore. Go up and pay your proper respects."

"Is . . . *she* up there? You know, I could come back later—"

"All visitors must pay their respects." The scar-faced man shut the door behind him and locked it. "All serve."

The view through the Witch's Eye showed the world in a rainbow of auras. The dancing, latent magic of the Bast Club, radiating from every wall and doorway, and the muddy-brown hearts of the men beyond the door. Two in the hallway, another two in the belly of the club, shooting pool and keeping casual watch. Another three talking in low voices by the bar. All of them human, all of them armed, toting pistols in calf-leather holsters.

The elevator chimed, hammered brass door rolling aside. Scudder stepped into the empty cage alone.

"I don't know if you can hear me," Scudder murmured into his wrist as the elevator began to whir, "but this is *fucked*. And you owe me big-time, assuming I survive this."

Beyond the open office door, al-Farsi sat in his high-backed chair. Shoulders slumped, head bowed, resigned to his fate. Nadine perched on the edge of his desk with one leg crossed over the other, high heels dangling as she studied her manicure.

Scudder knocked lightly on the door. They both looked his way.

He held up the stack of notebooks. "Delivery from the listening post, boss. It's, uh, that stuff you wanted on, uh . . ."

Don't blow this, I thought.

"Becke. Herbert Becke."

He mangled the first name, but the sudden look of relief in al-Farsi's eyes—and how he quickly hid it, putting on a face of despair when Nadine glanced his way—told me he'd gotten the message. He tapped the far side of his desk, out of Nadine's reach.

"Thank you, Anton. Just set it over here."

Scudder put the stack down and turned to leave.

"Hold on," Nadine said and hopped off the desk. "Come here."

He stepped toward her, every muscle in his body tense as a violin string.

"Did you just refer to this mewling worm, who isn't even one of our kind, as your superior?"

"Well, uh," Scudder said, "he—he pays me, I mean, I work here—"

"And did you just attempt to enter and leave a room without acknowledging *me*? You do know who I am, yes? You are aware that I am a noblewoman of your court, yes?"

"I just thought you were busy. No, uh . . . no offense intended, ma'am. Sorry. Won't happen again."

"But I am. I am very offended."

"Nadine," al-Farsi said softly, "please. He didn't mean anything by it. Just let him go."

She shot him a look that could cut glass. He sank deeper into his chair.

"That's curious. I don't recall giving you permission to speak. And yet there you are, speaking. Don't do it again." She turned back to Scudder. "There appears to be a speck of dust on my shoe. These are Louis Vuittons. Very expensive."

He shook his head, not following. "Sorry? I could, um, get a towel or something—"

She moved closer, almost nose to nose, looking deep into his eyes.

"I want you," she murmured, "to get down on your hands and knees and lick them clean. Do that, and I *might* consider it an adequate apology."

In the end, she didn't, but she got bored and sent him away with a dismissive wave. Scudder rode the elevator down, pale and trembling. He strode out past her men, nobody giving him a second glance, and I broke the connection.

"What did you see?" Jessie asked.

"Well, I think I know why Nyx was a seething bundle of homicidal rage. Her mother is a special kind of horrible. And now that I've seen her again—yeah, that *was* Nadine back in Oregon at the wine-tasting party when we were hunting the Red Knight. I think she was toying with us. That, or she wanted to get a good look at us, up close and personal, before she made her move."

"Joy. Is Nyx in there with her?"

I shook my head. "Thankfully, no, but she's not alone. I counted eight men, human, but all armed and ready. Everybody's on the first floor, one guy on entry, the rest scattered through the main club room. Nadine's up on two, in al-Farsi's office."

She held out her hand and pulled me to my feet.

"So," Jessie said, "as far as we know, the Bast Club only has one door. One way in, one way out. We breach and clear, take out her shooters, and hopefully lure her downstairs. I don't like the idea of getting into a fight on the second floor: tight halls and no cover up there."

"Agreed. Before we do that, though . . ."

When Scudder came back to his shop, grumbling under his breath and slamming the glass door behind him, we were waiting. Jessie hit him from the side, tackling him to the floor. She rolled him onto his belly, wrenching his wrists behind his back and zip-tieing them.

"What is this?" he gasped. "I did what you wanted! I did everything right!"

"You did," I told him. "And I'm grateful. Only, we have a little problem."

Jessie walked over to stand beside me, hands on her hips as she glared down at him.

"Namely," she said, "that you're a demonic bodyjacking piece of shit. And dealing with demonic bodyjacking pieces of shit is our job *and* our favorite hobby."

I nodded, turning to the desk to get my things ready. "Last time we were in town, you were figuratively bulletproof. You're al-Farsi's errand boy, and he wouldn't have given us the help we needed if we'd hurt you. But I really, really *wanted* to."

"This time," Jessie said, "he owes us. And after tonight he'll owe us twice. We're preemptively cashing one of those favors in. You're it."

His eyes bulged as he thrashed on the floor. "You promised—you promised I'd go free!"

"And you will," I told him.

I set the soul bottle down on the floor, right in front of his face.

"You're about to go free of that body."

# # #

The exorcism of Anton Scudder took seven minutes and thirty-eight seconds. Not my personal best, but I'd done worse jobs. The demon now resided in a corked soul bottle, nestled in the glove compartment of our surveillance van. Eventually we'd deliver it to the *Wunderkammer*, Vigilant Lock's repository for cursed objects, trapped demons, and other nasty and dangerous sundries, where it would stay under lock and key. Forever.

We were too late to save his host. He'd been wearing that body for decades, and even short-term possession can leave bone-deep scars. The real Anton Scudder had gone catatonic. Staring, mouth agape, lost in a madness too deep to comprehend. In the end, all we could do was give him a ride to Northwestern Memorial Hospital. I walked him into the lobby, flashed my credentials, told the orderly that he'd wandered into our crime scene and obviously needed some kind of help. Then I left him there.

Maybe, freed of the demon, his mind would heal. Days, weeks, months . . . or never, and the best help we could have given him was a mercy bullet. No way to know.

The van was very quiet on the ride across town.

"I don't know about you," Jessie finally said, breaking the stillness, "but I feel like kicking some ass."

"I'd use less colorful language," April said, "but I second the notion. While you and Harmony are clearing the building, I'll maintain surveillance on the lot. Keep your earpieces on: if I see any sign of backup arriving, I'll warn you at once."

"What's my job?" Kevin asked.

"If they can't contain Nadine," April told him, "and you see an extremely angry incarnate demon burst out the front door, I'll need you to drive us in the opposite direction. Very quickly."

I tugged the Velcro straps of my ballistic vest, fitting it snug, then reached for my jacket.

"Don't want to damper anyone's enthusiasm," I said, "but remember: in every documented case of a Vigilant team going up against an incarnate, the best outcome—ever—has been a draw. I know, I was there for three of them."

"That just tells me we need to work on our skills," Jessie replied. "Practice makes perfect. Let's start tonight."

We parked at the edge of the parking lot. Kevin killed the headlights.

I ran the final gear check. Kevlar in place. I tucked my bangs under a black baseball cap with a gold FBI logo. If the idea of shooting at the feds gave Nadine's men even a heartbeat's pause, it could be the split second we'd need to survive. Primary weapons were a pair of Heckler & Koch MP5 submachine guns, courtesy of the Chicago Bureau's armory, with thirty-round magazines. The black bulb of a Stinger grenade dangled from my belt opposite my pistol holster. In a utility pouch beside it, securely buttoned down, was my nonstandard gear. Herbs, sticks of ivory chalk, and the pouch of magically charged marrowgoode we'd taken from Vlad's secret stash.

It wasn't much, but it would have to be enough.

Jessie held out her hand. "You ready for this?"

I clasped it tight and looked her in the eye.

"Let's go."

NINETEEN

We hit the pavement, quiet as mice, and scoped out the parking lot as we hustled into the shadows. Jessie pointed at the neon-pink Maserati parked out front.

"Think that's Nadine's car?" she whispered.

"I'd bet a month's salary. Which wouldn't pay for one of those hubcaps," I said.

"Let's see if we can take care of the guy just inside the front door. Buy us a little breathing room."

Jessie stayed low, moving fast to the car, keeping her eyes on the front door.

Then she reached down, scooping up a loose chunk of asphalt, and hurled it through the driver's-side window. The rock punched through and landed in the front seat amid a spray of broken glass. The Maserati's alarm system wailed, its headlights strobing and horn bleating for help. Jessie ducked behind one of the panel vans as the club's door swung open, the doorman barreling into the lot.

He threw his hands up, staring at the broken glass. "Aw, come *on*. Son of a—"

CRAIG SCHAEFER

Jessie hit him from behind. She cupped a hand over his mouth, dragging him backward, and threw him down on the asphalt. I got hold of his wrists and zip-tied them, then grabbed his kicking ankles while Jessie ripped one of his jacket sleeves and gagged him with the torn cloth. He tried to scream as we hauled him off, setting him down on the far edge of the lot.

Jessie patted his head. "Stay put. We'll be back for you later."

I made a slow count to ten. No movement, nobody else poking their head out. Time to go in.

We eased through the steel door, into the dimly lit hallway beyond. Wooden tiles carved like puzzle pieces lined the baroque-wallpapered hallway, toward the main club room. I held up a hand for Jessie to pause and slung my MP5 over my shoulder while she kept watch.

With the pouch of marrowgoode, I drew a thin, gray line of powdered bone from one baseboard to the other, a few feet inside the doorway. Ever since our run-in with Nyx in Talbot Cove, I'd been doing my homework on incarnates. Allegedly—after all, magic was an art, not a science, and a craft laden with hearsay and lies—this stuff was like a titanium wall to demons. A summoning circle on steroids. That is, if the bones had the right provenance. And if they were enchanted correctly. Or any of a dozen other variables, any of which could leave the marrowgoode as useless as the ashes from a cigarette tray. Still, the theory was sound, and if it worked—big *if*—Nadine wouldn't be escaping out the front door. Not without getting one of her goons to break the line for her, and they were our next target.

We moved up the hall, Jessie taking point. Weapons braced to our shoulders, keeping the way ahead covered as our footsteps whispered against the hardwood floor. Reminders from my training at Quantico, a dozen plywood kill houses and a hundred paintball "deaths," ran through my mind. *Slow is smooth, smooth is fast.* We approached the lip of the club room, the floor opening wide, a red-velvet and green-glass Jules Verne wonderland. My last visit to the Bast Club, I'd seen the place

134

as a suspect pool. Now it was a newborn battleground, and instead of faces and profiles, my eyes saw angles and points of cover.

One cluster of targets by the bar, talking in low voices. Another to the right, playing pool on the vintage slate tables. I looked to Jessie and plucked the grenade from my belt. She did the same and pointed, calling our shots, then held up three fingers.

On the count of one, we pulled the pins and let fly.

Stinger grenades are made for riot dispersal. Flashbangs packed with an added payload: a fistful of tiny black rubber balls that blanket a fifty-foot radius when the grenade goes off, treating the unlucky targets to the sensation of kicking a wasps' nest. We fell back into the hallway, averting our eyes and bracing for the blast. My vision whited out when the stingers went off, for one blurry, heart-lurching second, and the brutal, ear-shattering sound washed away under sharp, shrill screams. Jessie and I burst from the corridor and ran for central cover—a cluster of divans at the heart of the room—while we broke left and right to cover each other's backs.

"Everybody down," Jessie roared. *"FBI!"*

I hit the floor as the gunmen by the pool table opened fire, bullets lancing over my head and chewing into red velvet cushions, feathers bursting and puffing out in all directions. I responded with two short, sharp bursts from the MP5. A vintage light fixture exploded, raining down stained glass, and one of Nadine's men fell back onto the pool table with three bullet holes in his chest. The pack at the bar clambered over it, one of them too slow as Jessie returned fire, shattering his spine and slumping him over the polished brass.

I broke cover in a dead run, turning sideways and firing burst after wild burst at the pool tables, keeping the shooters pinned down until I took cover behind a wide wooden pillar. We had two target clusters on opposite sides of the room: now, with me and Jessie split up, so did they. I leaned out to fire and clicked on empty. The dry magazine popped, hitting the floor at my feet. I kept my back to the pillar as I slammed a fresh one in.

Jessie was belly low, her cover between the divans chipping away one ragged chunk of wood and velvet at a time. She fired blind and a row of bottles behind the bar exploded. I saw one of the hitters break cover, moving low and fast, trying to flank her. He'd forgotten about me. Two quick bursts delivered a fatal reminder, dropping him dead on the puzzle-piece floor.

It didn't help. Jessie couldn't move, pinned behind the shrinking wreckage, and the two shooters left behind the bar were bunkered down. Then I saw the aftermath of Jessie's last frantic shots, the broken bottles, the leaking booze.

Earth, air, water, fire, surged the words in my mind. *Garb me in your raiment. Arm me with your weapons.*

"Jessie," I shouted, "the bottles! Shoot the rest of the bottles!"

I fired fast and wild, keeping the men behind the bar pinned down just long enough for her to take careful aim. She squeezed off a three-round burst that raked along the top shelf, shattering glass, raining spirits. Then I pointed my outstretched fingertips and exhaled.

A thin lance of fire arced across the club, hitting the shelves. And the rain of high-proof alcohol became an inferno. The gunmen shrieked as the burning waterfall crashed down on top of them and spread to the pool at their feet, turning their bunker into a flaming death trap. One staggered across the room, howling, his body ignited like a pitch-dipped torch.

We turned our aim onto the pool tables as one, bracketing the survivors under fire from two angles. I emptied my second magazine, slung the MP5, and pulled my Glock just as a gunman leaped from cover. Two bullets to the chest, one to the head, and he hit the floor like a bloody sack of rocks. The last man standing lost his nerve. He barreled for the exit, reckless, like hell was on his heels.

Jessie shot him in the back.

The room fell silent. She leaned against the wreckage of a divan, breathing heavy, muscle memory driving her hands as she swapped magazines. I slumped my shoulder against the bullet-riddled pillar just long enough to catch my breath. That was the plan, anyway. I didn't get the chance.

The elevator chimed softly. The hammered brass door rolled open, and Nadine stepped into the club. Her perfectly sculpted eyebrows arched as she surveyed the room, taking in the carnage.

"At the risk of a cliché," she said casually, "it's true. You just can't find good help these days."

"Hey, Nadine," I said, leaning into the post, "nice to see you again."

"*Harmony.* You'll forgive me if I don't call you Marilyn, won't you? Your silly little cover identity was cute, but I meant what I said back in Oregon: the name's just not a good fit for you. I hope your partner is with you?"

"Right here," Jessie said as she stood tall behind the wreckage, slinging the MP5 over her shoulder. She laced her fingers and cracked her knuckles.

Nadine smiled, impish, and took a step forward as the elevator rumbled shut at her back. "Ooh, are we doing *fisticuffs*? I'm generally more of a lover than a fighter, but there are times when exceptions need to be made. You two have caused me a great deal of trouble. A great deal of embarrassment. And while I've been ordered not to harm you, I believe this situation is the absolute definition of self-defense."

"About those orders," I said. "We know two of the hounds put out a no-kill order on us. Why? Why does hell want us alive?"

Nadine laughed, a sound like crystal wind chimes.

"Oh, dear, Harmony. Is this the part where I monologue while you stall and hope for a last-second miracle, or put your convoluted plan into play? Do I *look* like some kind of James Bond villain?"

"No," Jessie said, "you look like a second-rate pop star. What's the deal with that, anyway?"

137

Nadine's smile vanished.

"*Second-rate?*" She paused, holding up a hand and taking a deep breath. "Your lack of taste is not remotely surprising, considering your overall lack of anything resembling intelligence, culture, or good breeding. Harmony, you deserve a better partner."

"Have to disagree on that," I said, peeping out from behind the pillar. "It was shaky when we first started working together, but I've come to realize that we're basically chicken and waffles."

Nadine blinked. "What?"

"You wouldn't think the tastes would work together," Jessie said, flashing a grin at me, "but when you give it a try? *Delicious.*"

Nadine touched her chin with her fingertips. Then she flung her hand down. Her nails elongated, stretching, curling into black iron claws.

"You brought this on yourselves," she said. "I want you to understand that."

I stepped out from cover, feeling my strength surge back. Wisps of raw magic floated on the air around me, waiting for the call.

"Why? Because we didn't let Nyx win in Talbot Cove? You apparently didn't get the memo: helicopter parenting is *over.* How about you let her fight her own battles?"

"When you insulted her," Nadine said, "you insulted me. My bloodline. My house. I can't let a human get away with that."

I thought back to my talk with Fontaine, mind racing, looking for an angle. I wanted to throw her off balance. Anything to give us an edge here.

"Sure, but is this how you want to do it? Win or lose, you're going to look bad."

She squinted at me, uncertain. "How do you mean?"

"You're an aristocrat by demonic standards, right?"

"At least *somebody* around here recognizes that."

"So we busted in, killed your men, and you fought us in self-defense . . . even if you win, that sounds sketchy, doesn't it? I mean, that's not a victory—that's simple survival with your back to the wall. Playing us against Bobby Diehl, now that was a smart move. That took style."

Nadine scrunched up her lips, trying to read me. "Thank you . . ."

"A smart move you're about to totally ruin. Nobody's going to remember how you outfoxed us if this is how it all ends. Nobody's going to care. Killing us with your bare claws? A thug could do that. One of your *employees* could do that."

Emotions washed across Nadine's face. Turmoil, anger, doubt, more anger. Then, as she came to some silent resolution, she did the one thing that set my nerves on edge more than anything else.

She giggled.

And smiled, showing a mouth lined with shark teeth, as her blue eyes melted into swirling orbs of molten copper. Claws sprouted on her other hand, her slender and pale fingers tipped with razor-edged death.

"Oh, I'm not going to kill you, Harmony. You're right. You're absolutely right. Thank you for being the voice of reason here."

She took a step forward, her eyes glittering.

"What I'm going to do to you will be so much worse."

TWENTY

"I've studied you two. That's why I introduced myself in Oregon. Oh, I was playing, to be sure; there's nothing like the thrill of stalking your prey up close, but I wanted to get a feel for you. How you worked. How you *thought*."

I swallowed hard, rattled as her head turned my way and she fixed me with her molten eyes.

"Yeah?" I asked. "What'd you come up with?"

"Poor Harmony," she said, her voice a singsong taunt. "Spending her life in her dead father's shadow. You'll never escape him, and you didn't even really know him. He's fixed in your mind at six years old. Your hero, your strength, the brave man in the police uniform who went out every day to stop the bad guys. You want to be a champion of the just and the good, just like you imagined him to be, but the world can never live up to a little girl's fantasies. It can only destroy them. And so you strive, and you struggle, jousting windmills as you deny the truth: that you'll *never* be the woman you dream of becoming."

"Hey." Jessie unslung the MP5. "You can shut the fuck up now."

"Let's talk about *you*, then, Jessie. Dead mommy, killer daddy, and poor Jessie, all alone in the world. April Cassidy took you in, sure. Out of love? Compassion? No. You were a *science experiment*. You still are. And you know it, in your heart. You've never had anyone in your life you could truly trust, no one to love, no one you could even genuinely call a friend."

"*I'm* her friend." I stretched out my fingertips and called to the strands of raw magic in the air. Gathering them. Weaving them. "And she's right. This would be a good time for you to stop talking."

Nadine smiled. "I'm not going to kill you. I'm going to *help* you. First, though, I'm going to hurt you. I'm going to hurt you in ways you literally cannot imagine. I won't lie, that's for my own satisfaction after the frustration you've put me through, but also for your own good. You're wayward girls who need to be punished."

"Ooh, I get it." Jessie nodded slowly. "Should we be wearing Catholic-schoolgirl uniforms for this part, while you play the strict headmistress? Because, seriously, your sexual fetishes are showing. Hey, no judgment here. I've been known to get a little kinky in the bedroom. You're among friends."

The smile vanished.

"No," Nadine said, "this is the part where you pray for death, and *don't receive it*. Then I'll take you both with me, to a Dead Roses safe house not far from here, where I'll hurt you some more. And after a few months of hurting you, you'll start to see things my way. Believe me, when you finally get down on your knees and beg forgiveness for insulting my family, it won't be under duress. You'll mean every word of it."

A cold trickle of ice ran down my spine. Maybe it was her confidence. Maybe just the certainty that she was speaking from experience, that nothing she said was an empty bluff.

"I hear your beast, Jessie. The animal inside you, clawing to get out. And I know your happiest moments are those when it breaks free. So that's how I'll save you. By tearing everything human out of you, one scream at a time. When I'm done with you, there won't be anything left but the wolf. I think I'll keep you in a kennel and teach you tricks.

You won't even remember what it was like to be human. And you will discover that being my faithful lapdog is the most joyous time of your entire miserable existence."

"Harmony?" Jessie said. "If you have anything left to say to this bitch, say it now, because I'm about five seconds away from getting medieval on her ass."

"And you, Harmony. I'll grant a rare compliment: you have potential. Not like these feckless nothings at our feet. So when I'm finished breaking you, I'm going to rebuild you. You will be the newest and finest operative for the House of Dead Roses. You might even pose some healthy competition for my daughter."

"Never," I said. I tried to sound strong, but the word came out as a whisper.

"Oh, yes. I'm going to twist you around and scramble that lovely mind until you're mine. Faithful and true to the courts of hell, and to me. You're going to destroy everything you once loved, tear down everything you tried to build. And at the end of every day, your hands wet with the blood of innocent humans, you'll thank me with tears of joy in your eyes."

"That was five seconds," Jessie said. Then she shouldered the MP5 and opened fire.

Bullets raked across Nadine's chest, tearing her dress, spraying gouts of black ichor as she let out a shrill and feral hiss. She ran to the nearest wall, leaped and latched onto it, claws digging into the wood as she climbed like a spider. Jessie tracked her, firing burst after burst, and my Glock added a steady backbeat to the bullet percussion. Ichor and torn flesh rained down as Nadine skittered across the ceiling.

Jessie's gun ran dry. She tossed it aside, going for her sidearm, just as Nadine plunged down from above. She slammed into Jessie like a comet, both of them hitting the ground hard enough to shake the floor under my feet. As they untangled, rolling apart and jumping to their feet, I lashed out with a plume of occult fire. It hit Nadine in the breastbone, searing her bullet-riddled dress, and drew a furious yowl. Just enough time for Jessie to run in, swinging a brutal right hook that cracked across Nadine's jaw hard enough to knock any human out cold.

Nadine grabbed her by the shoulders and slammed her onto the floor, straddling her and raising a clenched fist high. I threw another lance of fire, my stomach clenching into knots as the energy coursed through me, and drew a yelp of pain as Nadine's hand broiled. Jessie twisted, flipping her around and trying to grab hold of her wrists. A savage kick, blindingly fast, sent Jessie onto her back again.

The elevator chimed. As the brass door rolled open, a flood of living shadows—wriggling, scuttling, crawling—poured out. Their master, al-Farsi, stood serenely in the elevator cage. Directing the shadow bugs with gentle motions of his fingertips.

They swarmed Nadine. She roared, peeling the centipedes from her dress one at a time, squeezing them in her fists until they burst in puffs of black smoke, tearing others in half and throwing them to the floor. She snarled at al-Farsi and charged at him, her claws hooked and going for his eyes.

He'd found the present we sent him, secreted inside the hollowed-out notebooks. Half my pouch of marrowgoode. He crouched and swung his hand across the elevator threshold, laying down a glittering line of ash. Nadine hit it like a car slamming into a brick wall, staggering back, her delicate nose broken and bleeding. When she turned, Jessie was waiting for her. They clinched, trading punches, Jessie driving her knee into Nadine's gut. Then Nadine got her arms around Jessie's waist and picked her up off the ground, spinning, throwing her across the room, where she crashed hard into the bullet-riddled debris.

Nadine let out a raw howl of frustration and barreled for the front door, picking shadows off her bloodied clothes and hurling them to the floor in her wake. Jessie stirred in the wreckage, alive but dazed. That left me. I gave chase, digging deep, on the edge of exhaustion but not giving up the fight.

Nadine jolted to a stop, inches from the line of marrowgoode that blocked the only way out. She wheeled around. I blocked the other end of the hall, cupping a roiling sphere of fire in my open right hand. My heart hammered, blood roaring in my ears, but I held my ground. Fighting not to show my fear.

She slumped against the baroque wallpaper, leaving a smear of black blood, and gave me a tired smile.

"You can't beat me. You're not as strong as your partner."

"There's more than one kind of strength," I said.

"True. True." She took a step toward me. I raised my hand, brandishing the flame. "I'll heal from these wounds in a few hours. Tomorrow, at the latest. I'll come after you then, when I'm nice and refreshed."

"You aren't going anywhere," I told her.

"Mmm." She glanced back over her shoulder. "Marrowgoode. Haven't seen that in a long, long time. I could smash a hole in the wall, claw my way through the wood and stone . . . but like I said, I'm a lover, not a fighter."

I didn't see it coming. She'd accused me of stalling earlier. *She* was the one stalling now, making small talk while she got her strength back. When she lunged for me, she moved like a blur, a lethal ripple in the blood-scented air. She slammed me against the wall, standing nose to nose, grinning as my concentration broke and my fire sputtered out. One hand clamped around my throat, fingers like cold iron squeezing tight.

Then she kissed me.

Her lips pressed to mine, fervent, demanding, leaving a lingering taste like cherries as her energy flooded into my body. A tidal wave of torrid, filthy heat. I pushed at her, shoving weakly, and then something flipped and the world went sideways and I was clawing at her shoulders now, returning the kiss, aching for more. Her tongue forced its way past my lips, twining with mine, and I didn't want it and it was an invasion and I hated her and then I suddenly didn't. I loved her, I wanted her, how could I do anything *but* want her? My soul ached as she pulled away, breaking the connection. The space of two inches was an infinite gulf.

"Break the line," she whispered. "Free me."

Of course I did. Of course I ran over, scattering the marrowgoode with my shoe, breaking the barrier. She had to be free. I wanted her to be free.

As she sauntered past, Nadine paused. Then she grabbed the front of my blouse and yanked me toward her, pulling me into another kiss. The flood of warmth hit my brain, lighting every neuron on fire. Pleasure I'd never dreamed of, couldn't have imagined existed, until that moment.

"You will make a *wonderful* slave." She pointed up the hall. I couldn't see clearly, the world blurred and going double. "That bad woman wants to hurt me. Protect me, Harmony. Kill her."

I remembered the crystal sound of Nadine's laughter, fading at my back. I remembered charging at the blur at the hallway's end, flailing wildly, desperate to protect my lover, my soul mate. Hands holding me back, voices shouting at me. Calm down? How could I calm down when Nadine was in danger?

"Sorry, babe," a voice echoed, sounding like I was a hundred feet underwater, "but you aren't yourself right now. Believe me—this is gonna hurt me more than it hurts you."

Then an arm curled around my throat, cutting off my breath, squeezing until everything went black.

TWENTY-ONE

"You should drink some water."

I sat on a stool at the edge of the ruined bar, surrounded by the bodies of the dead. I didn't really remember coming to. I was just *there*, all of a sudden, with a sore throat and an aching head and my shattered pride.

"I'm fine," I said.

Jessie touched my arm. I flinched. She pulled back, holding up her open hand.

"Babe, you're not okay. And that's okay, you get me?"

"I didn't . . . I didn't want her to do that, Jessie. I didn't want it."

"Of course not." She shook her head. "Nobody thinks you did."

I felt Nadine's lips against mine, her tongue worming its way into my mouth like a viper. Absent her magic, outside the heat of the moment, all I could feel was the violation. I cupped my hand over my mouth, leaning against the bar, squeezing my eyes shut until a sudden wave of nausea passed.

During my blackout, the rest of the team had moved in. April rolled herself across the hardwood floor, pausing here and there to snap pictures of the carnage, addendums for our final report. Kevin, looking queasy, had his laptop set up on the only undamaged pool table. He hunkered down so he didn't have to see anything but the screen. Al-Farsi stood off on the sidelines, surveying the damage in pained silence.

"Just sit there a second and catch your breath, okay?" Jessie said. "I'm gonna go talk to al-Farsi and find out what the hell happened here."

I was glad to be alone for a second. Then I didn't want to be alone. April picked up on that, I think. She pulled her chair alongside my stool, sitting at an angle.

"I've updated Nadine's profile," she told me. "Her effect on you, as Jessie described it, was consistent with the kinds of demons classed in the Vigilant archives as succubi or incubi. Now that we know what she's capable of, we can develop countermeasures for our next encounter."

I shrugged, fumbling for something to say. "Hooray for the scientific method."

"Indeed. Survivors of succubus attacks are quite rare, you know. It would be good to hear your account of what it felt like. When you're ready to talk about it, of course."

"Try asking the guy we jumped in the parking lot."

"I would, but he's dead." April glanced to the door. "Cyanide capsule hidden in a false tooth. I presume suicide looked more appealing than facing the consequences of failure."

"Huh."

She watched me for a moment, then turned to go.

"It was the best thing I've ever felt," I told her.

April paused.

"It was . . . you know how people say something is better than sex? It literally was. It was this rush that lit up my body, every inch, every nerve ending, just . . . absolute pleasure. It felt like heaven."

I looked away, dropping my gaze.

"And I know," I said, "I . . . I know that no matter how long I live, no matter what I do, no matter what I experience, I will never, *ever* feel that good again. And I'd say that's the worst part of it, but now all I can remember is the feeling of her . . . forcing herself on me, and believing, with all my heart and soul, that I *wanted* her to do it."

"But you didn't," April said. "That's part of the ruse. It's a trick. You didn't do anything wrong, Harmony."

I stared at my lap. My useless hands.

"I know. My head knows that. My heart just needs some time to figure it out." I looked across the room. "I'm gonna get back to work. Time to see what our host knows."

April took off her bifocals, polishing them with a pale cloth. "I'll finish documenting the scene. And, Harmony? Remember. You're part of a team now. If you need to talk, that's what I'm here for."

"Thanks." I hopped down from the stool and touched her shoulder. "I mean that."

I made my way over to Jessie, deep in conversation with al-Farsi. I thought back to the fight in Three Oaks, when she'd lost control and attacked me, and bit back a bitter laugh. I felt like I understood her better now. What she was feeling, her reluctance when I tried to console her afterward. I was all in favor of getting closer to my partner, but this wasn't how I wanted to do it.

Her turquoise eyes searched me as I stepped up. "Hey. It's okay, I got this."

"We got this," I said, and turned to al-Farsi.

He sighed. "As I was telling your partner, this was a trap, but not intended for you. Nadine wasn't satisfied with the damage done in Talbot Cove. We didn't know your friend had died in the attack, not until you called and told me. She hoped Mr. Diehl would reach out to me, requesting any other leads I could provide him."

"At which point you'd invite him to come over and talk in person, like you did with us," Jessie said.

Al-Farsi nodded. "Nadine was impatient. She felt that asserting direct control over Mr. Diehl would make him a better weapon against, well . . . you. When you contacted me first, she saw it as an attack of opportunity, and ordered me to ask you over."

"*Has* he called back?" I asked.

"No. I wouldn't doubt he has more than one iron in the fire, though, and multiple avenues of information. Now that he's struck a lethal blow—and again, I truly apologize about Mr. Winters—I expect he'll be even bolder."

I didn't bother correcting him. Given our host's selectively loose lips, maintaining the illusion that Cody was dead could only help us. And him. Between that convenient lie, and Fontaine keeping watch over him, Cody might actually stand a chance of surviving until we could take Bobby Diehl down.

"You owe us," Jessie said to al-Farsi. "For Cody, and for saving your life tonight. Don't even argue. Fortunately, there's an easy way to pay us back. We need intel."

His head bobbed, quickly, as he clasped his hands before him. "Of course, of course. Whatever you need."

"There's a disgraced private military company called Xerxes Security Solutions, operating illegally on American soil. Their leader is a former British SAS operative named Angus Caine. We need to find him."

Al-Farsi winced. As he began to reply, Jessie cut him off.

"Just so you know? If the next words out of your mouth are *I can't talk about my clients* or any variation on that theme whatsoever, my partner here is going to hold you down while I smack the living shit out of you. And when my arms get tired, we'll trade places."

He pursed his lips, weighing his options.

"I believe I can help," he said.

# # #

Caine's last known location wasn't far. Al-Farsi said he was on a recruiting drive over in Gary, Indiana, an hour southeast of Chicago and just a hop and a skip over the state line. Technically we didn't have the authority to take the surveillance van outside city limits. We did it anyway.

Gary was a relic of the Rust Belt. A steel town that still struggled to thrive and grow beyond the shadows of old, crumbling smokestacks. Kevin navigated the van down a stretch of broken road, where old cracker-box houses loomed over scraggly, yellowed lawns. Gary had a couple of nice neighborhoods, but by the looks of it, that wasn't where we were headed.

"No legal charter, no international PMC status, every known living member is a fugitive," Kevin mused from behind the wheel. "Xerxes used to be a big deal, but they're pretty much just a street gang with really big guns now. Gotta wonder what kind of people are looking to sign up with them."

We found our answer on a dead-end street, at a tap house called Foley's Place. Rusted pickups and motorcycles lined the street outside, pulled up to dead parking meters with smashed-out faces. From the street, we couldn't get a clear look inside: a Gadsden flag draped one window, bearing a coiled snake on a bilious yellow field. The other window's flag bore a grinning skull in a Viking hat, bone-white on black, flanked by Nordic runes.

"That doesn't look ominous or anything," Jessie muttered, staring at the feeds from the van's console. April rattled off a few quick keystrokes, tilting her bifocals as she read the screen.

"Hmm. Was afraid of that. Thought I recognized the general style."

"What've we got?" Jessie asked her.

"The flag on the right," April said, "is the symbol of the Aryan Cowboy Militia. They started in the Indiana prison system roughly fifteen years ago. Mostly stayed there. They're not a large organization, and they've had trouble getting a foothold, but they do have a small presence outside the walls. Mostly involved in the sale and manufacture of crystal methamphetamine."

Jessie arched an eyebrow. "Aryan, as in . . . ?"

"As in we should conduct our surveillance from *outside* the bar and wait for Caine to emerge."

Jessie leaned in closer over April's shoulder. "But we don't know if he's inside. Time is ticking. We need visual intel. Boots on the ground."

"Jessie," I said, hearing my own exhaustion in my voice, "are you making up reasons to go in there and mess with a bunch of racist tweakers?"

She looked my way, batting her eyelashes, the picture of innocence. "Why? Is it working?"

"I'm just trying to figure out if this is one of those things you *can* be talked out of, or if I should just assume it's going to happen regardless."

"Boots on the ground, Harmony."

Out on the street, as the van's side door rumbled shut behind us, I tasted the stench from the steel mills on the chilly air. Like rotten-egg fumes, catching in the back of my throat. Faint music drifted from the closed door of the bar and rattled the front windows. Speed-metal guitar playing on a cheap jukebox.

"Hey," Jessie said.

"Yeah?"

"You were pretty badass back there, you know that? The Witch's Eye thing, the bone dust, holding your own against that evil asshole."

"You trying to make me feel better about getting blindsided?" I asked.

"Why? Is it working?"

I had to smile. Just a little. "Maybe."

"We came closer to taking down an incarnate demon than we ever have before," she said. "Maybe closer than *anyone* has. And from the sound of it, even her own people think Nadine's pretty major league. This is how we learn, hon. Next time, we'll know what she's capable of, and we'll be ready for her."

"Suppose you're right." I looked to the bar, the dangling flags. "You really want to do this, huh?"

"This is gonna be good for you. I can tell when your confidence is shaken. This should fix you right up."

I laughed. "Oh, this is for *my* benefit, now?"

"Mmm-hmm. When's the last time you've been in a good old-fashioned barroom brawl?"

"Uh . . . never?"

Jessie grinned at me over the rims of her sunglasses, showing her teeth.

"You have no idea what you're missing. C'mon, let's introduce ourselves to the locals."

TWENTY-TWO

We pushed through the front door, into a maelstrom of grinding speed metal and stale smoke from cheap cigarettes. A weathered oak bar ran down the length of Foley's, opposite a few beer-sticky tables and booths where stuffing poked out through long, jagged knife scars. Almost as many scars as the men who crowded the room had. Scars and prison ink.

Every eye turned our way, and the din of conversation stopped dead.

The bartender muttered under his breath and found something to do at the far end of the room. As the jukebox played on, a screaming guitar rising to a crescendo, the welcoming committee sauntered over to greet us. Seven men, two of them openly carrying pistols in fat holsters on their belts, another two pulling back their vests to show us what they were packing. One of them, an emaciated tweaker with bad teeth and a double black thunderbolt tattooed on his neck, stepped ahead of the pack.

"Think you ladies walked into the wrong bar," he said. "How about you turn around and head back the way you came?"

"Sure, soon as we get a drink." Jessie turned and called out to the bartender. "I'll have a piña colada. Harmony?"

"Appletini," I deadpanned.

The men snorted at one another, moving in a little closer.

"Bitch, you got a hearing problem?" He stared Jessie down. "We don't serve your kind. Now get out of here before you get hurt."

We flashed our FBI credentials at the same time. Two of the thugs, the smarter-looking ones, took a step back.

"Boys," Jessie said, "you're looking at your worst nightmare. I'm a black lesbian from the government, and I'm here to take away your guns."

She gestured at my suit and tie.

"Yeah, she dresses like that, but I'm the gay one. I know, it's confusing."

"We're looking for a man named Angus Caine," I said. "British expatriate, about six foot two, fifty years old, salt-and-pepper hair in a military cut. We know he was here. Tell us where to find him, and this doesn't have to get unpleasant."

"Oh, it just *got* unpleasant," the closest one said, lunging for my jacket. I grabbed his wrist, spun him around, and twisted his arm hard, while my free hand snatched the revolver from his belt and put it to his head. Our greeter had the same idea, going for Jessie. Then he kept going—airborne, crashing headfirst through the bar window and hitting the sidewalk outside in a shower of glass. Three guns cleared their holsters in the same heartbeat, Jessie's and two of the thugs', and we all froze in a standoff.

"Guys?" said my hostage, his own gun barrel pressed to his skull as I held him fast. "C'mon, don't let her kill me."

"She ain't gonna do *shit*," said one of the gunmen, his weapon wavering as it swung between Jessie and me. I thumbed back the hammer on the revolver. Didn't need to—it was purely a TV cop-show move—but it got the message across.

As the jukebox went silent, the entire bar went motionless. Breaths held, waiting for the crack of the first bullet. Then a voice thick with a cockney drawl spoke up from the back of the room.

"I wouldn't bet on that, lads."

The crowd parted for Angus Caine. The broad-shouldered mercenary king had seen better days, with bloodshot eyes and stubble on his cheeks. He dressed in olive and khaki, a civilian take on a military uniform, and rugged climbing boots.

"I know these birds," he said. "Don't believe the badges. They're stone killers, both of 'em. Don't worry, they're just here to talk."

One of the gunmen gave him the side eye, still aiming at Jessie's face. "How do you know?"

Angus spat a toothpick onto the sticky floor.

"Because if they weren't, they'd have leveled this entire place without sayin' a word. Now put your guns up, and let's all be civilized for a minute or two."

Nobody moved.

"I said," Angus repeated, "*put* the bloody weapons *away*. *Now*."

Reluctantly, they holstered their steel. I let my hostage go, releasing his arm and giving him a little shove. I held on to his gun.

"If this is about the Red Knight," Angus told us, "I've got nothing for you. After that dustup at the shopping mall in Orlando, we lost track of you, that Russian chav and his pyro girlfriend, *and* the tablet."

When it came to the Wolves' paymaster, we'd narrowed down the list to just two names: Bobby Diehl and Alton Roth. Now was our chance to get all the answers. First, though, I needed to rattle Caine into giving up the goods. The best way to pry open suspects' lips, I've found, is to convince them you already have all the answers. So I rolled the dice.

"We're here about Alton Roth," I told him, "and the team of mercenaries he contracted from you."

And with the glint of recognition in his eyes, he told me exactly whom we were looking for. No denial. Instead, he nodded his head toward the back of the room.

"Let's chat in my office," he said.

His office was the booth in the back. We waded through the knot of barflies, all of them staring like they were sizing us up for nooses, and Angus paused on the way to wave over the bartender.

"Bring us three bottles of Stella. And get someone to pull the plug on that jukebox—can't hear myself think over that screeching-cat shite."

We sat down across from him. He took the seat that put his back to the wall. We took the one that put our backs to a bar filled with armed and angry men. I breathed slow and easy, trying not to look rattled. Jessie didn't have to try. If anything, she looked disappointed that she'd only gotten to smash *one* of the front windows.

"This just isn't my day," he told us. "I was hoping you were looking for a job. Turns out you're here to break my balls."

"Sorry, we're gainfully employed," Jessie said.

He smirked. "Not by the FBI. Come off it, I spent two decades in the SAS before I went private sector. Lots of undocumented missions, lots of hard men from no-name agencies along for the ride. I know the look."

"Trust me, the badges are real," I said. "And we've got some questions for you."

Angus spread his open hands. "What's in it for me?"

"You're a federal fugitive. You aren't in a position to negotiate."

"Really. Thirty lads behind you, half of them hopped up on cheap crank, the other half just itching to shiv somebody for the fun of it. You really think you can walk me out of here, alive and kicking, past all of 'em?" He looked Jessie over. "Hmm. You actually might. The way you strutted right in here and picked a fight? You're a special type of crazy, aren't you?"

"A very special type. We also aren't the kind of agents who have to take suspects alive," Jessie replied.

He pointed, grinning. "See? Gotcha. The badges might be real, but you answer to a higher calling."

The bartender came over with three green-glass bottles of beer. Angus tossed back a swig. I left mine untouched.

"Senator Roth—who hired your company once before, in Las Vegas—approached you with a new contract." I rested my hands on the table, palms flat. "He needed mercenaries to obtain a safe-deposit box from the National Equity Bank in midtown Manhattan."

"Which should have been an easy payday." He glanced at his bottle. "Well, you saw how *that* went."

"You gave him four mercs," Jessie said, "all of them touched by the King of Wolves. Are there others? And were they infected when you recruited them, or did you have something to do with it?"

Angus peered at her. "Your gums are flapping, but the words comin' out don't make a damn bit of sense. What the hell is the King of Wolves? Sounds like some occult-underground business. I'm *familiar* with magic, as a bit of an occupational specialty, but I don't do a lick of it myself. My boys are trained to lend support fire while the Merlin types do their business."

"I'll make it simple." Jessie pulled down her sunglasses. "They have eyes like mine."

Angus tossed back another swallow of beer. He wiped the back of his hand across his mouth, leaving faint, glistening stubble below his lips.

"No, they don't."

Jessie and I shared a glance.

"Yes," Jessie said, "they do."

"No," he replied, mimicking her voice, "they *don't*. I've known every lad who ever served under me, down to their birthdays and boot sizes. That's a commander's job. And in case you haven't noticed, I don't have as many soldiers as I used to. Sure, I knew Roth. Owed him, in a way. See, he tried to warn us off that sodding Vegas job. I didn't listen. Chased the money and lost damn near everything. So when he got in touch and said he needed a little snatch-and-grab done, I sent him four of my best men. Known all of 'em for years, and not a one had *normal* blue eyes, let alone peepers like yours. Two brown, one gray, one green."

It didn't make sense. How fast could the King's power turn a regular soldier into a superhuman? I drummed my fingers on the table.

"How much time passed," I asked him, "between accepting the contract and the bank heist?"

Angus shrugged. "Two days, maybe three? I told 'em to hit the bank when it was closed. Get in, get out, easy as peaches. Then I saw the news, same as everyone. No idea how they bungled the job so badly. The team went off the grid, zero communications, as soon as the contract came through—that's SOP, to make sure nothing comes back on me or mine. Meaning I can't reach them, and they still haven't gotten back in contact."

Jessie took out her phone. She flicked through her photos, hunting for the snapshot she took at Tucker's house in Three Oaks. The screen filled with the face of a dead man, his head turned in profile. She showed Angus the screen.

"We were on the same trail, looking for the suspect who looted the box before your team got there. We faced off in Michigan," said Jessie.

Angus pointed at the screen. "And that's him? That's the man?"

"No," Jessie said. "That's *your* man."

His eyebrows went up.

"Ladies, I don't know what this is all about, but I'll tell you this much and I'll swear it on my mother's grave: I've never seen that bloke in my life."

TWENTY-THREE

"Let me just make sure we're all on the same page here," I said. "Senator Roth hired you for the National Equity Bank heist."

Angus nodded. "Right."

"So you sent your best people—three men, one woman, none of whom have turquoise eyes—and this guy is *not* one of them."

"I said four *men*. That wasn't a grammatically vague statement." He looked between Jessie and me. "No offense to the fairer sex, but back before we fell on hard times, Xerxes mostly recruited from the special-forces community. Not a lot of skirts doing that kind of work. I don't have any women in my outfit. Never have."

"Hold on a second," Jessie said, and flicked through her list of contacts. She put the phone to her ear. "Yeah, this is Special Agent Temple. We spoke earlier? Right. That body, you don't still have it on ice, do you?"

She cupped her hand over the phone, listening.

"Local coroner in Three Oaks," she whispered to me, then took her hand off the phone. "Great, thanks. Listen, I need you to do something weird for me. Check his right arm. You're gonna see a tattoo, all black, looks like a wavy letter X with a triangle behind it. See it? Good. Go get some rubbing alcohol."

We waited. And when Jessie finally hung up, a fresh picture came across the line: the arm of a dead man, and the black smear of a freshly scrubbed-away temporary tattoo.

"Pull the other one," Angus said. "You tellin' me these people are pretending to be my men?"

"And doing the exact same job your people were hired for," I said.

"That doesn't make any sense. And if these phonies are running the mission, where are *my* people?"

I had a hunch, though part of me hoped I was wrong. My turn to make a phone call. I was routed across two police precincts, then to a mobile phone. I heard the sounds of traffic and a familiar, dour voice.

"Reinhart."

"Detective," I said, "this is Special Agent Black. We met at the bank, in Manhattan?"

"Of course. Any news?"

"We might be close to a break in the case. I've got a strange question: Do you have any record of any John Does turning up dead in the two days preceding the robbery?"

"There are eight million people in this city, Agent Black. When do we *not* have John Does popping up?"

"Specifically, four bodies at once, found at the same scene, all of them unidentified."

"That narrows it down. Hold on, I'll check."

I waited, and she checked, then I thanked her for her time.

"I'm sorry," I told Angus. "Your men are dead."

He set down his bottle of beer. "Tell me."

"The morning of the robbery, NYFD responded to a fire in the Bronx, at a boarded-up bodega. Four bodies in the wreckage. They'd been bound, executed at point-blank range, then doused in gasoline and lit on fire. Their teeth were pulled to prevent identification by dental records. They . . . aren't sure if that was done pre- or postmortem."

His hand tightened around the bottle. Knuckles turning white.

"That doesn't mean . . ." He shook his head, denial turning to bitter acceptance. "Why? Why kill my people, masquerade as them, just to do the same job? There's no money involved beyond the advance Roth paid me, no angle for anybody to turn a profit."

"We're working on that," I said. "Were they supposed to do anything else? What were their full orders?"

Angus sighed. Wrestling with himself for a few seconds before he spread his hands and came clean.

"Roth was involved in some seriously shady business, once upon a time. Some kind of black-bag program called Glass Predator. I don't know what it was about, didn't ask, not my business. He got wind that somebody might be close to blowing the whistle. He's looking at hardcore jail time, not to mention blowing his career to pieces. Man's got his eye on the presidency."

"So we hear," Jessie said. "What was the mission?"

"Hit that box, clear out the contents. Then work down a list of names, anybody and everybody who's in a position to talk about Glass Predator. They had to be liquidated, every last one of 'em."

"Murder for hire," I said. "You're moving up in the world."

Angus's lip curled. "I'm not talking about Boy Scouts here, all right? Nobody on Roth's hit list is an innocent man."

"I'd say that's a court's job to decide."

"And I'd say you're a hypocrite," he told me. "Or did you *not* come here fully prepared to put two slugs in the back of my head? Your phony badge doesn't make you any better than me. Doesn't matter if you kill for a cause or you kill for cash; believe me, I've done both. At the end of the day, all that matters is being the last man standing. Anyway, these people are as dirty as Roth is, or worse. That's why he wants them dead:

so they can't hold anything over his head when he makes his big play for the White House."

"Who were the targets?" Jessie asked.

"I'd tell you if I knew. Roth's paranoid. He demanded an encrypted channel, directly with the team, so he could pass the names to their ears only." He eyed Jessie. "You going after them?"

"This crew had four murders on their plate. Now they've got eight and counting. So, yeah. We're going after them."

"And Roth?"

"Why?" Jessie asked. "Is he a friend of yours?"

Angus gave her a look of disbelief. "Really? Men in my line of work don't have friends. We have clients. I said I owed him—I didn't say I *liked* him. Anyway, Roth's not the one you need to worry about. He's got a guardian angel."

"Meaning?" I asked.

"Man calls himself Calypso. Never met him myself, but word is, he runs a heavy firm."

"A gang?"

Angus shrugged. "Details are light on the ground, and people who go sniffing tend to get their noses chopped off. Calypso values his privacy. Almost as much as he values Roth. Near as I can figure, he's invested in the man. Strongly invested. Takes threats to his well-being very, very seriously."

"Where can we find this Calypso?" I asked.

"You don't find him. He finds you. And if you try to take Roth down, he *will* find you." His lips curled in a sarcastic smile. "I'd just *hate* to see you birds come to a bad end."

"You should be more worried about yourself right now," I told him.

Angus picked up his bottle and tilted his head back, draining the last of the beer. He smacked it back down on the table and shrugged.

"Sure," he said, "if you feel like picking a fight with every junkie and gunslinger in this bar, you can take me in, or kill me, do whatever you please. And you might be crazy enough to pull it off, I'll grant you that. But what if I made you a better offer?"

I glanced at Jessie. She gave me a subtle nod.

"We're listening," I told him.

"Like I said, I know your type. FBI creds means you're probably working on an FBI salary, which ain't bad, but your taskmasters expect you to pull off miracles on a shoestring. These black-bag ops always run on a razor-thin margin. You never have all the resources you want, am I right?"

I tilted my head at him. "Are you offering us a bribe?"

"Not money." He grinned. "A freebie."

"A free *what*?"

"A contract. The time may come when you need some serious firepower backing you up. And if you absolutely, positively need something destroyed overnight, we're the number one solution. Let me walk, and the next time you call me, Xerxes Security Solutions is at your disposal. No questions asked. You point, we shoot, free of charge."

Jessie held up a finger. "We need a moment."

"Take your time." He slid out of the booth, ambling past us. "I'm getting another beer."

"We don't actually have to fight everybody in the bar," Jessie murmured, "though, God, I really *want* to. We can just stake the place out and grab him when he leaves. That said, time's tight, and we've got other fish to fry."

She showed me her phone. A text had come in from Gerard Nowak while we were talking: Package is ready. Need to meet ASAP.

"You can't be serious," I said. "You want to make a deal? You weren't in Vegas with me, Jessie. This guy has worked for some truly evil people."

"Worked for. He's amoral. A hired gun. We're in the middle of a rogue op here—we might *need* some extra firepower soon. And how are we going to arrest him? We do that, we have to explain a lot of whys, starting with why we're even here. Which brings it all back to Roth and

Glass Predator and, oh, *our boss*, who may have had Douglas Bredford murdered. Look, for Caine to hold up his end of the deal, he has to give us a way to contact him, right? So he's effectively on a leash. Once we clear this whole mess up and things go back to normal, we can set up a sting and get him that way. Right now, finding out who the hell these impostors are is our number one priority."

She was right. I didn't like it, but she was right. If Roth was feeding these people names on a kill list, the sooner we caught them, the fewer corpses they'd add to their final tally. Which didn't explain why they were doing the job that Xerxes had been paid for, after murdering the original hit team and taking their place, but we weren't going to find any more answers here.

"And the verdict is?" Angus asked, sliding back into the booth with a fresh bottle. "Can we do business, or is it time to give one another a good kicking and see who's still standing when the dust settles?"

"We can do business," Jessie told him.

# # #

Chicago to New York was an hour and a half on a shuttle flight. Cutting through a stormy sky, dropping hard at the edge of the city, watching skyscrapers stand in ragged gray strips of cloud like tattered banners. We landed at LaGuardia in a shoe-box terminal at the back end of the airport—the whole team this time. April taking the lead as the four of us crossed the concourse. Jessie seemed a little more relaxed, less insistent on keeping April and Kevin at arm's length. She didn't frenzy when we went up against Nadine, and I think we both hoped her control over her powers was gradually coming back.

While she got them set up at the hotel, I reached out to Nowak. **Same place, one hour**, was his terse response.

Black clouds loomed over the Hudson and smothered the late-afternoon sun, turning the sky over Chelsea Piers to a smoky amber gloom. Not many people out on the cold, choppy waters now, just a lone sailboat gamely making its way upriver, trying to get ahead of the rain. Icy driblets pelted my face as I got out of the cab, a promise of storms to come.

Gerard Nowak stood at the water's edge, a thick cardboard binder under one arm, the collar of his gray trench coat turned up against the cold.

"It's Roth," I told him, "and he's looking to wipe the slate clean."

He nodded, resigned. He wore every year and every sleepless night in the lines on his face.

"I suspected as such," Gerard said. "This is a complete copy of the Glass Predator dossier—minus, of course, anything that could incriminate me. Do as you will. I'm leaving. I have a flight to Belize, and I won't be back until the dust settles. Under no circumstances will we meet again."

Jessie took the binder and shook his hand.

"Thanks for the help."

"Don't thank me," he said. "I didn't hand you a gun, I handed you a ticking bomb. You have to remember the thing about bombs. They're nondiscriminatory. It doesn't matter if you're just or unjust, deserving or undeserving, only how close you're standing when it goes off. Now if you'll excuse me, I have a plane to catch."

A storm cloud swallowed the sun whole. Out on the water, I caught a glimmer of light. Just a pinprick—pulling my gaze to the lone sailboat as it caught a gust and picked up speed, skating the Hudson.

Then came a distant *crack*, like the snap of the wind against canvas sails. And Nowak crumpled to the ground in a fine red mist with his skull perforated by a bullet.

TWENTY-FOUR

Jessie threw herself at me, both of us hitting the pavement hard as a second shot rang out. A couple of joggers, getting their exercise in before the downpour, covered their heads and ran screaming. Halfway up the block, shoppers paused, pointing, trying to figure out the commotion.

I came up on one knee, sweeping my Glock from the holster, drawing a bead on the sailboat. No chance. It was good as gone, riding the choppy waters and turning toward the Jersey side of the river, too far out of range. A handgun couldn't make that shot.

A sniper rifle, in skilled hands, could.

Jessie grabbed the fallen binder and pulled my sleeve. "C'mon, we gotta go."

"We have to call the Port Authority," I said, holstering my gun and running alongside her as she raced up the pier. "Get local PD on the scene, have them waiting every place that boat might put in—"

"We don't and we can't. We aren't supposed to *be* here, Harmony. Anything we do through official channels has a chance of landing on Linder's desk, and we already pushed our luck back in Chicago. Getting placed at the scene of his old buddy Gerard's murder is pretty high on the list of things we do not want right now."

I ran to keep up with her. We darted across the street, toward a warehouse where empty trailers stood silent beside a row of shuttered loading doors. A hard right took us onto a parallel street, out of sight and earshot from the crime scene. Jessie held up a hand and slowed down, a chance to catch our breath.

"Okay, nobody's behind us," she said. "Now we walk cool and easy. Two more blocks and we catch a cab."

She held the binder in her hands like it was the Holy Grail.

"Then we figure out what to do with this."

# # #

Once we got back to the hotel room, my hopes for a big, juicy smoking gun were easily shattered. Government memorandums tended to be overwritten and obtuse, and a program like Glass Predator doubled down on expectations: the binder held at least two hundred pages of tiny type and jargon, acronyms that pointed to a glossary filled with new acronyms that pointed to a second glossary. Worse, the page order was scrambled.

"Camouflage, Washington-style," April said as I divided the dossier into four stacks and passed them out. "Make it dense enough, someone might not even realize what they're reading."

She had a point. As I took a chair by the window, sitting across from Jessie at a small reading table, I fell into a cesspool of small print and euphemisms: page after page of risk assessments, debating the value of "the forcible cessation of domestic insurgency with the assistance of select military assets."

It was just damning enough, though, and Alton Roth's name was all over it.

After twenty minutes, my eyes fought to stay focused. Then I turned the page and everything changed. I'd found a service record for one of the killers Glass Predator recruited. Half of it redacted, but what remained still raised my eyebrows. He was a Delta op, with service in Iraq, Afghanistan, a smattering of third-world hellholes I didn't even know we had troops in—a man born to the battlefield. And his psychiatric evaluation, judging from what few words hadn't been blacked out, suggested he wasn't capable of living anywhere else.

That wasn't what made me grab Jessie's hand, pulling her attention to the page as I set it down between us and turned it toward her. It was the photograph.

We'd seen the man before, him and his bright-turquoise eyes. Jessie had killed him in Three Oaks, at Tucker Pearlman's house. And now he was lying on a coroner's slab with the fake Xerxes tattoo scrubbed from his pale arm.

"The original Glass Predator hit team," Jessie said. "They're behind this. They're still alive."

I compared his picture to our photo of the corpse, just to be sure, holding them up side by side. Same man.

"He's got the eyes in his original photo. So whatever contact these people had with the King of Wolves happened before they were recruited into the program. Maybe it happened during their military service? This guy's been damn near everywhere. Let's find the other three service records—they've gotta be in here somewhere."

"They're still alive," Jessie said, "and back, ten years later. Why? It doesn't make sense."

I needed to move. I stood up and paced the floor, thinking through it.

"It does," I said. "It makes perfect sense."

April glanced over at me, a stack of pages on her lap. "Explain."

"Let's put ourselves in their shoes. Four combat vets, recruited for a secret assassination program. And by all indications, the kind of people who enjoy the work. The program is canceled. Then somebody slips a bomb in their helicopter and sends them off over the ocean to die. Nowak thought they'd been blown up, everybody had; maybe they found the bomb and defused it, maybe they bailed out over the ocean, maybe they just got lucky and the charge was a dud. Regardless of how it happened, they survived. Now, you've just been thrown away by your employer. Worse than thrown away: they tried to murder you. What's your first reaction?"

"Payback," Jessie said.

"But not immediately," April said. "Beyond the chance that some of them were injured in the explosion and needed time to heal, they'd have found themselves completely cut off. No financial support, no lines of communication or assets they could draw upon—at least, not without revealing their survival and provoking another attack. They'd been kicked from the shadows with a steel-toed boot. It would take time to rebuild."

"But, eventually," Jessie said, "payback. I'd wanna track down every last person who signed off on my death warrant."

Sitting cross-legged on the hotel bed, pages spread out around him like tarot cards, Kevin frowned. "But they wouldn't know, would they? It sounds like the whole program was tightly controlled for everyone's safety. Nowak talked to the NSA, who fed names to RedEye, and Burton Webb channeled the information, but he never even *met* the assassins."

April gave him a thin smile. "You're almost there. Follow that thread."

"But Roth knows." Kevin snapped his fingers. "Roth has the whole list of names, everybody involved in Glass Predator. He wants the same thing the assassins want, just for different reasons. He's having everybody killed to protect his political career. They're just out for revenge."

Jessie nodded slowly. "So they kill the Xerxes team, take their place, and follow Roth's hit list. He has no idea that the people working for him are the same people *he* tried to have murdered ten years ago."

"They're following his list," I said, "but theirs has one more name on it. Senator Roth is their final target."

"And while I won't shed any tears over Roth's grave," Jessie said, "that list is the only reason the Wolves are sticking around. If they finish their mission before we hunt them down, they'll most likely disappear. Either they'll go to ground or just vanish overseas, back to wherever they've been licking their wounds for the last ten years. I want these people. Not just for the crimes they've gotta pay for, but *somebody* out there is infecting people with the King of Wolves's power. We need to know who and how, and this is our only lead."

"Check your stacks," I said. "There should be service records for the other three assassins somewhere in this mess. We need to know who we're dealing with."

Riffling through his pages with mechanical speed, Kevin found one in less than thirty seconds. Baker, a blue-eyed killer with a background in explosives and demolitions. April found the third man on the team a moment later.

"Lovely," she said. "Meet SFC Ferrara, formerly of the Seventy-Fifth Ranger Regiment. A sniper, with thirty-eight confirmed kills. *Before* he came stateside, that is."

I thought back to the pier. The glint of light from the scope, the sound of the bullet whistling over the water. It was a long-range shot from a moving boat—not just moving but bouncing on the choppy river—with a strong wind blowing, and the bullet landed with pinpoint precision. An ordinary person, even one with a decent amount of hands-on training, couldn't dream of making that shot. Someone like Ferrara, though? He did it for a living.

"So we've got a bomber and a sniper running loose," I said. "Great. April, what are you gathering from the psych evals?"

"Mostly redacted, but I can read between the lines. And they don't fit my expected profile."

"How so?"

April's fingertips dragged across a dense block of text. "Professional contract killers tend to display high levels of detachment, and are driven by financial needs rather than emotional gratification. In short, they're sociopaths who have found a career perfectly suited to their lack of empathy."

"So, these two—they're not sociopaths?" I asked.

"Oh, I wouldn't doubt it, but I'm seeing other traits. Fantasy-driven personalities, kills tied to sexual gratification . . . Hand me the dossier on the dead one, would you please?"

She looked it over quickly, comparing the three pages side by side.

"An unpleasant confirmation," she said. "I don't know how much this will help us from a practical standpoint, but these men aren't assassins by nature."

I tilted my head at her. "What are they, then?"

"Serial killers," she said. "They didn't join Glass Predator for the money, or out of any patriotic drive. They joined because they fundamentally crave and enjoy the act of murder."

"Wait a second," Kevin said. "I thought serial killers didn't normally team up together."

April nodded. "Pairings are rare. Generally you have a dominant killer and a weaker, submissive partner. Here we have three strong, aggressive personalities, each with their own favored victim types and favored methods of killing. Normally they'd be at one another's throats in a heartbeat—but they not only worked together, they *stayed* together long after Glass Predator was shut down. Something, someone, had to be holding them together. Someone capable of bringing all three of these men to heel."

That's when I realized Jessie wasn't moving.

She stared at the page in her hands, lips parted, not even blinking. Reading it again and again, as if the words might change.

"Jessie?" I said. "You okay?"

Her response was a murmur, under her breath, almost too soft to hear: "He told me he killed her. He told me. He told me he killed her."

"Jessie?"

I pushed my chair back and walked around the table, to stand by her side. She looked up at me. Tears glistened in her eyes.

"We found the vector for the King of Wolves," she said, her voice on the edge of breaking. "We found patient zero."

The woman in the photograph dominated the page, as if she could force her way off the paper by sheer will. It wasn't just size, though she was broad-shouldered and tall, muscular—it was the steel in her turquoise eyes, her expression of pure, raw determination. A force of nature who wouldn't be stopped by anything or anyone.

I looked at the name at the top of the service record: *Althea Temple-Sinclair, Sergeant First Class.*

"Harmony," Jessie said, "it's . . . it's my mom."

TWENTY-FIVE

"My oldest memory," Jessie said. "I was . . . five, maybe six. That was the day my father told me that my mom was dead. That she'd 'disobeyed the King.' So he'd sacrificed her, in the ritual pen behind our cabin in the woods. He . . . he showed me the bloody knife. Said he'd already burned her body, and the same thing would happen to me if I was bad."

She crumpled the page in her hand.

"That son of a *bitch*. That *fucking* . . ." Her voice trailed off as tears trickled down her cheeks, dripping onto the paper, welling over the ink.

I put my hands on her shoulders, standing with her. I didn't know what else to do. April rolled her chair over, reaching out to gently take the crumpled service record from Jessie's hand. She smoothed it on her lap, eyes intent behind her bifocals, comparing it to the other three.

"So maybe, she . . . took off?" Kevin said, uncertain. "And your dad used that story as a way to scare you, to keep you in line?"

"It holds," April said to Jessie, her voice unusually gentle. "He had infected her, the same way he infected you as a child. These records overlap: all four soldiers were assigned to a joint task force in Mogadishu at the same time. That's probably when she spread her power to the other three."

"She took off," Jessie echoed faintly.

She rubbed her fist against her cheek, smearing her tears, and took a deep breath. When she raised her head, the look of raw fury in her eyes almost drove me back a step.

"Then why the *fuck*," Jessie snapped, "did she leave me with him? The things he did, the—the things he made me *do*. She would have known. She would have known what would *happen* to me. What kind of mother does that to her child? Why didn't she take me with her?"

April chose her words carefully. "Back when I was with the Bureau, when we raided your father's cabin . . . Jessie, there was photographic evidence implicating your mother in his earliest murders. We know she was an accomplice, very likely a willing one. *You* know that. No, no woman in her right mind would abandon her child to a monster like Russell Lee Sinclair. But Althea wasn't—"

"Abandoned." Jessie's cheek twitched, a nervous tic as she spread a humorless smile. "How clinical. She threw me away like a piece of garbage. And then she went off to have adventures overseas, never looking back, and left me in *hell*."

Her fist slammed down on the table, papers scattering, a jagged crack in the cheap wood erupting like a fault line.

"She wants an overseas adventure? Fine. I've got one for her: a cell at Detention Site Burgundy, for her *and* her buddies. Angus Caine said Roth had a direct communication line with them. So we go after Roth, we squeeze him until he pops, and we use his encrypted channel to set up a trap."

"You realize you're talking about going after a sitting United States senator," April said.

"I'm talking about doing our jobs. Just because they're not the hit men he *thinks* he hired doesn't change the fact that Alton Roth is responsible for their victims. His title can't protect him. Not from us."

"Jessie." My hands tightened, just a little, on her shoulders. "You're in shock, and you're furious, and you're *right*—you're right to be feeling everything you're feeling right now. We've got to be careful, though. You remember what Nowak told us: these are deeper waters than we've ever been in, and Roth has a lot of powerful friends."

She turned in her chair, rubbing her damp cheek with the heel of her hand, and looked me in the eye. "You don't think we should take Roth down?"

"No," I said, "I *absolutely* think we should. And using his encrypted line to lure the killers is a good play. I'm just saying we need to take it slow, step by step, and come up with a bulletproof plan before we make our move."

Jessie inhaled, deep, and let out the breath with a tired nod of her head.

"Yeah," she said. "Yeah. Okay. Let's work it out. Number one threat is Linder. He's also on Roth's target list, but . . . hell, *we* don't know how to find him, and he's our boss. If there's one thing Linder is good at, it's turning ghost. We'll have to anticipate the blowback if he figures out that we know he was involved in Glass Predator."

"We've obfuscated our tracks so far," April said. "He believes we're still in Michigan, by the way. Or at least he's pretending to believe it. What else?"

"Calypso," I said.

Jessie glanced my way. "Roth's mysterious protector."

"Gerard Nowak and Angus Caine both warned us about him. Nowak was *frightened* of him. I think we need to get eyes on this guy and find out what his angle is before we make a move on Senator Roth."

"He'll be close." Jessie pointed at Kevin. "Jump on the laptop and get me Roth's public itinerary. If he's making any appearances, lectures, kissing babies, whatever. We need a venue where Harmony and I can get near him without drawing his attention."

"On it, boss." Kevin reached for his computer, leaning across the bed.

"There's one piece out of place," I said, "and it's sticking out like a sore thumb. RedEye. Somebody posed as Nowak and fed the system a fresh name—that Hamas suspect, Yousef Masalha."

"Given the timing, probably the Wolves," Jessie said. "We know, from how they handled the security cameras at the bank, they've got access to a grade-A hacker."

"Right, but why?" I gestured to the dossiers on April's lap. "Yousef's allegedly a bomb maker. Well, they already have one. According to his service record, this Baker guy can juggle explosives blindfolded. So why go out of their way, and risk drawing the NSA's attention, to find Yousef?"

Kevin's fingertips rattled across the keyboard. "Got something here. Looks like Senator Roth is gearing up for a fund-raising tour. He's in DC right now; tomorrow night he's hosting a big-ticket banquet at the Jefferson Hotel. Damn. A thousand dollars a plate."

Jessie winced. "And we can't use Vigilant funds or Linder will figure out what we're up to. Gonna have to find another way."

"Or," April said, "this is one of those rare occasions when it becomes prudent to break into one's retirement piggy bank. I think I can foot the bill, just this once."

Jessie and I turned to stare at her.

"*Just* this once," April said. "And if you don't come back with solid results, 'extremely cross' will not adequately encompass my reaction."

# # #

DC and tomorrow night felt like a world away, and we were all coasting on fumes. Jessie and I decamped to the room next door, looking for a few hours of sleep before we got back to work. I unfurled my tie, rolled it up, neatly stashed it in my suitcase. We brushed our teeth in side-by-side sinks, and she shot a look at my reflection in the bathroom mirror.

"What?" she said.

"Sorry. Was I staring?"

"You were staring."

"Just . . . are you okay?" I asked. "You kinda got hit with a bombshell today."

Her gaze dropped. She finished brushing her teeth. She spat into the sink, then leaned forward, both hands pressed to the cold laminate.

"I'm tired and I'm angry and I'm . . ." Her voice trailed off. She shook her head. "It's funny. I'd been thinking about the gunfight at Tucker's house. You drew a bead on her, and that's when my brain flipped. I thought it was something to do with our, y'know, shared condition."

"The musk you smelled. You said it made it hard to fight them."

"Yeah. But I couldn't figure out why the woman, in particular, was hands off. Like it was impossible for me to attack her. Hell, I jumped you to save her life." Jessie let out a short, bitter laugh. "Guess we know now. Harmony, I'm sorry, but I've gotta drop something heavy on you."

"Go for it."

Jessie looked my way. At me, not my reflection. "Even knowing the cause, I don't know how to fix it. I don't know how to stop going feral at the drop of a hat—"

"You didn't against Nadine."

"I got lucky. One time out of the last three? Those are crap odds. And as I was about to say, I don't know how to fight the . . . pack scent. When we go up against these creeps again, I'm not gonna be a hundred percent."

She took a deep breath.

"There's a very real chance that you're gonna have to kill my mother."

I wasn't sure how to answer that. I gave a tiny nod.

"Okay."

"I just want you to know," she said, "there's no . . . there's no sentimentality here. There's no love. She abandoned me and left me with a monster. What I'm saying is, what you and me have, our friendship? That stays solid, no matter what."

Jessie rinsed her mouth and reached for a hand towel.

"If you get a chance to kill the bitch," she told me, "you take the shot."

I tried to sleep. The glowing numbers on the clock between our beds read 12:42, and I was still wide-awake, tossing and turning, the mattress too hard and the pillow too flat. Or maybe it was the temperature in the room—too hot one minute, then too cold the next.

Or maybe it was because every time I closed my eyes, I was back in the Bast Club. Shoved up against the wall, Nadine's hand squeezing my throat, her lips pressed to mine.

I remembered the rush of energy flowing through my veins, a burning red line that shot straight to my brain, lighting every neuron on fire. Wave after wave of pleasure crashing down, each one stronger than the last. And then . . . nothing. I remembered it, but I couldn't *feel* it.

I felt hollow. And hungry.

It was three in the morning before my body finally gave out from sheer exhaustion, and I slept on an empty stomach.

TWENTY-SIX

A ghost stared back at me from the bathroom mirror. I had bags under my eyes, my skin paler than it should have been, my hair stringy and unkempt. I looked about as good as I felt. Still drowsy, I stood under the shower on full blast, letting the pulse of the spray massage my aching scalp.

I'm not big on makeup in general, but I still know some things. A little foundation, a little concealer, and I looked like a functional human being again. Jessie passed me on my way out of the bathroom, shambling and half-asleep.

"Morning, sunshine," I said.

She growled at me and shut the door.

We flew into Reagan National on the earliest flight we could get. The fund-raiser was scheduled for seven o'clock, which gave us plenty of time to scout ahead. We decided to go in under civilian cover. Oceanic Polymer was an old front company, established years ago as part of a discontinued DEA operation and left to gather dust. Jessie's team had scooped it up and made it their own. April made a few quick phone calls and secured two plates at tonight's banquet in Oceanic's name, and

Jessie and I—as two of the company's senior executives—would happily be attending to show our support for Senator Roth's reelection.

"Considering we're trying to stay low profile," I said to April, "any chance Linder's going to notice if we start throwing Oceanic Polymer's name around?"

"Vigilant Lock may have acquired the front initially, but we've made it our own since then. The addresses, accounts, and phone numbers have all been altered and suitably obfuscated, to the point that they shouldn't trip any red flags."

"You're welcome," Kevin said, strolling past us.

The Jefferson stood in the heart of DC, half a mile from the White House. A monument worthy of its name, the vintage '20s architecture stood tall and blocky and pristine against the city skyline, white stone with a touch of art deco. A restored skylight illuminated the lobby, the room appointed with marble and vintage tapestry, delicate but strong. Faint piano music drifted from an open lounge door, an elegant counterpoint to the rumble of suitcase wheels and the click of guests' footsteps on black-and-white marble.

We rented a pair of rooms on the fifth floor. The windows offered a sweeping view of the DC skyline, but we didn't have time to take it in. While April finalized our reservations and routed cash through the Oceanic Polymer bank account, Kevin got to work infiltrating the hotel's computer system.

"This is a recon mission," Jessie said. "Top priority: get access to Roth's encrypted channel so we can reach out to the Wolves. Kevin, what have you got for me?"

"Cracking the reservation database now—that'll give us intel on everybody staying at the hotel, including credit-card info. Roth's probably using his phone to talk to them—that or a secure laptop. Coin toss. If it's his phone, I can run a man-in-the-middle attack. Basically spoof the hotel's Wi-Fi, get him on *my* network, and drill in that way. One catch: I need to know which phone is his."

"So we have to get his phone number?"

"Uh-huh. His personal phone, not his business line—he might not want to give that out."

"I can be very persuasive. Okay, so we get his number, you jack his phone, we lure the Wolves into a trap. Once we take care of them, we can decide how to handle the senator."

I emerged from the bathroom with a glass of tap water from the sink. I'd been thirsty all day. "Agreed," I said. "Second, we have to get an angle on this Calypso person. Find out who he is, what he knows, what he's capable of."

Kevin looked up from his laptop. "If he's staying in the hotel, get me his room number and I'll dig up everything I can on him."

"A possibility," April said. "It sounds as though Calypso—for reasons yet unknown—has appointed himself Roth's protector. If you were to rattle the senator a bit, *without* compromising your identities, it's possible he'll run straight to his guardian angel."

Jessie nodded. "Put a scare into him. I like that."

"Focus on his specific fears," April told us. "He's terrified of exposure, of damage to his political ambitions. That's his pressure point."

"Sounds like a plan. Just have one thing to do first." Jessie looked my way.

"What's that?" I asked, sipping my water.

"Black-tie affair, a thousand dollars a plate, and the rich and famous in attendance. We can't go in there looking like FBI agents." Jessie put her hand on my shoulder, her face grave, like a doctor about to deliver a terminal diagnosis. "Brace yourself, Harmony. We have to find . . . dresses."

# # #

It wasn't hard to hunt down a place that rented formal wear. If there were three things DC had in abundant supply, they were fund-raisers, banquets, and reasons to dress to the nines. We walked along racks of glittering gowns with price tags that made my eyes blurry. Jessie gave a dubious eye to a sequined frock.

"Gonna need handbags," she muttered. "I don't think I can hide a gun under *any* of these."

Eventually, she gamely picked out a gown and tried it on. Then another one. Then a third.

"They all look amazing on you," I said, fidgeting with my hands as she turned in front of a three-way mirror. "Just pick something."

Jessie glanced over her shoulder at me. "Hey, I don't get to dress up that often. I'm having fun. Indulge me. And have you even tried anything on yet?"

I gave a helpless shrug at the racks. "Nothing's . . . me."

"Well, something's gotta fit. Just give it a shot, okay?"

I wandered the aisles, frowning. Nothing felt right, or maybe all the gowns were fine and it was just me that didn't fit. Then I got an idea and went looking for a salesclerk.

Later, Jessie knocked at my dressing-room door. "You okay in there, Harmony? You've been gone awhile."

"Yeah," I said, hedging with my hand on the doorknob. "I think I found something. I don't know."

"Well, come out and let me see!"

I opened the door. Jessie's mouth hung open. Then she laughed. "You have got to be kidding me."

My face fell. "You . . . don't like it?"

"Don't like it?"

She took my hand, her smile growing, and led me to the mirror.

"I *love* it," she told me.

She'd settled on a Faviana gown in blazing emerald, sleeveless, with a long pleated skirt that almost brushed the floor. The willowy folds were accented with shimmering sequins, making her look like a Hollywood starlet from the golden age. And I stood beside her in my sleek black tuxedo and bow tie, the puff of an ivory handkerchief poking from my breast pocket.

"It's very you." Jessie put her arm around my waist. "And we are definitely gonna be the best-dressed spies at the fund-raiser."

# # #

The ballroom at the Jefferson Hotel put the "class" in "classic." Glittering crystal chandeliers dangled along the heart of the room from an ivory ceiling filigreed in scallops that evoked Greco-Roman temples. Bronze curtains adorned tall window arches, draped like a theater stage, and wall sconces cast light across a vivid carpet painted in swirls of turquoise, scarlet, and gold.

Men in dark suits at both doors checked credentials, moving fast through a line of luminaries. They looked up our invitations and waved us through without a second glance. I tapped my earpiece.

"April," I murmured, "what do we have on Roth's security detail?"

"Checking on it," her voice echoed in my ear.

Conversation swirled around the room as Roth's supporters gathered to see and be seen, clinking glasses and catching up with old acquaintances. Half the room was in the pocket of one lobby or another, looking to hitch a ride on the senator's rising star. I spotted the man of the hour. He was busy glad-handing his way from one end of the room to the other, flashing a perfect ivory smile. Roth was a big man with big moves, in his late fifties but built for lifting weights, and his broad shoulders filled out a custom-tailored suit with an American-flag pin on one lapel.

"Let's divide and conquer," Jessie said, keeping her voice low. "Scout the room and try to figure out a way to spook Roth without giving the game away."

I mingled without mingling, drifting through the room alone. The back end of the ballroom was all set for the senator's speech, with a regal wood podium and a small, unobtrusive teleprompter off to one side.

"Kevin," I whispered, "are you inside the hotel's network yet?"

His voice crackled over the earpiece. "Am I awesome? The answer to both questions is yes."

"I've got an idea. There's a teleprompter down here. Can you see if it's hooked up to the hotel's Wi-Fi? Can you get access to it?"

"I can find out. What's the plan?"

I allowed myself a tiny smile. "A little last-minute rewrite."

I told him what I had in mind. We'd just finished the fine details when the crowd parted. And at the far corner of the room, surrounded by a cluster of doting, wide-eyed men, stood the last person I expected to see.

Nadine.

She wore a gown of shimmering pink, her hair pinned up, her face radiant. An angel who laughed and sipped champagne. And all the hunger that kept me up last night, all the pangs of loss and need, hit me like a fist to the gut. One kiss. Just one kiss and she could make me feel good again. One kiss and I wouldn't be aching like this.

I took a deep breath. Looking past the hunger to why I felt it in the first place. Remembering what she did to me, how she violated me. Dark alchemy bubbled in the pit of my heart, transforming desire into pure, burning anger.

"Excuse me," I said to a passing waiter with a tray of champagne flutes, "do you know who that woman is?"

He looked her way, suddenly as enraptured as every other man in the room. "Yes, ma'am. Nadine . . . Aston, I think. She runs a charity, the Rose Foundation for Underprivileged Youth? Big supporter of the senator."

I headed straight for her, like a shark cutting through the water. Smelling blood. I made eye contact with Jessie on the other side of the crowd. She saw where I was headed, her eyebrows lifting, and moved on an interception course. Nadine turned as I came up behind her, and for a fleeting moment, just a moment, I saw something new in her eyes.

Fear.

The look vanished, replaced by a cruel smirk. She looked to the man she'd been chatting with, handed him her empty glass, and patted him on the cheek.

"Go be a dear and fetch me another drink."

Nadine looked back to me, sizing me up. "Harmony. Have you been *following* me? I hoped that you would. That was my plan all along."

"You and I both know that's a lie. Nice to see you, Nadine. Or should I say, Nadine Aston, of the Rose Foundation for Underprivileged Youth. Huh. Looks like we know the full name you go by, and the 'charity' you work for."

Jessie closed in, moving to stand beside me. "We might have to come and visit your office sometime," she said. "You know, just to chat. In any case, we're gonna find out *all* about you—or at least the human you're pretending to be—and what you've been up to."

Nadine's bottom lip twitched, her smile frozen on her face and her eyes as cold as dead coals.

"You can make an appointment," she told Jessie, then looked back to me. "You, on the other hand, can drop by anytime. This doesn't change anything, Harmony. I've always been easy to find. And I feel . . . close to you now."

Her boy toy came back over with a fresh flute of champagne. She took the glass with a smile and a twinkle in her eye, getting her footing back. She leaned in close, her voice soft, and I felt her warm breath against my ear.

"After all," she whispered, "I've been *inside* you. I carved my initials into you. That's forever."

I clenched my hands into fists, nails digging into the meat of my palms to keep myself from reaching for my gun.

She giggled and stepped back, taking the man's arm.

"Let's go mingle," she told him. "I'll be seeing you two later."

She vanished into the crowd. I stood there, frozen, nails digging angry red welts. The sting was the only thing I could feel.

"Hey." Jessie touched my sleeve. "You okay?"

I forced my fingers open, forced myself to smile, forced myself to function.

"Fine," I told her.

"I have an update," April's voice said in my ear. "Senator Roth's personal security is provided by A-1 Protection, a local DC firm; he uses a different company when he's in his home district in Nevada. Nothing belowboard, perfectly ordinary business record. I presume you'll be wanting a full dossier on this Rose Foundation?"

Jessie's eyes narrowed, hard and hot as burning coals. "You know it. Soon as we're done with this mission, we're paying Nadine a little courtesy call."

"On that note," Kevin said, "I'm good to launch the attack on Roth's phone as soon as you get me a number."

Alton Roth swaggered our way, on a mission to shake every hand in the room. I shoved all the turmoil in my heart, all the hunger and hate, into a tiny box and locked the lid down. Nadine would keep for later. We had work to do.

TWENTY-SEVEN

Nevada might have been his home state, but Roth still hadn't lost his Texas twang. He took our hands in a gentlemanly grip, spending a little too much time looking up and down the front of Jessie's gown.

"I'll tell ya," he said, "I hate fund-raisers, but I love meeting new friends. My girl Charlene says you two are from . . . hold on, don't tell me, testing my memory here . . . Oceanic Polymer, is that right?"

"That's right," I told him, pretending to be impressed. "We're based in New York, but we're looking at a major expansion, and Nevada is on our short list."

Roth grinned. "That's a smart move, miss. Nevada is officially open for business, and I'm championing some new tax reforms that'll make our great state even more welcoming for investors."

"That's why we're here," Jessie said. "You know, we'd love to discuss our plans when you're free. Could you take a phone call in a few days?"

He nodded, already looking past us to his next handshake target. "Sure, sure, just call my office. Charlene can set up an appointment."

I had five seconds to keep him from leaving, keep him on track, and wring his personal number out of him. Speed chess, then.

My mind raced back, riffling through everything we knew about Alton Roth as if there was a dossier in my hands. I pictured the pages as if they were real, an old memory trick, reading lists of facts and figures. I'd never met him in person, but I'd used him all the same, when Vigilant called on Roth's connections to get me placed on a Las Vegas task force. Bredford's blackmail file was a litany of dirty connections to dirty people. I couldn't call him out directly and reveal that we knew about Bredford's research, though—couldn't break our cover. Of course, that didn't mean that a pair of crooked businesspeople from Oceanic Polymer couldn't be working their own angle.

"We were actually hoping," I said, moving my body to get between Roth and the person he was looking at, "for a more . . . off-the-record discussion."

One eyebrow lifted as I captured his gaze. Suspicious but interested. "Off the record?" he asked.

"We're given to understand that you have access to certain back-channel opportunities in Las Vegas. That you might be able to help us grease the wheels when it comes to building permits and the like. For an appropriate incentive, of course."

He gave me a nervous smile and ran his finger along the inside of his collar. "I, uh, don't know what you're getting at, but I can't do anything outside the bounds of the law, you understand—"

"Not even for a generous donation to the Nevada Heritage Coalition?" I asked. "Say, in the five-figure range?"

The lights glinted off a tiny bead of sweat on his forehead. "The PAC? That's not mine—I mean, they help, and we'd all be thankful for your support, but they're just a coalition of concerned citizens who value good civic leadership."

"Right," I said, holding his gaze unblinking. "I must have been given some faulty information."

"And may I ask, um, for curiosity's sake, where you heard that info?"

"Lauren Carmichael," I told him, and watched him freeze.

"I . . . uh . . . ," he stammered. "I don't—"

"The Carmichael-Sterling Corporation handled all of our real estate acquisitions until that . . . unpleasantness in Las Vegas and Lauren's disappearance. We were actually quite close," I told him.

April's voice crackled in my ear. "Well done, Harmony. Remember his pressure points. Keep him on the ropes, then appeal to his greed. Give him a lifeline and make him *want* to help you."

"I don't really know anything about that," he said, inching away from me.

I smiled as warmly as I could and gently touched his arm. Making human contact and keeping him calm. A tiny, calculated manipulation.

"*Relax*, Senator. You're among friends here. We don't want to make any trouble for you, or the slightest inconvenience."

"We're big fans," Jessie said. "All we need is a little special consideration, just like you did for Carmichael-Sterling."

"Just like Lauren documented via e-mail," I added, "quite thoroughly, actually. Like I said, we were close. And I want you to be our man in the Senate. Which means we'd better make sure you get reelected, hadn't we?"

"Did she say a five-figure donation?" Jessie asked. "What my partner meant was, we'd *start* in the five-figure range. The more you can do for Oceanic Polymer, the more we can do for you."

Roth licked his lips. Vacillating between his fear of exposure and the promise of easy money, he gave me a long, close look.

"I think," he said slowly, "we might be able to build a relationship."

I touched him again. Rewarding him with positive feedback.

"This could be the start of a beautiful friendship," I told him.

"We should take this to the back channels," he said, tugging out his cell phone. "Let me give you my private number. I'm heading back to Nevada in the morning. Give me a call and we'll set something up."

As he walked off, finishing his circuit of the room, Jessie flashed a smile.

"Nice moves," she said. "Kevin, did you get that?"

"Loud and clear, boss," he said over the earpiece. "And, Harmony, I just finished that little last-minute speech rewrite you asked for."

"Good," I murmured as Roth made his way to the podium. "I think we're just in time."

Conversations dissolved into applause as Roth gave a big, friendly wave. He squared himself behind the podium, back straight, chin high, flashing a plastic smile that was made for winning elections.

"What a wonderful evening, am I right, folks? I can't tell you how happy I am to see so many of you fine, upstanding citizens coming out to lend your support." He paused, mischievous. "And, of course, your generous donations don't hurt, either."

After a round of polite laughs, he glanced to the teleprompter.

"Before I tell you what I'm going to do in my next term, lemme tell you what I did in my last one. I brought thousands of new jobs to Nevada. I oversaw an unprecedented period of economic growth. I killed American—"

He froze. Reading the new addition Kevin had made to his speech on the teleprompter, a message for his eyes only: *I killed American citizens as part of Glass Predator, an illegal assassination program.*

The crowd fell into a confused hush as he stumbled over his words. He got his footing back fast, recovering like a pro.

"That is to say," he continued, "when American Airlines wanted tax concessions that would hurt our state, I killed that deal. Because I'm not just your man in the Senate, I'm your *fighter* in the Senate."

He tugged out his phone, tilting it as if reading fast.

"Ladies and gentlemen, I'm . . . I'm so sorry. Just got a text, and apparently there's been a family emergency. Nothing to worry about! But I've got to deal with this. Family has to come first, that's a principle I've always stood by, and I'll be back as soon as I can."

He scurried from the podium, face etched with panic. Jessie and I skirted along the edge of the audience, following him with our eyes, ready to move fast if he left the party.

I had checked out every face in the room, making my rounds. At least I thought I had, but Roth made a beeline for a man idling in the corner, someone I swore I hadn't seen come in. He was just *there*, as if he'd been there, leaning casually against the wall, unseen and unnoticed the entire time. He was tall and lean, with deep-umber skin and an ivory linen suit. He stared at Roth, utterly dispassionate as the senator gestured wildly at the teleprompter and barraged his ear with frantic whispers.

The tall man pushed away from the wall, shaking his head. I couldn't hear what he was saying, but his body language read, *Calm down, it's under control.* He waved over a pair of bodyguards, gesturing to Roth, giving low-voiced orders.

"I think we just found Calypso," Jessie murmured. "Whoever he is, he's definitely calling the shots."

I tugged my chunky black glasses from my inside pocket, slipping them on and looking their way. Two quick presses of a gimmicked pen, and the concealed camera in the frame snapped a perfect shot.

"Photos coming your way," I said. "April, can you run them through facial recognition, see if we get any hits?"

As the bodyguards hustled Roth to the door, the tall man gamely followed without a care in the world.

Kevin's voice cut in. "Guys? We've got a problem. I've lassoed Roth's phone onto my dummy network, but the hack isn't finished. If you want me to clone his cell, you've gotta keep him in range."

We shouldered our way through the crowd, moving fast.

"How close and for how long?" Jessie asked.

"Don't let him leave the building, or at least not more than a few feet off the front sidewalk," he said. "I'm piggybacking off the hotel's

191

Wi-Fi. No connection to Wi-Fi, no hack. Maybe . . . ten minutes? Fifteen, tops, I promise."

That wasn't going to be easy, not with Roth and his party heading for the lobby, and from there, I could guess, the valet-parking stand.

"Jessie," I said fast, "stall them. Just buy me a couple of minutes."

We broke ranks. She came up alongside the group, and I jogged past her, using a small pack of tourists for cover. The bodyguards tensed as she reached for Roth's sleeve.

"Senator," she said, "I'm sorry about your emergency. Do you have just one moment to talk before you leave? I wanted to make sure you have my information—"

My jog broke into an all-out run, racing across the lobby, drawing curious looks from the bell clerks. I burst out onto the sidewalk, standing under the hotel's vast art-deco awning, and looked for the valet stand.

I flashed my credentials in a valet's face. "FBI. There's been a threat against Senator Roth. I need his car pulled around immediately."

The kid blinked at me. "Do you have the ticket?"

"It's *Senator Roth*. Are you really going to tell me you don't know which car is his? And are you going to do that while there's been an active threat against his life? Think carefully before you answer."

He ran off to get the car. I paced the sidewalk, looking back over my shoulder, hoping Jessie could keep them inside long enough for me to get the job done. My plan was simple: no ride, no way out. All I had to do was disable Roth's wheels. By the time they lined up a replacement car, Kevin's work would be done, and we'd have everything we needed.

A black Grand Cherokee rumbled up the block, the valet looking tense behind the wheel. *Earth, air, water, fire,* I softly intoned. *Garb me in your raiment. Arm me with your weapons.* I slowed my breath, reaching deep inside myself, calling to my magic.

Nothing happened.

TWENTY-EIGHT

My power sparked, fluttered, and died.

I looked over my shoulder. Roth and company had shaken Jessie off, crossing the lobby with long strides. I had thirty seconds, maybe less.

As the Jeep rolled closer, I dug deeper. Scouring my heart, repeating the ritual trigger, grasping for the threads of magic.

All I felt was a gulf of hunger. And the memory of Nadine's kiss, and her voice: *I carved my initials into you.*

I banished the thought, locking my mind down, summoning every trick of discipline I'd ever learned. In my mind's eye I stood in a cyclone, the winds buffeting me every which way, confusing me and slipping from my grasp.

Then I moved into the eye of the storm, the center of tranquillity, untouched by the chaos. Now the spark ignited. Now the air was mine to command. I felt the pressure in the Jeep's tires as it rolled up to the curb, felt the air yearning to break free from its rubber prison. I reached to the trapped air and fed it.

"I have no idea . . . ," Roth said as he led the way outside. "Lobbyists are all crazy, you know that—"

All four of the Jeep's tires exploded at once.

One of the bodyguards threw himself on top of Roth, hitting the pavement, while the other drew his pistol. By the time they realized it wasn't a gunshot, the valet was clambering out of the Jeep and staring, horrified, at the shredded tires.

As the tires burst, something wrenched inside my stomach. And snapped.

I was used to paying the price for channeling power, the pain and nausea that followed in the wake of a potent spell, but this was something different, something darker. The residue of Nadine's poison touch throbbed under my skin—an oily, dirty itch.

I fought to catch my breath, leaning against the valet podium until the worst of it passed and I could stand on my own feet again. Roth, the bodyguards, and the valet were all shouting at one another, angry, confused—and not going anywhere for a few minutes. Only one man was untouched by the chaos.

Calypso stared at me.

I met his gaze. He tilted his head, curious . . . then cracked the faintest ghost of a smile.

I walked past him, without a word, and headed inside.

Jessie met up with me just inside the lobby doors. She'd been keeping out of sight. "How'd it go?"

"He's going to need another car. Kevin? How's it coming?"

"Thirty seconds," his voice replied. "By the time you get back to the room, I should have total ownage over Roth's phone. You coming back soon?"

"We're on our way," I said. I heard the strain in my own voice, fraying at the edges.

Jessie gave me a sidelong glance. "You all right?"

I wasn't all right. I played it off, giving her a tired smile. "Just had to move a lot of power around. You know it takes a lot out of me."

"Yeah, but . . ." She shook her head. "Never mind."

We'd almost reached the elevators when Nadine planted herself square in my path. She crossed her arms, chin raised high as she stared me down.

I stepped to my left. So did she. I stepped right. So did she, graceful as a ballerina.

"Really?" Jessie asked her. "You want to do this here? In public? Right now? Sure, I'm your Huckleberry."

Nadine ignored her. She only had eyes for me.

"You've been having a rough night, Harmony. I can see your soul, did you know that? It's all tattered and frayed at the edges, and aching. And hungry." Her lips curled into a cruel smile. "Would you like me to kiss it and make it better?"

I took a deep breath, counting to five, slow, as I let it out.

"I would like you to get out of my way."

She didn't move.

"What you're feeling," she said, "by the way, is withdrawal. The first pangs of it. It only gets worse from here. But I can fix it. I can take the pain away, make you feel right inside again. Just one little kiss. I certainly understand if you don't feel comfortable with public displays of affection. We can go up to your room, or mine . . ."

Jessie stepped in, getting between us. "Listen up. The next time we meet is the *last* time we meet: *know* that. And you better believe that day's coming fast. There's nowhere you can hide from us."

"Why on earth would I hide?" She eased her way around Jessie, closing the distance between us while I stood there, paralyzed. "I'm just offering your partner a bit of pain relief. After all, she helped me escape. Such a good little slave deserves a reward. Would you like your reward now, Harmony?"

My stomach tightened, and I tasted bile in the back of my throat. My guts were a knot of twisting, biting snakes.

And all I had to do, to make it all go away, was lean in and kiss her.

"I don't want anything from you," I snarled, forcing out the words. "So unless you're ready to finish this once and for all, right here and now, get the *fuck* out of my way."

"For when you change your mind . . . ," Nadine said, turning so Jessie couldn't see her left hand. She pressed something into my palm, a rectangle of plastic.

A room key.

"Six oh five," she murmured as she turned to leave. "I'll be up all night long. Leave your partner behind."

We watched her saunter off. Jessie hadn't seen her pass me the card.

I slipped it into my pocket.

"Hey," Jessie said, her brow etched with concern, "is it that bad?"

I shook my head. "It's . . . I'm just aching a little."

"If it was worse than a little, you'd tell me, right?"

Sure. While Jessie's powers were running out of control and she'd just found out we were on the trail of her own mother, I'd be happy to throw more problems onto the pile. No, she had her own pain to deal with, and I needed to be there for her. I could keep my misery to myself.

"Let's go back to the room," I said.

The lights of the DC skyline shone through a gossamer-veiled window. Kevin sat at the worktable, typing furiously, a USB cable tethering an old phone to his laptop like an umbilical cord.

"Who," he asked as we walked in the door, "is the most brilliant person you know?"

"April is," Jessie said. From her seat by the table, April offered her a tip of an imaginary hat.

"Okay, *besides* the doc."

"Oh, easy," Jessie told him, pointing my way. "Harmony."

"Third most brilliant."

"Well," she said, "I don't want to brag . . ."

He sighed and held up the tethered phone. "Point is, I'm the man, and this is Senator Roth's phone. Which I've just started digging into, but it's just laden with *oodles* of barely legal nastiness. His unlock code, by the way, was his birthday. Literally the first thing I tried. People really have to stop doing that."

I walked over, happy for something to distract me. "How does it work?"

"It's a clone. Identical to the phone in his pocket in every way. All the same data, and to the network, any calls I make from this cell will look like they're coming from Roth. Just have to figure out how he's reaching the Wolves, and we can do the same."

"I've put the photo of the man we believe to be Calypso through the IPS," April said. "We'll know if he's in any government databases soon enough, but I don't expect they'll get back to us before tomorrow."

"It's late, I'm famished, and we deserve a team dinner." Jessie looked me up and down. "Besides, these clothes have to go back to the rental place tomorrow, and you and I haven't turned nearly enough heads yet. Did I mention we look amazing?"

My phone rang. I glanced at the screen. "One second. Sorry, I have to take this."

I stepped out into the hallway, out of earshot.

"Hey there, darlin'," Fontaine drawled. "Just calling in with a little status update on your boy. Deputy Cody split town five minutes after you did, and the only tail on him was the one I put there. Bobby can hunt, but he's got no idea where to start looking."

I closed my eyes. Some of my pent-up tension slid out on a faint sigh of breath. "Good. Where is he now?"

"Detroit. Though I should warn you, Bobby Diehl's not the only one looking to do some hunting." Fontaine paused. "Cody just bought himself a gun. Not like his legal, registered police special, either. A street piece."

Cody had told me, back in Talbot Cove, what he had in mind. That he was going after Diehl, planning on making him pay for what he'd done. I'd hoped it was just talk, the kind of heat-of-the-moment promise that would fade once he got some distance and some time to work through his grief.

His grief and his anger were still burning hot, and now he had a black-market gun in his hand. Only one thing he could be planning to do with it. I had to stop him. To save him from himself, somehow.

I just wasn't sure if I was trying to save him from getting himself killed, or to save him from turning into me.

The door opened, and Jessie poked her head out. "Harmony? Dinner? Yes?"

"Thanks," I told Fontaine. "Keep me posted, okay? I gotta go."

# # #

We ate at Quill, a lounge inside the hotel, where a live grand piano played rolling jazz across a stretch of polished parquet floor. Faded maps adorned the walls, charting the vineyards of eighteenth-century Europe. I ordered a romaine wedge salad and a ginger ale.

"Not a Diet Coke?" Jessie asked in mock bewilderment. "First you go from a suit to a tux, now you're changing up your choice in soft drinks . . . I just don't know who you are anymore."

"Stomach's a little upset," I told her, offering up a smile I couldn't feel.

"The prime fillet looks lovely," April said. "And I think I'll indulge in a glass of cabernet."

"Make it two," Jessie said.

"Three," Kevin added. "C'mon, we're celebrating."

"I'll happily buy you a glass," April said, "as soon as you turn twenty-one. Remind me, will you?"

"I've been thinking about our approach," Jessie said. "Let's look at what we're up against. We know what they're physically capable of because, well . . . they're *me*. More training, more combat experience, but I squared off with one of their guys in Three Oaks and took him down. They're not any more bulletproof than I am. That said? Two against three isn't the kind of odds I like."

She didn't mention the head-fogging musk that turned her against me, in a heartbeat, when I tried to shoot at her mother. I didn't bring it up, either.

"We don't have to go close quarters unless we're trying to capture them," I said. "So . . . *are* we trying to capture them?"

A hush fell over the table, all eyes on Jessie. The waiter brought our drinks.

"We're still in the woods here when it comes to Douglas Bredford and Cold Spectrum and hiding what we know from Linder," she said. "Hell, we just keep going *deeper* into the woods. Safest solution is to terminate all three of them. Dead men tell no tales."

"But," Kevin said, hearing the edge in her voice.

"Jessie," April said.

Jessie looked her way.

April studied her, gazing into her eyes.

"Existing Vigilant Lock protocol allows for a temporary change of cell leadership, if it's deemed necessary. You can transfer that command for the remainder of this mission."

"Meaning?" Jessie asked.

"Meaning," April replied, "if you need that authority to rest in someone else's hands—if you need someone, who isn't you, to issue a kill order on your mother—I'll carry that burden for you."

Jessie stared at her glass of wine. Rolling the stem in her fingertips, catching the light in its scarlet depths.

"I'm still the one who's gotta pull the trigger."

"There's a difference between following the order and giving it. You're our general. If you need to be a soldier for a little while, I think we all understand."

Jessie looked up from her glass. She shook her head.

"No. Thank you, I mean that. But this is my team, my responsibility, my call. We'll take prisoners if it's possible. If not? We sanction all three. That said, I *do* want one of them alive. Somebody out there knows exactly what Cold Spectrum was and why everybody involved had to die. I think we should ask the people who pulled the trigger."

TWENTY-NINE

After the waiter came back with our entrées, Jessie sliced off a chunk of rare steak and held it up on her fork like a conductor's baton.

"So," she said, popping it into her mouth, "how do we take on three assassins who have spec-ops training and my powers, hopefully keep one alive to interrogate, and also not die in the process?"

"I'm loath to say this," April said, "but we need to see the world from your mother's point of view. Althea's training and fields of expertise were largely redacted, but we know what assets she can deploy."

"Baker and Ferrara," I said. "Baker's an explosives expert, and we've seen what Ferrara can do with a sniper rifle."

"We also know what they're after," Kevin offered, lifting his hamburger. "Work their way down Roth's hit list, hit *Roth* for a grand finale, and . . . I don't know. Revenge complete. Probably go back to whatever they've been doing for the last decade."

"They're goal-oriented killers," April said. "They won't want to deviate from the plan."

I swirled my straw in my ginger ale, bouncing glaciers of ice against the side of the glass. I'd poked at my salad, but I didn't have the stomach to do much more than nibble.

"Meaning when Roth—meaning us—contacts them, they'll probably be suspicious."

We ate in silence, thinking.

"Maybe we can use that," Jessie mused. "Okay. You're Althea. You get a message from Roth asking for a meet, and it feels hinky. What do you do?"

Kevin shrugged. "Can't ignore it. If they think they've been compromised, or Roth has, they've gotta find out for sure."

"And it wouldn't be the first time someone's set them up to be killed," April added.

"So they have to show up, but not on Roth's terms. Get the intel without sticking their necks out." Jessie looked my way. "Harmony. Tactics."

"She'll use Ferrara," I said. "Put him somewhere with a good vantage point so he can eliminate any threats from a safe distance. She'll also want to scout the meeting site well in advance. The last time the NSA tried to kill them, they planted a bomb. She'll suspect they'd pull the same move twice. She might even try to flip that idea on whoever shows up: have Baker wire the entire site with explosives, or just strategic access points. That would give her control of the battlefield and an escape route."

Jessie tapped her chin with the tip of her finger, thinking it over.

"So what if we let them? We deliberately send them a meeting request that doesn't sound right. But we pick a location that has an ideal sniper's nest overlooking the scene. Instead of showing up, we ambush Ferrara. From there, we pick off the other two at long range. Hell, we can use Ferrara's rifle to do it."

We spent the rest of the meal debating, batting plans and ideas back and forth. I slipped farther and farther away. The emptiness in the pit of my stomach was a gnawing, frustrated knot, and I kept reliving the moment at the valet stand when my magic, for the first time since I was a child, refused my call. Short-circuited by the residue of Nadine's kiss.

Or by the lack of it. The more time passed since our forced kiss, the hungrier the memory made me, the more my skin crawled. The world felt sideways, and the only thing that could put me back on my feet was the touch of my worst enemy. It felt like water torture. A slow, ceaseless drip that set my nerves on edge and made my teeth itch.

Kevin went back to the room. Jessie discovered that they served cigars on the terrace and wanted to try one; April was game, too. I begged off, telling them I had a headache. Truth was, I just couldn't talk anymore. I couldn't think straight. I couldn't think of anything but the rush I'd felt and how badly I needed to feel it again.

I got on the elevator, reached for the button for our floor, and froze. Nadine was here. In the hotel. I had her room key, and an invitation.

Would she kill me? Was it a trap? I didn't think so. She was obviously enjoying herself. Addicting me to her toxic kiss was a game to her. She wouldn't spoil the fun by taking me out so quickly. No, she'd give me exactly what she promised, knowing I'd be back for more.

So I could go to her. I could swallow my pride, go to Nadine, and get some relief. And considering the effect the withdrawal was having on my magic, and we needed my magic to take down the Wolves, it was actually a smart tactical decision. I'd be letting down the entire team if I *didn't* go to her room. Possibly putting us all in danger.

My finger touched the button for the sixth floor.

I didn't press it.

"Harmony," I said out loud, "you are acting like a goddamn junkie. And you are not a junkie. *Stop.*"

I pulled my hand away. Then I touched the button again.

I marched back into the lobby and showed my FBI credentials to a desk clerk.

"I need to get onto the roof," I told her.

A little badgering and a few incoherent excuses later, I emerged from an access stairwell and out onto the hotel rooftop. A long, flat plain studded with thrumming air-conditioning units, bathed in moonlight. The DC skyline blazed in the dark, white diamonds glowing all around me.

This was where I needed to be. Away from everything and everyone. Somewhere I couldn't hurt anybody. Or myself. I stumbled across the rooftop, my legs shaky, and sat down on the dirty concrete with my back to an AC unit. The maintenance crew had left their tools behind, and I grabbed an empty plastic bucket, hauling it onto my lap.

I stuck my head inside and screamed. As loud as I could, as long as I could, until there was nothing left. Screaming out my anger and my hurt and my hunger—everything I'd bottled up inside me.

The bucket tumbled from my limp hand and onto the rooftop beside me. I leaned back and stared at the city lights.

"Needed that, huh?" Jessie asked.

She was standing a few feet away, watching me.

"How'd you find me?"

"I knew something was wrong," she said. "So I asked around. Front desk sent me up here."

She walked over, the sequins on her gown shimmering in the moonlight, and sat down next to me. She leaned her head back against the dented metal and shared the view.

"It's peaceful up here," she said.

"Yeah."

"I wish you'd talked to me."

"Jessie," I said, "you just found out your mother is alive. And tomorrow we might have to take her out. That's more weight than anybody should have to carry. I don't want to add to it."

"It's not adding. It's sharing. You carry as much as I do." She turned her head and looked at me. "I'm gonna get a little tough love on your ass right now. Come down off the cross, Harmony. Nobody asked you to nail yourself up there. This team only works, we only hold together, if we *talk* to one another. And you and me, we made a deal."

I tilted my head. "Deal?"

"Uh-huh. Remember our first trip to Talbot Cove? When we got jacked by that . . . psychic parasite thing in the mayor's basement?"

I remembered. The creature had blindsided us, drawing us into hallucinations fueled by our fears and insecurities.

"You rescued me," Jessie said. "And do you remember what you said? 'If you fight my demons, I'll fight yours.'"

She put her arm around my shoulder, pulling me close, letting me lean against her.

"Did you really think I wouldn't hold up my end of the bargain?"

I shoved my hand into my pocket, tugging out Nadine's room key.

"I need you to take this away from me," I told her.

She did. And then she helped me to my feet, and we walked across the rooftop to stand at the edge. She flicked the card away, letting it spiral through the air, falling, gone.

"Come on," she said. "It's late, and we've got a lot of work ahead of us. Let's try to get some sleep."

# # #

Things looked a little better in the morning.

I still ached, still hungered, still worried my magic wouldn't come when I needed it, blocked by the remnants of Nadine's touch, but it wasn't so bad now. I wasn't fighting alone.

Kevin was unusually chipper for this early in the day. He'd cracked the code, finding the line between Roth and the Wolves.

"It's a custom text-messaging app," he told us, demonstrating on the cloned cell phone. "Pretty slick. Two-way channel, encrypts outbound and inbound texts, and autodeletes messages within twenty-four hours of receipt. And I mean it scrubs them *clean*: there's no way I can recover any of their past conversations. On the plus side, there hasn't been any traffic since last night in either direction, meaning Roth hasn't tried to contact them. He's probably afraid to, after how we spooked him with the teleprompter switch."

"But you can reach out to the Wolves with this thing?" Jessie asked.

"Yeah, but if they had any nonelectronic security—like, if they were supposed to start each message with a password or a key phrase to prove it was Roth on the line—they'll know it's not really him."

"That's fine. We're going with plan A, then. Let them think something's up. We won't be at the meeting: we'll be in the sniper perch, jumping Ferrara from behind."

April spread a map of the city across the table, and I tugged back the curtains to flood the room with morning light.

"On that note," she said, "I've looked over a number of possible locations. I suggest this one: Dupont Circle."

She rested her finger on the folded page. Streets radiated out from her fingernail in geometric precision, like the spokes of a bicycle wheel.

"A traffic roundabout?" I asked.

"Indeed. With a public fountain and pavilion right at the center."

Jessie shook her head. "We need to predict where they're gonna put their sniper. They could post him in any one of those surrounding buildings and he'd have a perfect vantage point."

April said, "They could, if not for the large trees planted all around the fountain to provide shade. None of the surrounding buildings are particularly tall, so the trees would make things difficult for a sniper, even at this time of year. Not a lot of leaves, but the branches could still obscure a clear shot." She pointed to a small X on the map, drawn in ballpoint pen. "Except here. I called the Department of Parks and Recreation; they had to remove a tree last week after a bark-disease outbreak, and they haven't planted a replacement yet."

She set her pen to the map, drawing a razor-sharp line toward the east side of the traffic circle.

"This is the Patterson Mansion. Four stories, and thanks to the tree removal, these central windows offer a perfect line of sight to the fountain. The *only* perfect line of sight."

I leaned in, following the stroke of her pen. "Who lives there?"

"That's the best part," April said. "Nobody. The building has been on the market since 2013. There's a proposal to convert it into apartment space, but construction hasn't begun. All Ferrara has to do is break in, make his way to the fourth floor, and set up his perch. It's the perfect spot."

"It's the perfect trap," Jessie said. "All right. Let's do it. Lay out the bait."

THIRTY

Kevin booted up the encrypted-text app on his cloned cell. "What do you want me to tell 'em?"

Jessie paced the hotel room, thinking it over. "Let's tell them the truth. Somebody messed with Roth's speech last night, he's scared, and he wants to meet in person to talk about it."

April folded her street map neatly. "Give them the address in the initial message before they suggest a meeting place of their own. Set the rules of engagement."

The answer came back in a heartbeat: Thought you were in NV.

Nevada, Roth's home state. I thought back to what he'd told us last night.

"He's supposed to fly back this morning. Tell them he canceled the flight—he's too afraid to leave town until he finds out what's going on."

1700, came the response, and nothing more.

"Seventeen hundred hours," Jessie said. "So, five p.m. They'll have to get there earlier than that. Let's beat 'em to it."

# # #

A fountain burbled at the heart of Dupont Circle. Three classical nudes posed gracefully on its central pillar, embodying the wind, the sea, and the stars. Around them, a paved pavilion stretched out in a clean circle, surrounded by thick, leafy trees.

All except the one missing tree, the lawn marred by churned-up dirt next to a maintenance worker's wheelbarrow, offering a line of sight straight to a mansion of pristine white stone.

Connected by our earpieces, we split up. April rolled her chair past the fountain, finding a shady spot near the benches that ringed the pavilion's edge, and unfurled a copy of the *Washington Post*. She gazed over the newspaper's edge, studying the passersby, keeping a lookout. Thanks to their service records, we knew exactly what Althea, Ferrara, and Baker looked like. We just had to pick them out of the crowds.

Jessie, Kevin, and I patrolled the street around the outer circle, just ordinary locals out for a morning walk. We staggered our rounds and spread out so that one of us was always close to the Patterson Mansion's front steps, but never for so long that we'd stand out. I had to assume that Althea or one of her men would be studying the scene before they moved in, expecting a trap. They were right. They'd just be expecting the trap in the wrong place.

I kept my eyes open, watching for the telltale signs of a countersur-veillance operation. Cars with tinted windows or panel vans, lingering too long or passing the same street too many times. I noted license plates, memorized the digits, and watched to see if they came back around. I'd pause now and then, pretending to look into a store window when I was really checking the glass, scanning the reflections of people on my tail.

The hours dragged on. We were pushing four o'clock when Kevin's breathless whisper crackled over my earpiece. "Oh, shit, oh, shit, it's him. Ferrara. I've got eyes on him."

"Easy," Jessie responded. "Slow your roll, big man. Don't give the game away. Is he carrying?"

"Well, he's got a guitar case, and I don't think he's a musician. He's headed for the Patterson place. Oh, shit, he's slowing down, I think he's doing that store-window reflection trick you taught me."

"Break off," I murmured, "*now*. Is there a shop near you? Anywhere you can get off the sidewalk?"

"Yeah, a Starbucks—"

"Stop talking. Go inside. Buy something to drink, sit down, and drink it. Do not look behind you, do not look at the door, and don't talk on this channel again until we say so. Jessie, you're closer than me."

"Already moving," she said.

Kevin wasn't trained for this. We were—and so were the Wolves. We needed him earlier, to cover more ground, but now taking Kevin off the board was our safest option.

"He's doubling back," Jessie said, watching from a safe distance. "Yeah, he's checking Kevin out, poking his head in the door."

"Oh, shit—"

"Do *not* talk," Jessie said. "Just drink your latte or whatever. Yeah, it's cool. He's moving on. Talking into his sleeve—I see his lips moving."

I circled around from the other direction. He wasn't hard to spot at a distance, wearing dark glasses like Jessie's and lugging his black guitar case along the sidewalk. He paused, scoping out the scene, then skirted the back of the mansion. The place earned its name: four stories of white marble and brick with dozens of ornate windows, all decorated in a neoclassic, Italianate style. It looked like the kind of place where the Great Gatsby might have thrown a party once or twice.

"Let's give him twenty minutes," I said softly. "Enough time to get in, find his perch, and hopefully be staring out the window through a rifle scope when we sneak up behind him."

"On that note," April said, "I'm exposed here. Moving to the north end of the circle. Kevin, come meet me, and we'll take a cab back to the hotel. We can provide logistics support from there."

I caught up with Jessie on the sidewalk. She touched her earpiece.

"Good," Jessie said. "April, I want every possible escape route planned out. Kevin, I want you on top of the traffic situation. Things are liable to get very loud and very messy out here."

We walked together, killing a few minutes, marking time. I focused on my breathing, working to keep my nerves in check. Sometimes on a mission, I'd find a strange moment of tranquillity. A place where I really felt like myself. Alive. At peace. It was always just before the moment of truth: the moment when the hammer thundered down, the first bullet flew, and the blood began to spill.

Maybe Cody was right. Maybe something was wrong with me. Maybe I didn't react to violence, to death, like a normal human being should. Maybe I couldn't worry about that right now.

"So, we jump Ferrara, take him alive, and use his rifle to snipe the other two when they show up at the fountain. Then we get the hell out of Dodge." Jessie looked me over. "You're gonna have to do it. I'm sorry. I don't think the . . . pack scent . . . thing is going to let me. I can't even be in the room, just in case I flip out like I did last time."

I shrugged. "I'm the best markswoman on the team, anyway. I'm qualified with a Remington 700. Whatever rifle Ferrara is using, it can't be much different."

"I'm hearing an unspoken reservation."

"Jessie . . . don't you even want to *talk* to her?"

"Althea?" She took off her sunglasses and pinched the bridge of her nose, as if staving off a headache. I watched years of bitterness and pain flicker across her face in the span of a heartbeat. She put the glasses back on and pursed her lips. "No. There's no excuse for what she did to me. No excuse for what she did with my father, and no excuse for the four dead civvies at that bank in Manhattan. No excuse I want to hear. She's not my mother, Harmony. She's Hostile Entity 144, and we are gonna do our damn job."

We circled the mansion. Ferrara hadn't bothered to cover his tracks. The windows on the first floor were all covered in curving, decorative iron bars, except for one: there, the bars hung bent and twisted, the entire grate wrenched to one side and pressed to the ivory brickwork. I checked out the broken ends of the bars, corroded and drooling faint wisps of foul-smelling smoke.

"Acid," I told Jessie. "He treated the tops of the bars to weaken them, waited a few minutes, then used his muscle to haul the whole thing down."

"I'll have to remember that trick," she said, clambering through the window. She gave me a hand up and over, my feet landing light on a desolate span of hardwood floor.

Faint impressions in the dust hinted at where classic furniture used to stand. Now there was nothing but empty galleries and empty walls, with the occasional ladder or bundled-up painter's tarp. We crept through the mansion slow and soft, ears perked. A grand staircase of pristine white marble, overseen by a Grecian fountain, took us up to the second floor. A back staircase, just a hall away, wound its way straight to the top.

Guns drawn, moving in single file and covering every angle of attack, we emerged onto the fourth-floor landing.

The light outside had started to fade. Long shadows stretched across the empty floors like ghosts of the mansion's past, and the air took on a dusty amber hue. The halls smelled like old cedarwood, clean and rich and sturdy.

Open doorway on our right. Jessie looked back, nodded at me, and we took up positions on either side of the door. I heard movement inside, footsteps on softly groaning wood, someone pacing. Waiting.

Jessie held up three fingers. On the count of one, I was first through the door. Moving in, smooth and fast, finger on the trigger and sweeping the muzzle of my Glock across the room while Jessie followed on my heels.

Four windows lined the empty gallery, letting in the dying sunlight, casting glowing pools between patches of shadow. The windows were all closed tight. No sniper's nest. No sniper.

Just Althea Temple-Sinclair. Stepping from the darkness at the far end of the room to stand, exposed, in the light.

THIRTY-ONE

"I wouldn't," Althea said, and my trigger finger froze even as I locked her in my sights. In her left hand she carried a .45 automatic, loosely pointed our way. In the other, a slim steel box with a spring lever, squeezed in her curled fingers.

A dead-man switch.

"There are ten pounds of C-4 remotely connected to this switch," she said casually, her voice carrying an easy, singsong cadence. "I let go, explosives go boom. You don't want that."

Althea was bigger than she looked in her photograph. Not just taller, broader-shouldered, but emotionally bigger. Something in her burning blue eyes nearly pushed me a step back, like her sheer force of will could fill the entire room. She wore her hair in tight dreadlocks, and the buckles of a tactical holster crossed the ribs of her olive sweater.

I took a step toward her. The second I neared the closest pool of light, a bullet cracked through the antique window and dug a splintered hole in the floor two inches from my foot.

"You should also stay right where you are," Althea said. "While you were coming in the back, my man Ferrara was going out the front. Moving to the real sniper perch on the eighth floor of an office building about two blocks from here. Yeah, after our little dustup in Michigan, we knew somebody was on our tail. We were sitting in a room with Roth, listening to him whine, at the same time 'he' texted us for a meet. Had to be a trap. And if you knew I had a sniper on my team, you'd know I'd want to use him. So you made him the priority target. That's exactly what I would have done."

"You were never coming to the fountain," I said.

"Nope. And unless you're about to reveal that this is a *double*-double reversal, and you've got men moving to intercept Ferrara at the real sniper post . . . I think you've got to admit, you just got outplayed."

Jessie hadn't said a word. Standing beside me, holding Althea in her sights. The muzzle of her gun wavered but held steady. Her eyes narrowed, hard, behind her sunglasses.

"I'm calling your bluff," Jessie told her. "We've had surveillance on the mansion all day long, and we know what all four of you—excuse me, all *three* of you now—look like. No way your guy got in here and planted explosives without us seeing him."

Althea laughed, flashing a darkly amused smile.

"When did I say the explosives are here? No, girl. They're planted in a trash can over at 4500 Van Ness. Friendship Park. The locals call it Turtle Park, I think. Mmm, big ol' playground there. Swings, slides, things to climb . . . the kids love it. And it's not that late in the day. Probably a whole bunch of the little rug rats clambering around, no idea they're about to become front-page news."

April's voice crackled over my earpiece. "Contacting the bomb squad now. Harmony, she may be lying about the explosives' location, or the number of bombs they planted. Do *not* let her release that switch."

"Are you insane?" I said to Althea. "Why a *playground?*"

"Because I'm playing the odds. I don't know who you folks are, but most people don't like having dead children on their conscience. Which is exactly what you'll have if you shoot me and I let go of this switch.

So let's lower the guns and have a little conversation." She holstered her pistol and nodded across the room at Jessie. "You, I want to know more about. Why do you smell like one of mine?"

Jessie took off her sunglasses. She stared her mother down, eyes hard, neither one blinking.

"It's funny," Jessie said. "I kinda thought you might recognize me."

Althea squinted at her. "You weren't one of those witches with the Coven of Everlasting Night in Morocco who I met back in 2011, were you? I know they were trying to reach out to the King, but last I heard they all got eaten by something they called up from the pits."

"Try again. Try real hard."

It dawned on her then. Althea's mouth slowly fell open. Her eyes widened, shimmering, and she finally found the breath to speak the name on her lips.

"Jessie?"

Jessie raised her gun an inch higher. Sighting the barrel right between Althea's eyes.

"Hi, Mom."

Althea stared at her, in shock. Her nose twitched. *Smelling* Jessie, from across the room. Whatever hung in the air between them, the invisible musk they shared, it seemed to tell her the truth.

"Jessie, I . . ." Her mouth opened, closed again, and she shook her head. Her free hand, balled into a fist, wiped at one of her eyes as it began to glisten. "He told me . . . Jessie, he told me you were *dead.*"

Jessie blinked. "What?"

"Your father. That son of a bitch. He took you into the woods to do the rite—to bless you with the nectar of the King of Wolves. He came back and told me that the King had rejected you, that you'd died. He showed me a child's body, all burned up. I thought it was *you.*"

"He . . . did the same thing to me," Jessie said, her voice a pale whisper now.

"I left. I couldn't be with him after that, couldn't stand to look at him. He knew I would. He must have . . . wanted you for himself. We had arguments, about how to spread the good word, how to do the King's work. And that's how he solved it. He stole you from me. Sweet misery, Jessie. My baby girl. Did you think I *abandoned* you? You must have."

Jessie's bottom lip trembled. Her eyes as wet as Althea's, tears pooling and threatening to fall. "You left me with that monster—"

"I didn't know!" Althea cried. She paced the floor, clenching the dead-man switch, flailing with her other hand. "I would never, never, *never* have left if I'd known. Never. You're my daughter. My beautiful baby girl. You should have been with *me.*"

Before Jessie could respond, Althea turned, fixing her with a desperate and trembling smile.

"But it's all right now. You're coming home." She flung out her outstretched hand. "Come with me."

Jessie didn't lower her gun.

"I don't think you understand the situation," she said. "Harmony? Do the honors."

"Althea Temple-Sinclair," I said, holding her in my sights, "you are responsible for the deaths of two bank employees and two police officers at the National Equity Bank in Manhattan, the attempted murder of Tucker Pearlman, and the murder of Gerard Nowak. You were a known accomplice of Russell Lee Sinclair, aka the Dixie Butcher, and you were a key figure in an illegal program that carried out the assassinations of multiple United States citizens. This is your one, only, and final chance to surrender. We *will* use lethal force."

Althea's smile faded as she looked my way. Her eyes narrowing, reptilian, as she slowly licked her lips.

"Well, just look at you, sitting up there on your fancy high horse. Does it feel good, looking down on me? Know what you look like to me, little girl? Dinner. Bet you've got some tasty meat on those bones. Maybe I'll find out."

"How can you do this?" Jessie demanded. "How can you just go through life . . . *hurting* people like this?"

Althea looked confused by the question. "Because of what we are, because of what your father made us. Jessie, you're the same as me."

"I am nothing like you," she snapped.

Althea gave her a gentle smile.

"Oh, bless your heart. You've got the beast all bottled up inside you, trapped. Know what a trapped wolf does, baby girl? Chews its own leg off if it has to. That's what you're doing. Probably what you've been doing your whole life. The power of the King of Wolves is in our *souls*, Jessie. If you don't let that power run free, if you don't embrace it with all that you are, it's gonna eat you alive from the inside out."

"I'd rather be dead than turn into a monster."

Althea rolled her eyes. "Monster? Really? Your father was a very dim man, Jessie. He never taught you right. We aren't monsters."

"You hurt people. Murder people. You just put a bomb on a playground. So tell me, *Mom*, what the fuck would you call that?"

"Survival of the fittest. We are the children of the King. Our role, our purpose in this world, is to spread his truths. We are apex predators. Hunters and killers. The next stage of human evolution. We are the preparers of the way, here to teach humanity that there are only two roles in all of nature: predator and prey. You're a predator." She gestured at me. "Your little friend here? She's prey."

"Bullshit," Jessie said. "Who you are is defined by the choices you make. You chose to spend your life hurting people. I chose to spend mine saving them."

Althea cupped one hand to her ear, leaning in a little, pretending to listen.

"Mmm, hear that? That is the sound of a lifetime of denial. I was like you once. Do you think I was born this way, Jessie? No. Before your father took me into the woods, before the rite, I had never harmed a hair on any man's head no matter what he did to deserve it. I would chase flies out of the house because I was too timid to swat one. Then the King of Wolves entered my heart, and everything changed. Violence is easy for you, isn't it? I bet it's hard to hold back. You hit somebody and you just want to keep hitting. Tearing. Ripping. Biting. There's nothing in the world like the taste of hot blood, and you know it."

"Yeah," Jessie said, "you know what? You're right. But unlike you, I've got my shit under control. I'm the one running the show, not the monster inside me. You took the easy way out."

"Is that true? Is that really true? You don't have blackouts? Uncontrollable rages? Moments where the beast takes control no matter how hard you fight?"

Althea read the look on Jessie's face, her momentary uncertainty, and smiled.

"You do," Althea said. "And it's only going to get worse. If you don't embrace the beast, it's eventually going to kill you. Jessie, you are my daughter, and I love you. You have to come with me. I can teach you. Help you."

I thought it was the shadows, the shift of the dying light, but Jessie's face wasn't the same. Her cheeks seemed to lengthen, deepen, her jaw just a fraction longer than it was a moment ago. As if her features were shifting under the weight of Althea's musk, trying to reshape themselves into something more bestial. Something more like a wolf than a woman.

"Make me just like you, you mean?" Jessie's eyes narrowed, her resolve flooding back. "No, thanks. Hard pass."

"You'll change your mind. And now that I know you're alive, baby girl? I'm not letting you go. We *will* be a family again."

Jessie gave me a sidelong glance. "I already have a family."

"Not the one you belong in." Althea brandished the dead-man switch in front of her, sidestepping across the room. "Now let me tell you how this is going to go down. I'm leaving. You're gonna stay right here, sitting pretty, and give me a twenty-minute head start. If my man sees you leave this room before the twenty are up, I drop the switch and you just created a whole mess of dead kids."

"This isn't over," Jessie said. "You *will* see us again."

Althea paused on the threshold. She looked back at Jessie with a soft, sad smile, but her eyes blazed like radioactive sapphires.

"Oh, baby girl," she replied, "you're goddamn right I will. Real soon now."

THIRTY-TWO

The bomb squad combed Turtle Park, all the civilians evacuated—April gave us a play-by-play over our earpieces—but we couldn't risk the chance that Althea had lied about where the bomb had been stashed. Our only choice was to stay put and wait the twenty minutes, just like she'd told us to.

Jessie sat on the dusty hardwood floor with her chin in her hand, staring at the shadows where her mother had been standing.

"I feel like 'Are you okay' is the worst, stupidest thing I could say right now," I told her. "But I'm saying it, anyway."

She didn't turn her head.

"Say she was wrong."

"She was." I moved to stand behind her. "Jessie, you were right. She took the easy way out, giving in, while you fight every single day to keep this thing inside you under control. Your way is better."

She let out a small, bitter laugh.

"Yeah, I fight. Been fighting a war with myself for years." She fell silent for a moment. "And I'm losing."

"No, you aren't—"

Jessie turned my way, frowning. "Yes, I *am*. Come on, Harmony. When we went up against Dr. Carnes and I went feral when she started throwing fire around, I nearly got both of us killed. At Tucker's house, I nearly killed *you*. I'm getting worse. It's only a matter of time now before we go out on a mission and only one of us makes it back alive—or neither of us. Because of me."

She pinched the bridge of her nose, squeezing her eyes shut.

"And my mother and her pals don't have that problem. Because they embraced the beast. It's the only difference between us, so that has to be the reason why. So that's my choice. I can be like them, or I can get us killed fighting a war I can't win."

"You're not fighting on your own," I told her. "And you're not giving up. Because I'm not letting you."

Jessie sighed. She gave me a tired smile and held out her hand. I helped her to her feet.

"God, look at us, huh?"

I shrugged. "We get the job done."

"Think we'd better prove it." She checked her phone. "It's been twenty minutes. C'mon, let's get back to the brain trust and figure out our next move."

# # #

On our way out, we kept our heads on a swivel. We switched cabs twice, doubling back, taking every precaution in case Althea had someone tailing us. Back at the hotel, Kevin's laptop shared table space with two steaming cardboard boxes, and the aroma of fresh-baked dough and pepperoni filled the room. Kevin gave us an awkward shrug as he opened the door.

"I, uh, figured you guys would be hungry, and maybe you wouldn't feel like going out," he said.

Jessie gravitated toward the pizza boxes like her nose was on a tether. "You are now my favorite nerd. Meat lover's?"

"Well, yeah. Of course. The other one's a veggie combo."

I loosened my tie and sat down on the edge of the bed. Now that I was out of the action, back in safety, all the stress of the day hit me at once. Pouring on, weighing me down.

"The bomb squad came up empty," April said. "No explosives at Turtle Park."

"So she was bluffing," I said.

She shook her head, cradling a slice of pepperoni-laden pizza on a folded paper napkin. "I doubt it. The Wolves have no compunction about murdering innocents. I suspect the bomb was in another park entirely. She simply kept her word and didn't set it off."

"I'm keeping my word, too," Jessie said. "I don't care if my father tricked her. I wouldn't have been any better off growing up with Althea. She's just as bad as he was, and she's going down the same way."

"Before we get to that," April replied, "Kevin?"

Kevin walked over to his laptop, looking anxious. "Yeah, about that. We ran a full search on Harmony's pictures, trying to figure out who this Calypso guy is. Nothing on the Interstate Photo Service, nothing in immigration or the passport registry, pretty much a ghost. Then we got a hit someplace I didn't expect: a Google image search."

He turned the screen to show us a grainy, faded photograph from a website archiving back issues of the *Reno Evening Gazette*. Roth's man stood on a stage backed by scarlet curtains, his eyes shut as he leaned back and played an ice-white Fender Telecaster. He cradled the guitar in his hands like it was made of solid gold. Beneath, a caption read: "Webster 'Calypso' Scratch tears it up at the Sequin Room."

"Roth's guardian angel is a musician?" I asked.

"Well, there's the problem," Kevin told me. "This photograph was taken in 1978."

Jessie paused in midbite, a doubled-up slice of pizza poking between her teeth. "So either this guy's got *amazing* genes . . ."

"Or he hasn't aged a day in almost forty years," I said.

"Since we can assume the latter," April said, "Harmony? Your occult assessment?"

"Too little information. Could be a demon, could be some kind of monster we haven't run into yet, could be a human sorcerer—Edwin Kite was, what, two hundred years old when we dragged him out of the House of Closets?" I paused, staring at the caption. "No. He's a demon."

Jessie tilted her head at me. "You can tell from his photograph?"

"Nope, because he's too cute for his own good. Webster Scratch— Old Scratch is a nickname for the devil in old Southern folktales. Also used in a classic short story by Stephen Vincent Benét called—wait for it—'The Devil and Daniel Webster.' Folks, we have a problem here. Possession victims age naturally, so Calypso has to be an incarnate, like Nadine."

"We're getting pretty good at beating up incarnates," Jessie said through a mouthful of pizza. "I wouldn't mind going again."

"No. Think about it. Before he died, Nowak told us that Senator Roth is under Calypso's personal protection. And it looks like Nadine's funneling money into Roth's campaign coffers through this 'charity' of hers." I looked across the room, meeting my teammates' eyes. "We also know that Roth is gearing up for a run at the White House. And the powers of hell want him to win."

Jessie finished shoveling down her first slice and reached for a second one. "I'm starting to think our best course of action is to stand back, *let* Althea murder Roth and Bobby Diehl, then mop up after. I mean, we want Bobby dead, but we're not allowed to touch him. And we all know Roth's gotta go. We could just . . . let the chips fall how they're gonna fall."

"Too risky," I said. "If they go underground the second their hit list is complete, we'll never find them again. Roth and Diehl will get theirs when the time's right, and soon, but the Wolves are an active threat here and now. And . . . I keep thinking we're missing something. One element stands out: this Hamas guy, Yousef Masalha. The Wolves hacked into Nowak's account so they could access the RedEye system and get Masalha's location. Why? He's not involved with Glass Predator, he shouldn't be on their target list . . . so who is he, and why is Althea after him?"

April raised a finger. "There's another question we should consider: Why is Senator Roth still alive?"

"He's the last name on the list," Kevin said with a shrug.

"Indeed. He provided the Wolves with the names of everyone involved in Glass Predator—everyone who attempted to have them murdered ten years ago when the program shut down. Which would be the exact moment at which Roth was no longer useful to them. Yet they've stayed in contact with him, and continued this charade of pretending to be the Xerxes mercenaries he hired. Wouldn't it have been infinitely simpler to meet him, get the list, then terminate him on the spot?"

"They need him for something," Jessie said. "Roth is still part of the master plan."

I rose from the bed, pacing.

"Meaning the master plan *isn't* just simple revenge. They've got something bigger in mind. And the loose end is Yousef Masalha. What do we know about him?"

Kevin swung his laptop around, rattling off a few quick keystrokes. "Well, he's in the country on an expired work visa. He's an H-1B, person in a specialty occupation. A mechanical engineer, to be specific."

"How did he qualify for a visa if he's a member of Hamas?" Jessie asked.

"Alleged," Kevin replied. "I guess there's a bomb maker with the exact same name, but Yousef convinced Homeland that he's not the guy. Helped that his brother, Walid, is a solid citizen. American born, and a judge on Boston's court of appeals. Yousef was living with Walid and his wife. A few months ago he didn't show up to renew his visa, then he just went dark. Walid says he has no idea where the guy went."

"The RedEye system found him fast enough," Jessie said, "but with Burton Webb in hiding, we can't get that intel."

"We might not have to," I told her. "The NSA isn't the only agency who'd be interested in a guest worker going missing, and you know what the federal government's like, especially when it comes to the intelligence agencies: the right hand never knows what the left hand's doing. Except we've got eight hundred hands."

"You think somebody else might have a line on him?"

"For all we know, he might already be in custody." I took out my phone and hunted down a number. "Hello? Yes, this is Special Agent Harmony Black with the Critical Incident Response Group. Could you put me through to SAC Mueller, please?"

Twenty minutes later we were headed out the door, bound for a red-eye flight and an appointment at the FBI's Boston field office.

THIRTY-THREE

Special Agent in Charge Mueller didn't like us very much.

I couldn't blame him, considering the last time we were in town, Kevin ran over a fleeing suspect with a Bureau-issue surveillance van, leading to a very unhappy fifteen minutes of YouTube fame. I hoped Mueller wasn't the kind of man who held grudges.

He wasted very little time crushing my hopes.

"What I want to know is," he demanded, leaning toward us with both palms flat on his desk, "how the hell did you two keep your badges?"

The monochrome clock on the wall read 8:04, and fluorescent light from the office filtered through the slats of Mueller's half-closed window blinds. We'd slept on the plane, and our rumpled clothes showed it. We'd landed at Logan, dropped Kevin and April at a hotel, and gotten to the field office at 1 Center Plaza—a tall beige rectangle studded with hundreds of windows, parked on a bustling intersection—just in time for our morning meeting.

"We're part of a secret program that hunts demons and other occult threats to national security," Jessie told him. "We're hard to fire."

Mueller stared at her. The lights glistened off his bald scalp.

"Is that a joke? Are you trying to be *funny*, Agent?"

I jumped in, fast. "What my partner is trying to say, sir, is that we did make a formal apology, in writing, after the incident. You should have been forwarded a copy."

"Oh, I got your apology. Want to see where I filed it?"

He reached down, yanked a black plastic waste bin from under his desk, and held it up for my inspection.

"See? I can make jokes, too. Now what's this about Yousef Masalha? You are *not* commandeering my investigation, I'll tell you that right now."

"So he's a person of interest. Do you have eyes on him?"

"Your intel first," Mueller told me, setting his waste bin down with a thump. "Why do you want him?"

Jessie and I had worked on our story on the ride over, deciding just how much to share and which details to spin. Technically, with the aid of SAC Walburgh—our fictitious supervisor—I could push the issue and twist Mueller's arm into cooperating, but that would take time we didn't have, and I didn't need any more enemies in the Bureau. Better to get him on our side, if I could manage it.

"We're following up on a terror tip," I told him. "A cell of radicalized former American military members. We know they're planning an attack, but details are thin. Our only lead is that we know they're trying to make contact with Masalha. Or, possibly, already have."

"An attack in Boston? Why wasn't I notified about this?"

I shook my head. "They've got nationwide reach, so we don't know the target site—that's why CIRG is taking the lead on the investigation. We're hoping Masalha can tell us more."

He rubbed his cheek slowly, squinting as he stared me down.

"Sir, whatever you're working on here, we don't want to steal it out from under you, and we don't want to trample on an active investigation. That's why we came directly to you, in the hopes that we can coordinate our efforts. We have absolute respect for the Boston office and your work here. We just want to help," I told him.

"All right," Mueller sighed. "Fine. I've got something tangential going, and if we pool info, maybe you won't blunder in and wreck it."

He walked over to his office door and poked his head out.

"Acker? Anyone, is Acker here yet? Yeah, *you*, Acker, not your imaginary twin brother. Come in here and bring the Vukovic case file."

Acker was a pink-eared kid fresh out of Quantico, with a black jacket too big for his shoulders and a fat manila folder tucked under his arm. He pumped our hands with the enthusiasm of a cocker-spaniel puppy, and we all gathered around Mueller's desk as he laid out his files.

"Oh, yeah," Mueller said, "our perp is an old buddy of yours. Maybe you can hit him with another van and finish him off this time."

The stack began with a familiar mug shot: Ranko Vukovic, Serbian gunrunner and explosives connoisseur. He wore the scars of his trade—two fingers missing and a lobster-red, puddle-shaped burn scar along his jaw. Last time we'd crossed paths—and Kevin hit him with the surveillance van—Vukovic was working for a mercenary hacker named Roman Steranko; apparently his subsequent arrest hadn't steered him to the path of the righteous.

"Ranko walked on his last set of weapons charges," Acker told us. "Went right back to his usual line of business, supplying weapons to Boston's finest gangbangers and creeps. I'm heading up a small surveillance op, trying to build an ironclad case against him. We've already got enough to put him and his whole crew behind bars, but we're holding out for a *big* deal, something that'll lock him away until he's ready to collect Social Security."

"What's the connection to Masalha?" Jessie asked.

Acker riffled through surveillance photos, most of them fixed on the facade of a run-down auto-body shop. He stopped on a picture showing two men, one of them Vukovic, shaking hands in the shade of an open bay door.

"That's Yousef Masalha," he said. "Taken two weeks ago. We didn't know who he was at the time, and the team let him go. You can see, he's leaving empty-handed. Still, once we found out the guy's in the country on an expired visa and a terror suspect, well . . . he's a priority now."

"I thought he was cleared?" I asked. "I mean, he got the visa legally."

Acker shook his head, flipping through the pictures. "Because he's not the Hamas guy with the same name, right? You ask me, I think Homeland Security screwed the pooch. Check this out: here's a file photo taken in Ramallah, three years ago. CIA confirmed that this guy here *is* the Yousef Masalha with a penchant for blowing things up. Mostly civilians."

He held it next to the auto-body picture, and I leaned in, squinting hard. The man in the second photo—shot at a distance, in a crowded marketplace—wore a bushy black beard and a checkered kaffiyeh head scarf, while the Yousef meeting Vukovic was clean shaven.

"Hard to tell," I said. "I mean, it *could* be the same man."

The more I studied the picture from the auto-body shop, the more I focused on Yousef's face.

"He looks . . . terrified," I said.

"Wouldn't you be?" Acker said. "You don't mess with these Serbian crews—they're crazy. They'll cut your hands off over a two-dollar debt. You know where Vukovic got that beauty mark on his jaw? He was wiring a bomb to a car to kill a guy who cut him off in traffic."

"An ordinary person would be scared, sure. A terrorist, though?"

Acker spread his hands. "Why would he be visiting an arms dealer—an arms dealer who specializes in explosives, no less—if he wasn't one?"

"But he didn't buy anything," Jessie pointed out.

"What's he doing, then? Playing chess with the guy? Yousef hasn't shown his face since, but the second he does, I've got people in place ready to grab him."

"What about family?" I asked. "Wasn't he living with his brother?"

"Yeah," Acker said, checking his notes. "Judge Walid Masalha and his wife, Bella. They're clean. Trust me, we checked them out from end to end."

"Would you mind if we took a run at them?" Jessie asked.

Acker gave Mueller a look, asking a silent question. Mueller answered with an irritated shrug.

"I think you're wasting your time," Acker said, "but sure, suit yourself. All I ask is that you keep me in the loop, and don't go anywhere near Ranko Vukovic without talking to me first. Deal?"

"Deal," Jessie said, shaking his hand.

# # #

"Now, I'm not saying we *should* go run Vukovic over—" Jessie said as we stepped out of Mueller's office.

"Jessie."

"I'm just saying, hey, wouldn't it be *funny* if we just happened to run him over? By accident, on purpose?"

"Let's go have a chat with the Masalha family. Acker's a little too quick to close the book on Yousef, and I'm wondering how thorough he was."

"You think he's innocent?"

I pushed open the door to the motor pool and held it open for her.

"Don't know," I said. "But a hard-core Hamas bomb builder isn't going to look like a scared, whipped dog coming out of a meeting with a bottom-feeder like Ranko Vukovic. When we busted Vukovic, did he seem intimidating to you?"

"Spent most of it whining about how he was going to sue us."

"A real terrorist would eat Ranko for lunch. Something else is going on here, something deeper than the surface details. And I still don't know why the Wolves are looking for a guy who makes bombs when they already *have* one on their own team."

Mueller had reluctantly granted us a service vehicle, something to get around in during our (brief, he vocally hoped) stay in Boston. Second time we'd drawn on Bureau resources since Chicago, and April could only run interference for so long. Sooner or later, Linder was going to start asking hard questions. We needed this case wrapped up, and fast, so we could invent a few good answers.

Jessie stopped dead at the designated parking spot, marked in yellow paint. She stared at the keys in her hand, then at the car, with tired resignation.

It might have been a station wagon, once. Before the back bumper had fallen off and been reattached with twine, before two doors were spray-painted matte-black, and a hairline crack had drawn its way from one end of the windshield to the other.

"Every time," Jessie said. "They do this to us every damn time."

I took the keys. I didn't even have to ask.

The Masalhas lived out in the suburbs, in Lexington, where garrison colonial–style homes lined quiet, shady streets. I didn't know what Walid's wife did for a living, but apparently his seat on the court paid off: they lived in a center-entrance colonial with black eaves and powder-blue siding, sparkling-clean bay windows looking out over the doors of a four-car garage.

"What do you think?" Jessie asked as our car sputtered up the driveway. "One million? A million five?"

"More than we make. How do you want to play this?"

"Keep it friendly," she said. "Odds are they've got no idea where Yousef is, but we'll see if any stray details shake loose. Hopefully they know more than they think."

We rang the bell, a pleasant chime ringing out from behind the front door. Then we waited. Up in the corner eave, a tiny security camera watched us with a black glass lens. I took out my FBI credentials and held them up for the camera.

We waited some more. Jessie gave me the side eye as she rang the bell a second time.

"I hear people moving around in there," she murmured. "Stay sharp. Something smells fishy about this."

THIRTY-FOUR

When the door finally opened, the smell that wafted out definitely wasn't fish. More like rich, spiced chicken, steaming hot. The woman behind the door was petite, small voiced, with her delicate features wrapped in a lavender head scarf. We showed her our shields.

"Good afternoon, ma'am," I said. "We're with the FBI. May we have a few minutes of your time?"

She frowned. "But . . . we already talked to the FBI two weeks ago."

"I know. We just have a few follow-up questions. It won't take long at all, I promise."

Reluctantly, she ushered us in. Baby-blue wall panels offset with ivory crown molding lined a long foyer, the hardwood draped in a lush storm-gray carpet. A bearded man in a three-piece suit poked his head from an open archway up ahead.

"Bella?"

"More people from the FBI," she said with a helpless shrug. "This is my husband, Walid."

I inclined my head. "Your Honor. Thank you for your time."

"We already talked to the FBI," he said as we followed Bella into the dining room. "Two weeks ago."

Jessie and I shared a glance. Their reactions were all wrong. If I had a brother who'd gone missing—a suspected terrorist, no less—my first reaction to finding the FBI on my doorstep would be to ask if we had news on the case. Not only did neither of the Masalhas ask, their body language was tight. Flustered. Like they couldn't get us out of there fast enough.

"We were just sitting down to lunch," Walid said, gesturing to the long oak table. Two plates were set out, a meal of roasted chicken and onion with sides of creamy wild rice. Jessie took out her phone and pulled up the photos from the Wolves's service records.

"I do apologize for that. Could you just look at these pictures and let me know if you ever saw your brother associating with any of these people?"

My gaze wandered across the table. My instincts were shouting in my ear, telling me a puzzle piece was out of place, that I had to find it.

Two grains of rice.

Two grains of rice spilled on the smooth, clean wood, nowhere near the serving dish or the two place settings.

"Mrs. Masalha, may I speak to you for a moment? Let's step into the kitchen."

Legally, we had no right to be in their house without permission. Searching the place was out of the question. That meant it was time to break out an old law-enforcement trick, projecting my authority and politely, firmly, herding the flustered Bella into the room I wanted a peek at. I didn't have any real reason to talk to her alone, and she could have stopped me at any moment: I just didn't give her time to think about it.

I showed her my own copy of the pictures, and while her head was bent toward my phone, I scanned the room. Marble counters, white-washed fixtures, a big tub-size stainless-steel sink . . . and in the sink, an extra glass and an extra plate, residue of a hastily scraped-off meal still clinging to the ceramic.

"No, I'm sorry," she said, handing me the phone. "I've never seen any of those people in my life. We really should get back to my husband—"

"Sure, of course." I stepped around her, toward a stainless-steel trash can. "We should get going so you can enjoy your lunch before it gets cold. You know, it really does smell amazing. Are you the chef?"

She smiled. "I am. I love to cook."

"Well, if it tastes half as good as it smells, I imagine you're great at it."

I stepped down on the can's black-rubber foot, the lever popping the lid up. And looked in at the remains of a third meal, still piping hot.

"So why, Mrs. Masalha, would you throw an entire plate's worth in the garbage?"

The blood drained from her face.

"That . . . that portion was bad. It wasn't good."

"Looks fine to me. You know, it took you a while to come to the door when we rang the bell."

She wrung her hands, clutching them close to her chest. "We were . . . we were busy. Cooking."

I lifted my foot. The lid fell shut with a metallic clang.

"Mrs. Masalha, beyond the expired visa, which might be something we can fix, your brother-in-law hasn't done anything illegal that we know of. Yet. Personally, I think he's mixed up in something, he's in over his head, and he needs help. Help that you and your husband can't give him. We can."

"But—but we haven't seen him—"

"You and your husband, on the other hand, *are* doing something illegal by harboring him. Again, maybe a charge that can quietly go away. But if you push this, and we have to escalate to an arrest, your husband's career as a judge is over. Oh, and considering you two are hiding Yousef in your house, you might want to look up the federal laws on asset forfeiture."

"Asset . . ." She put her hand over her mouth. "We could lose the house?"

"You could lose a lot more than that. We don't want to hurt Yousef, and if he hasn't done anything wrong, we don't want to arrest him. We just need to talk."

Jessie was stalling for time when we returned to the dining room, showing Walid mug shots from a totally unrelated case. I gave her a quiet thumbs-up from across the room.

"Walid," Bella said, "they know."

He looked up at her, his eyes going wide. "You *told* them?"

"They know. They already know. We have to give them your brother."

"We just want to talk to him," I said.

"No." Walid chopped the air with the flat of his hand. "You won't believe him. You just want to lock him away because he's an Arab—"

"We want the truth," Jessie told him.

"You won't *believe* the truth."

"Try us," she said. "You'd be amazed, the things we might believe."

# # #

They fetched Yousef from the guest bedroom, where he'd been hiding in the closet since the moment we rang the doorbell. The small man made me think of a rabbit: twitchy, jumping at every outside noise, sitting at the oak table with his shoulders hunched and his head ducked low. While his brother paced the room, muttering under his breath, Bella sat beside Yousef and rested a comforting hand on his shoulder. We pulled back chairs on the opposite side of the table.

"I am not that man" was the first thing he told us.

"The other Yousef Masalha," Jessie said.

"When I applied for my work visa, your Department of Homeland Security turned my life inside out. They *knew* I wasn't that man.

I'm an engineer, I have a degree from the University College of Applied Sciences—"

"Why did you let your work visa expire?"

He sighed. "Someone found a photograph of the other Yousef and decided it looked like me. I got word from a friend of mine who works in the Bureau of Consular Affairs that they might reopen the investigation. Have to verify me, dig into my life all over again. You have to understand: If I'm banished from the United States on suspicion of being a terrorist? For *Hamas*? What do you think will happen to me when I get off the airplane in Jerusalem? Or maybe your CIA will put a bag over my head and take me to Guantanamo Bay. Maybe they'll torture me, I don't know. I *don't know*."

"He was frightened," Bella said. "We all were. We knew it was wrong, but we had to hide him while Walid looked for a way to guarantee his safety."

"I've never hurt anyone in my life," Yousef said, miserable, slumping lower in his chair. "I'm an engineer. I make parts for airplanes. That's all."

"If that's true, why were you seen with Ranko Vukovic?" Jessie asked.

Still pacing, Walid pointed at his wife. "You see? You see? They're going to take him away, Bella. Your fault!"

"Just tell us the truth," I told Yousef. "Even if you don't think we'll believe you. Trust us, okay?"

He clasped his hands on the table, took a deep breath, and nodded. "A little over two weeks ago, I got a phone call from a blocked number. It was a woman. She knew I was here, and she said that if I didn't do exactly what she told me to . . . she'd come here and kill me. And kill Walid and Bella."

Jessie looked my way, thinking the same thing I was. *Althea.*

"What did she tell you to do?" I asked.

"She told me to drive into the city and look for a trash can in one specific alley, under a patch of graffiti with a white arrow pointing at the lid. Like something from a spy movie. An envelope was taped under the lid. It was stuffed full of money."

"How much?" Jessie asked.

"Thousands. Tens of thousands. Not from a bank, either. The money was old, rumpled."

"Used bills," Jessie said, glancing at me. "Nonconsecutive serials, probably laundered."

"She told me to take it to an auto shop and talk to the owner, Vukovic. I had to . . ."

His voice trailed off, and his gaze dropped to the table. Bella held him closer.

"It's all right," she said. "Tell them."

"I had to pretend to be that man, from Hamas. And use the money to buy explosives."

I leaned in. "How many explosives? What kind?"

"Semtex," he said.

He shook his head, staring at the table.

"How much, Yousef?"

Yousef slowly looked up, meeting my gaze.

"One hundred pounds."

The room fell silent.

"He locked me in a room with one of his men for three hours," Yousef said, "while he 'made sure I was who I said I was.' He said if I didn't check out, they'd . . . cut me up and feed me to his dogs. Whoever he asked, they must have vouched for me. But he said he didn't have that kind of firepower just sitting around. He'd have to call in favors. So I paid him the money and left. He called me a few days ago and said he'd have it ready by tomorrow at the latest."

"So you're supposed to go back and pick it up?" Jessie asked.

Yousef shook his head. "No. I mean, originally, yes. I was supposed to pick it up and bring it back here, where the woman would come and get it from me. Then she called and told me to stay here, stay hidden, and not leave for any reason. She said she'd take care of the pickup, and my job was done. As long as I didn't go to the police, she wouldn't hurt my family."

Jessie and I eased back from the table. We stepped out in the hall, keeping our voices low.

"This guy's a patsy," Jessie said.

"Agreed. I'm more worried about what your mother wants to do with a hundred pounds of plastic explosive. This is too elaborate, though: Why force this poor guy to go through with a charade when she could just do business with Vukovic personally? Surviving this long in the shadows, she's *gotta* have the underworld contacts to merit an introduction."

"And why set up the buy, arrange for Yousef to pick up the goods, then call it off?"

"Acker," I said. "This guy running the surveillance op. Do you think he's good?"

"I think I've got milk in my refrigerator older than that kid."

"The Wolves are trained in countersurveillance. If they spotted Acker's team, they'd know that Yousef's gonna get arrested if he shows his face again."

"So, last-minute change of plans. Althea's going to pick up the Semtex." Jessie's eyes hardened. "And if Acker's team tries to move in and make a bust, she and her men are gonna carve those poor bastards to ribbons. Harmony, we gotta *go*."

THIRTY-FIVE

We strode into the dining room. Yousef looked up at us like we were his executioners and he was just waiting for the ax to fall.

"We know the woman who called you," I told him. "We know you're telling the truth."

Relief washed over his face, and Bella hugged him tight.

"Bad news is, she's not the kind of person who leaves loose ends dangling around," Jessie said, "and she knows where you live. All three of you are in serious danger. You've got to get out of here right now . . . and stay gone for a while."

"What?" Walid said. "But my job—I can't just pack up and leave. Gone for how long?"

"This should all be over in a few days," Jessie said.

I gave Yousef my business card. The unofficial version, with nothing but my number on it. "If you think you see anyone following you, or anything suspicious at all, call me."

"And . . . my legal status?" he asked.

"I'm sorry, we can't help you with immigration. You're going to have to sort the visa problem out on your own. On the plus side, as soon as we deal with this woman and the Semtex, everyone's going to know you're innocent. I'll make sure of that."

Jessie held out her hands as we jogged to the car. I tossed her the keys. Bella watched us from the open front door, hand raised in a curious, frozen wave, as we peeled out of the driveway.

As we lurched onto Concord Avenue, tires squealing, I called the Boston field office and had them patch me through to Acker. When he finally picked up, he sounded pleased with himself.

"Agent! Good timing, we're about to saddle up here. Vukovic's crew has been sitting on a big shipment from one of the New York *Bratva* families for a couple of days now; no sign of Masalha, but some new faces just showed, and it looks like the buy is about to go down."

"Stand down," I said. "Those may be our suspects. Hold off until we get there."

"'Your' suspects are about to walk off with about six crates of God knows what," Acker said. "No can do. I'm not letting those weapons get out into the wild."

"Listen to me: these people are *extremely* dangerous, they have special-forces training and—"

"It's two guys, and half of Vukovic's crew is sloppy drunk. I've got a SWAT team on standby. I think we can handle ourselves, Agent."

Jessie cursed under her breath and pumped on the brakes as we screeched nose first into a wall of traffic. She glanced over her shoulder, flicking the turn signal, and veered one lane over. Then she hit a button on the dash, triggering the car's police package: red-and-blue lights strobed behind the front grille, the whine of a siren splitting the air, and the bumper-to-bumper traffic grudgingly, sluggishly, parted for us.

"Acker," I said, "those suspects are key to an ongoing investigation. Our interests here supersede yours. I'm sorry, but I am *ordering* you to stand down. If you have a problem with that, we can argue it out in front of SAC Mueller, but for now—"

He talked over me, cutting me off. "Sorry! Didn't catch that. Lots of static on my end. Bad reception, the line's breaking up. Can't hear you. I'll call you back in a little bit."

I stared at my phone.

"What?" Jessie said.

"Idiot hung up on me."

Even with the lights and sirens, fighting through traffic was like swimming in syrup. By the time we broke free, turning off onto a jumble of side streets and run-down tenement rows, I'd tried to call Acker back seven times. Straight to voice mail.

The car swerved, taking a hard right, and I jolted against the seat belt as we slammed to a dead stop.

The street outside Roxbury Auto Body was a war zone.

Bodies of fallen SWAT officers littered the blood-streaked pavement, not far from the smoking ruin of an armored personnel carrier, its tires perforated and black smoke gusting from its ruptured hood. Another corpse, tattooed and dressed in a gore-soaked tank top, lay prone in front of the bullet-riddled loading bay doors.

"Requesting immediate backup," I shouted into my phone as we threw open the car doors. "We have multiple officers down, repeat, multiple officers down."

We jogged across the open street, serpentine, guns drawn as we closed in on the front door of the garage. Jessie stepped carefully through the shattered frame, her shoes crunching on broken glass. I followed her in. Another one of Vukovic's men slumped over the cashier's counter, the back of his head blown open. Chips of bone and matted hair decorated the cash register.

Through an open door, in the garage bay, we found the heart of the massacre. My stomach lurched at the stench of dead meat, so strong it stole my breath. More of Vukovic's thugs lay scattered around a flipped-over card table, some shot, some bludgeoned, one beaten against the dirty brick wall until his head had turned to bloody paste.

Vukovic—what was left of him—had been tossed to the oil-stained concrete next to the open door of an old junker. From the looks of him, they'd shoved his head inside and then slammed the car door on his neck a few dozen times until his spine had crumbled to powder.

Jessie's ears twitched. She scanned the room, following a sound too faint for me to hear.

"Live one," she said, racing toward the far end of the garage. A lone figure slumped near the open bay door, propped up against the brick wall. Acker. I didn't know how he was still alive, not with his legs and arms and wrists all bent the wrong way, more blood outside his body than in it. He stared at nothing with his one good eye and let out a rasping hiss of breath. I crouched down beside him.

"Acker. Hey, Acker, it's okay. We're here. Backup is inbound."

He lolled his head, trying to see me. His jaw worked as he struggled to talk, but no words came out.

"Shh," I said. "Just sit still. We've got a bus coming, okay? You're going to be all right."

He wheezed, forcing the words out. "They weren't . . . human."

His eye closed. Jessie took his wrist, feeling for a pulse, her fingers peeling away scarlet and sticky as she let his hand fall. She shook her head at me.

We stood silently in the chaos. Looking out the bay door at the bullet-riddled APC, the fallen officers who'd died at the hands of a force they couldn't understand. All for nothing. My heart screamed out for order, for reason, but there wasn't any to be found here. Althea and her men sowed pain and discord everywhere they went, as easily as breathing, leaving corpses in their wake.

The nozzle of a security camera poked down from the rafters of the garage. I pointed it out to Jessie. We went back to the hunt.

A security console stood in a small back room, a cheap setup with a tiny, flickery monitor and a shelf of backups on bulky cassette tapes. I slowly spun a black plastic dial, rewinding the day's events.

"There," Jessie said. "Stop there."

The tape showed two things we didn't see out in the garage: a pair of wooden pallets laden with bulky wooden crates, and the tail end of a pickup truck, pulled back and ready to be loaded.

". . . don't like changes to the plan," Vukovic was saying as Ferrara and Baker surveyed the merchandise. Baker used a crowbar to pry back a crate lid. His beetle brows furrowed as he reached inside, fiddling with something just out of the camera's eye, and gave Ferrara an approving nod. Behind them, Vukovic's thugs played poker at the table, slapping down cards and passing around a half-empty bottle of cheap vodka.

"Where's Althea?" Jessie murmured.

I squinted at the screen. Acker hadn't mentioned seeing a woman, either. He'd said, "It's two guys."

Ferrara spread his hands and flashed a cocky grin. "Hey, you think we like playing errand boy? Believe me, no argument."

Baker hefted one of the crates all by himself and tossed it into the back of the pickup. It rumbled hard against the metal, the truck bouncing on its suspension.

"I make a deal with a man, I expect that same man to take delivery," Vukovic told him, agitated.

"I hear you, pal. Like I said, last-minute changes of plan are a real pain in the ass. Hell, originally, we were gonna let you live. Those asshole feds camped outside spoiled the whole plan, and now we've gotta kill *everybody*."

Vukovic squinted at him like a cow in a truck's headlights, not sure what part of that statement to question first. The best he could manage was, "Wait. What?"

Baker's hand sprouted a pistol as it came up from behind the crates. He opened fire on the table, sending a thug falling back in his folding chair with three slugs in his chest as Ferrara effortlessly grabbed Vukovic, spun him with his arm around the gunrunner's neck, and snatched the revolver from his belt.

The squawk of a bullhorn announced the impending raid, and from there—well, we'd already seen the aftermath. The Wolves slaughtered their way through the garage with brutal efficiency, more gunfire crackling out of frame as they turned the street outside into a shooting gallery. The lucky victims ate a bullet; for the rest, the Wolves used their hands and teeth. They hadn't run out of ammo, they just *wanted* to kill them that way. Vukovic was the last to go, and they took their time with him.

Standing in the carnage, Ferrara and Baker shared a feral smile and a fist bump. Then they loaded the rest of the crates and drove away.

"I'm calling in an APB," I told Jessie. "Can't see the plate on that pickup, but at least we've got a make and model."

"But where's Althea?" she asked again.

My phone chimed. I didn't recognize the number. Before I could get a word out, Bella's voice came over the line in a terrified, rambling gush. "Agent, please, you have to help, I think we're in trouble, and there's a woman outside—"

I headed for the car, long strides, waving for Jessie to follow.

"Bella? Slow down. What's going on?"

"We did what you said, we packed a bag and left. We went to a motel. There's a woman parked outside, just . . . staring at the window. Like she's waiting for something, or she's waiting for us to come out."

"Okay. Bella? Listen carefully. Do *not* leave that room. I want you to shut the curtains, bolt the door, and slide whatever you can in front of it. A chair, the bed if you can move it, anything. Then I want all three of you to lock yourselves in the bathroom, okay? Give me the address—we'll be right there. I'll call you when we arrive."

I hung up as we jumped into the car. Jessie looked my way.

"Althea found her patsy," I told her. "I think she's waiting for her buddies to show up before she goes after him."

Jessie hit the sirens and lights. "Then we'll just have to drive faster than they do. Let's roll."

If we beat the clock, if we got there ahead of the other Wolves and faced off against Althea alone, we might have a chance of taking her down. Then I looked at Jessie's face. She was changing again. Her features shifting subtly, just like they had when we faced her mother for the first time in DC. Her jaw, just a fraction of an inch longer. Her cheekbones a millimeter higher.

"Jessie," I said, "when we go up against Althea, are you—"

"I'll be fine," she said through gritted teeth.

"Are you positive? We're only going to get one—"

"*Harmony.* Trust me, okay? Just . . . trust me."

For the first time since we met, I wasn't sure if I could.

THIRTY-SIX

The Masalha family had made their escape to the outskirts of Boston, to a motel on a lonely strip of highway north of the city. As we swung into the parking lot, tires squealing, I looked across the black pavement. A few scattered cars, but no pickup.

We'd beaten Ferrara and Baker to the scene, but that didn't mean we weren't too late. The door to room three hung open, swaying in a cold breeze, a torn brass chain dangling from the splintered wood.

I jumped out of the car and took point, drawing my Glock as I ran for the door, sweeping inside. Details registered fast, like flickers imprinted on my mind: Walid lying dead on the bloodstained mattress, his throat torn out. Yousef and Bella sitting on the cheap, thin carpet, their wrists and ankles bound with zip ties, tears glistening on Bella's cheeks.

And the inhumanly fast blur coming at me from the left as Althea lunged, snatching the gun from my hand and throwing a punch that slammed into my stomach with the force of a sledgehammer. She got her hand on the back of my neck as I doubled over, hurling me to the floor and going for Jessie. I thumped to the carpet hard on my shoulder, rolling. Jessie was faster on the draw. She dodged, leaping to one side, getting Althea in her gun sights.

Althea had a weapon in each hand, hers and mine, and she aimed them both at the hostages.

"Uh-uh," she said as Jessie froze. "You shoot me, I shoot them. I'll probably live. I've been shot before. These two? Not gonna be so lucky. Now put it down, baby girl."

Propping myself up on my elbows and struggling to catch my breath, I reached to my magic. This was my one chance to disarm Althea and take her out before the others got here. I dug down, calling to the water and wind, reaching . . . and felt nothing but the howling gulf of hunger Nadine had hollowed out inside of me. I could hear her crystal laughter as my connection to the universe sputtered out and died.

Jessie raised her sights, just an inch.

"You haven't been shot by *me* yet," she told Althea.

"You think you can pull your trigger faster than I can pull mine? Think you can pull it at all? I don't think so."

Jessie bit her bottom lip, holding fast, her grip starting to waver. She was changing again. This was no illusion, no trick of the light. I watched as the bones of her face began to shift under the skin, crackling softly, her jaw trembling as the muscles of her gun hand knotted and pulled. Her body in open rebellion against her mind. Althea broke into a big, toothy grin.

"Mmm, you feel that? Sure, you do. See, you and me, we're having two conversations at once. There's the one where we're talking out loud, then there's the *other* conversation. The one where my beast is talking to yours. Telling it how *good* you'd feel if you'd just stop fighting. And your beast is listening. Give it up, baby girl. You can't fight me. Your heart might be willing, but your flesh belongs to the King of Wolves, just like I do. Soon enough, your heart's gonna see the light, too."

The barrel of the gun slowly drooped, shuddering in Jessie's rebellious hand. Althea's grin grew even broader.

"Make it easy on yourself," she said in a low, raspy voice. "Stop resisting me, Jessie. Don't *make* me hurt you. Our bodies can recover from a whole lot of damage, and I've spent a long, long time learning how to deal that damage. Put. The weapon. Down."

Jessie rested her gun on the dresser and bowed her head in silent defeat. Althea motioned for her to sit on the floor beside me, keeping the hostages covered until she obeyed.

The pickup rumbled to a stop outside. Ferrara and Baker poked their heads in, and Ferrara glanced from us to the broken body on the mattress.

"What, did we miss a party?"

"Party's just getting started," Althea said. "We've got a couple live ones to play with, if you feel inclined. Gotta get moving, though. And we're taking my daughter with us."

Baker sighed at her. "Seriously? Now we gotta babysit *two* hostages?"

A storm brewed behind Althea's eyes. While I feverishly struggled inside myself, feeling snap after snap of raw magic in my heart like I was cranking the key on a car that refused to start, she stepped up and stood nose to nose with him. Baker's eyes widened, like he'd just woken a sleeping rattlesnake.

"Who rules this pack, Baker?"

"Y-you do. We all know that."

"You stepping to me, boy? You feel like throwing down a challenge?"

He shook his head. "No! No, never. It's your pack."

"Good," Althea said.

Then she turned, raised her pistol—the long barrel of a sound suppressor screwed to the muzzle—and shot Yousef between the eyes. Bella shrieked as the bound man's head slumped forward, blood drooling down his leg.

"There," Althea said. "Now you don't have to worry about him running away. Aren't I nice? Dig the bullet out and carry him to the truck. And shut that cow up."

Baker grumbled, trudging across the room. He silenced Bella's screams with a backhanded slap, sending her crumpling to the carpet, then dug into his pocket for a folding tool as he grabbed a fistful of Yousef's hair and yanked his head back.

Althea stood over us. Her gaze fell upon me.

"You've been a bad influence on my kid," she said.

"I don't think you're in a position to judge."

Althea chuckled. "I'm in a position to do whatever I damn well please. That's the whole point of being me."

She crouched down, and her smile spread into a feral, toothy grin.

"And what I want to do, right now, is find out what your skin tastes like."

"Don't," Jessie said, her eyes wide as she pressed her back to the dresser. "Don't hurt her."

Althea reached out and trailed a fingernail along my cheek.

"Predators and prey, baby girl. That's all the world is."

"Let her go," Jessie stammered, "and I'll come with you."

Althea looked her way. "You're coming with me no matter what. You don't get a say in the matter."

"*Willingly,*" Jessie said.

Althea paused. She stood up, staring down at her, contemplating.

"Willingly," Jessie repeated. "Right now, yeah, I'm a hostage. I'll get away if I can, kill you if I can. Let Harmony go, unhurt, and I'll come of my own free will. You want us to be a family again? That's the only way you're ever gonna get it."

"Jessie, no—" I told her.

Althea glanced to Ferrara. "Get 'em on their feet."

Rough hands hauled me up as Jessie pleaded with her mother.

"Whatever you want to teach me, I'll learn. I'll surrender to the King of Wolves. I won't fight you. But you have to let her go."

"Jessie," I said, "don't do this."

Althea nodded to the dresser. "Leave your phone. And that fancy little earpiece, don't think I didn't notice that. You don't need those anymore."

Baker shambled past us with Yousef's corpse draped over his shoulder, hauling it out to the truck. Jessie's earpiece clinked against the cheap wood as she dropped it.

"You made the right choice today," Althea told her, "and a few weeks from now? Maybe a few days? You're gonna thank me. Jessie, this is how it always should've been. Now let's get going. We got a lot of miles ahead of us."

"Let me say good-bye."

Althea put her hands on her hips and nodded. "Make it fast."

Jessie turned toward me. The light from outside the shattered door caught a faint, wet glint in her turquoise eyes.

"Jessie—"

"It's the only way," she said. "You know that. They had me no matter what. One of us was going to get away, or neither of us. I told you this would happen eventually."

"I'll never stop looking for you."

She gave me a faint, lopsided smile.

"I know you won't. I'd tell you not to, but you're too goddamn stubborn to listen. If you ever see me again, will you do something for me?"

"Name it."

She reached up, touching her finger to my forehead. "See me with your head, not your heart. Because there's a real good chance that I won't be the Jessie you know anymore. And if that's the case, you'd better put me down, hard and fast. Kill me before I kill you."

"That's not going to happen. You're going to fight this."

"You can only fight so hard, for so long, Harmony."

She put her hands on my shoulders. Leaned in, and gently kissed my cheek.

"Daylight's burning, baby girl," Althea said behind her. She stood in the doorway, an expectant silhouette.

Jessie didn't say good-bye. She turned and walked away, taking her mother's hand.

# # #

Baker or Ferrara had paused just long enough to shred two of my tires, leaving me stranded. Apparently they weren't worried about me calling for backup, so long as they got a good head start. I watched them leave from the motel-room door, peeling out in a pair of vehicles, Althea and Jessie leaving in a dirty black Charger. License plates stripped. I called it in, anyway, along with an ambulance for Bella. She came to, saw the bloody patch of carpet where her brother-in-law had been, her husband's torn corpse on the bed, and started screaming until she hyperventilated.

I went numb. Full lockdown, battening my psychic hatches so I didn't feel too much. Or anything at all. Nothing mattered but the mission.

And now, Jessie was the mission.

"Did . . . that just happen?" Kevin asked softly, his voice crackling on my earpiece.

Local police rolled in with the ambulance. I flashed my credentials and took charge of the scene, getting Bella out of there and cordoning off the room. A white Crown Vic swooped in, and Mueller jumped out with a flustered aide on his heels, coming at me like a charging bull.

"What the hell did you do, Agent? I've got a goddamn massacre in Roxbury, reports of—"

I cut him off and got in his face. Whatever he saw in my eyes, it stopped him dead in his tracks.

"What you've got, Agent Mueller, is what happens when you let a rookie oversee a surveillance op he was in no way fit to command. Then that same rookie went in against my orders, after I *told* him the situation was too volatile. It was a failure of leadership on every level, and now a field agent has been abducted. The Crisis Management Unit is taking charge of this situation, and you are going to shut up, *listen*, and do *exactly* what I tell you."

"Abducted?" His hard eyes narrowed to slits. "One of ours?"

"Abducted by the same people who murdered the SWAT team at the auto shop."

It doesn't matter what kind of badge you wear: the only thing in the world that mobilizes the law faster than a call of "officer down" is an officer taken. Mueller turned to his aide without missing a beat and snapped, "Call in the entire field office. Pull 'em off vacation, cancel field ops, do whatever you have to do. And I want the police commissioner on the phone, stat."

"We've got their vehicle makes," I said. "No license plates, and presumably they'll steal some to minimize their chances of getting pulled over. We'll want to flag any reports of stolen plates within five miles of this address. They're carrying several large, heavy crates, so if they switch vehicles, they'll need a truck or a big SUV."

"I'll have roadblocks set up within the hour. And the suspects?"

I held up my phone. "Sending you their pictures now. I cannot emphasize this enough: these people are *extremely* dangerous. If they're spotted, no officers are to approach without my say-so. I'll coordinate the takedown."

How I was going to do that, I had no idea. Althea had stolen my service weapon. My magic, thanks to Nadine's toxic touch, was still short-circuiting like it had back in DC, and I couldn't count on it being there when I needed it. My mind was all I had left to fight with.

It would have to be enough. Jessie needed me. I wasn't going to let her down.

THIRTY-SEVEN

Kevin and April were on their way in a rental car, texting me updates every five minutes like clockwork. While uniforms swirled around me and paramedics rolled out the remains of Walid Masalha under a white sheet, I decided it was time to take a risk. I called Linder.

"Agent Black?" he said. "What's going on out there? According to Dr. Cassidy, you're in Michigan, I'm showing you pinging FBI resources in Boston, I haven't gotten a mission update from Agent Temple in days—"

"Jessie is MIA. She's been taken by our targets, and the situation is worse than expected. I need Vigilant-trained and qualified backup, and I need them yesterday. Occult *and* combat support."

"Impossible," he said.

"Excuse me? That's not a good word to use right now."

"Beach Cell is in deep cover at Diehl Innovations—it's too dangerous to contact them right now, especially with Bobby Diehl trying to sniff out the traitor in his ranks. The trainees for Redbird Cell are still being vetted, and they're nowhere near ready to tackle a real mission yet."

"Panic Cell?"

"Out of the country. I'm sorry, Agent Black. You have to go it alone."

"You can provide material support, then. Every second counts right now, and I can't waste time flying commercial. I need a charter jet at Logan International, fueled and ready to go."

"To go where?" he asked.

"Wherever I tell it to. I also need weapons. High caliber, automatics, and incendiary rounds if we can get them on short notice."

"Agent, please," Linder sighed. "You know Vigilant Lock has to covertly siphon all its funding from various public programs. We don't have an unlimited cash flow, and I'm afraid the Diehl operation is demanding the lion's share of resources—"

"Sir," I said, "Agent Temple is missing. The odds of getting her back alive and unhurt go down with every minute you waste bullshitting me. You are going to get me that jet, within the hour, or God help you, because everything that happens to her is going to happen to *you*."

He fell silent.

"Well?" I demanded.

"That's just . . . the sort of response I'd normally expect from Agent Temple, not from you."

"We have an operative missing. *Act* like it, and start doing your job. Jet. Logan. Fully fueled. One hour."

I hung up on him.

Kevin and April roared up in a dirt-brown Explorer. I hopped in the backseat, and Kevin punched the gas.

"You've got a hundred pounds of Semtex and a dead body in your luggage," I said, "and you know a dragnet is closing in fast. Where do you go?"

"I'd switch vehicles," Kevin said. "Semis are easy to find. Kill the driver, take the truck, load everything and everyone in back. They have to keep Jessie under control, too, and make sure she doesn't leave any clues behind for us: locking her in a trailer, especially if her mother's there to keep an eye on her, would take care of that problem."

April shook her head. "You're still running the risk of being stopped at a roadblock. Commercial flight wouldn't work, but what about a private charter? A small, sturdy plane could take them four hundred miles or more before they'd have to land and refuel."

I thought back to their service records. Althea and Baker were both certified to fly.

"How many airports around the greater Boston area?" I asked.

With Kevin's laptop on her knees, April rattled off a few quick keystrokes. "Sixteen, plus one seaplane port."

"Pull over."

The wheels rumbled as Kevin parked on the side of the highway. We split up the list, and all three of us started calling airports. I climbed out of the SUV and paced the roadside, a cold wind that smelled like diesel fumes ruffling my hair. I had just gotten off the phone with my second airport, convincing them to shut down all traffic, when Kevin swung his door open and leaned out.

"Harmony! The doc's got something."

"What I've got," April said, "is a bad feeling. I'm trying to contact someone—anyone—at the Plum Island Airport. No answer. I just reached out to the Newbury Police Department, and they can't get an answer, either. They're sending a car around to check it out."

"Kevin, drive. April, call them back and tell them to stand down. Two of the Wolves chewed through an entire SWAT team, and now they've got Althea with them; ordinary patrol cops don't stand a chance against them."

"Uh, do you have a plan?" Kevin asked. "Because when it comes to taking on heavy hitters, that's usually Jessie's job. And she's not on our side right now."

I shot him a glare. "She's still on our side."

We hit the outer limits of Newbury in a little under an hour. The airport was the size of a postage stamp, with training Cessnas lining the grass not far from the single, short strip of runway. Newbury PD was too slow or just didn't listen: the squad car they'd dispatched was parked up ahead, near the lip of the tarmac. One cop hung out the side window, arms dangling limp, neck broken. His partner was a few feet away, facedown, his blood soaking into the dark pavement and turning it the color of ripe raspberries.

"Stop here," I said. "Keep the engine running. If you see anything move that isn't me, take off fast."

I got out of the SUV alone.

The airport stood silent. Just the rustling of a chilly breeze, ruffling the grass along the runway.

I needed a weapon. I jogged up to the patrol car, circling to the dead man dangling out the window, and crouched. His bulky service revolver lay a few inches from his dangling fingers, down on the tarmac. Snatching it up, I checked the load. He'd only gotten a single shot off.

Circling the big, curving aluminum arc of the hangar, I spotted the pickup and Charger parked out front. No crates in the back. Another pair of bodies, dressed in maintenance coveralls, lay flat on their backs on the concrete. Their bullet-riddled faces looked up to the cold October sun.

Inside the cavernous hangar, all I found was a conspicuous absence where a plane had once stood, and the remains of their final victim. I stood over the body, revolver tight in my grip, the stench of rotten meat and excrement shoving its fingers down my throat.

They'd eaten him.

The man was naked, his clothes shredded and thrown over by a cluttered workbench, his dead eyes wide and his jaw wrenched open in a silent howl. From his chest to his groin, he'd been torn open and turned into a living feast table, ropy guts yanked out by the strand, blood gulped down and his organs gnawed, like he'd been set upon by a pack of wild beasts. A soup bowl made of living, screaming flesh and bone. His heart lay discarded over by his shoulder, half-eaten and tossed away like a bad apple.

"Did they make you join in, Jessie?" I asked the silence. "Was this your initiation?"

I called Newbury PD for backup, then notified SAC Mueller to call off the dogs. No need for roadblocks now: the Wolves were long gone, and they weren't coming back.

A long line of ambulances filed along the airport, their flashers silent, grim-faced paramedics carrying out the dead one by one. I walked along the grass, breathing deep and letting the cold wind wash away the stench of death. Still, it followed me.

"We have to work the targets," I told April and Kevin. "It's the only lead we have left. Who was involved in Glass Predator and hasn't been killed yet? Linder, but they won't be able to find him. Burton Webb we sent out of the country. That leaves Bobby Diehl and Senator Roth. Kevin, see if you can find Roth's itinerary online: Is he making any public appearances in the near future?"

Two minutes later, Kevin stopped typing. His mouth hung open.

"Uh, guys? I think I found something. Looks like the Wolves might get a two-for-one special. Roth's back in Nevada, working the fund-raising and publicity circuit for his reelection campaign. There's a brand-new Diehl Innovations plant that just finished construction in Vegas—Roth is gonna cut the ribbon tomorrow night. Big party after, and Bobby's going to be there personally."

Everything clicked.

"This is what they've been building up to," I said. "Their grand finale."

I locked eyes with April.

"They're going to stage a terrorist attack. They're not just going to kill Roth and Diehl. They're going to blow up the building and murder everybody in it."

"The hundred pounds of Semtex," April said.

"And Yousef Masalha. Althea could have made the deal for the explosives herself, but she didn't. And Yousef was more than just a convenient patsy; when we watched the security footage from the garage, the Wolves said the original plan was to let Vukovic and his gang survive. Then, the motel. Althea shot Yousef and told Baker to dig the bullet out of his skull—"

"So that when his charred remains are found at the bomb site," April said, "it'll be assumed he was responsible for the attack and died in the explosion."

"And investigators would follow the explosives back to Vukovic, who had been convinced he was dealing with a Hamas operative," I said. "More 'evidence,' carefully planted and intended to be found. The Bureau already believed Yousef was guilty, and that would just be another nail in the coffin."

"But why?" Kevin asked, glancing between us. "Why go to all that trouble when they could just *shoot* Roth and Diehl from a safe distance? I mean . . . beyond the fact that they just really enjoy killing people."

"They like killing people," I said, "and they like getting paid to do it. Remember, Glass Predator was created under a sealed presidential order, then it shut down when the brass got cold feet."

April nodded. "We have a new president now. A new administration."

"I think they want their old jobs back," I said. "Revenge is only half the story. They'll simulate a major terrorist attack, cause a mass panic, and at the same time finish checking names off their hit list. If they can throw a big enough scare into the Oval Office, bringing Glass Predator back online might seem like a reasonable idea."

"They'll go through the back channels, approach the powers that be, and make their sales pitch," April mused. "Try to get the program reinstated. Not likely to succeed, but then again, they've got nothing to lose. If they're turned down flat, they still took their vengeance. Either way, the Wolves win."

I stared at the far horizon. The sun shimmered downward, casting the sky in a lonely violet haze. I thought of Jessie, somewhere up in that sky, trapped and cornered and needing a rescue.

"Over my dead body," I said. "Let's see if Linder came through with that plane. We're going to Las Vegas."

THIRTY-EIGHT

For once, management delivered. A Citation VII waited for us at Logan International, the midsize jet fueled up and ready to fly. I wasn't sure what the pilot had been told: he just gave us a nervous look and helped clear space as we wrestled April's chair up the short flight of steps into a wood-walled cabin with plush ivory leather seats.

"I can get us there in seven, eight hours if the weather's good," he said, "but we can't take off until traffic control clears us. There's bad storms over Atlanta. Backs up the whole system."

I took out my phone. "Oh, they'll clear us."

The crew ran their preflight checks while I called the tower. An hour later we were airborne, lifting off the tarmac and soaring into the dark, a steel raptor on the hunt. A call came in as we lifted off.

"Your beau is on the move," Fontaine told me.

"Let me guess," I said. "Cody's flying to Las Vegas."

"Mmm-hmm. Used his police credentials to bring that shiny new gun along for the ride."

"He's doing what he promised in Talbot Cove." I leaned back against the cool leather headrest, closing my eyes. "He's going after Bobby Diehl."

"How do you rate his odds?" Fontaine drawled.

"Against a man with a million-dollar security detail and black magic up his sleeve? Cody's no assassin, he's not . . ." I trailed off, looking for the words.

"Not a natural-born killer," Fontaine said. "Not like you and me."

"I'm not a—" I paused, shaking my head, brushing the comment off. "We've got to stop him. He's going to get himself killed."

"Well, I'd suggest you put some hustle in your step. I don't reckon he'll be waiting too long. Don't worry, my girl's got her eye on him. She's sitting two seats behind him on the plane right now. She'll keep tabs on him until you rendezvous."

There wasn't anything left to say. Nothing else I could do until we landed. I knew I should try to sleep, just like I knew I wouldn't be able to. The jet was roomy enough for us to spread out, and I walked the aisle to burn off some nervous tension. Kevin had passed out already, slumped against his window. April sat silent, staring at her phone, the blurry flicker of a video playing against the glass of her bifocals.

I felt like I should say something to her. She'd taken Jessie in, raised her as her own. She had to be hurting right now. I just wasn't sure what I could tell her and hoped something would come if I paced long enough. As I paused near her chair, turning, she glanced up and caught my eye.

"Sorry," I said. It was the best I could do.

"*Sorry.* One of the most useless words in the human vocabulary. Don't you think it's funny, how we feel compelled to apologize for pains we didn't inflict?"

She glanced down.

"I'm the one who should apologize. This entire situation is my doing."

I frowned, slipping into the seat beside her. "How can you say that? Jessie told me that when you and your team killed her father, Linder wanted to sanction her on the spot. You adopted her instead."

"I had leeway. Bear in mind that Vigilant Lock didn't technically exist yet. Back then, it was just Linder with a phone and a loose network of friendlies, myself included. No rules, no cells or formal teams, just the very rare call to duty. Linder was busy with other things, after all."

"Like Glass Predator."

She nodded. "And who knows what other dirty business. That was my first and only time working with him. Then, years later—after I'd raised Jessie as best I could, and gotten her into the Bureau—he came calling once more. Vigilant Lock was officially active, as much as an illegal program funded through black-bag methods can be. And I volunteered both of us for the job. Jessie is in this life because of me. Meaning she's in enemy hands because of me."

"You can't hold yourself responsible for that. We all volunteered. We knew what we were signing up for. And we all know the risks. Operatives are taken. Operatives die. We know that, but we do it anyway, because the job is too important not to."

"There's our Harmony," April said, her voice dry. "That sterling sense of duty. I suppose next you'll say something optimistic about never losing hope."

"Do I need to?"

She sighed. "What you need to do, as I am doing, is prepare yourself for a worst-case scenario. Surrounded by Wolf cultists, encouraged to indulge her beast . . . Jessie may already be lost to us."

"How can you say that?" I stared at her as my buried fears fed a streak of anger. "You had faith in Jessie when nobody else did. Her father buried an *ax* in your spine, and your first reaction—when everybody thought she needed to be put down right alongside him—was to take her in."

April met my gaze. A slow, wry smile played on her lips.

"A fascinating presumption."

"What do you mean?" I asked her.

"Agent Black . . . did you really believe it was her *father* who put me in this wheelchair?"

Silence fell between us. The jet engine droned, muffled by the cabin walls as they closed in on me.

"Jessie did it?" I asked, my voice soft.

"I had her father in my sights. She was defending him. Just as she'd been trained to. Jessie was never taught morality as a girl. Concepts of right and wrong were alien to her. There was only predator and prey, the survival of the fittest." She paused. "Decades of studying abnormal psychology, and I'd never seen the like. *Could* she be rehabilitated, turned into a model citizen? I had to find out."

"I know Jessie," I told her. "She's my partner. My friend. She's a good person, in her heart. I *know* this."

"I've been watching some old home movies. Look at this one. You may find it informational. I took this when Jessie was seventeen, at a tactical training facility."

She leaned toward me and turned her phone so we could both watch as she rewound the clip. I didn't recognize the place, but I'd clocked time in plenty of ranges just like it: simulated towns filled with pop-up targets, designed to teach movement and clear thinking in a gunfight. The camera looked down from a narrow catwalk as Jessie—young, bright-eyed, and bouncing from foot to foot—waited for the starting buzzer.

She hit the course like a wrecking ball, barreling through at blinding speed, pistol blazing. She made up for untrained, crude technique with brutal ferocity, using her fists and feet as much as her gun, leaping over barricades to tear her simulated opponents in half. Target after target went down in a barrage of splinters and shredded paper.

April climbed down to meet her at the end of the course. A buzzer rang out. Jessie panted, leaning over with her hands on her thighs, catching her breath. She looked up and beamed.

"Auntie April! Did I kill them all? Did I win?"

The camera's eye slowly panned over the carnage. One target, a civilian carrying a sack of groceries, had a perfect kill shot drilled through his paper forehead. A silhouette of a mother with a baby in her arms had been torn in two, straight across the middle.

"Jessie . . . ," April's voice said from off camera, hesitant. "These were innocent people. You were only supposed to hurt the ones posing an active threat."

Jessie's smile fell.

"But you didn't *tell* me that," she said, showing hurt in her eyes. "How was I supposed to know that?"

April ended the playback.

"But you did teach her," I said. "You got through to her. All she needed was for someone to heal the damage her father inflicted, to show her a better way to live."

April gave me a faint shrug. "I'm not sure how much that amounts to, if her inner beast is encouraged to go unchecked. The longer she spends with Althea, the harder it'll be to bring her back."

"Will it? Look, you're talking about nature versus nurture. You, and the care you took in raising her, made Jessie the woman she is today. The power of the King of Wolves . . . that's just a thing she *has*, not who she *is*."

"Her mother would disagree with you," April said. "To hear Althea tell it, she was a meek little saint before Russell Lee Sinclair infected her. And now look at what she's become. She's living proof of her own claims."

"She's a monster," I said. "And that's fine. Dealing with monsters is what we do. I'll take Althea down and bring Jessie home safe and sound."

"Without your magic?"

I blinked. April stared at me, her gaze steady.

"How did you . . ."

"By paying careful attention. I wasn't sure, but your body language at the airport—almost timid until you'd snatched up that fallen officer's weapon—confirmed it."

"Althea stole my gun, and you know my magic's mostly defensive. I *can* deal damage with it, but—"

"You may not want to hear this, Harmony, but you and your predecessor have something in common. Mikki was a prime example of a phenomenon I've observed with several other magicians. It's a certain level of confidence that comes from knowing you're never unarmed. A confidence you suddenly stopped displaying right around your encounter with Nadine. What she did to you—it's interfering with your powers, isn't it?"

I slumped back in the plush leather seat.

"It's *me* that's interfering. I keep thinking about what it felt like. I keep . . ." I trailed off. I was too ashamed to say another word.

She rested her hand over mine. "Harmony, no one thinks you wanted Nadine to do that to you. And no one thinks that you want her to do it again. What you're craving is the chemical by-product of the attack: the rush you felt. It's exactly the same as if Nadine had injected heroin into your veins or forced you to smoke crack at gunpoint."

"Which doesn't change the fact that I'm acting like a junkie." I clenched and unclenched my other hand, balling it into a fist. "To call my magic, I have to go to a place deep inside me. It feels like . . . standing in a mountain spring, as the cool, pure water washes past you and over you, cleansing everything. Now? All I feel is how hungry I am. I smell this . . . toxic scent, like a pile of rotting garbage doused in a bucket of rose oil. That's what I feel like inside."

April looked me over, taking me in.

"You know the most important thing about addictions, Harmony? They can be beaten. And while you may not have a conventional obstacle to overcome, you're not a conventional woman. You'll find your center again. For now, you should probably get some sleep."

"Should," I said, "but I don't think it's happening. Hey, do you have the old Sinclair case files?"

April adjusted her glasses, thinking. "I should be able to dig them up. Why?"

"Know thy enemy. You said there was evidence that Althea was helping Russell Lee, before her 'death.' I want to learn everything there is to know about her."

"I'll send them to your phone," April told me. "I'll warn you, they don't make for pleasant reading."

That was an understatement. And if I hadn't been inclined to stay awake, the first few pages—scanned copies of old witness statements and field reports, typed up in a clunky typewriter font—would have kept me up anyway. Russell Lee Sinclair was equal parts prolific and sadistic, and he led his family across half of the Deep South as he racked up victims. He had a preferred victim type—young, pretty, and blonde—mostly grabbing hitchhikers and making attacks of opportunity.

And he liked to take pictures.

Hundreds of them sat in my phone, seized from the crime scene, stamped into evidence. Tiny windows into a man-made hell, daring me to open them. Here was a teenager bound to a makeshift altar while Russell carved ritual symbols into her skin, laughing at her pain. Another victim hung upside down, ankles snared by a rope slung over a tree. Russell posed for the shot and held up a skinning knife, grinning, like a hunter with a trophy buck. Every shot was out of focus, faded, blurry: I could barely make out Russell's face. His eyes lost in shadow, his teeth white and sharp.

"He's in most of the pictures," I murmured. "You were behind the camera, Althea. Documenting the tortures, the kills. What were you thinking about? Come out from behind the camera. Let me get a good look at you."

I made my way back to one of Russell's first documented murders. Althea stood beside him at the killing table. From the time stamp, Jessie would have only been two or three years old, and the lens held perfectly stable for a long string of photos. They must have set up a tripod and a timer, letting the camera snap away as they slowly dissected a screaming teenage runaway. The angle was bad, and their faces weren't even in the frame: just their bloody hands, and the tools they used.

I studied the details as I paged through the endless photographs, looking for a clue, something I could use, then froze.

The victim's flailing arm must have bumped the tripod. The camera's nose had lurched up, capturing one perfect frozen frame in crystal-clear focus.

I clicked my seat belt and jumped to my feet, racing to the back of the plane. April jolted awake, startled by the sound. She rubbed her eyes and slipped her glasses on.

"April. The pictures you found at the murder house: Did you look at them? All of them?"

"As many as I had to. There were nearly a thousand of them, and a good chunk of them were misfiled until long after the case was officially closed. Why?"

I thrust the camera in her face. "Look. This picture. *Look.*"

April leaned forward, her eyebrows lifting in surprise.

"This . . . changes everything," she said.

THIRTY-NINE

We landed in Las Vegas at sunrise. I stood in the jet's lavatory and looked at myself in the mirror. Knotting a bloodred silk tie around my neck, pulling on my black suit jacket, preparing for battle.

I didn't have a gun, and I couldn't rely on my magic. Requisitioning support from the Vegas Bureau office was an option, but that would take time I didn't have—and if I was going up against Althea and her pack, three against one, I needed heavier firepower than they could give me. All I had was a photograph. A photograph I could turn into a deadly weapon and save my partner, if I played my cards right.

I wasn't going to rely on luck, though, especially not in this town. I'd never liked Vegas. Too many memories, most of them bad ones. Still, I'd spent a few months in a frustrating struggle to bring a little virtue to Sin City, and those days had left me with some contacts I could rely on. As we touched down on a landing strip at McCarran Airport, I called one of them from the plane.

"Detective Kemper," said a tired-sounding voice.

"Detective, it's Agent Black. Is this a bad time?"

"*Harmony?* I haven't heard from you since the task force broke up. I, uh, tried calling you—I guess you got promoted or something?"

"Transferred out of the Seattle field office," I said. "I'm with the Critical Incident Response Group now. Same job, a lot more travel."

"Hey, good for you. And to answer your question, this city is a complete shit show, and I haven't slept since . . . I don't even know. Ever since Nicky Agnelli went on the lam, the natives have gone from restless to murderously unhinged. I've got a gang war, multiple homicides—I don't suppose you're here to help out?"

"Afraid I'm working my own case. Tell me something: If I was a criminal in Vegas and I needed to get my hands on some heavy firepower, who would I talk to?"

"Are you working an arms-smuggling investigation?" he asked. "Because we really should make this official and get my captain in the loop, maybe pool our intel."

"No," I said, "I just need to know where someone can acquire high-caliber firearms, discreetly, and with no questions asked."

He didn't answer right away. I heard the sounds of a staff room behind him, phones ringing, faint and muffled voices.

"I've been hearing things about you," he told me.

"Really."

"Not that it's any of my business."

"And yet," I said.

He let out a heavy sigh. "Harmony, I'm barely treading water here. My city's going nuts, and I've got bodies dropping left and right. Will you answer me one question?"

"Shoot."

"Are you here to make things better, or worse?"

"I'm still an FBI agent, if that's what you're asking."

"That isn't even remotely what I'm asking. All right. All right, fine. *Allegedly*, because we've never been able to get more than a penny-ante bust here and there, the big weapon conduit in town is an outlaw motorcycle club called the Blood Eagles. I'm not talking about suburban dads and their midlife Harleys, all right? These guys are the real thing, and serious trouble. The club president is a guy who goes by Winslow. Personally, I wouldn't try to roust him without half of Metro backing me up."

"If I wanted to try my luck," I said, "where would I find him?"

"You mean, if you were completely insane and wanted to get curb stomped?"

"Just the facts, Detective."

"Place called the Sunset Garage. I'll text you the address. Do me a favor? Be smart and bring backup. I'm pulling sheets over bodies all over town this week; don't add yours to the pile."

#

"You want to go *where?*" the cabbie asked me. I repeated myself. He stared at his fare meter and chewed his lip. "I can take you there, but you find your own way back. I'm not sticking around, not in that neighborhood."

"That's fine," I told him.

While I rode across the city, April and Kevin were nested inside the jet we'd turned into a flying command center, frantically mining for data.

"The Blood Eagles are local," April said over my earpiece. "Minimal out-of-state presence, but a fair representation in Nevada's prison system. If you recall that dramatic escape from Eisenberg Correctional a few days before their big riot, two of those men were soldiers for the club."

"Isn't George Clooney doing a movie about that?" Kevin asked.

"Get me a lever I can use," I told her. "What do we have on the top dog?"

"Full name, Winslow Sciavelli. Extensive rap sheet including multiple weapons charges, manufacture and distribution of crystal methamphetamine, assault with a deadly weapon—he's been in and out of the system his entire life."

"Any family? There has to be somebody he cares about."

"One sister, Lisa. Oh, this is potentially relevant. She's currently serving time in maximum security at the Florence McClure Women's Correctional Center on two murder charges. She insisted, during her trial, that she'd been possessed by a demon during the killings. She let slip that her brother hired a sorcerer to drive it out of her. Of course, that excuse went over about as well as one could expect."

I furrowed my brow, staring out the window at the silent, sleeping monoliths along South Las Vegas Boulevard. At the far end of the Strip, the grim black-glass shadow of the Enclave Resort still stood, a reminder of my last visit to the city. Considered unsellable at any price, the place had been earmarked for demolition in a month or so. I vaguely considered booking a return trip, assuming I lived to see tomorrow, just to watch it fall.

"Any chance she was telling the truth?" I asked.

"We've certainly seen possession victims kill before," April said. "Impossible to tell, given the data, but by all accounts she's been a model prisoner since she went inside. No disciplinary infractions, and she spends most of her free hours in the prison chapel."

Praying she wouldn't relapse. Interesting. I filed the information away.

The casinos and the tourist traps fell behind us as the cab turned onto a long stretch of rough and broken road. The driver gave a nervous eye to rows of boarded-up, graffiti-spattered storefronts, rolling past stop signs with only the slightest tap on the brakes. The end of the line, the Sunset Garage, lurked in the shadow of a rumbling overpass. A neon sign stood atop a concrete pillar grimy with age and exhaust smoke, the tubing burned out long ago and encircling the image of a pale-green sedan from the '50s. As my shoes crunched on loose gravel, the cabbie driving off the second I shut the door and leaving me stranded, I heard dogs yowling and hurling themselves against a long chain fence. The air smelled like gasoline. The whine of power tools and tinny rock music washed out from an open garage bay.

I adjusted my tie and invited myself inside.

A pack of grizzled men—most of them bearded, all of them wearing black leather vests with the symbol of a skeletal, diving eagle on the back—were working on a Harley Fat Boy. One glanced up from his work, giving his buddy an arm tap with a socket wrench and pointing my way.

"Nice chopper," I said.

They spread out, not sure what to make of me or the intrusion. Forming a ragged semicircle but not getting too close.

"You know bikes?" one asked me.

I shrugged. "Not enough to repair one, but I know how to ride."

One of the men sniggered, elbow jostling. "Yeah, I *bet* you do. I bet you can ride all day long."

"I'm looking for Winslow," I said with a thin, unaffected smile.

The biker with the socket wrench stepped toward me, the steel dangling loose in his grip. An unspoken threat.

"I don't think he's looking for you."

"He'll want to meet me," I said.

"Yeah? Why's that?"

"Your little club is the biggest supplier of firearms in Las Vegas," I said, "and I'm looking to buy."

The bikers glanced at one another, brows furrowed. Not sure if they should laugh or be concerned. I kept the thin smile on my face, eyes fixed and unblinking.

"You look like a cop." The biker with the socket wrench leaned in and took a big, loud sniff. "Smell like one, too. Mmm, bacon."

"Huh." I tapped my lips, pretending to think it over. "Good point. And a cop, walking into the heart of Blood Eagles turf completely alone, asking about an illegal buy? Why, that'd mean I'm either completely crazy . . . or I'm not alone, and I probably have at least two SWAT teams for backup hiding less than ten seconds away."

He tried to stare me down. I met his gaze, and he took a halting half step backward.

"So let's hope I'm not a cop," I said. "And let's decide to accept that I'm exactly who I say I am: a new customer who wants to put a nice bundle of cash in your club president's hand. Call him. Now."

A few of the Eagles fell back, murmuring in low, worried voices. One took out his phone.

Then we waited, passing the time by staring each other down. After what felt like an hour, I finally heard the rumble of engines. A pack of choppers, five in all, pulled up to the open garage doors in a perfect V formation. The man at the head of the pack swung a dusty, denim-clad leg over his bike, running callused fingers through stringy gray hair. He was built like a lumberjack, with sunburned, chapped skin and a voice like wind-scoured gravel.

"This some kind of a fuckin' joke?"

Winslow and his men closed in from the doorway while his boys behind me did the same. I knew the look I was getting from all directions. Predators' eyes. And without a gun or my magic, no badge was going to save my life.

I had to count on my wits to do that. My wits, and a little audacity.

"No joke," I said, "just business."

"This might come as a shock, lady, but I don't just do business with any stranger who comes strutting into my garage. I don't know you. I don't know who knows you. My boys checked out the block before we rolled up. If you even have any backup, they're too far away to help you. I don't think you're local law, no. That suit, that attitude? I'm thinking *fed*. So give me one good reason I shouldn't put two rounds in the back of your skull and bury you in the junkyard."

"You want a reason? Sure. I'll give you one."

I moved in, getting up close and personal.

"Lisa," I said, "your sister."

FORTY

Winslow's eyes narrowed to icy slits. He brushed his leather vest back, his hand resting on the walnut grip of a revolver. His voice dropped to a graveyard whisper.

"Only one thing on God's green earth I care about more than my club. That's my sister. And you walk in here, stand in *my* garage, and threaten her? You just dug your own grave."

"You've got it backward," I said. "For starters, that whole demonic-possession alibi? I know she was telling the truth."

He squinted at me, hard.

"Bullshit."

"I know it, and from what I hear, you know it, too. You hired someone, someone from the local underground, to cast it out of her. That tells me you saw something. Something you couldn't explain."

"It's Vegas. Lots of unexplainable shit going down. Like this, right here. What do you know about Lisa?"

"I know she's in maximum security, and she shouldn't be."

I reached into my breast pocket. The room tensed, hands slipping behind backs, closing on guns tucked into belts or dangling on cheap holsters, but nobody drew. Slow and easy, I pulled out my FBI credentials. They unfolded in Winslow's face, giving him a good look.

"You're right. I am a fed. Not the ordinary kind, but considering I not only know about your sister's situation but I *believe* her, you can probably guess that much."

I shut the credentials and put them back.

"I'm the kind of fed with influence in a lot of strange corners," I told him. "And if we can do business, I can put that to work. Help me out and I'll try to get Lisa moved to minimum security. See about getting her some privileges to make her time behind bars go easier. No promises, and it'll take a while—I can't just pick up the phone and make it happen—but I'll give it my best shot. My word on it."

"If this is a setup," he said, "it's the strangest fuckin' setup I've seen in my entire life. Tell me this, though: Why's an FBI agent need to make a purchase from a guy like me?"

Telling the truth had worked so far, so I looked him in the eye and gave him my honest answer.

"Because I don't feel like following the rules today. And some people are looking to hurt my best friend. So I'm going to kill them."

Winslow paused. Then he barked out a raspy laugh, his eyes opening wide.

"You," he said, pointing at me, "may have a deal. Let's see if I can put some steel in those angry little hands of yours."

His men parted ranks to let us through. Winslow pulled back a tarp on the floor in the back corner of the room, then hauled on a rough twist of rope tied to a ring in the floor. A trapdoor groaned up, over, then fell on its back with a *clang* that reverberated through the garage. I followed him down into darkness, along a rickety wooden staircase. Winslow tugged a string and clicked on a single overhead bulb cased in an orange plastic cage. Hard white light flooded the small cinder-block cellar, glinting off enough guns to arm a company of marines. They lined the walls, suspended from hooks on wire-frame racks, everything from pistols to submachine guns to modified, kitted-out battle rifles.

Winslow spread his hands, taking in the room, eyeing me like a used-car salesman. "So what's your pleasure?"

"I'm looking for something along the lines of a fully automatic shotgun, an AA-12 or a Saiga, with a thirty-two-shell drum magazine."

He blinked at me. "What are you hunting, a tank?"

"Three tanks," I said. "And they need to go down and stay down."

Winslow chuckled, rubbing the stubble on his cheeks as he surveyed the racks, looking for something to offer me.

"You remind me of this guy I know. He came in here once, same as you, looking like his back was up against the wall and he had some serious killing to do. Ain't got an AA-12 in stock, but . . . you ever handle a Taurus Judge? Might be your kinda weapon. I got a pair of 'em if you feel like doing some John Woo shit."

My gaze drifted across the wire racks and settled in the corner. The curves of a tall, olive-painted canister festooned with straps and buckles caught my eye.

"Is . . . *that* for sale?"

Winslow followed my gaze and cracked a grin. "Hell, you'd be doing me a favor, taking it off my hands. Damn thing's been just sitting there forever. You know how to use one of those?"

"I'll throw in another twenty bucks for a tutorial."

We lugged my weapon of choice up the steps and out back, where Winslow showed me how to fire it at a wall of junked cars. I turned a rusted-out sedan into a smoking ruin and nodded with grim approval.

"Don't suppose you sell any working vehicles? Doesn't need to be anything fancy, just fast." I'd had to clean out my bank account for this—and more of April's retirement fund—but I still had some cash to spare.

"Two wheels or four?" he asked me.

"What do you think?"

With my purchase slung over my shoulder, I puttered out of the garage on a jet-black Harley Street Glide. The rebuilt engine revved, rumbling and hungry between my legs. I gave Winslow and his buddies a wave, hooked a left, and poured on the throttle as I hit the open road. My jacket's tails billowed out behind me, the wind catching my scarlet necktie and flipping it back over my shoulder, and I leaned in low against the handlebars with my eyes shielded behind a pair of tinted riding goggles.

Jessie would love this, I thought, and a pang of heartache spurred me along. I swerved onto an on-ramp and hit Interstate 15 hard and fast. Up in Apex Industrial Park, twenty minutes north of the city, they'd be getting ready to cut the ribbon on Bobby Diehl's new production facility. The Wolves would be there. So would Jessie.

Along with a hundred pounds of high-powered plastic explosive, primed and ready to kill.

# # #

The Diehl Innovations plant gleamed like a hundred burning diamonds. Long and low, solar panels studded its rooftop and feasted on the setting sun, reflecting its shimmering glow. I expected crowds and reporters, a parking lot filled with cars, a party ready to begin.

The place was deserted.

I rolled the Harley to a stop out front, flipped down the kickstand, and swung off the saddle. I tapped my earpiece and peeled off the riding goggles.

"April, Kevin? Did you call for an evacuation?"

"Absolutely not," April said. "I thought we agreed that might provoke them. We were waiting until you arrived and evaluated the scene."

I looked over the lobby's glass facade. One of the front doors hung open just an inch, blocked by a wedge of brown leather jammed against the lock.

Jessie's holster.

"I think I'm being invited to dance," I said, striding toward the door.

"It's almost certainly a trap."

I opened the door and stepped inside, closing it gently behind me.

"God, I hope so," I whispered. "Just find out what happened to the party. And where Diehl and Roth are."

Bobby hadn't spared any expense on the lobby. It was a lavish cavern of green Italian marble, polished to a mirror gloss, studded with square pillars and elongated rectangles of black glass about as tall as I was. A pair of big, bubbling fountains, encased by foot-high marble walls, flanked a bank of elevators. I crept across the room, eyes sharp under the dead overhead lights, checking every shadow for movement.

I edged too close to one of the glass panels. It suddenly erupted in a burst of light and sound, and I found myself face-to-face with Bobby Diehl's maniacal grin.

"You know your coffeemaker," the recording said, "but does your coffeemaker know *you*? It will now—"

An elevator chimed, and the doors rumbled open. I darted behind a pillar, pressing myself flush to the cold stone.

"—interfaces with your alarm clock, ensuring that when you get up in the morning, a piping-hot cup of coffee prepared just the way you like it is ready and waiting," the recording droned on, almost covering the sound of footsteps. Two pairs. Heavy, and moving slow.

"Oh, *Harrrmonyyy*," Ferrara called out in a singsong chant, "come out and *playyy* . . ."

"Althea figured you'd follow us," Baker said. "What's wrong? Not what you expected to find here?"

They knew exactly where I was. They could smell me. I heard them, spreading out, flanking my hiding place as my heart pounded against the hard green marble.

"Where's Jessie?" My voice echoed through the room, ringing off the stone.

"With her mom, where she belongs," Ferrara said. "Seems they had to move the party, though. Somebody called in a bomb threat. Fortunately, the good senator was able to relocate the event to a much larger venue at the last minute."

Baker chuckled. "You didn't think we were going to blow *this* dump up, did you? C'mon, that'd make some headlines, but it just doesn't have that . . . air of a nation under siege we're looking to cultivate."

"A casino, on the other hand," Ferrara added. "Right in the heart of the Las Vegas Strip? That has potential."

They were coming closer. Taking their time. Enjoying themselves.

"So I was right. You're trying to convince the government that Glass Predator should be reactivated, and get your old jobs back."

"That's Althea's crazy idea," Baker said. "Me? I just want to blow some shit up. I don't care either way. Ferrara? You care, bro?"

"Not even a little. Now, skinning this bitch alive? *That* I care about. I care about that so much I'm getting hard just thinking about it."

I took a deep breath. No more stalling. Time to do or die.

"I'm giving you one last chance to surrender," I called out.

The Wolves's laughter filled the room, harsh and braying.

"And what," Baker said, stumbling over his words as he giggled in disbelief, "are you gonna do if we don't?"

I stepped out from behind the pillar and showed them what I'd bought from Winslow: the heavy olive steel tank of a Vietnam-era M9 flamethrower strapped to my back.

I remembered how Jessie had locked up when we fought Dr. Carnes back in Nashville, her beast driven into a helpless panic by the mad doctor's flames. Safe bet that Althea and her pack would have the same reaction. I could conjure a little fire, too—but with my magic in a muddled twist, I couldn't count on it.

There was more than one way to burn a Wolf.

The two men stood to my left and right, about ten feet away, frozen in place where they'd been moving to flank me. I reached back, unslung the flamethrower's wand, and slapped it into my open palm.

"You know, usually it's my partner who comes up with the clever things to say," I told them. "I don't have the knack for it. She says I'm too serious. I don't know. But seeing as Jessie isn't here—seeing as she isn't here because you murderous pieces of dirt kidnapped her—I'll give this my best shot. What am I going to do if you don't surrender?"

As I squeezed the safety-release trigger, the faint odor of gasoline wafted from the wand's bulbous nozzle.

"I thought I'd invite you to a barbecue."

FORTY-ONE

Baker charged me, roaring, hands hooked into killing claws as he lunged for my eyes. I spun, squeezed the fuel-release and ignition triggers, and the flamethrower roared back. A gout of blazing gasoline hit him full on and engulfed him in an inferno. He went up like a Roman candle, shrieking in agony as he stumbled across the lobby, his arms pinwheeling. His foot hit the rim of the shallow fountain. Water splashed across the marble floor as he plunged in, his back still burning, eyes staring dead and blank from his charred, smoldering face.

Ferrara was faster. He leaped sideways, dodging a lance of fire, and threw himself behind a pillar. I squeezed the triggers again as he broke cover, and a glass panel shattered, its jagged shards bubbling and melting down. He ran from panel to panel, darting around pillars, cheetah fast. The air rippled as I chased him with blast after blast from the wand, and sweat beaded on my skin as the room turned into a sauna reeking of spilled gasoline.

Then the tank ran dry.

He tackled me and we hit the ground hard together, the tank clanging, cracking the marble floor. His fist smashed into my jaw hard enough to blur my vision, stunning me while he wrestled my arms out of the straps.

I thumped onto my back, a lance of pain jolting up my spine. Ferrara straddled my chest, pinning my arms under his knees, his weight squeezing the air from my lungs. Then he reached into his pocket and tugged out a folding knife, his turquoise eyes gleaming in anticipation as he opened the serrated blade.

"You've got a pretty face," he panted. "Think I'm gonna hang it on my wall."

Earth, air, fire, water . . . My magic sparked and sputtered, failing to ignite again and again. It was inside me, I knew it was, but the howling void of hunger Nadine had left in my heart drowned it out.

Ferrara put his knife to my throat, just under the jawline, and started to cut.

Blood welled under the blade, sudden white-hot pain mixed with the hot, wet trickle as it rolled down my neck. I thrashed my head, trying to escape, and he clamped his free hand down on my scalp to hold me still.

"One nice, long, deep oval incision," he said, spittle glistening on his lips as he leered down at me, "and it'll peel right off."

As the blade dug in, cutting a slow red line under my jaw, my frantic mind grasped at shadows. Sparks of power that crashed and died inside my heart, the connection to the universe that used to come so naturally now impossible, mocking me. I grasped as deep as I could, reaching inward, tumbling into darkness.

# # #

I was nine years old again. Sitting in our cottage on Long Island Sound, the fresh, clean breeze of a summer morning wafting through an open window and ruffling the lace curtains. Grizabella, just a little puffball of a kitten then, batted at my toes as my mother arranged a tea set.

"It's important that you understand," she told me, "that there are many people in the world with abilities like ours. But they're not always good people. In fact, most of them aren't, so you need to be very careful."

I frowned, hearing my voice in my ears as I relived the memory.

"Why aren't they?"

"Well, magic . . . changes people. It can make them greedy, or cruel, and magnify the worst things inside them."

"They turn into monsters?" I asked.

My mother smiled gently. She poured two cups of tea, filling the parlor with the scent of chamomile.

"They do on the inside, even if they look pretty, or nice, on the outside. So you need to learn to look past the surface. Never let your guard down. And always remember, it could happen to you, too. Once you start to slip, it's a very long way down, and it just gets easier and easier."

I hugged myself with my tiny arms.

"I don't want to turn into a monster," I told her.

"Good. So always remember the first lesson: Why do we call it the gift?"

"Because it's a present," I recited, "but it's not for us. It's for the people we help."

She beamed. "That's right. So if you ever feel confused, or like you're wandering off the path, don't think about yourself. Think about the people you love, the people the gift is really for. They'll show you the way."

# # #

A vicious slap brought me back to reality, snapping my head to the side, one cheek stinging and the other pressed to the cold marble floor. Ferrara grabbed me by the chin, jerked my face back toward him, and leered down at me.

"You serious? One little cut and you pass out?" He held the bloody knife in front of my eyes, then put it back to my throat. "This is going to be a long night. I haven't *started* to hurt you yet."

I didn't feel it. I didn't see him, or the knife, or my blood as it trickled down my throat and pooled on the imported marble. All I saw was Jessie's face.

She needed me to find my center, to break Nadine's grasp. She needed me to fight my way to her, wherever she was, and save her from her nightmare of a mother.

She needed me. And if I died here, I'd be letting her down. That was the real spark for the flame, the push to give me the strength I needed.

I found the quiet place inside me, where my magic slept.

"One word," I grunted, wriggling my right hand out from under Ferrara's knee, wrenching it loose.

"Yeah?" he said. "What's that?"

I pressed my open palm to his face, fingers curling over his eyes.

"Burn."

The dam burst and the universe flooded in, turning me into its surrogate. A conduit for raw power, channeled and shaped, breaking loose as my hand ignited hotter than white phosphorus. Ferrara shrieked, rolling away from me, clutching his burning face. He flailed at himself, trying to beat out the fire as it spread to his shirt and rippled down his shoulders. I stood over him, without a shred of mercy in my heart, and hefted the empty flamethrower tank.

Then I lifted it high and brought it crashing down on his skull. I heard the bone fracture, flames billowing around the olive-painted steel. Then I raised it up again and plunged it down as hard as I could, smashing the tank into his blistered face like a pile driver.

Two more hits and he stopped moving. His leg gave a last, desperate twitch, and finally he fell still, his corpse smoldering in silence.

The tank fell from my limp fingertips. It clattered on the marble at my feet. I staggered away from the corpses, leaning on a pillar as I tried to catch my breath. Blood rolled down from the inch-long cut on my neck, staining my ivory blouse the same shade of red as my necktie, and I pressed my sleeve against the torn skin to try and stanch it. I tapped my earpiece.

"The Wolves conned Roth into moving the party," I gasped. "They want a bigger boom. And I need a location in the next thirty seconds."

"Harmony?" Kevin said. "You okay? You don't sound so good."

"*Location*, Kevin."

I'd done the best I could with the cut, bunching the bloody neck of my blouse against the tear, holding it tight while I waited for Kevin to get back to me. The wound still bled, a slow, hot trickle running down my shoulder. I stumbled out the lobby doors and into the gathering dusk, breathing in the clean desert air under a tangerine sky and finding my footing again. By the time I swung back into the saddle, slipping my goggles on and shoving back the kickstand, he was on the line again.

"It's the Monaco. The party's already getting started, and Roth and Diehl are both on-site. Should we call the police and have them evacuate the building?"

I hit the highway, leaning low into the handlebars as I swerved through traffic, setting my sights on the Vegas Strip. Fitting, considering I was about to gamble with hundreds of innocent lives.

"April, it's just Althea and Jessie now, and I was right about Althea's motive: she's staging a terrorist attack to try to pressure the government into reactivating the Glass Predator program. Which is insane, but she doesn't care about collateral damage. She also just pushed me into a showdown with Baker and Ferrara—if we evacuate, she'll know I survived, which means her pack is dead. What do you think she'll do?"

"She's highly mission oriented," April said, "with no regard for human life. If she feels her opportunity is slipping away, she may detonate the explosives ahead of schedule. Frankly, if she discovers she's lost her men, she may begin killing as many innocents as possible just to spite you."

It was all on my shoulders, then. At least the element of surprise was on my side for a change.

"A mass evacuation is too risky," I said. "Call the Vegas Bureau office, have them set up a cordon around the property, but tell them I'm going in first. Then get in touch with the Monaco. Have hotel security waiting for me when I get there, but tell them to act like nothing is out of the ordinary. We'll get everybody out, but we'll do it carefully, right under Althea's nose."

"And then?" April asked.

I revved the throttle. Up ahead, the lights of the Strip blazed to life, white and hot like a thousand miniature explosions.

"And then I get my partner back."

FORTY-TWO

I climbed a flight of ivory steps, past towering Grecian pillars, and entered the Monaco through the casino. It wasn't the low-profile entrance I'd been hoping for. The casinos had a loose dress code, but a woman with a blood-soaked blouse, skewed necktie, mussed hair, and a few fresh bruises tended to draw attention. I looked straight ahead, ignored the stares and uncomfortable murmurs, and kept going. Slot machines buzzed and trilled, their raw chaos setting my teeth on edge as I crossed the crimson-and-black carpet. My contact wasn't hard to spot: he wore a cheap suit, his black hair slicked to one side with a fistful of grease that shone under the hot casino lights. Not much to look at, but the two gorilla-size bruisers on his heels followed him with an air of deference.

"I was told to keep my eyes peeled for a woman in a suit and tie." He looked me up and down. "They didn't say she'd look like she just got the shit kicked out of her."

I flashed my credentials. "Special Agent Black, FBI."

"Greenbriar. Director of Special Security for CMC Entertainment." He licked his wormy lips, squinting. "You wanna tell me what's going on, Agent? When I get a phone call telling me to act like nothing's wrong, that usually means something's very, very wrong. I don't need *more* problems this week."

"You're hosting a party for Diehl Innovations tonight, correct?"

"Yeah, it was a last-minute thing—I guess the new plant got a bomb threat or something. The girls in catering had to work their asses off, but hey, personal request from Senator Roth. You don't say no to that, right?"

"Please listen carefully." I leaned in close, holding his gaze as I lowered my voice. "The threat is real, but the bomber is *here* and may already have explosives on-site. If she knows we're evacuating, she may set them off early and kill as many people as she can. Where, *exactly*, is the party being held?"

His eyes bulged. "The . . . the grand ballroom. Second floor, right above the lobby."

A hundred pounds of Semtex might not be enough to level the entire hotel and casino, especially without Baker around to help Althea with the wiring. She'd want to do as much damage as she could, take as many lives as she could, and make sure she killed Roth and Diehl in the blast. So she'd have to make her stand close to the party. Under it. And since she couldn't be wiring the lobby itself . . .

"Is there a basement sublevel?" I asked. "Anything underneath us?"

"Sure, this whole place is honeycombed with tunnels. Electrical, the hotel water reservoir, HVAC ducts—it's a rat maze."

"I need you to get me down there. As soon as I leave, you and your men need to clear this building *without* using any intercoms or alarm systems. CMC owns more than this one casino?"

"You kidding? We own half the Strip."

I gazed across the crowded casino floor, tables packed shoulder to shoulder by gambling tourists and eager onlookers.

"Good. Shut this place down, table by table, and give everybody vouchers to a different casino. Free drinks, comped rooms, anything you have to offer them. Make them leave, but make them *happy*: if anybody panics, it could trigger a stampede. Same with the lobby. Say your registration system is down, whatever—just get those people on a shuttle to a different hotel."

I half expected him to argue about the money involved. To his credit, Greenbriar gave me a sharp nod, shooting a look of concern at a pack of elderly tourists as they passed us on the carpet.

"Got it," he said. "Can I bring housekeeping in on this? They can hit the hotel floors, room to room, and knock on every door. We can tell 'em there's a gas leak or something, move everybody out nice and quiet."

"If you can trust them, do it. Try to move the guests out through multiple exits, and *no* fire doors. If any kind of an alarm sounds, the bomber will know what we're up to."

"You know this is gonna take a while, right?" He gave me a dubious eye. "As in, hours? I mean, this is a three-thousand-room hotel. Even with all hands on deck, it's gonna be slow going."

I knew. Just like I knew Althea wouldn't give us the time we needed. The best we could do was minimize casualties.

No, I told myself, *the best I can do is stop her.*

"Work from the ground floor up," I told him.

Greenbriar led me to a back stairwell, the casino glitz giving way to a cinder-block corridor with a bare metal door at the end. Greenbriar looked to the door, hanging open a crack, and frowned.

"This is supposed to stay locked," he said.

The door creaked open, and a gust of hot air laden with the coppery stench of blood washed over us. Greenbriar threw his hand over his mouth and nose, reeling.

At the bottom of a dark flight of steps, a maintenance worker lay sprawled on the concrete, his throat torn out and his overalls stained as dark as the spatters that painted the walls around him.

"Jesus," Greenbriar said, his voice muffled by his palm, "they got a wild dog with 'em or something?"

"Something like that. Close the door behind me."

He stared at me. "You're not going down there by *yourself*. Shouldn't you call a, you know, a SWAT team or something?"

"Close the door behind me," I repeated, and left him there as I descended the blood-slicked steps one at a time. Down into the bowels of the hotel, alone.

# # #

Faint safety lights glowed through the winding concrete tunnels, little squares of amber set into the ceiling every twenty feet or so. Beacons in the dark. I crept between puddles of dirty yellow light, ears perked, the sound of my own footsteps swallowed by the hiss of steam pipes and faint clanking from the fat aluminum conduits that ran along the walls at waist height.

I paused at an intersection, not sure which way to go, when another light caught my eye. A faint cherry-red eye, winking silently from the shadows. I inched forward, holding my breath. Three bricks of orange Semtex, each about the size of a stick of butter, were duct-taped together and fixed to a support column. A metal plate secured the blasting caps, and a thin line of bloodred detonation cord snaked off into the darkness.

I didn't touch it. I didn't have bomb-squad training, and there was no telling what kind of traps Althea had left behind to protect her mad designs. Instead, I followed the cord, turning a corner and finding a second trio of bricks on another support beam. The tunnels ahead were a maze of tiny blinking lights and long strands of unspooled cord, strung from pillar to pillar like a poisonous spider's web.

As I edged toward an opening, five more lines of cord winding their way past me and slipping around the bend, I heard voices muffled by the mechanical thrumming of the pipes. The smell of mildew hung heavy in the air, like damp and moldy socks.

". . . hand me the screwdriver."

"Mom, please, don't do this."

I peeked around the corner. The tunnel opened into a wide room, one wall dominated by steel pipes stenciled NATURAL GAS MAIN A/B. Althea had her back to me, hunched over a metal box on the floor. Jessie stood near her, her sunglasses gone and tears in her eyes, an open tool chest at her feet. Althea turned and froze her with a glare.

"Do you think those are *people* up there? They're not alive, not like us. They've never been alive. This is a mercy. Hand me the screwdriver, Jessie. *Now.*"

Cowed, her head drooped as she obeyed, meekly passing Althea the tool.

I had to get her attention. I leaned out from hiding and waved. Jessie's head snapped my way. She shook her head, suddenly terrified, and mouthed the word, *Go.*

I stood my ground and beckoned her toward me.

"You two," Althea said without looking up from her work, "are too much, you know that? Jessie, you smelled that girl as soon as I did. Don't pretend otherwise. Now bring her to me."

Jessie shot toward me. I hoped, for a second, running from Althea. She'd grab my hand and we'd go, get out of there—

She wrenched my arm behind my back and slammed me against the wall.

"Why," she growled into my ear, "couldn't you *listen*? Why didn't you kill me when you had the chance?"

Althea stood, dusting her hands off, and stepped to one side. The box was a detonation panel, the heart of the det-cord spiderweb, set with a keypad and a digital timer. A tiny green button pulsed patiently, waiting for the command.

"Because she's a weakling," Althea said.

"I'm here to *save* you," I grunted as Jessie yanked my arm, hauling me toward her mother. "This isn't who you are, Jessie! You have to fight this."

I felt her ragged breath gust across the back of my neck, her voice tortured.

"I'm done fighting, Harmony. I can't. I just can't anymore. It hurts too much."

Althea folded her arms, staring me up and down. "Well, now, this is a wrinkle. If you're here . . ."

"Your men are dead," I told her.

"Good."

I blinked. *"Good?"*

She shrugged. "They were weak, too. And starting to question my authority. That welcoming party at the Diehl plant would either kill *you*, solving a problem, or kill *them*, solving a problem. That's what we call a win-win situation. See, Jessie being alive, that changes everything. We're starting a new pack. Blood this time, only blood, and I could hardly ask my daughter to mate with one of *those* men."

She gave me a smug smile, her gaze drifting to meet Jessie's eyes.

"I always wanted grandchildren." She looked back at me. "You cut away the deadweight. I owe you a favor. Don't think a fast death is going to be it, though. Jessie, take her gun."

Jessie's rough hand patted me down, feeling the contours of my jacket, my thighs, and came up empty.

"She's not carrying."

Althea tilted her head. "Excuse me?"

"No gun," Jessie told her.

Althea's eyes, blazing in the shadows, bored into mine as if she could peer inside my thoughts.

"You came down here to face us, to face *me*—the living emissary of the King of Wolves—and you didn't even bring a weapon? Why?"

I met her gaze, meeting her fire with cold, collected ice.

"Because you're a spineless coward who only kills unarmed people," I told her, "especially if they're helpless and can't even *try* to fight back. I wouldn't want to make you uncomfortable."

Her lip curled, quivering. One of her hands folded into a fist as she stepped toward me. Then she paused. Taking a deep breath, unclenching her hand, and letting out an uneasy laugh.

"Oh, no. I'm not letting you goad me into a fight. Not when you're a link to Jessie's old life. Know what you are, girl? *Baggage.* Loose ends and baggage."

She looked to Jessie.

"Time to let that baggage drop. Prove you're my daughter, Jessie. Kill her."

FORTY-THREE

Jessie's arm hooked around my neck. Trembling as it squeezed.

"I'm sorry," she whispered. I felt hot, wet tears against the back of my neck. "Why didn't you kill me when you had the chance? I'm so sorry."

"Jessie," I croaked, struggling to breathe, "you don't have to do this."

"It's been so loud since I left with her. That voice telling me to lose myself, to give in, to serve the beast. I can't fight it anymore."

With my last breath, vision blurring, I said, "You can, and I can *prove* it."

Her arm stopped tightening against my throat. Althea looked at her, uncertain. "Jessie, do as I say. Kill her."

"Let me go, just for a second," I said. Her hands still held me fast. "Jessie, you're faster than I am, and you know I'm unarmed. I can't get away. Just let me go so I can show you something."

"*Jessie,*" Althea said, frowning as her daughter released me.

I turned to face her. And reached up, brushing a tear from her cheek with the tip of my finger.

"This is who I am," she told me. "I never had a choice, not after my father put this . . . *thing* inside me. My mom and me, neither one of us had a choice. The King controls us, makes us whatever it wants us to be. And it wants us to be killers. The only way to make this pain stop is to surrender to it, like she did."

"That's not true."

"I thought I could be one of the good guys. Thought I could use this curse for good." She shook her head. "I was never anything but a monster playing make-believe."

"Jessie," I said, "there's something you need to see."

Althea pointed at me, her face etched with sudden worry.

"Jessie, kill her. Do as I say!"

I took out my phone. Slid through a line of photographs, the evidence I'd sifted through on the jet, and held one up to Jessie's face as I looked Althea's way.

"You were only half-right," I told her. "I don't have a gun. But I *did* bring a weapon."

Jessie's lips slowly parted. She looked from the picture, to her mother, and back again.

The photo showed a young hitchhiker who'd fallen into Russell Lee Sinclair's hands, bound to a butcher-block table, screaming as he and his wife gleefully took her apart. One perfect shot of two serial killers sharing their passion together, the light capturing their leering faces in crystal-clear focus.

Showing their big, bright brown eyes.

"Althea lied to you, Jessie. What was it she claimed—she'd chase flies out of the house because she was too timid to swat one? She and your father had murdered their third victim before they even *heard* of the King of Wolves. The King didn't make them evil. They were already evil. The power didn't change anything about them, just like it didn't change you. Just like it *can't* change you unless you let it, unless you surrender to it, just like Althea's trying to con you into doing."

Jessie turned and stared at her mother, her face a mask of sheer disgust.

"You. Fucking. *Liar.*"

"Jessie," Althea said, backing away from her, "you don't understand. I'm helping you. This is—this is for your own good."

"The King of Wolves doesn't get to decide who you are," I told Jessie, "and neither does your mother. You do. Your actions do. And you know what your actions tell me? That you're one of the most kind-hearted people I've ever met. This power can't corrupt you, or transform you, or whatever crap she's been filling your head with, unless you open the door. The only person in control of your choices is *you.*"

Jessie fell silent as I lowered the phone. Her gaze swept across the room, and she stared her mother down.

"Harmony," she said after a moment's deliberation, "you've been running around town, taking down perps without me, having all the fun. Speaking as your partner, I just don't think that's fair."

I nodded, eyeing her. "Maybe so. How do you propose we rectify the situation?"

"I think you should stand behind me. Because this one here? She's all mine."

Althea gritted her teeth. She rolled her head around and stretched her arms, limbering up. She filled the tunnel junction with her presence, seeming to loom over us, to starve the air out of the place with the raw force of her anger.

"You sure you can take her?" I asked in a low voice. "What about the pack-scent thing?"

Jessie glanced my way, giving me a lopsided smile.

"Funny thing. I can still smell it . . . but it's a lot less like roses now, and a lot more like bullshit. Naw, I think I'll do just fine."

Althea spread her open hands wide. "I don't want to hurt you, but if you don't fall into line right now, I'll show you *everything* I can do. You sure you want it like that, baby girl?"

"Let's see," Jessie said. "Taking into account that you filled my head with lies, made me an accessory to your crimes, tried to turn me against everything I believe in, and tried to make me kill my partner . . ."

Jessie punched her fist into her palm.

"Yeah. I *absolutely* want it like that."

Althea shot me a venomous glare. "This is all your fault. This could have been so perfect, but no, you had to ruin *everything*. You want to play the hero? Fine. Here you go. Save the day."

Before we could move, she hit the green button on the detonator box. The LED display blinked to life, starting the countdown.

Three minutes on the clock.

Jessie blazed toward her, a blur in motion. Althea leaped in the air as she charged, snarling, hurling a savage punch. Her knuckles slammed into Jessie's eye hard enough to knock her to the concrete, and she rolled out of the way a heartbeat before Althea's boot slashed down. Skirting the edge of the room, I tugged my glasses from my breast pocket, slipped them on, and activated the internal camera.

"Brain trust, I hope one of you knows how to disarm a bomb, because I don't. Sending video now."

Kevin's voice crackled across my earpiece in fits and starts, the underground tunnels muffling reception. "—buffering, hold on. Crap, you're—only fragments—"

"Kevin? Can you hear me?"

Althea grabbed hold of Jessie's belt and the front of her blouse, hoisted her up, and whirled her around like she was weightless. Jessie went flying across the room, hitting the gas pipes hard enough to dent the metal, and crashing to the floor.

"This better?" Kevin said, his voice still faint but a little clearer now. "Don't know bombs, but electronics I can do. Pry open the faceplate."

I fumbled for the fallen screwdriver, snatching it up, working at the tiny screws at the four corners of the detonator box. The clock ticked down, as relentless as Althea as she stomped her boot down onto Jessie's ribs. I heard a bone snap. Jessie writhed on the floor, groaning, and her mother hauled her to her feet.

"Only way you can beat me is by letting the beast loose." Her fist slammed into Jessie's face, snapping her head back against the pipes. "And the second you do, it'll know its own and bow down to me. Once again, because you two children still don't seem to get it: either way, no matter what happens, *I win*."

The brushed-steel faceplate pried back, baring the guts of the detonator: a circuit board hooked to a ribbon cable and a tangled nest of colored wires.

"Okay, okay," Kevin's voice said, "electrical runs to the keypad, routes to the main board and also to the timer, timer's on a separate power supply . . . yeah, got it, find something to cut wires with."

I reached over and dragged the toolbox toward me, scraping across the concrete floor. I rummaged through the box, tossing hammers and wrenches aside, searching for a tool I could use. Five feet from me, Althea hurled Jessie against the concrete wall. Jessie reeled, stunned and bleary-eyed, blood trickling from a cut on her lip.

"How much of this can you take, huh?" Althea hammered Jessie's stomach like a punching bag, throwing punch after rock-fisted punch. "Let it out, baby girl. Give in."

A pair of wire cutters nestled at the bottom of the box. I snatched them up and turned my glasses toward the detonator. The timer ticked down. Ninety seconds left.

"Got it. What now?"

"Okay, you're gonna want to clip that green wire," Kevin said.

I reached for it, tugging the wire from the rat's nest and putting it between the cutter's jaws.

"Wait!" he shouted in my ear. "Wait, wait, that's wrong. Don't do that. Shit. Sorry."

Jessie was limp as a rag doll as Althea threw her again, her body crashing against the pipes, dropping to the concrete. Her mother kicked her in the gut, snarling, and dragged her back to her feet. I watched, helpless, struggling to stop the countdown while my partner died by inches.

"What are you waiting for, huh?" She punctuated that with another punch, smashing her fist into Jessie's jaw. "Let it *out*."

Jessie's hand shot out and grabbed Althea by the throat.

And hoisted her off her feet, her boots dangling an inch over the concrete floor, as Jessie's eyes burned like blue fire.

"I already did," Jessie growled. "And guess what: *I'm* in control."

She slammed Althea down onto the concrete. Althea rolled, getting up on her knees just in time for Jessie to spin like a top and lash out with a lightning-fast kick, pulping Althea's nose under her heel. Althea roared, jumping to her feet and charging at her, getting her hands on Jessie's shoulders and trying to haul her down.

The last minute blinked from the LED timer. Fifty-nine seconds to detonation.

"Kevin," I said, "help me out here, okay?"

Althea went sailing, hurled aside as Jessie spun hard and let her go. The back of her skull cracked against the tunnel wall and she hit the floor as Jessie moved in, relentless. Jessie grabbed her neck and dragged her up to her knees, her other fist raining down blow after blow.

"That battery in the upper-right corner of the box," Kevin said. "Little round thing, looks like a watch battery? Yank that."

"Are you sure?"

"Yes. No. I mean, yeah, that's the power supply for the timer, which sends the detonation signal to the main board, so *theoretically*—"

"*Kevin.*"

Jessie forced Althea to her feet. Her mother wavered, dazed, bleeding, and Jessie yanked her close with both fists clenched around the neck of her shirt.

"You know what?" Jessie hissed. "I'm *glad* I never knew you, growing up. You're a piece of shit just like my father was. I don't need either of you. I've got a family of my own."

Althea spat out a broken tooth and curled her swollen lips into a cruel smile.

"You'll always be mine, baby girl. You'll always be *his*. It's only a matter of time."

"Before I bow down to the King of Wolves, right? Here's the thing: only one person here is gonna bow down tonight."

Jessie pulled back her fist and let it fly, throwing a roundhouse punch that sent Althea crumpling to the ground at her feet. She stood over her, bloody knuckled and battered, staring down with her eyes blazing.

"And it ain't gonna be me," Jessie said. "It will *never* be me."

The timer ticked down. Fifteen seconds.

"Kevin," I said, "are you *sure*?"

"Yeah, yeah, I'm sure, do it. Pull the battery!"

I held my breath, got my fingernails around the tiny silver disk, and tugged it loose.

FORTY-FOUR

The timer froze at 0:09.

I counted down in my head, ticking off the seconds, all the way to zero.

Nothing happened.

As I exhaled, relief washing over me, Althea groaned at Jessie's feet. Jessie had Althea's pistol. She squared her stance, taking aim.

Althea flopped onto her back, breathless, and stared into the barrel of the gun.

"Go ahead," she said, tapping her forehead. "Put it right here. Let's see if you can murder your own mother in cold blood. Just like I taught you, it's all about survival of the fittest. You won the fight. Now make the kill."

The pistol wavered in her hand. Her resolve cracking, Jessie looked from her, to me, and back again.

"Jessie." I stood up, dropping the tiny battery, hearing it plink against the floor. "I'll make the shot. Give me the gun."

Althea let out a raspy chuckle. "Yeah, Jessie. Let your little girl-friend do it, if you don't have the spine. We all know you're not woman enough to get the job done."

Jessie stared at her. Then she lowered the gun.

"I can't. I . . . *hate* her, I hate everything she is, everything she's done, but . . ." Jessie shook her head. "No. I've got a better idea."

She kicked Althea onto her stomach, straddling her as she yanked her wrists back and zip-tied them.

"Harmony, call for an extraction team. She's going to Site Burgundy." She loomed over Althea. "It's a prison, offshore, designed just for people like you. And you're going to be there for a long, long time."

"Jessie," I said, "are you sure? If we send her to Burgundy, Linder's going to know. Which means he'll know what *we* know—about Glass Predator, about his involvement, everything. We won't be able to cover our tracks."

Althea spat a gobbet of blood onto the concrete and lifted her head to give me a bleary-eyed grin. "Oh, are you two keeping secrets from the boss? That's a dangerous game, especially when you've got a talkative prisoner on your hands. You know, if I were you, I'd put a bullet in me."

Jessie grabbed her by the wrists and hauled her to her feet.

"I'm *not* you, and I never will be." She looked to me. "And let him. I'm done hiding from Linder. Us and him are gonna have a nice, long sit-down after this, face-to-face. Time to lay all the cards on the table."

# # #

I walked Althea out, pushing her ahead of me with one hand on her shoulder and the other on the cuffs, Jessie limping at my side. We'd called ahead to give the all clear. The Monaco's doors swung wide, and two streams of SWAT officers hustled through the abandoned casino, weapons shouldered, trailed by a team of disposal experts in bulky bomb suits.

Flashing lights cast Las Vegas Boulevard in flickering red and blue, the street cordoned by a fleet of squad cars. A stoic wall of uniformed cops held the teeming crowds back. Dark-suited agents raced over, taking Althea off my hands, marching her to an unmarked car. I had met the woman leading the pack: SAC Brannon, a steel-haired woman in her fifties with eyes as sharp as the cut of her blazer.

"Agent Black," she said, "things always get interesting when you're in town."

"Sorry about that, ma'am."

She smiled. "You got the perp, no lives lost . . . good catch. Just do me one favor?"

"Yes, ma'am?"

"Next time you take a few vacation days? Go somewhere *else*. You're making me nervous." She looked Jessie up and down. "And you both need medical treatment. Come on, we've got paramedics on standby."

"I'm fine," Jessie said. Then she shrank under our combined glares. "Okay, maybe I've been better."

As she led Jessie off, frantic waving from the edge of the cordon caught my eye. I slipped past the police line, into the crowd of onlookers, and met up with Greenbriar.

"So we good?" he asked. "Problem solved?"

"Problem solved. I'm sorry for the inconvenience."

He blinked at me. "*Inconvenience?* No, inconvenience is having one of our flagship properties go up in smoke, literally. You did my bosses right, and we're gonna do you right. You ever sleep in a penthouse suite?"

"I . . . haven't, actually."

"Well, you are tonight. And anytime you need a place to stay, just call ahead, I'll make it happen. CMC Entertainment wants to express its gratitude."

"As do I," said the man cutting through the crowd, dressed in a black tuxedo and lime-green sneakers.

Bobby Diehl.

His lips curled in a serpentine smile as we stood face-to-face. "I just had to meet the hero of the hour. If I understand correctly . . . you're the woman who just saved my life. Funny how the world turns, isn't it?"

"Sure." My jaw clenched. "Funny."

"I mean, life and death, it's so arbitrary. One day, a terrorist attack in Michigan causes the deaths of so many poor, innocent people. The next, an even worse one is foiled in the act. Too bad there wasn't a hero like you in Talbot Cove, to save those victims like you just saved me."

I leaned in, dropping my voice to a whisper.

"You're living on borrowed time. I hope you know that."

Bobby's smile only grew bigger. "What's the matter, Agent? Can't take a joke? You should learn to loosen up a little. I have to get back to my amazing life, but I'll be seeing you soon. We are going to have *so* much fun together."

He sauntered off. I let him. My eyes were already on the crowd, the skin on the back of my neck prickling. Telling me something was wrong, my subconscious picking up on the danger before my waking mind could spot it.

"Three o'clock," said a small voice to my left. A little girl, maybe eight or nine, in pigtails and a frilly white smock. Her skin was pale, almost jaundiced, and she had the eyes of a dead fish.

"Excuse me?"

"Your *boyfriend*," she said, glaring. "I'm being paid to follow him, not stop him from shooting up the place. And Fontaine says you're welcome."

I saw him now. Cody, dressed as one of the Monaco's waiters, hot on Bobby's heels with murder in his eyes and a bulge under his jacket. I shouldered my way through the crowd and planted myself like a brick wall in his path.

"Not tonight, Cody."

His tortured eyes met mine. His voice almost pleading.

"Harmony, get out of my way."

"No," I told him. "Not tonight. Cody, this street is swarming with police and FBI agents. If you gun him down, they *will* kill you. I'm not letting that happen."

"Oh, please. You're protecting him."

"What I'm doing," I said, "is stopping you from throwing your life away. Diehl's going down, and soon, but not tonight. And you won't be the one pulling the trigger."

He shook his head at me, uncomprehending. "Why not?"

"Because you were right, back in Talbot Cove. I'm not normal, Cody. I don't process things the way normal people do. Part of that, I don't know, maybe I was born that way. Part of it I can blame on this job and the things I've had to do. You've been in a gunfight, but there's a big difference between pulling the trigger in self-defense and killing in cold blood."

I moved an inch closer to him. Feeling frustrated, trying to find the right words.

"There's a difference between killing and being a killer," I told him. "I don't want you to find out what that feels like."

"Maybe it's not your choice."

"It is tonight. Cody, this isn't who you are."

"Who I am?" He wore his anguish on his face. "I'll tell you who I am. I'm the man who watched almost a dozen people he's known his entire life *die* right in front of him, right on Main Street. They died in agony, and they died because that son of a bitch thinks he's above the law. That he can do whatever he wants and nobody can touch him. And maybe he's right. But one bullet can fix all that. One bullet, and Bobby Diehl can never hurt another innocent person."

"Don't you think I know that? Don't you think I want to stop him?"

"Then why *don't* you?" he asked me.

The chaos of the last few days washed over me as I fumbled for a reason, all of it hitting me at once. Government-recruited killers. Illegal surveillance programs. A candidate for the White House, backed and funded by the powers of hell. All of it connected to Bobby Diehl, and to Linder. And to the dead operatives of Cold Spectrum, assassinated to conceal a secret worse than anything we'd already uncovered.

A secret we were going to crack wide-open.

"We're on the edge of something," I said. "Something big, and we're only going to get one shot. One shot at the truth, and one shot to survive. From here on out, every move we make has to be the right one. Cody, listen. Diehl's going down, just not tonight. If I *promise* you that when the time is right, we'll bring you with us, will you stand down?"

He searched my eyes, looking for a hint of a lie.

"You promise?"

"You're not pulling the trigger. But you'll be there when it happens."

Cody nodded, slowly. He took a step back.

"I won't wait forever, Harmony."

"Trust me," I told him. "It won't be much longer now."

He walked away without saying good-bye. I watched him go. The little girl with the dead-fish eyes blended into the crowd at his back as she silently followed, his invisible guardian.

I found Jessie sitting on the back ramp of an ambulance, bandaged up, talking to April and Kevin as a paramedic finished checking her out. I didn't hear what they said, but as I wandered over, Jessie bent down and gave April a hug. April's arms clung to her, tight. Not an aunt hugging her adopted niece, but a mother—her real mother—relieved to see her daughter safe and sound.

"I'm gonna have a beauty of a shiner," Jessie told me, "plus she busted two ribs and loosened a few teeth, but all in all? I think I gave better than I got."

"Linder's burning up my phone," Kevin said. "He wants a mission report, like, as of an hour ago. How are we going to explain all this?"

"Over the phone?" Jessie said. "We aren't. He's gonna come talk to us in person, and I'm choosing the meeting ground. I think we need to clear the air, once and for all. But we'll be doing it *after* we pay a little visit to RedEye. We're leaving for New York first thing in the morning."

"And tonight," I said, "we're staying in a penthouse suite, apparently. Looks like we made a new friend."

"Did that friend also offer us dinner?" Jessie asked. "I'm thinking something four-star and expensive, preferably cooked by a celebrity chef."

I looked out across the boulevard, taking in the neon and the crowds, the din of voices and the excitement that crackled through the street like raw electricity. I had a lot of bad memories in this town. But with Althea and her pack defeated, and Cody safe—for now—maybe I could spare one night to make a few good ones.

"Sure," I told her. "Let's live a little."

FORTY-FIVE

Greenbriar came through. Attendants whisked us up to Hotel 28, the boutique hotel inside a hotel hidden on the top floor of the Monaco. Double doors opened onto a penthouse suite, marble floors stretching from a wall with three wide-screen televisions to a tournament-quality pool table to a glass-topped bar stocked with brands of liquor I couldn't even pronounce.

"Yes," Jessie said, "this is how we live now."

"It's only one night," I told her, wheeling my suitcase in.

"Don't break the illusion."

Kevin shouted from the bathroom, "Oh my God. Guys. Guys. You could have a party in this shower."

April rolled past him, one eyebrow arched.

"This suite may have a dubious history," she said. "There's some fresh plaster behind the hot tub. If I didn't know better, I'd say it looks like someone dug a bullet out of the wall."

"Not to worry." Jessie threw her arm around my shoulder. "If there are any ghosts lurking around, leave it to my girl here. She's got her mojo back, I've got my shit sorted, and everything is roses."

"Yeah," I said, offering up a smile I didn't really feel.

I sealed myself in one of the bedrooms. Showering, changing into a clean suit and a salamander-green necktie, putting a fresh bandage over the angry red cut on my neck. Looked like it was going to scar. That was fine. Just another for the collection.

I tasted magic on the air. The invisible winds swirling around me, waiting to be called upon. And I felt the void inside me, the hunger, the memory of Nadine's laughter echoing in my ears. Biting my bottom lip, I sent a message to Vigilant Lock's archival officer.

Requesting info on all active suspects believed to possess incubus/succubus abilities.

The response pinged back: Reason for request?

Pertinent to an ongoing investigation, I texted back.

Understood. Dossiers forthcoming.

The bedroom door swung open, and Jessie poked her head inside. I fumbled with my phone, shoving it in my pocket. Feeling like a criminal who'd been caught in the act. Or a closet junkie, looking for a new dealer where she could get her fix.

"Hey," Jessie said, "just making sure you're okay."

"I'm okay. Hey. Got you a present."

Her eyebrows lifted. "You did?"

"Uh-huh. Come with me."

April gave us a knowing smile as we left the penthouse. While the paramedics were finishing up with Jessie, I'd told April my plan and made a few phone calls to my local contacts. Jessie and I hopped into a taxi and rode across town to a police impound yard over on A Street. Harsh white lights crackled from posts at each corner of the razor-wire fence, casting shadows across row after row of slumbering, dusty cars and a trio of tow trucks.

"So what's this about?" Jessie asked. Our footsteps echoed on the worn asphalt as we walked between the rows.

"Well, you've had kind of a shitty week."

"Yeah, fair, fair."

"I wanted to do something. And you know how every time we request a car from a field office, they give us the worst one they've got?"

Jessie scrunched up her face. "Yeah. I'm aware."

"Last time I was in town, I busted this one sorcerer, and he had incriminating materials in his trunk—"

"Faust, right? You told me about that."

I nodded. "Well, okay, understand that we can't *keep* this, it's technically evidence, but . . ."

I led her to a spot at the edge of the fence and pointed. A midnight-black muscle car, freshly washed and waxed, gleamed in the darkness. It was long, low, and razor edged, built for street races and long, fast nights.

I jangled the keys in my hand.

"It's a 1970 Barracuda," I said. "That's good, right?"

Jessie's mouth hung open. The most she could manage was a faint, high-pitched squeak.

"Jessie?"

She draped herself over the hood, hugging the car. "It's a *Hemi*cuda. And it is now my baby. And I will pamper it and cherish it and love it forever."

"We're just borrowing it."

She held out her open palm, making grabbing motions. I tossed her the keys.

"Get in," she told me. "Let's see what this baby can do. Fair warning: I might have to break my rule against dating coworkers, because I am definitely jumping *somebody's* bones tonight."

I laughed, for what felt like the first time in weeks, and slipped into the passenger seat for a change. We traded the city lights for the desert dark, the Barracuda's beams cutting across long ribbons of highway and winding through red-rock canyons, the world whipping past at the speed of joy.

The mission had gotten messy, a tangled cluster of loose ends and lies. We'd inherited secrets that people would kill to bury, including, just maybe, our own boss. It was going to take everything we had, all our skills and our wits, to survive the fallout and get to the truth. I knew we were dancing on a razor's edge.

But tonight, we were just dancing.

# # #

We said a reluctant good-bye to the penthouse life and boarded a plane the next morning. Cross-country, nonstop, back to New York City.

"Invite you to a barbecue?" Jessie asked as we walked into the lobby of RedEye Infometrics. "You really said that?"

I shrugged. "I'm not good at quips."

"No, that wasn't half-bad. For you, I mean. I figured you would have gone with something like"—she dropped her voice and put on a thick accent—"'I ahm here to turn up da heat.'"

The receptionist stared at us, one hand concealed behind her desk. I glanced sidelong at Jessie.

"Is that supposed to be Schwarzenegger?"

"Jean-Claude Van Damme. C'mon, get with the program." She turned to the receptionist. "We're here to see Burton Webb."

"I'm afraid Mr. Webb is out of the country."

Getting a message to Burton on his Caribbean cruise had been hard. Getting him to cut his vacation short and book a flight back to the States had been harder, but he was desperate for some good news.

"No, he's not," I said. "He just got back this morning and passed through JFK customs at 9:17 a.m."

"You're not the only branch of the government that spies on people," Jessie told her.

She paled. "This is a private civilian company—"

Jessie groaned and leaned against the desk, striking a dramatic pose.

"Webb. Now. Please. *God.*"

She called him.

Burton ushered us into his office, nervously glancing over his shoulder until the door was shut and locked. He sat down on the far side of his desk, wringing his hands.

"So, it's over?" he asked us.

"As over as it's going to get, for now," I told him. "Senator Roth is about to find out that three of his hit men are dead, and the fourth just got busted trying to blow up a hotel. The one he was standing in at the time. If and when he digs into it, he'll find out she's been taken into federal custody on charges of attempted terrorism, the murder of a judge, several homicides committed during a bank robbery, about a dozen conspiracy charges—they're going to have to write entirely new books just to throw at her. She's been relocated to a special maximum-security facility, no contact with the outside world."

"What, like, Guantanamo Bay?"

"Something like that. Let's just say she's buried someplace deep, dark, and out of the senator's reach. Permanently."

He shifted in his chair, still twitchy. "So that's *one* team of killers down. Won't he just hire more?"

"Probably not. The whole plan blew up in his face and made things even worse: now he's got a killer sitting in a secure facility—too secure for him to get at her—and she can expose him anytime she likes. After that debacle, I think he'll be too afraid to double down and try again."

I didn't mention that we'd anonymously e-mailed a little present to the senator earlier that morning: a chunk of data from Bredford's blackmail file, just enough to let him know a sword was dangling over his head, and a single sentence.

We'll be in touch.

We hadn't decided how to use Alton Roth to our advantage, but from here on out, he was *our* playing piece. And we'd move him, or sacrifice him, when the time was right.

"Well, thanks for keeping me out of it," Burton said. "And, uh, thanks for being understanding about that little embezzlement issue."

Jessie leaned forward in her chair. "You can repay us with information. You said there were two survivors of Operation Cold Spectrum concealed inside your system."

"*Potential* survivors. The whole point of the patch is that RedEye can't find them. They could be dead by now, out of the country—anything's possible. All I know is that they weren't assassinated with the rest of their team."

"We want them," I said.

"Are you sure? If I remove the patch, they instantly go back on the NSA's radar. Glass Predator's been disbanded, but these names could flag if they're still on some analyst's watch list. Bottom line, invisibility is an all-or-nothing deal: if you can find them, anyone can find them."

I thought back to our first meeting and Burton's story about meeting Douglas Bredford on the day his team was marked for death. And Bredford's words: *"I'm the soldier who fired the last shot, at the last battle, for the future of humanity. The war is over. Humanity lost.*"

Jessie and I locked eyes. I gave her a firm nod.

"It's time for the truth to come out," she told him. "Do it."

It didn't take long. Just a few keystrokes, and RedEye saw all. Burton's printer rattled as it reeled off page after page, dense with data. Addresses, registrations, tracking coordinates. He handed it over.

"That's all I've got," he said. "If they're still alive, I hope you find them before . . . well, before anybody else does."

As we left the building, my phone chimed. Linder. I let it go to voice mail. Out on the bustling street, Jessie hailed a cab to take us straight to the airport.

The race was on.

EPILOGUE

Men in suits and dark glasses swarmed the halls of the Rose Foundation for Underprivileged Youth. Carrying boxes, emptying safes, shoving fistfuls of printouts into paper shredders. The oblivious volunteers had all been given their walking papers and one week's severance pay, sent home ahead of the newcomers' arrival. Nadine stalked through the charity's headquarters, eyes blazing as she pointed an accusing finger.

"If everything in those file cabinets isn't shredded in the next fifteen minutes, one of you imbeciles is getting flayed! And where is my fucking *coffee*?"

She hadn't noticed him until that moment: the tall, dark man in the ivory linen suit, leaning against the wall with his arms and ankles crossed, watching the proceedings. He let out a low, rumbling chuckle.

"Better make that decaf," Calypso told her.

She stopped in her tracks. "I'm sorry, do you find this amusing? My cover was blown at that damned fund-raiser, and I'm expecting a strike team to kick down those doors at any second. *Not funny.* What are you doing here, anyway? Shouldn't you be haunting some crossroads somewhere, making deals with blues musicians?"

"Only on Saturday nights. Like to give 'em something to think about when they're shuffling off to church on Sunday morning. And you need to lighten up a little, baby. Eternity's a long, long time. Gotta take things easy, see the humor in life."

He twirled his hand. His once-empty fingers now cradled a long, thin cigarette and a silver lighter.

"Easy for you to say," Nadine told him. "You're a peon. You have no idea what I'm trying to accomplish here, the sheer scale of my ambitions."

Calypso shrugged as he lit up, puffing the cigarette to life.

"Take advantage of an impending scandal to make Prince Malphas's hound look incompetent, depose him and take his place, putting you a heartbeat from Malphas's throne. Then lay the groundwork for a coup so you can become a princess." He lifted an eyebrow. "Is that about the size of it? Stop me if I'm wrong."

Her bottom lip twitched. "You think you're so smart."

"Smart enough to deal with a couple of wayward humans. Now, you and I are generally copacetic, are we not? I mind my business and you tend to yours. But now I've got outsiders sniffing around Senator Roth. Smelling smoke and looking for the fire. And that's on you. You just made your business *my* business."

She strode toward him, glaring daggers, and stood toe to toe. Her eyes melted to swirls of molten copper as she stared up at the tall man.

"Then serve me," she said. "Serve me and you'll be well rewarded."

Another rumbling, basso chuckle. He tilted his head to one side and exhaled a plume of silver smoke.

"Same old song and dance. But are you so sure you're the one calling the shots, baby? Think you're a player, but you might just be somebody's pawn."

"Pawn?" she said. "I am a *queen*."

"And the queen still gets played, just like every other piece on the board. We're living in interesting times. You got a plan for dealing with our two curious do-gooders?"

"Harmony," Nadine said. "I left her with an itch she won't be able to scratch. She won't come to me—she still has her pride, for now—but she'll go looking for someone who can ease her pain. When she does, I'll be there waiting."

"Fair enough. Just make sure you deep-six those two before they can step on my man's toes again. Senator Roth has great things ahead of him. Great things indeed."

Nadine smiled now. A slow, predatory grin.

"Kill them? Oh, no. I made them a promise, and I intend to keep it."

Her voice dropped to a slithering whisper.

"I'm not going to kill them. I'm going to *break* them."

#

The black stretch limousine was a fortress on wheels, with ballistic armor, run-flat tires, and door handles that could be electrified at the press of a button. It was also Linder's rolling office, and half of the passenger compartment had been converted into a surveillance-and-command suite. He even had a fax machine for dealing with the tech Neanderthals in DC.

He sat slumped in the leather bucket seat, tie loose and dangling, a glass with three fingers of scotch on ice in his weary hand. *Clusterfuck.* That was the only word for it. If he'd had any inkling that those Manhattan bank robbers were the assassins he'd recruited back in the day, he'd . . . well, he wasn't sure what he would have done, but setting Temple and Black on their trail didn't even make the top ten possibilities. At least three were dead—for real, this time—and the fourth was on permanent ice.

Garbled reports, lying about their location, the mess of contradictions—Temple and Black knew about Glass Predator. And they knew he was involved. No question. And he could live with that. He'd gotten his hands dirtier than that back in the day. No stable government survived without men like Linder, rolling up their sleeves to keep the secret wheels of politics greased with blood. He was proud of his service.

But knowing about Glass Predator put them one shy heartbeat from knowing about Cold Spectrum. And that, he couldn't live with.

That, he wouldn't survive.

He tapped his phone and put it to his ear. The man on the other end picked up, wordless, in one ring.

"It's me," Linder said. "Call Panic Cell back from Beirut. I might have some . . . housekeeping for them. I want the team stateside, geared up and ready for a sanitation job in the next twenty-four hours. I also want a word with Althea Temple, *alone*, before she's sent to Site Burgundy. I need to know exactly what she told my operatives."

He paused, listening to the terse reply, and a wave of ice water crashed through his veins.

"Repeat that," he said. "What do you mean, *we don't have her?*"

# # #

Althea had spent six of the last twelve hours with a black bag over her head. Shuffled from car to car in stony silence, handled by men with callused hands and dead eyes. She knew their type: soldiers, not attached to any real unit, recruited into the shadows and willing to do whatever needed doing with no questions asked.

Now she rode in the back of a windowless van. They weren't taking any chances: they locked a straitjacket over her jumpsuit and a bite mask over her face, her body strapped to a gurney and belted down with hospital restraints. She could barely wriggle more than her toes. Three men, toting slim black rifles, sat on a bench across from her. They weren't much for conversation. She didn't mind. The long ride gave her time to think.

Mostly, she thought about Jessie.

The girl was weak, but it wasn't her fault. She'd been raised by weaklings, surrounded by them. A wolf fooled into thinking she was a sheepdog. That could be fixed. It could all be fixed. They could still be a family again.

They *would* be a family again.

Althea was still thinking about Jessie, and all the ways she was going to show her the light, when the van hit a land mine at fifty miles an hour.

The van flipped, lurching onto its side, going into a roll as steel screamed and the air filled with the stench of burning rubber and leaking fuel. None of Althea's guardians were belted in: the crash threw them like rag dolls, slamming them against the steel roof and sidewalls, pulping faces and snapping bones. Althea just closed her eyes and rolled with it. The locked-down gurney and restraints kept her snug in the sudden chaos, and the only bruise she took came from a collision-tossed body slapping her in the shoulder on his way to the floor, crumpled and dead.

The van rocked one last time, and squealed to a rest on its shredded tires. A new smell hung in the air. Fresh blood. Althea's mouth started to water.

The back doors wrenched open, flooding the compartment with harsh daylight. The men outside, four of them, wore jet-black tactical gear and ballistic helmets with opaque faceplates. One of Althea's overseers was still alive, groaning as he reached for a fallen rifle. A three-round burst of machine-pistol fire raked across his back.

The invaders climbed over the wreckage and the dead, fast and efficient, unstrapping her restraints and unbuckling the bite mask. One checked her eyes with a penlight.

"We're friendlies," he said, his voice muffled under the helmet. "You understand? You hurt? Follow the light with your eyes."

They got the straitjacket off her. She flexed her arms, kneading the life back into her skin, as they led her out of the wreck and onto the edge of a lonely desert highway. A Humvee with tinted windows sat ten feet behind the crumpled van. One of the men ran to the backseat and came back with a bundle of clothes. Civilian clothing, jeans and a gray flannel hoodie, a pair of sneakers in Althea's size.

"For you," he said, pressing the bundle into her arms. She stared at him, still a little dazed from the crash.

"Who are you people?" she said. "Why are you rescuing me?"

"Told you. Friendlies." He waved an envelope at her, then slapped it onto the pile. "Ten thousand dollars. Clean, unmarked cash. That's incentive money. Our boss wants to give you a job."

He added one last thing to the pile in her arms: a business card. No name, no phone number, just a Los Angeles address in crisp black type.

"Who's your boss?"

"Go to that address. You'll learn everything you need to know."

Althea's brow furrowed. "What if I don't? I might be busy. Got a family reunion to plan. I don't need your money. Already got a nice little rainy-day fund stashed away—"

"In the Caymans, right? No, you don't. What you have is a *frozen* account in the Caymans, a stack of federal warrants, and, in an hour from now, when you don't show up at the cargo plane waiting to haul you to a black-site prison, a price on your head bigger than your body weight in solid gold. Even with all your skills, you'll be dead or recaptured within a week. But our boss can make it all go away."

Althea put a meaty hand on her hip, frowning down at him. "And how's he going to do that? He some kind of a genie? Gonna grant me three wishes?"

"*One* wish. That family reunion you've been wanting. How does you, your daughter, your own private island, and all the time in the world sound? Oh, and more money than you can spend."

Althea scowled at her distorted reflection in the gunman's onyx faceplate. "Nothing's free. What's the catch?"

"No catch. The boss wants what you want. It'll be the easiest job you've ever had, and the best-paying, with all the resources you need to get it done."

"What about her partner?" Althea's eyes blazed, hard turquoise. "What about Harmony Black?"

A low chuckle echoed from beneath the helmet. "Like I said . . . the boss wants what you want."

Althea glanced down at the business card.

"You've got my attention."

"Thought so." He pointed a black-gloved hand down the road. "Walk that way. Fifteen minutes back, you'll find a rest stop where you can catch a ride."

They boarded the Humvee, peeling out, leaving Althea standing by the side of the road. Dazed and squinting at the distant sun, holding her clothes and her money and a world of possibilities in her arms.

She shrugged. Then she looked to the west, toward Los Angeles, and started to walk.

AFTERWORD

I'd say we've come to the end of another adventure, but really, this one is just getting started.

In times like these, in the brief pause between manuscripts, I often sit back and wonder at how lucky I am—to have found an audience, and to be able to share my stories with readers who enjoy them as much as I enjoy writing them. I'm thankful for you. So: Ready for the next one? I'll warn you, things only get more dangerous from here.

Special thanks to Adrienne Procaccini at 47North, my developmental editor Andrea Hurst, my copyeditor Sara Brady, and the audiobook skills of Christina Traister. Every finished novel is a team project, and my team is at the top of their game. These are the folks who make me look like I actually know what I'm doing.

Also, I want to give a big shout-out to Susannah Jones, who introduced me to the wonders of NYC and helped with location scouting; all the folks at Hattie B's in Nashville (that's cluckin' hot, folks); the experts at Battlefield Vegas (where I get hands-on with all the things that go bang); and the staff at the Monte Carlo, my home away from home, where they never fail to make my research trips memorable (even though they are fully aware, at this point, that my arrival can only herald a fresh batch of fictional trouble for their establishment).

Want a heads-up when new stories are on the way? Head over to www.craigschaeferbooks.com/mailing-list/. Once-a-month newsletters, zero spam. If you want to reach out, you can find me at www.facebook.com/CraigSchaeferBooks, on Twitter as @craig_schaefer, or just drop me an email at craig@craigschaeferbooks.com. Always happy to hear from you.

ABOUT THE AUTHOR

Photo © 2014 Karen Forsythe

Craig Schaefer's books have taken readers to the seamy edge of a criminal underworld drenched in shadow through the Daniel Faust series; to a world torn by war, poison, and witchcraft by way of the Revanche Cycle series; and across a modern America mired in occult mysteries and a conspiracy of lies in the Harmony Black series. Despite this, people say he's strangely normal. He lives in Illinois with a small retinue of cats, all of whom try to interrupt his writing schedule and/or kill him on a regular basis. He practices sleight of hand in his spare time, although he's not very good at it.